Praise for *The Love Thief*

"The Love Thief *is a rip-rollicking spiritual love story that leaves you gasping with all the feels and clamoring for the sequel. Complete with a narcissist villain and magnetic healers and sages, what a tale Arielle Ford has cooked up as she guides us on a delicious trip to magical India.* The Love Thief *is a must-read."*

— **Sheri Salata**, former executive producer of *The Oprah Winfrey Show*

"Just like life, The Love Thief *takes us on a sometimes dark, unexpected, and ultimately illuminating ride through one woman's fairy tale romance, that becomes a nightmare of heartbreak and betrayal. Like many of us, the heroine of this story discovers what it takes to heal a broken heart, pick up the pieces of a broken life, and move forward to find purpose, peace, and love. Well done, Arielle! Thank you for the many reminders."*

— **Iyanla Vanzant**, author, spiritual life coach, and executive producer of *Iyanla: Fix My Life*

"Wow! What a ride! Arielle Ford has managed to weave life lessons and transformation into a captivating story that has it all—betrayal, love, revenge, and vindication. Be prepared to be enchanted!"

— **Natalie Ledwell**, best-selling author and co-founder of MindMovies.com

"Some people have to kiss a sociopath or two before they start to realize what real love is. For Holly, the fake version felt so good—until it didn't. This book is true to its title: the story of a love thief, and the repair of the trust that was stolen. What she learned, and how she learned it, leads at last to the love that was there all along but hidden. Most people will see themselves somewhere in this story and learn more than they might imagine about how to get love right."

— **Marianne Williamson**, best-selling author, political activist, and spiritual thought leader

"Arielle Ford's debut novel The Love Thief *is a spiritual book sure to inspire women to move on beyond life's heartbreaks and disappointments and reclaim their power to fulfill their heart's desires. A fast-moving heroine's journey of love, betrayal, deceit and final justice, it paints a wonderful picture of what BIG LOVE looks like and the miracles of that are possible when we let go of control and self-judgement and trust in the ultimate goodness and flow of the universe."*

— **Claire Zammit, Ph.D.**, founder of Feminine Power

"When what she thought she wanted isn't what she gets, Holly finds herself on an unexpected journey through the world of love, loss, and heartbreak, only to discover the power of a spiritual awakening to provide both hope and healing."

— **Cheryl Richardson**, *New York Times* best-selling author of *Take Time for Your Life*

"From page one of The Love Thief *you'll be hooked. Like many of us, the story's heroine is called to surrender her ideas of what her life should look like and embarks on a wild ride into the unknown. You'll be mesmerized and enchanted by the spiritual discoveries she makes along the way."*

— **Kute Blackson**, best-selling author of *The Magic of Surrender*

"The Love Thief *is a dream read. It's a gripping tale of love, intrigue, and adventure—and a soul-stirring journey of spiritual renewal. Ford's genius is that she evokes the ineffable—you actually experience the states of soul-healing she captures so beautifully. It's a luscious beach-read and an exquisite meditation retreat all in one. Don't miss it!"*

— **Ken Page**, author of *Deeper Dating*

"In Chef Holly's journey from a wronged woman and a broken life to self-knowledge and self-love, Arielle Ford serves up a delectable and deeply satisfying treat. Heartburn *meets* Eat, Pray, Love *in this gripping page-turner."*

— **Lynne McTaggart**, internationally best-selling author of *The Field, The Intention Experiment,* and *The Power of Eight*

"Arielle Ford has always been a strong and beautiful voice that acts as a guiding light for women wanting to find and maintain lasting love. With her debut novel, Arielle takes us on another soulful journey of self-discovery."

— **Dr. Laura Berman**, author of *Quantum Love* and host of the *Language of Love* podcast

"Arielle Ford is a master storyteller. I was completely moved by this book and inspired by the big lessons it reveals."

— **Marci Shimoff**, *New York Times* best-selling author of *Happy for No Reason*

"Arielle's wisdom speaks through her characters in this soulful, immersive novel that will inspire the gamut of emotions within you."

— **Damona Hoffman**, host of *The Dates & Mates Podcast* and resident love expert on *The Drew Barrymore Show*

"I can't wait for The Love Thief *to become a movie! This is one book I'll never forget."*

— **Linda Sivertsen**, best-selling author and host of the podcast *Beautiful Writers*

"This compelling page-turner, set in San Diego, Budapest, and India, will engage your emotions, tempt your taste buds, restore your hope and swing your heart wide open. I didn't want it to end!"

— **Nancy Levin**, author of *The Art of Change* and founder of Levin Life Coach Academy

"For anyone whose heart longs for healing and believes in the power of love, hope, and surrender, this book will stir your heart and remind you of the impact of the eternal power of self-worth, resiliency, and the Divine."

— **Marni Battista**, author and CEO for the Institute for Living Courageously

"The Love Thief *is a sumptuous meal! The characters are real and amazing, and the plot is fresh and filled with transformation. Don't miss this fabulous read—it will become one of your favorite novels!"*

— **Dr. Diana Kirschner**, best-selling author of *Love in 90 Days*

"Magic and spiritual wisdom are afoot in this page-turner that offers a delightful mix of romance, revenge, and the eternal nature of love."

— **Colette Baron-Reid**, best-selling author of *The Map*

"Arielle Ford's fun and breezy style grabs you from the first page, taking you on a roller coaster ride of love lost and found that will surprise and delight any romantic."

— **Donald Altman**, psychotherapist, former Buddhist monk, and author of *Travelers*

"The Love Thief *is a charming story in three delicious parts: a revenge fantasy tale of a woman scorned, a travelogue that makes the magic and mystery (and culinary delights!) of India come to life, and a deeply spiritual guide that reveals the answers to life's most important questions . . . including what is happiness, and how can we mere mortals attain it? (Without having to hike to a cave in the Himalayas.)"*

— **Carol Allen**, Vedic astrologer and author of *Love Is in the Stars*

"The Love Thief *is one of those books I wished would never end. Holly's journey masterfully blends adventure, color, smell, taste, travel, and juicy romance, proving that a crisis might just be the beginning of a life much better than the one we had planned."*

— **Kelly Sullivan Walden**, award-winning best-selling author of *A Crisis Is a Terrible Thing to Waste*

"I loved the twists and turns of this story! Painted on a vivid backdrop of the sights, sounds, tastes and smells of life on the Ganges River in the holy city of Rishikesh, India, we accompany Holly through the exhilaration of finding 'the one,' the unbearable betrayal of love lost, and ultimately, the reclamation of her dreams."

— **Debra Poneman**, best-selling author and founder of Yes to Success Seminars, Inc.

"Arielle Ford has knocked it out of the park with The Love Thief, *a stunning spiritual adventure illuminating the beautiful perfection of our lives."*

— **Liz Dawn**, CEO of Mishka Productions and Celebrate Your Life Events

"In The Love Thief, *Arielle Ford masterfully portrays how a broken heart can be the beginning of something magical when we have the courage to heal and allow its gift to be revealed."*

— **Terri Britt**, spiritual coach, author, and former Miss USA

"The Love Thief *is a thoroughly enjoyable page-turner, a delightful read that transports us to India for inquiry and revelation on what love truly is."*

— **Julie Ferman**, legendary matchmaker and dating coach

"The Love Thief *is a fascinating and gripping story of love, betrayal, suspense, healing, and forgiveness. Arielle Ford has a poetic way of drawing the reader in, and you can't help yourself from finishing this book as soon as you pick it up.* The Love Thief *is a must-read if you've ever felt the world is against you."*

— **Jonathon Aslay**, author of *What the Heck Is Self-Love Anyway?*

"The Love Thief *is an invitation into a private world where wealth, decadence, love, betrayal, spirituality and women's empowerment are all on display. I read it through in one sitting and gobbled up every morsel—a perfect combination of hilarious moments and magnificently written scenes, rounded out with some heartbreaking relationship issues. Witty and cleverly told, it's the kind of book about love every woman needs to read."*

— **Crystal Andrus Morissette**, best-selling author of *The Emotional Edge*

"The Love Thief *took my breath away. I could relate to every facet of Holly's journey and found myself cheering for her growth and healing. Bravo, Arielle Ford."*

— **Cynthia James**, author, speaker, and coach

"The Love Thief *is a fun and engaging read. Once again Arielle Ford's wisdom and talent shines forth."*

— **Barbara Biziou**, personal transformation and vision coach

"I loved every part of this story: the journey, the characters, the intrigue, the suspense and the satisfying conclusion. Rarely have I read a book that captivates and inspires me at the same time."

— **Peggy McColl**, *New York Times* best-selling author

"Like a great TV series that you end up bingeing on or the cake you devoured, not able to stop at just one slice, once I started The Love Thief, *I could not put it down."*

— **Heide Banks**, relationship coach

"The Love Thief *takes you on a delightful, transformative journey that provides a deeper understanding of love in all its forms and unveils secrets for and finding contentment and inner joy."*

— **Susie Collins**, co-author of *Big Fat Love*

"This is a powerful story of what it takes to move from betrayal to transformation, from pain to peace, and from confusion to clarity. Schedule some time for this exciting read, dive in, and enjoy where it takes you."

— **Dr. Debi Silber**, founder and CEO of the Post Betrayal Transformation Institute

"There are many lessons waiting for anyone lucky enough to read this book. Thank you for reuniting me with the truth and reigniting my relationship with Santosha."

— **Kurt Koontz**, author of *A Million Steps*

"Warning: The Love Thief *will steal every free moment you have as you won't be able to put it down! Each discovery on Holly's journey keeps you on your toes. This unique love story has a twist that does not disappoint."*

— **Puja Shaw**, author of *For My Sister*

"In The Love Thief, *we are transported to one of the holiest places on earth as Holly, the heroine of the story, struggles to heal from a heart-shattering betrayal and experiences a spiritual awakening and rebirth. Arielle Ford does an excellent job of bringing all the colors, flavors, magic and spirituality of India to life."*

— **Mary Morrissey**, global thought leader
and founder of Brave Thinking Institute

"The Love Thief *is an intense and page-turning fiction story with real-life depth and heart. I couldn't put it down."*

— **Christy Whitman**, *New York Times* best-selling author of *The Art of Having It All*

"The Love Thief *takes us to the intersection where the suffering that seemingly crushes our soul meets the mystical forces that conspire for our healing and return to love. Arielle Ford's writing drops us into a sense of place—in the internal landscape of our hearts as well as the external landscapes that call us home to ourselves."*

— **Peggy Fitzsimmons, Ph.D.**, author of *Release*

"The Love Thief *is a beautiful, highly riveting, deeply intuitive and breathtaking story that takes you on a powerful journey of awakening and love only found through rediscovering oneself."*

— **Kailen Rosenberg**, *Celebrity Love Architect*
and author of *Real Love, Right Now*

The Love Thief

Also by Arielle Ford

The Soulmate Secret

Turn Your Mate into Your Soulmate

Wabi Sabi Love

Hot Chocolate for the Mystical Soul

More Hot Chocolate for the Mystical Soul

Hot Chocolate for the Mystical Teenage Soul

Hot Chocolate for the Mystical Lover

Magical Souvenirs

Inkspirations Love by Design

Love on the Other Side

The Everything Book

All of the above are available at your local bookstore.

The Love Thief

A NOVEL

Arielle Ford

HAY HOUSE

Carlsbad, California • New York City
London • Sydney • New Delhi

Published in the United Kingdom by:
Hay House UK Ltd, 1st Floor, Crawford Corner,
91–93 Baker Street, London W1U 6QQ
Tel: +44 (0)20 3927 7290; www.hayhouse.co.uk

Cover design: Mary Luna
Interior design: Bryn Starr Best
Author Photo Credit: Jeremiah Sullivan

A catalogue record for this book is available from the British Library.

Tradepaper ISBN: 978-1-83782-623-0
E-book ISBN: 978-1-4019-9907-0
Audiobook ISBN: 978-1-4019-9908-7

10 9 8 7 6 5 4 3 2 1

This product uses responsibly sourced papers, including recycled materials and materials from other controlled sources. For more information, see www.hayhouse.co.uk

The authorized representative in the EU for product safety and compliance is Penguin Random House Ireland, Morrison Chambers, 32 Nassau Street, Dublin D02 YH68, Ireland. https://eu-contact.penguin.ie

Printed and bound by CPI Group (UK) Ltd, Croydon CR0 4YY

MIX
Paper | Supporting responsible forestry
FSC® C018179

For Debbie

Your love, light, and desire to heal others

shines brightly on every page.

Contents

RECIPES

CHAPTER ONE

Hell

My mother was right. Shit.

As I began my descent back into the real world, I wanted to laugh at this thought, but I wasn't sure why.

Now, where am I?

I could hear rhythmic mechanical beeping.

My eyes were closed, and my mouth was so tight I couldn't open it.

I must be dreaming.

I felt a heaviness as if I were stuck in some mucky quicksand.

Thoughts floated by and disappeared.

Am I asleep?

My mother was right.

There was that thought again.

Right about what?

"Holly, Holly, are you in there? Can you open your eyes? It's me, Mom."

Did I want to open my eyes? I wasn't sure . . .

"Holly, you're in a hospital. You had an accident. You are going to be okay. Please open your eyes."

I willed my eyes to open. They felt sticky, but I slowly coaxed them to half-mast.

My mother's face hovered above me . . . she looked terrible. Not a smidgen of lipstick.

This must be bad. She never goes out in public without her lipstick.

Something pulled me away, luring me to return to sleep. Whatever this was could not be good.

"Holly, please open your eyes. You're going to be okay," Mom pleaded. Footsteps. Pushing through the grogginess, I opened my heavy eyelids enough to see a middle-aged woman in a white coat above me. She said her name was Dr. Something. She explained that my jaw was wired shut because it had been broken in the car accident. *A car accident?* She told me I had eighteen stitches over my right eyebrow and my right wrist was fractured and would be in a cast for four to five weeks and, if all goes well, my jaw would heal in six weeks. She said I was a very lucky woman.

It could have been much worse.

It could have been worse? I still did not understand. Worse than what?

This was all too much. I dove back into the comforting, safe, silky darkness of morphine-laced sleep.

I'm not sure how much time later, I came to again, sensing warmth in my left hand . . . it felt like something big was squishing it. Someone was holding my hand and I needed it to stop. I did my best to pull away.

"Holly, Baby, thank God you are alive! What happened? You scared me to death. Your mom is here, too. We're here for you! Don't worry about that big gash and stitches over your eye. We'll find the best plastic surgeon and have you looking great in time for the wedding."

It was Barry, my fiancé, talking at his usual over-caffeinated pace, not bothering to come up for air.

My addiction to playing online jigsaw puzzles seems to have paid off. Flashes of scenes rapidly clicked into place and the events that landed me here in this hospital bed became a string of memories.

All bad. Without wanting to, I visualized the last screenshot I took on my phone before the car crash. It was all I could see in my mind.

My stomach clenched and a zillion images suddenly tumbled into my head. Tears slid out of the corners of my eyes, and I felt crushed as if a jumbo jet had crash-landed into my heart. Once again that thought circled like a buzzard through the fog in my brain: *Mom was right.*

A half hour before my plane had landed in Phoenix, I looked in my briefcase to review my notes for the morning meeting and realized the hard copy of the Feinberg contract was missing. I must have left it at home. Shoot! If Barry could scan the document, I could print it out before the meeting and all would be well.

While waiting in the rental car line, I called Barry multiple times; I kept getting voicemail. I recalled his mentioning something about his wanting to go to bed early, but all I needed was for him to scan the document and email it to me before morning.

As I got behind the wheel, I remembered the new security system we had installed recently. It came with a phone app for remote viewing. When I couldn't reach Barry, I decided to see if I could locate the document in its red folder in the Great Room.

What I found instead shattered my world: Barry and Carly, my longtime friend and business partner, were sitting nearly naked at our dining room table. Dinner laid out and candles glowing; clearly a prelude to sex. My heart dropped like an elevator in free fall to the bottom of my soul. Incomprehensible. I thought I must be hallucinating, yet somehow I had managed to snap a screenshot just in case this was all real. I looked up from my phone just in time to see the back of the eighteen-wheeler I was about to plow into.

What is that awful guttural sound? It sounded like whimpering from a gravely wounded animal. Something in pain. Utter despair.

Where was it coming from?

Oh my God. It's coming from me.

Mom panicked, calling for a nurse, something about my needing more morphine.

Barry still had a death grip on my hand, mumbling shit like, "Don't worry, Babe, you're gonna be fine. Just breathe. The doctor is on the way. Don't worry about that nasty stitching on your forehead. I'll get you the best plastic surgeon. You'll look great for the wedding . . . it's gonna be okay."

Dear God, I thought. *This is not just meaningless drivel. It's* repetitive*, meaningless drivel.*

I pulled back from his grip, opened my eyes as best I could, and tried to think.

I couldn't talk. My jaw was wired shut. I couldn't write. My wrist was broken and in a sling. And, more than anything, I needed to get this motherfucker away from me as quickly as possible.

The pain in my body wasn't what was causing these horrible sounds. These were the tormented wails of the realization that my life was over. Not only was my body broken but my heart was also shattered. Every dream I had nurtured for my nearly thirty-eight years on Earth had been decimated.

I might as well be dead.

My eyes opened as a pretty young attendant walked in wearing peacock blueprint scrubs. She smiled at me and with a lilting accent I couldn't quite place beyond possibly Caribbean, said, "Hi, Holly. I'm your nurse, Kiyana."

She gently took my left hand and placed it on a small switch and pressed my thumb, which clicked while she instructed, "Okay, honey. You can control the pain medication dosage yourself. Just push this button."

I was in a small private room. The walls were a comforting shade of steel blue. I could see a whiteboard on the wall that said in big block letters, "Today is Sept. 15th. Your nurse is Kiyana. Your help call button is RED." Barry was now on my right, Mom on my left, looking more stressed than I'd ever seen her.

Despite IV lines and other wires protruding from my left arm, I motioned to my mother that I needed my phone. She handed it to me and I fumbled, eventually finding a one-handed way to retrieve the screenshot and make it full screen.

I gave the phone back to Mom with Barry leaning across me trying to see the screen.

Her eyes widened. A look of disbelief, followed by horror, followed by a rage that transformed her face.

At that moment, I remembered what she was right about. In her own way, she had tried to warn me about Barry.

It was all too much, so I allowed myself to give in to the morphine haze . . . the last thing I heard before I disappeared into the comforting sea of nothingness was Barry pleading, "Babe, I can explain!"

CHAPTER TWO

Some Enchanted Evening

The night sky exploded into a glittering array of red, white, and gold pops of light as the fireworks began. I was standing alone at the far end of the sprawling estate, feeling suitably satisfied with the success of the hospital gala. The five-bedroom mansion looming in the background was illuminated by a golden light, a perfect background for the big spenders milling about the five-acre garden.

We had fought hard to secure the catering contract, and the "Gala Chairwoman," Mrs. Phyllis Tavers, had been nothing short of a nightmare of a diva. Her lifestyle of privilege was mirrored in the gilded frames of the art lining the marble entrance hall. If I had to give her a title, it would be the Sir Edmund Hillary of social climbing.

A mash-up of Rothschildian opulence, her home featured a formal dining room that would seat up to twenty-two local, deep-pocketed kings and queens with even deeper desires to see, be seen, and, in many cases, be heard, a little too loudly. Ornate, throne-like chairs at each end of the table gleamed and were reflected in the wall of smoky mirrors. A row of smaller, leather-cushioned mahogany chairs lined up on both sides.

As I neared the building, knowing what was inside, I paused a moment to breathe in the air of wealth surrounding the place. Moving toward the dining room, I straightened myself, hoping that my small frame would measure up to the tall stakes this evening held for me and my partner Carly.

Rumor around town was that the powder room featured a gold-plated toilet, but I didn't have the nerve to sneak a peek. *A Marie Antoinette complex*? I mused as I bustled toward the platters of food warming on the sideboards. I caught my image in the mirror on the wall before me. Assuming an air of professionalism, I tried hard to concentrate on my goal for the task at hand: to throw the greatest event in town.

However, my thoughts drifted back to the moneyed crowd and, in particular, Mrs. Tavers's demanding expectations over the past weeks.

You're gonna be fine.

I straightened my chef's coat with a quick jerk.

These people are human beings, too, I reasoned.

Besides, I had guests to serve. Now was no time to be fantasizing about the rich and famous.

Despite some initial resistance to moving away from the familiar beef or chicken, once Mrs. Tavers and her small planning team tasted our pistachio-crusted mini lamb chops, they were all in. She had discovered us through the same local society tabloid in whose photographs she regularly appeared, attending various soirees, always decked out in the latest designer duds.

Our little startup catering business had been highlighted in an article for a pop-up foodie night we had thrown where the writer not only loved the flavors but was also knocked out by my artistic plating. Through the use of small edible flowers and swirls of sauces, each dish gleamed with the broad, unbroken fields of color of postimpressionism.

Not only did we get a stellar review of our food, but the headline also read, "San Diego's Hottest New Chef," and featured a large photograph of me, as well as additional pictures of our appetizers, main course, and dessert. It was easily the best photo of me ever taken. I looked sophisticated, joyful, and I had a coy smile on my face. Unfortunately, the photo they took of Carly and me together never made it into print. It was an oversight that Carly insisted was okay, but I always wondered if she felt otherwise.

Hopefully, this gala would be the launching pad Carly and I needed as we went off on our own to compete with the big-boy caterers in San Diego. For the past several years we had worked for the best caterer in town. I was now head chef and Carly was head of sales; we were also best friends. We were taking a giant leap of faith together.

I've always had a thing for fireworks. In my overly romanticized fantasy world, I dreamed that my prince would someday come and our first kiss would be underneath a sky exploding with neon bursts of color. Fireworks equal love. And not just any kind of love, but big, soul-stirring, major heart-tingling, explosive, legendary love.

As I stood on the slightly damp expanse of perfectly manicured grass, I had my arms wrapped tightly around me trying to stave off the slight chill in the air when I felt someone approach me from behind. I turned around and, in the dim light, saw a tall, well-dressed man smiling at me. "It's gotten chilly," he said, taking a step toward me. For a second, I forgot the cold as my heart skipped a beat. He emanated an intoxicating warmth mixed with an air of extreme wealth.

"You look cold," he said gently. I took a step back, wondering where this divine creature had come from. I wordlessly nodded, unclutching myself as he slipped his navy cashmere jacket off his shoulders. "May I?" he asked, moving a little closer. I nodded and shuddered slightly as he draped it across my shoulders. The jacket was as soft as puppy ears, but it smelled of expensive cologne.

"I've noticed you dashing about all night," he continued. "You're the caterer, right?" My face flushed as I looked down at my old chef's clogs. Suddenly, an awkward silence ensued.

Why was this princely man talking to me?

A niggling, familiar sense of doubt clouded my vision as I blinked hard.

He is just being nice, I reasoned, pulling the jacket ends closer to my body.

Really, I'm just the hired help.

"I'm just crazy about those bacon-wrapped scallops, and the truffle risotto was amazing," he said encouragingly. He flashed a set of white teeth that would have illuminated the night sky. I could feel my shoulders loosen ever so slightly.

"Yes, they are indeed our specialty," I offered, cocking my head to one side as I grinned at him.

"I could live on that! Oh, forgive my manners. My name is Barry Tavers," he said, smiling at me with the confidence only Prince Charming could have.

Tavers was a name everyone in town knew. It was plastered on hospitals, symphony halls, and education centers. *Anonymous* giving was not what this family was about.

"I suppose you are related to Phyllis Tavers?" I asked, hoping my face didn't reveal the loathing I had developed for her over the past few weeks. The man looked at me apologetically.

"Oh yes." He sighed, holding his hands out to his sides. "That's my mother. I hope she didn't torture you too much. She can be a bit difficult as I'm sure you now know," he said with a smile. With that, he clapped his hands together and laughed so infectiously that I just had to join him. I could feel the tension escaping my limbs for the first time all month. Phyllis had put Carly and me through living hell with all her demands. Looking at Barry now, I wondered how such a dragon could have produced such a lovely son.

Not wanting to risk saying anything negative about my first, and so far, biggest client, I remained silent. Even though Barry seemed to share at least some of my opinion about his mom, she was paying us well to put on this gala. I felt at ease with his gentle manner, but I didn't want to make a wrong move by agreeing with him. Besides, I didn't even know him!

Yet something about him made me trust him immediately in a destiny-driven kind of way. It wasn't just his dashing good looks and well-manicured hands. He exuded a charm that put me off balance. Erecting myself within the warmth of his jacket, I lifted my eyes back to the brilliant lights in the sky, trying hard to settle my racing heart.

For this event, Mrs. Tavers had been talked into using "reduced noise fireworks" at the behest of her neighbors, many of whom had horses. It was rumored that she once had four small, fluffy, designer dogs—all white—but she had their voice boxes removed so she wouldn't be disturbed by their barking. As much as I loved fireworks, I certainly appreciated their lack of *Boom, Boom, Boom*.

Barry continued his polite banter, looking me directly in the eye as he easily shared stories about his background. The conversation was easy, and in the scope of less than ten minutes, I learned he was a lawyer, a divorced father of twin teenage girls, and anxious to find his soulmate and have more children. His hobbies included tracking down rare art in Europe for his parents' collection, playing tennis, having a passion for design and architecture, and fine dining, the latter being something we definitely had in common.

My phone began buzzing in my bra, which made me gasp. How embarrassing to have to reach through his jacket underneath my shirt to retrieve it! I saw a text. The kitchen needed me—NOW.

"Gotta run, Barry. Lovely to meet you," I said as I slipped off his jacket and turned to hurry away. For a split second, our hands touched. An electric shock raced through my entire torso down to my toes as our eyes met.

"Do you want to get together sometime?" He looked at me intensely.

My mouth went dry as I swallowed hard.

"Uh, sure," I stammered. "Sounds like fun!" I faked a casual tone as I looked at my phone again to distract myself from this force of nature. "I really have to go," I apologized as I backed up, nearly stumbling into a potted plant behind me.

I swerved around, heading for the kitchen as thoughts raced through my mind. *Was this my fantasy coming true? Was my prince the son of a nasty, wealthy witch?*

The next morning at 7:08 A.M., my phone was shimmying on the bedside table. Not ready to wake up, I nearly ignored it until curiosity got the best of me and I found a text: "Good morning, Holly, this is Barry. Ready for a walk on the beach?"

Jolting upright, I nearly dropped my phone onto the bedcovers. I had indeed agreed to get together with him. But so soon?

I texted him back. "How did you get my number?"

Within twenty seconds, he responded. "My mother kindly provided it. Normally I am not this forward, so I apologize for the short notice, but I have an opening in my schedule and couldn't resist the chance to see you."

Pausing a moment, I typed back, "You're in luck! I have an opening in my schedule as well."

I had to smile at the irony. His witchy mother had facilitated her son meeting with the kitchen help without her even knowing it! I shook my head from side to side.

No, I am more than that, I said to myself in the mirror.

Something tells me Barry sees that, too. My phone vibrated in my hand.

"Meet me at 9 A.M. at the pier? How do you like your coffee?"

"Okay, and I'd love an almond milk latte. No sugar. Ciao."

There was so much adrenaline pumping through my system that drinking coffee seemed redundant, but I slid out of bed and headed to make a big mug of hazelnut brew. I started thinking about what to wear for a walk on the beach with a handsome stranger who didn't seem strange at all. In fact, he seemed perfectly wonderful.

Handsome. Hmm. Strong jawline, lightly tanned. I noticed the slight crow's feet around his eyes that gave him a permanent look of joviality. His thick dark hair suggested an air of prowess and strength. I imagined his height would cast a protective shadow over me in the sunlight.

I rummaged my closet to find something appropriate for a morning jaunt along the shore. My normal beach-walking attire included my faded, shredded, oldest pair of yoga pants, my high school boyfriend's football jersey (also old, stained, torn, and worn), a floppy hat, and a big slathering of SPF to protect my face. Fortunately, my hair still looked pretty decent from the blowout I had gotten two days ago, so I figured some makeup, a favorite wide-brim hat, and my light blue lululemon top and bottoms from Mom for my birthday would be cute and casual.

Heading down to the pier, I recognized his silhouette against the shimmering water. As I drew closer, my breath shallowed. Aviator sunglasses, a clean white polo shirt, khaki pants, and boating shoes matched the scenery perfectly. I found myself fantasizing about running my fingers through his thick dark hair. As he approached me, his smile revealed those perfectly white teeth and two dimples, one on each side.

"Holly," he whispered as he drew me close.

I hadn't really noticed his smooth skin and high cheekbones until this very moment. How broad his shoulders were! He definitely worked out. I could feel my knees buckle ever so slightly. It was the first time we'd been this close to one another. My insides tingled.

Holly! I warned myself. *Don't act so eager.*

I smiled shyly, looking up at the towering man before me.

"You look stunning," he said with a playful growl, his green eyes scanning me from my floppy hat to my thighs. "Do you do yoga?" His gaze rested on my buttocks for what felt like an eternity. *Oh my.* A rush of pleasure coursed down my spine and a smile lit up my face.

"I . . . I . . . I . . ."

How could a person be so disarming? I asked myself. I couldn't answer before he offered me a warm smile.

We walked and talked for hours. He showed me dozens of photos of his twin girls, Tiffany and Lily, presenting himself as a Proud Papa, a Father of the Year. He reveled in their academic accomplishments, their athletic awards, and their dutiful service work for the underprivileged. He made time to attend their events, cook for them, and support their dreams. They would soon be leaving for college.

I felt a twang of jealousy. He was living the life I'd always dreamed of. The girls had lived with him most of the time, and their mother, his ex-wife, was apparently an "unfortunate basket case who regularly makes bad decisions."

As we walked along the sun-drenched beach, he held my hand, and it seemed like a million-watt glowing orb of light was emanating from the center of my being. I had never felt so seen, heard, understood or at "home" with a man. Ever. He seemed genuinely interested in my goals and dreams and asked me unusual questions, including, "What's your superpower?"

"I have super facial recognition abilities," I said. "I can see a face once, for just a second, and never forget it. Sometimes it scares people because I will run into someone from my childhood and now, years and many pounds later, I recognize them despite a lot of outward changes."

He offered no response so I quickly pivoted the conversation back to him. I asked him what he would claim as his superpower.

"Well, forgive me if this sounds arrogant, but I am a master strategist and I always win." He gave a nervous laugh. "I can always figure out a way to make things go my way."

"Does that include conjuring up winning lottery numbers?" I asked him with a tinge of snark.

"Oh, Holly, look where I am right now! If this isn't winning the lottery, walking on a beach in paradise with a smart, beautiful woman, then what is?" he asked as he put his arm around me and pulled me in close.

He was wearing the same cologne from last night. Its fragrance drove me to the edge as it overpowered my senses. I was on the verge of swooning. I shared with him my lifelong vision of being a mother and a wife, including vignettes of summers rowing on a lake and winters skiing in Tahoe. I also confessed that one of my nicknames was "Queen of TMI." He listened intently and then said, "You've just described my dream life." He proceeded to tell me he wanted to have more children, too. An electric jolt ran through my body, as if we were speaking directly to my ovaries. Barry continued, "I admire you for knowing that family is more important to you than becoming a celebrity chef on the Food Channel and I can't wait to have you spoil me with your incredible culinary skills."

He then embraced me and whispered in my ear, "I think I've been looking for you my entire life."

Oh my God. Was this actually happening? Could it be that I had finally found a mature man who wanted what I wanted?

Before I could luxuriate in this possibility, he asked me that most dreaded question.

"Holly, why are you still single? You should have been scooped up long ago."

There was no good answer to that question.

Raised by a single, baby-boomer mother with hippie leanings, I had a perfectly happy, seemingly normal childhood. I never knew my father. All Mom would tell me was that I was the result of a one-night stand where the only conscious thing she did was swallow a quaalude. Even if I wanted to find my dad, she didn't know his last name, but she did recall that he had worn a wedding ring.

My friends often suggested I should take a DNA test and search for my biological father. I always shrugged it off, saying it was no big deal that I didn't know him.

Well, that was a lie. The truth was I knew he was married at the time. *Shit, he may still be married, and I wouldn't want to throw a monkey wrench into his family life.*

Okay, that was a half-truth.

The bigger truth was my fear of rejection. What if he slammed the door in my face? What if he couldn't care less about me? What if he didn't even know I existed? *No, no. It was better this way—not knowing.*

At this point in my life, I was grateful to have been raised by a loving mom, maternal grandparents, and my mom's boss, Auntie Geeta, plus an assortment of aunts, uncles, and cousins. I wasn't sure I needed to risk being rejected by someone who didn't realize he had a daughter from a one-night stand.

Being single at nearly thirty-eight was one of the biggest pain points in my life. I knew I was attractive enough, I was fun, I had an active social life, a lot of interests, and a variety of dates. And yet, real love seemed to evade me. As a lifelong "planner" who had every other aspect of my life under control, I was way behind schedule.

Mom would tell you that I was a typical Virgo: a perfectionist, traditional, systematic, dependable, and responsible, albeit given to wild romantic fantasies due to my Pisces moon and Libra rising. Mom was a New Age type who loved all things mystical and magical—she'd watched the movie *The Secret* a zillion times. I was not exactly an atheist, but I was not sure I believed in God, Goddess, the Universe, or whatever. I believed in hard work, detailed planning, and, maybe, four-leaf clovers.

While I didn't necessarily believe in fate or destiny or karma, I had always believed I was meant to be a mother. And, not just any mother, but the "fun mom." The mom all the other kids wish they had. A stay-at-home mom who would bake cookies and let all the neighborhood kids invade every inch of the house and yard. Unlike my mom, who was loving and sweet but had always worked a very demanding full-time job as a paralegal and had never baked me cookies, I planned to be my kids' *everything*. Yes, I would readily admit that.

My future had become crystal clear to me on my seventh birthday.

My grandparents had come to our apartment while I had been sleeping and set up a surprise for me in the spare bedroom. Gramps had built me a big, multi-level, three-bedroom dream dollhouse, complete with Barbie and Ken and basic furniture. Over the years I added carpet, artwork, needlepoint pillows, and more.

My mother's contribution to the dollhouse was to show me how to feng shui it, which included putting miniature dream catchers over the beds in the kids' rooms and telling me that at the right time we would put a sacred romance altar in the "love corner" of the house. I wondered now if that would have saved me from my predicament of still being single at nearly forty.

Nearly every day, I played with my fantasy family and made up stories about their life together and the kids I would have and the things we would do as a big happy family.

While my girlfriends were dreaming of big careers in law or medicine or finance, I was never that ambitious, nor was I a particularly good student. I managed to maintain a solid "C" in high school and somehow even got into a decent college.

My plan was simple: score a degree and work for a few years before marrying by twenty-eight or twenty-nine at the latest, and then having at least three kids before age thirty-six. My husband would be a professional who loved his work but also made time for the family and would revel in my supermom capabilities. And of course, we would have an electrifying sex life!

My beach walk with Barry never really ended. From that first morning walk, things accelerated faster than a Formula One Ferrari at Monza. We became inseparable and, when we weren't together, we were on the phone as if we had lifetimes to catch up on.

Three days after the beach walk, Barry called to ask me a question that would alter the course of my life.

"Hey, Holly, ever been to Budapest?"

"Not lately," I said as I quickly tried to figure out where in the world Budapest was.

"I'm going next week for a quick five days on my annual art-collecting trip. Wanna come? You'll love it, it's one of the most beautiful and romantic cities in Europe, and it will give me a chance to spoil you," he said in a husky, sexy voice.

My entire body vibrated at the thought of taking a flight with him to a place I had never been before.

"Give me a sec to check my calendar." I stalled as I felt butterflies swirling in my stomach. Even though the gala had been a huge success, Carly and I had yet to book our next event, so technically my calendar was wide open.

"Well, it appears the timing is perfect. I would love to go," I said, trying to sound a whole lot cooler than I felt.

Little did I know how fatal my agreeing to accompany him would be.

CHAPTER THREE

Shattered

Three in the morning. I could see on the monitor that my heart was beating at a steady pace. And my blood pressure was a decent 121 over 92. My mother was sound asleep on a cot next to me. Barry, thankfully, was not here.

My jaw was very sore and tight and uncomfortable, but I was not in any extreme physical pain. My mouth felt like a disgusting desert; I couldn't remember ever being more parched. With my left hand I reached for a cup of water with a straw and slowly, carefully, did my best to position it on my lips. Somehow I managed to suck up a little wetness.

My head felt clear for the moment, nearly alert, and I wanted to figure out how I was doing physically, as well as how to "be" with whatever I discovered next. I wiggled my toes, bent my knees a bit, and moved my legs. All seemed well there. I arched my back. Check. Moved my head a little from side to side. Okay there, too.

I remembered someone saying my jaw would take six weeks to heal, my wrist sometime sooner. I hadn't seen a mirror so I didn't know how bad the gash and stitches were over my right eye, but I assumed, since Barry mentioned plastic surgery, it didn't look good.

In so many ways I had led a charmed life. I had never had a serious *I just want to die* kind of heartbreak before. Yes, I had had breakups and lots of upsets and disappointment, but nothing like this.

Sure, like most folks, I had lost friends, but I had never been betrayed by someone I considered a sister. Carly and I had been BFFs since seventh grade when we bonded at our first school dance. We showed up in the same dress, and even though physically we could not be more different— me with a tall, thin, athletic frame and Carly very curvy and busty—we took the coincidence as a sign that we were meant to be friends.

The youngest of five from a dysfunctional family that often had money troubles, Carly was a wild child—some would even say promiscuous—but I always found her to be fun, adventurous, and exciting to be around. That is, until now. In many ways, she was the sister I never had. Losing the love of my life, my BFF and business partner, and nearly dying in a car accident was a trio of tragedies I didn't think I would ever recover from. The only word to describe this feeling of tremendous loss was the term *shattered*. My biggest dreams had been blown into a million bits. My dollhouse life was a smoldering wreckage.

Now, I couldn't talk or type or cook, making it impossible for me to work, so I would most likely be broke in the very near future, too. Usually, when something bad happened, my natural tendency was to go into denial and look for the positive.

But lying on the sterile sheets in a hospital bed, I was certain I would never get there again. Right now I felt like I had sunk to the bottom of an inky, cold, black sea.

I was, perhaps for the first time ever, all alone.

Hopeless.

Nothing to live for.

How could he have done this to me? How could she?

What did I ever do to deserve this?

Confusion arched over my head, swallowing me whole. A part of me hoped beyond hope that I was stuck in a terrible nightmare and I would wake up and my old life would be waiting for me.

The practical part of me was channeling Dr. Laura Schlessinger who whispered encouraging no-nonsense messages in my ear. At least I had discovered this before Barry and I married and had kids. I had dodged a bullet. Big time.

My heart ran a video loop of our uber-romantic early days, remembering so many moments of our whirlwind trip to Budapest not even two weeks after we met.

Two hours after I had said "Yes," to going with him, he'd sent me a detailed Excel file that had tips on what to pack and outlined nearly every hour of the trip, including suggestions on what to wear.

Our itinerary covered visits to castles, parks, monuments, museums, cafés, a private boat ride on the Danube, and an afternoon of pampering at an ancient mineral bathhouse. When Barry had sent me the Excel file with packing instructions, I took it as a romantic and thoughtful gesture, but Mom surprised me when she responded quite negatively, telling me she saw that as a sign of control issues.

I thanked her for sharing and ignored her warning.

Carly and I googled fashion in Budapest and decided I needed a more European look for this sophisticated city. From the packing list, it was clear that my usual Southern California casual style was inappropriate for our sophisticated outings.

Fortunately, Carly was more than happy to become my personal travel stylist. "Holly, I have the perfect vision for your Budapest wardrobe," she said, flipping her long brown hair to the side. "We are going to transform you into a sleek and sexy version of Rene Russo in *The Thomas Crown Affair*. You're going to look fabulous." Her chubby cheeks flushed a slight crimson as she grabbed my arm in excitement.

"What are you talking about?" I said, pulling away. "That movie with all the guys in bowler hats who steal art for a living? I don't remember Rene's clothes at all."

"Of course, you don't! Your idea of fashion is anything with a stretch waist for your almost nonexistent one," Carly said, peering down at her own plump frame. At five feet four inches, Carly found it hard to find flattering clothes to accentuate what I liked to call her "more positive attributes." She had lovely green eyes that sparkled with mischief. And she seemed to know everything about the fashion industry, which I clearly did not.

"I'm taking you to a designer resale shop in La Jolla where all the socialites place their barely worn Gucci, Prada, and Chanel. Eleganza has the best selection, and European tailoring is made for your perfect size six body," Carly teased, her envy showing.

Carly's passion for fashion, as I called it, was one thing we didn't share. For me, clothes were first and foremost about comfort and function with a dash of cute. While I did care about my appearance, I couldn't have cared less about trends or fancy labels.

My daily work outfit consisted of a white chef's jacket, polyester black-and-white houndstooth pull-on pants, and beat-up clogs with rubber soles. On my days off, I traded the chef look for my most comfortable well-worn yoga pants and colorful hoodies.

"I'll pick you up in an hour," Carly continued. I could see the wheels turning in her head as her breathing accelerated. "Be sure to bring your mother's Big Bang scarf with you," she instructed.

"Her big what?"

"Remember that dude she was dating a few years ago who bought her an original Hermès scarf? The one in the iconic orange box? It's called the Big Bang and it's going to be the centerpiece of your new look." Carly spun toward me. "Oh, and don't forget your credit card."

As promised, she picked me up within the hour. Luckily, we found parking on Girard Avenue just a few doors south of the store. I was instantly impressed with the marble floors, the gleaming crystal chandeliers, the elegant glass displays of jewelry, and the well-spaced clothing racks featuring velvet hangers.

The air smelled expensive and the fabrics gleamed with a pristine, nearly ridiculous perfection. As I thumbed through the first rack, I wondered where these clothes had been. *And on whom. What did these ladies have that I did not?* I smiled to myself, realizing at that moment that I was entering a whole new league of living. A surge of juicy anticipation overcame me.

My prior shopping ventures into secondhand stores and shoddy-looking bargain basement outlets where haphazardly jammed racks overflowed with clothes were everything but pleasant. A musty odor would cling not only to the clothing, but also to my skin as I rushed out of the place, gasping for air.

Eleganza was the exact opposite: It was not only beautiful but it exuded something exotic: a blend of fresh clean citrus and a promise—no, an invitation—to a world of ease and pleasure. A calming classical piano soundtrack arose from an invisible speaker nestled somewhere in the background.

We were greeted by a fifty-something woman with a mane of gorgeous, thick, shoulder-length silver hair. Wearing all-black Issey Miyake and an impressive amount of string pearls around her neck, she glided to us in her stylish, gold-quilted Chanel ballet flats.

"Welcome, ladies, my name is Juliet. Can I serve you a glass of champagne or rosé?" she offered.

"Yes, champagne for us both," Carly said before I could answer.

"I'd love some sparkling water," I said, giving my friend a side glance. "It's too early in the day for me."

"Holly, we have to get you in the mood, and champagne is exactly what this occasion calls for," Carly confidently explained to Juliet, signaling two glasses were needed. Moments later a young woman approached with two flutes atop a round silver platter and a small silver bowl of smoked nuts.

"Now, what can I help you two with today?"

With that, Carly launched into my needs for the upcoming trip to Budapest while she dug into my large brown faux leather shoulder tote and pulled out the orange Hermès box, handing it to Juliet.

Juliet set the box on the counter and delicately pulled the scarf out to its full glory.

"Ah, the Big Bang. What a stunning treasure," Juliet said, while draping it around my neck. "The navy and blue tones really accentuate your eyes," she noted.

Carly moved between us, holding her champagne flute casually in one hand while beaming oddly at me. I shifted my weight from one foot to the other, not knowing what to say.

"Holly," Juliet continued, "with your friend's vision, we are going to create a beautiful travel wardrobe that will take you from the streets of Budapest by day to the elegant evenings you have planned."

I gave Carly a puzzled look as if to say, *How does Juliet know about my specific plans?*

"I called ahead to prepare your visit here," Carly whispered as she pushed me toward a rack of dresses. She picked through the selection, piling one thing after another onto her left arm.

Carrying a stack of clothes, we entered the largest dressing room I'd ever been in. Mirrors adorned three walls and a settee was neatly located against the fourth. A delicate chandelier hung daintily from the ornate ceiling. Looking at myself in the mirror, something I rarely did, reminded me of my teenage days when I often wished to be shorter, curvier, and sexier. I had despised it when the boys at school teased me about my long, skinny legs, relentlessly calling me chicken legs or bird legs.

Mom often told me I was blessed to have been born with her legs, her brains, and her high metabolism. I always knew that Carly was jealous of my ability to eat anything, at any time of the day or night, and never gain an ounce. There, underneath the bright lights, I was pleased with my fashionably slim reflection.

For the next forty-five minutes, I became a living mannequin. Juliet and Carly stripped me down to my bra and panties and had me stepping in and out of clothes all while speaking a language of color, print, texture, and fabric that was mostly foreign to me. Every item they had me try on was something I would have never selected for myself and yet, I was delighted with how everything looked and enjoyed the feel of real silk and cashmere against my skin.

My favorite of the three outfits I bought included a pair of skinny dark brown leather pants topped with a pale gold, scoop-neck silk blouse, accompanied by the Hermès scarf, a navy Burberry car jacket, and gorgeous navy suede three-inch LK Bennett pumps.

It took both Juliet and Carly a while to convince me that I absolutely could not enter Budapest carrying my schleppy old brown shoulder sack. I was now the proud owner of a slightly used Celine calfskin shoulder bag.

For perhaps the first time in my life, I felt chic and classy and surprisingly comfortable. I also felt a bit nauseous, not just from the champagne, but also when it came time to pay up.

My shopping spree came in at just under $1,800. Even though I realized everything was heavily discounted from the original retail price, this was easily the most I had ever spent on clothes in one day.

Carly assured me that my new wardrobe was classic, timeless, and of the highest quality, and it would most certainly last me through dozens of future European adventures. As I thrust the shopping bags into Carly's trunk, my thoughts wandered to my pending travels with Barry. I had never been on an airplane for longer than a couple of hours. For a brief moment, I wondered if I could smuggle my yoga pants into my bag without Carly looking. Closing the trunk, I saw a strange look cross her face. Then it vanished without a trace. Had I just thought out loud?

"We'd better get you home, Holly," Carly said in a quiet voice. "You have a big adventure ahead of you."

The fourteen-hour nonstop Los Angeles business class flight to Budapest was my first adventure out of coach and out of the country except for my trips over the border to Tijuana and Rosarito by car. The flight was mostly fun, except for Barry's crazy notion that we should join the milehigh club, which I absolutely declined. Instead, I tried to dig in and get some information on what kind of business he had to conduct in Hungary. He explained that it was an annual trip to collect some art his parents had acquired through their broker and he would be hand-carrying it back home since it was so rare and precious.

After clearing customs, we found our driver with a sign that read "Tavers." Fully decked out in a knee-length, double-breasted, brass-buttoned uniform complete with cap, our driver escorted us to a newly minted black Mercedes sedan. In less than a half hour, we pulled up to our hotel, the Four Seasons Gresham Palace, a grand art nouveau building that promised extreme luxury. There were definitely advantages to dating a wealthy man. In our family, when we did stay in a hotel, it was generally at the Holiday Inn level.

As we walked up to the reception, a handsome gray-haired man dressed in a dark gray suit smiled and offered his hand to Barry with a warm, "Welcome back, Mr. Tavers. So nice to see you again. We have you in your favorite suite with the Danube view."

Exhausted from the long flight and the time zone change, my mood brightened the moment I walked into the suite. Long hot baths were my passion and I was completely smitten when I discovered the giant soaking tub in the pristine black-and-taupe marble bathroom. Barry informed me that I had options for dinner. We could order room service (he recommended his favorite dish, the Chicken Paprika with Kapaa Pepper Sauce and Baked Gnocchi) or we could take a short walk around the river and go to a casual café for a light supper.

As much as I wanted to see Budapest, a bath and room service was all I was up for. Having seen the itinerary for the next day, I figured I needed to rest up and get ready for prolonged cultural sightseeing.

Before I even opened my eyes the next morning, I could smell brewing coffee and feel the sun streaming through the window as it warmed my face. I heard the crunchy sound of a newspaper page turning and assumed it was Barry. I was incredibly cozy under the down comforter and was enjoying a few moments alone in bed, taking in the incredible circumstances I was enjoying. It all seemed too good to be true and yet, here I was, wrapped in luxury with the man of my dreams—for real.

Barry brought me a small tray with coffee and a warm chocolate croissant (my number one guilty pleasure). He had a gigantic smile on his face and the most loving look in his eyes as he said to me, "You are so beautiful and I love your adorable bedhead morning look. I don't remember a time in my life when I was happier than I am right now."

I was speechless. The insides of my thighs were still moist from the pleasures of the night before. Moving the tray to the floor, I rolled toward him. He took both of my hands in his.

"This will be a trip you will never forget," he promised. At that moment, I had no idea how right he was.

Our first adventure for the day was scheduled to begin at the very reasonable hour of 11 A.M.: a private boat tour down the Danube. As we were walking through the lobby, I saw a familiar face out of the corner of my eye. Without meaning to, I waved to him.

It happened often. I would get this hit—"Oh, I know them"—and I instinctively wanted to connect. I remember thinking that this man was all-American with his standard beige khakis and blue button-down oxford shirt when I had first seen him yesterday at our departure gate. In his mid-forties, he had attempted an earnest sweep of his thinning hair across his brow. He looked away when he saw me wave and then Barry asked me who I waving at and I reminded him about my super facial-recognition abilities.

"Well, it's not surprising that people on our flight would also be staying at this hotel," he said a bit dismissively. Then he gave me a big smile, took me by the hand and guided me out the ornate iron doors of the Gresham Palace.

We walked the short distance to the dock where our own private boat awaited us. It was a water version of a limousine, a sleek mahogany speedboat with super plush leather seats. Barry let the captain do the driving while he became my personal tour guide and pointed out the landmarks on both sides of the river.

He regaled me with the history of the city and stories of the Habsburg royal family. He promised he had a treat planned for later in the day when we would have an amazing cake loved by Elisabeth Habsburg at the 150-year-old Gerbeaud Café, known to have the finest pastries in all of Hungary. We cruised under a variety of beautiful bridges, all of which had a different look and feel to them. I found myself wondering if perhaps Barry had lived in Budapest in an earlier life because he seemed so at home here. I giggled to myself that I was starting to think like my mom. *Did I believe in past lives after all?* Blinded by the romance unfolding before me, I brushed off the thought immediately.

Later that afternoon, after an indulgent feast at the café, Barry insisted that we sit for charcoal caricature portraits with a street artist set up in front of St. Stephen's Basilica. He thought it would be fun to have the two of us pose together. He sat down on a small metal chair and pulled me onto his lap and we snuggled together for fifteen minutes while we were being sketched. The end result was surprisingly adorable and then Barry decided we should each have an individual portrait. While I was seated, trying to hold still for the artist, I noticed a man standing under a tree across the street and, even though the sun was in my eyes, I was pretty sure it was the American who had been both on our flight and in our hotel.

Is he following us? I wondered.

Naw. Why in the world would anyone do that? I figured it was just another coincidence since we were hanging out in front of the basilica, one of the major tourist sites of Budapest. I decided not to mention it to Barry, since he was clearly not impressed with my superpower.

Our sightseeing included a visit to Barry's favorite sculpture garden at the Koller Gallery, the oldest private gallery in Budapest located in the historic Castle District. The gallery had a wide array of art for sale, but the sculpture garden was a permanent exhibition. Barry had a particular attraction to a sculpture of two masks, a man and a woman puckered up for a kiss. He positioned us to mimic the pose. I was quickly discovering that Barry had quite the sentimental side and wasted no time setting up selfies of the two of us to do what he called "capturing the moment." They turned out brilliantly.

I loved everything about Budapest. It was beautiful, charming, romantic, and steeped in art and history. Barry had been coming to Budapest since he was a teenager. He grew up hearing exaggerated stories about his family connection to Hungarian royalty and he seemed eager to share the few stories he knew with me.

Barry's parents had honeymooned in Budapest and Vienna in 1965 with directions from Phyllis's mother to connect with the family still living in Budapest. What they discovered when they arrived in Hungary was that there was only one relative still alive, a young man named Laszlo Varga, whom everyone called Lassie (like the dog).

He was the son of Mrs. Tavers's cousin, a woman of exceptional beauty and style named Ilona, who after World War II had an affair with a prominent art dealer, which resulted in a son. Ilona died when Lassie was nearly twenty years old. While his biological father never publicly accepted his son, he did see him a few times each year and, eventually, he made Lassie an apprentice in the family art business. It was on their honeymoon that Mrs. Tavers acquired her interest in collecting postimpressionist art, but it would be many years before the Tavers had enough money to indulge her obsession.

Barry did mention that over the past decade he had made an annual pilgrimage to Budapest to bring his parents back a new piece for their collection. When and where the Tavers struck it rich was still a mystery to me. I had heard stories that they were slumlords in Detroit before selling off their tenement buildings for demolition to make room for a huge development project that made them zillionaires.

The next day we were invited to lunch at Lassie's villa in the Castle District. A three-story sandstone structure that had a castle-like vibe to it with seven bedrooms, six bathrooms, a gorgeous garden, and a swimming pool that was half indoors and half out. The entryway had a soaring ceiling and an eclectic art collection that included a Flemish master, a Rauschenberg, and what might possibly have been a Pissarro just on one wall!

A surprisingly strange mix of art for an art dealer, I thought. I was captivated by the gorgeous gold-veined, pale pink marble floor, and the peachy pink walls. The carved furniture looked like mahogany with gold accessories everywhere. Giant Chinese-style pots held massive indoor greenery. High above, light streamed in from several skylights positioned in such a way as to not potentially fade the art on the walls. It was unusual, feminine, and screamed big money and yet, it somehow felt warm and inviting.

The beeping machines shook me awake from my daydream, bringing me back to the cold hospital room. Budapest now felt like a distant hallucination. At the moment, I was hanging out in the seventh circle of hell trying to figure out was any of this real? *Did he ever love me? And, ultimately, who the hell was he?*

I was strong. I could figure out how to endure the physical healing process. But of something else I was not so certain . . . would I survive what came after that?

CHAPTER FOUR

More Lies

I told Barry no.

No, you can't explain.

No, you can't come see me.

No, you can't talk to me (and even if I wanted to talk with my jaw wired shut most of what I could say would be incomprehensible), and most importantly, no fucking way am I going home with you.

Going home!

Now, this was a major dilemma. After three days in the hospital, I was told I was ready to be discharged. But to what home would I go?

Less than four months after we'd met, we had had a very public and very dramatic Fourth of July engagement at Petco Park. Barry had arranged for us to be center field at the end of the Padres game while the fireworks were going off. Then he got down on one knee on the pitcher's mound.

The entire stadium had watched and, of course, we had been on the jumbotron. He had chosen Petco Park because his parents owned most of the land upon which the parking lot was built and they had connections. He had presented me with a stunning five-carat, cushion-cut diamond ring with a pavé diamond-studded double band, in a platinum setting.

I, naturally, had said, "Yes!"

The crowd had roared wildly. We made the Ten O'Clock News on KUSI, which is how my mother heard about it. When we made it back to his home, Barry had a few more surprises for me: three-dozen red roses on the dining room table, a bottle of chilled champagne, and a small plate of my favorite Teuscher milk chocolate champagne truffles.

Then, as he raised a glass of champagne, he announced that as an engagement present he had arranged for me to have a boob job. He seemed very pleased and excited as he told me this. He proceeded to give me the doctor's credentials listing all the women he knew that had found breast bliss with his handiwork. We had never discussed plastic surgery and it wasn't something I had ever seriously considered doing.

Sure, I'd been insecure about my body as a teenager, but by now I was pretty much at peace with my slim athletic swimmer's body and almost 34B chest.

"A boob job?" I repeated slowly, feeling both a little flattered and deeply insulted by the grandiosity of the gesture. "Are there any other imperfections about me that you'd like to change while you're at it?"

"Oh, God, no," he said, grabbing me in a tight embrace. "I love you the way you are! I just want you to feel more comfortable in your wedding dress." My body stiffened, not sure how to react. As if sensing my reluctance, he quickly added, "We'll just make you one cup size larger. It is a very special day and I want it to be perfect for you!" His tone sounded genuine enough. I mean, *he really was trying to be generous, right?*

"Oh, and think of how you will look then in your bikini on the beaches of Hawaii!" His green eyes glistened. Hawaii? It was his favorite getaway, yet another surprise he had in store for us.

The champagne made me lightheaded. What a night, filled with over-the-top surprises! My lifelong dream of becoming a bride, wife, and mother was finally coming true and then some. Not knowing how to process all of it, I quickly drank two more glasses of champagne.

The day after the engagement, Mom called and invited me to lunch, saying she couldn't wait to see the ring. I suspected she had a bigger agenda since she generally had lunch at her desk at Auntie

Geeta's super-busy law practice. Mom and Auntie Geeta had been friends and a working team for longer than I had been on the planet, and Auntie Geeta had always treated me like one of her own.

It was Geeta, in fact, who had first awakened in me a passion for Indian food. One of my earliest memories was that of being seated on her lap as she fed me bites of gulab jamun, a yummy, syrupy dessert made from fried dough, sweet cream, and aromatic spices. Every August, Auntie Geeta and I would go together to the Indian Heritage street fair, where we'd sample all the delicious food, play with the colorful jewelry, and get our hands painted with henna. She was like a second mother to me, and a sister to my mom.

Mom and I met at our favorite place and ordered our usual Lounge Burgers with gluten-free buns and we split the glutenous half-and-half order of yummy onion rings and fries with extra BBQ sauce. In our line of thinking, we figured the gluten-free buns canceled out the gluten in the batter-covered onion rings.

She seemed genuinely wowed with the ring and then launched into a long speech about how it might be wise for us to have a very long engagement before the wedding since we'd really only known each other a relatively short time.

"Holly, honey, Dr. Pat always says you can't really know someone until you've spent a year with them," referencing Dr. Pat Allen, one of Mom's favorite love experts. "You are about to make the biggest decision of your life. What's the rush?" she asked before biting into a golden crusty onion ring.

"Well, Dr. Pat never dealt with eggs that are about to take their last breath and I know in every cell of my being that Barry is *the One*. Besides, aren't you a little interested in finally becoming a grandmother?" I asked a bit too deviously.

Mom smiled and laughed, "Please don't ever call me Grandma. I want to be called Gigi."

"Huh? What's the matter with *Grandma*?"

"I'm much too young and hot. Besides, Gigi stands for gorgeous grandmother, which is much more fitting."

Thinking this was the end of the conversation, I dug into an onion ring with a big dollop of BBQ sauce. She then asked if I wanted her to give me a tarot reading, but I declined.

Seconds later she offered up an astrology compatibility reading with her friend Carol, but on my oxytocin, dopamine, adrenaline, being-in-love drug high, I assured her I was 100 percent certain that Barry was my one. I explained that we planned to have a spring wedding on the grounds of the Tavers Estate in Rancho Santa Fe, a good six months from now, so technically we would have known each other a full year by the wedding day.

I thought somehow this would assuage her concern. What I didn't yet know was that Mom had already consulted the tarot many times on my behalf since Barry first showed up in my life. She was freaked out because each time she read the cards, the dreaded Tower card appeared, signifying potential disaster and imminent disruption.

Barry decided it was only logical that once we were engaged, we would move in together to share his recently completed "dream home." The twins would be leaving for college in six weeks, and he saw it as an opportunity for me to do some bonding with them and to get our new life together up and running.

He also dropped a bomb. He told me that his parents would insist on a prenuptial agreement because of his role as executor of their massive estate, the family trusts, and so on, and they wanted to make sure the family was protected. As a justification, he said to me, "I will make sure we will never, ever need to use the prenuptial agreement and it will be more than fair. One thing we can do right now, as an act of faith on both our parts, is for you to invest your retirement account into the house, and then I will put you on the deed. We will co-own the house, which is valued at over $2.5 million. Isn't that fair?" he asked.

At the time, in my naiveté, it sounded more than fair. How generous to be able to buy into a multimillion dollar home for a mere $100,000, even though it was the entirety of the inheritance my grandfather had left me plus my retirement account. I didn't bother to consult my paralegal mother or my auntie who was an attorney, or even Carly. I simply agreed to it.

At that moment, it felt right to use the inheritance money from my grandfather who had built me a dollhouse to buy a life-sized one. Besides, Barry reminded me that he was an Ivy-league-trained attorney and could easily handle all the paperwork. Within weeks, I had moved in with him, given him my money, and signed a bunch of legal documents with little plastic adhesive tabs with arrows that said, "Sign Here."

I vividly remember the day I signed the papers, because we went to lunch at a beautiful ocean-view restaurant. He wanted to celebrate and so ordered a bottle of champagne. It was a gorgeous day, warm and sunny, with a very gentle breeze. I could hear the seagulls squawking as they were diving for fish in the surf. The champagne was delicious and matched the bubbly, loving feeling I had running through my veins, plus it gave me quite a buzz before our whole grilled sea bass arrived.

After lunch, we walked the two blocks to his office where a quiet, dowdy, grandmother type in sensible shoes notarized the papers as soon as I signed them.

And yes, I did have the thought, *Perhaps I should read these documents or at least have them reviewed?* and then moved on to thoughts about what I wanted for dinner.

Now I had to figure out where I was going to live during my recovery and when I could get Barry to return my life savings.

Mom came to the rescue and insisted that I move into her home, and she would oversee my care for however long I needed her. She also offered to go to "our" house to pick up whatever I needed. I didn't know how or when I would be up for confessing to her my financial predicament.

A few hours before I was discharged from the hospital, an aide walked in with a large orchid plant, and he handed me an envelope that contained a note from Carly:

Dear Holly,

You have been my best friend and sister for more than twenty years, and I can't tell you how much I love and adore you. I am so grateful you survived the accident and to know that you will have a full recovery.

I am beyond sorry for the pain I have caused you. I never meant to hurt you.

Barry has been flirting with me forever, and the truth is I was jealous of all the good things that were happening to you. I should have been a better friend and told you what he was doing.

When he invited me over that night, I had no idea he was going to seduce me. He texted and asked me to stop by to help him plan a surprise for you. When I got there, he opened a bottle of wine and then showed me some lingerie he had bought for you and asked me to try it on so he could see what it looked like. It was a bit of a stretch because you know how much bigger I am than you. But he insisted and, well, with several glasses of wine in me on an empty stomach, I wasn't thinking straight. And then things got out of control.

I hope you can find it in your heart to forgive me. Please forgive me. I can't imagine my life without you.

Love, Carly

I literally felt like I was going to throw up in my mouth, which would have been a nightmare with my jaw wired shut. I closed my eyes and willed my stomach to settle down.

How did I not see this coming? From the day we met, I suspected Carly was jealous of me. She had always wanted what I had. Deep down, I knew this but never wanted to confront it. So, of course, she shows up at *my* house and seduces *my* fiancé. I should have known she would jump at the first chance to take something that was mine.

Waves of rage coursed through me, unlike anything I had ever felt before. The skin on my arms turned pink, my cheeks flared an angry shade of red, my heart raced, and I wanted to scream in the worst way.

If only I could scream.

I would get into her face and, at the top of my voice, yell, "You stupid, mean-spirited, low-life bitch! How could you throw away a lifetime of friendship? How could you betray me like this? How could you dare to think I will ever forgive you?"

If only my right wrist wasn't broken. I would grab her by the neck and slap her as hard as I could and then kick her with everything I had.

If only this wasn't happening.

With my very clumsy left hand, I sent Carly a text that read, "Never contact me again." Then I blocked her number on my phone.

Carly and I were done forever. I mumbled to the aide to get rid of the plant.

Barry was blowing up my phone with voicemails and text messages. I ignored them for days. After my mailbox was full, I knew I needed to begin deleting the messages. I began listening to the voicemails, almost all of them from Barry.

His first message said, "Babe, I know I fucked up. I am beyond sorry, completely ashamed of myself that I could do anything that would hurt you. I love you beyond the stars, the moon, and the sun. I have never loved anyone the way I love you. I am begging you to forgive me, to give me another chance, to focus on all the amazing times we have had and will have for the rest of our lives.

"Maybe I was subconsciously driven to 'sow my wild oats' just one more time. I have a strong appetite that way. But it was a terrible misstep, and you have my word that it was just that—a foolish mistake that will never happen again. Please call me. I miss you so much. I need you so much. Our future children need you."

A few messages later, he changed his tone. "Listen, be reasonable. We have built a life together already. I am asking that you call me. We have to talk."

A day later, he switched tactics. Again. "I keep thinking about how this could have happened. And I think I was drawn to Carly because she is your oldest and dearest friend, like knowing her most intimately was a way to know *you* more intimately. I know it sounds crazy. And what's even crazier is that I think the same was true for Carly. Her getting close to me was a way to be even closer to you.

"We had been talking about you all evening, both of us expressing our love for you. And the more we laughed and the more Carly told me stories about you, the closer we got—until there was an unfortunate blurring of the lines. Yeah, I know it sounds nuts. But I think it really was our mutual adoration for you that lit the flame. I'm so sorry I allowed it to ever get that far."

When I did not respond, he flipped the story once again.

"I didn't want to tell you this, but the truth is Carly has been chasing me for months. When you weren't looking, she would blow me kisses across the room. It was unreal! She just couldn't resist the temptation. I only meant well by allowing her to have a taste of your life and showing her the house and the pretty things I had gotten you. She is so jealous of us! How could you let her ruin our lives like this?"

In his final message, Barry said, "Holly, we're done. I can't believe what an arrogant and unforgiving bitch you are. Clearly, you are not capable of real adult love. For your sake, I hope you find a good shrink to work through your extensive and deep emotional wounds and issues.

"The love we shared was rare and precious and special and you have now thrown away your only chance at happiness and a real family. I am arranging to have your things packed up and sent to your mother's house, and I fully expect you to return the ring."

Shit, Mom was right, and it was worse than she could have imagined. The fucker was a toxic narcissist. And then, as much as I didn't want to, I was overtaken with body-racking sobs and snotty tears and a feeling that I might as well be dead.

I decided it was time to block him on my phone, and as I did, I sent him a psychic vow: *By the power vested in me, I now pronounce you blocked and deleted. You may now kiss my ass.*

If only that was enough to soothe my misery.

When I wasn't in physical pain or emotional pain or both, my thoughts would turn to memories of Barry and all the ways in which he said and did things that made me feel, for the first time in my life, cherished, treasured, and protected.

He was a master of big and small romantic gestures, and it sometimes felt like he could reach inside my heart and discover the words

I most wanted to hear. I had visualized him as my safe place to land, my true home, wrapped in the big, strong arms of my real-life knight in shining armor, always there claiming he would take a bullet for me.

If only. I never, ever expected he would be the one shooting at me with an AK-47 to the heart.

I wondered how I had missed signs of trouble, and then I beat myself up for falling for what I now saw was a fantasy. I tried hard to make sense of the conflicting feelings of love and obsession and desire for the Barry *I thought I knew* with the reality of the Barry I got.

My thirty-eighth birthday arrived just in time for my second day at Mom's. It was by far the worst birthday ever. Mom did her best to make things festive. She brought me a bowl of my favorite hot fudge–covered coffee ice cream, nicely softened to near-soup consistency, with a birthday candle in it. I felt nothing but misery, certain that I was now damaged goods on all levels.

My mind was on a negative feedback loop that screamed nonstop insults at me, such as, "You are a stupid, naïve airhead who should have known you are unlovable, unmarriageable, ugly, and possibly destined to be an angry cat woman."

Mom couldn't have been sweeter or kinder to me. She made me delicious chocolate protein shakes to sip through a straw for breakfast, and she left me nutritious pureed chicken and veggie soups to enjoy for lunch and dinner. Each day, she came home from work as early as she could to drive me to the park to take long, slow walks. And she didn't force me to attempt to talk, knowing that I hated sounding like a drunken Aussie when I did.

We watched movies together every evening. One of our movies was a comedy from the 1970s called *Heaven Can Wait,* starring Warren Beatty. Mom confessed she had been crazy in lust with Warren back in the day and that he was the Ryan Gosling of her generation. I had to agree with her that he was quite the sexy specimen and the movie was fun. It's the story about a quarterback for the L.A. Rams, Joe Pendleton, who is about to play in the Super Bowl.

After practicing in the stadium, Joe rides his bike along Kanan-Dume Road in Malibu on his way back to his home. We see him pedal into a long dark tunnel, and then there is a big truck headed toward him. It appears he is about to get crushed. The scene jumps to what looks like heaven, and we see Joe in his tracksuit and sneakers walking around, looking baffled and lost. An overanxious man in a suit, the "escort," tells Joe he is there to lead him to his next destination.

Joe argues with the guy, telling him he needs to get back to where he was because he has the Super Bowl coming up in a few days. The escort tells him that is impossible. Joe continues to protest until the escort's supervisor, Mr. Jordan, arrives. Mr. Jordan questions the escort who, on his first day on the job, was certain that Joe was about to be crushed by the truck. He didn't want to witness the accident, so he snatched Joe out of his body a second before impact.

Mr. Jordan then gently explains to the escort that Joe, being the elite athlete he was, would have swerved and avoided the collision and that, technically, he wasn't supposed to die until much later—10:17 A.M. on March 20, 2025, to be exact.

Mr. Jordan now has to tell Joe that his highly tuned athletic body has been cremated, and it is impossible for him to return. Joe, while slightly relieved to discover that this was all a big mistake, continues to insist that a NEW body be found, pronto. Because he has to play in the Super Bowl.

The comedy continues with Joe inhabiting not one but ultimately two new bodies. In the end, he does get to play in the Super Bowl.

Watching *Heaven Can Wait* with Mom was entertaining, and it did have a sweet love story intertwined into it, but what really got me thinking was, *What if God does make mistakes??? Is it possible this whole disaster with Barry was a mistake? Maybe we should have never met?*

That night I barely slept. I kept thinking about the mistakes I had made along the way with Barry, especially signing those legal documents without reading them or having them reviewed. I realized that I needed to ask Mom and Auntie for help to recover my $100,000. There was no way I wanted to be an investor in a home, no matter how great the potential financial upside, with a man I would never speak to again.

The next day on our walk through the park, I slowly filled Mom in on what I had done with my retirement account and explained that I didn't even have a copy of the papers I had signed. While she didn't say so, I could see the look of shock and disappointment on her face, and then she confessed something horrifying to me. "Holly, there's no easy way to tell you this," she began slowly. "You know I have always had my suspicions about Barry, so I hired Auntie's investigator to do a background check on him. I think you're going to want to sit down to hear what I'm about to say."

We walked in silence to a nearby bench. Mom paused briefly to gather her thoughts and then proceeded to drop a bomb—several of them, in fact, in rapid-fire succession.

"Holly, Barry did not go to an Ivy League law school. He graduated from a law school neither Geeta nor I have ever heard of, and ranked close to the bottom of his class. He was disbarred within three years of practicing law for fraud: commingling and stealing funds from his clients. And for several other unscrupulous offenses.

"For the past twenty years, Barry has earned his living filing frivolous lawsuits against wealthy people and major corporations, and he currently has over a hundred active lawsuits just in San Diego County alone. His career, if you can call it that, is weaponizing the legal system against the innocent. Generally, people settle with him because it's ultimately cheaper than litigating. Some of these settlements have been more than a half-million dollars."

We sat in silence for several minutes as I tried my best to absorb the news.

I asked her to give me a copy of the report. She said, "I will, but first, let me prepare you for the rest of it. There's more. We discovered Barry is forty-nine, not forty-two, like he told you. And we also found out that he has been married three times. In addition to the twins, he has a son who was born with severe multiple defects whom he abandoned within days of the birth. This left the mother and infant homeless and living in a shelter for several weeks. A generous citizen then took them in and gave them a home."

Mom told me all of it in a whisper. No response was possible.

I felt paralyzed and a bit dizzy. Unable to formulate a single sentence, I put my head between my knees and sobbed.

Mom held me as I cried until I gasped for air.

"Holly, I'm so sorry . . . there is no way you could have known. He is a true sociopath. He turned on the charm, and you became his prey. This isn't your fault. You will get past this, and tomorrow I will ask Auntie to start working on getting your money back from him."

I didn't just want my money. I wanted revenge to ensure Barry would never be able to con another person for the rest of his life.

CHAPTER FIVE

Fire!

Blood-curdling screams arose from the head bobbing out of the enormous black iron pot perched on a serene, deserted beach. Palm fronds dangled above. Seagulls circled overhead like vultures as reddish-tinged yellow flames licked and leaped up the sides of the pot. I closed my eyes and covered my ears, hoping not to hear the excruciating yelps of this poor soul, and yet I was pulled to walk closer and see that a man was burning alive in a vat of boiling oil.

And then the biggest, widest, most gleeful smile spread from cheek to cheek on my face. A wave of something akin to pleasure rushed through my body. It was Barry, and I was thrilled to see him in his final dying moments!

My jaw ached as I began to wake up, and I realized I had been dreaming. My face was sore from trying to smile despite the wires.

I had no idea I was capable of such violent thoughts and surprised by how happy the vision of Barry burning alive had made me.

Mom's soul-crushing revelations the day before about Barry, the real Barry, the criminal, predatory Barry, had taken me to a new level of despair and misery. I had spent the time since hiding deep under my comforter, crying endlessly, fighting to breathe at times. Now, this crazy, revenge-filled dream had offered an unexpected sense of possibility.

Maybe, I thought, there really was justice in the Universe. Maybe I would get revenge. And, for sure, this dream was an omen that karma was at work, and he would someday suffer for the intolerable pain he was causing me.

This feeling of righteousness didn't last long enough. As the day wore on, waves of anger replaced my usual waves of grief and sadness. It was as if a hot red rash was erupting under my skin, and my stomach was sending up volcanic burps of acid indigestion, despite my very bland, mild diet of smoothies.

Thank God for liquid Maalox. I quickly sipped a dose to quell the burning in my gut.

I had heard that depression is a symptom of unexpressed anger but had never really allowed myself to experience anger. Being "sunny and psychotically optimistic," I never allowed anger in my self-created persona, nurtured in the world I had created through my fantasy dollhouse. The good dollhouse mom was a cheerful, loving, nurturing being, willing to sacrifice everything for the good of her family. If she was anything at all, she was not an angry bitch.

Now anger was upon me. My arms tingled uncomfortably and I felt lightheaded as my mind raced with all the different possibilities for exacting revenge upon this less-than-human asshole who had ruined my life.

As much as I hated feeling sad and depressed, anger wasn't any better.

My feelings rocketed through me like pinballs in an out-of-control pinball machine.

I craved serenity. Balance. Relief.

I fucking want my life back. My delusional life, where the man of my dreams loves me and can't wait to give me everything I've ever asked for.

My phone vibrated and slithered across the nightstand with a text from Mikey, one of my oldest and dearest friends, who was gifted with a wicked sense of humor and a shocking ability to behave inappropriately and get away with it. Mikey and I had met in a playground sandbox as toddlers, and ended up in the same schools from kindergarten through our senior year. Mom always called us the "soul siblings." He was the closest thing to a brother I had ever had.

In fact, we'd probably be married by now were it not for the minor detail that he's gay. Mikey moved to Los Angeles after college and, even though we had drifted apart physically, technology and social media had kept us enmeshed in each other's lives.

Mikey was a professional fundraiser who was extremely talented at talking rich folks into giving him giant donations for very good causes. As he once explained it to me, "I metaphorically turn them upside down, hold them by the ankles and shake until all the gold falls out of their pockets."

"I'm in town to visit my parents. Got time for a catch-up visit?"

"Yes, yes, yes," I slowly typed with my left hand. "Come soon? Walk on the beach? Need you desperately."

Seconds later, Mikey responded: "Of course, my sweet. See you in an hour or less. Lace up your shoes."

I ran to the mirror, something I had been avoiding during my recovery. My reflection surprised me . . . I nearly didn't recognize myself. My normally gorgeous, thick, honey-blonde-streaked hair, by far my best feature, was so dirty that the color defied description. And it was plastered to my head. The stitches over my eye needed to remain dry, and I had been too lazy to take the time to take the necessary measures to wash my hair. The bags under my eyes were frightening, and my skin tone was dry and dull.

Ugh . . . I'd never looked worse.

I shoved my hair on top of my head and plopped my favorite broadbrimmed, yellow-and-white-striped beach hat on. To distract Mikey from my face, I donned my biggest Anna Wintour–inspired sunglasses. I dug out my favorite workout/walking gear, which consisted of a bright yellow-and-white-striped hoodie and white leggings. I grabbed a handful of tissues and stuffed them into my pocket, convincing myself that I was presentable.

Mikey is one of the most loving, giving people on the planet, and just knowing that I would soon be with him was filling me with something resembling happiness. We had been connecting on FaceTime several times since I'd left the hospital, and he was up to speed on the horror and drama of my life. Although he was technically only 5 feet 6 inches (tops!), I always described him as the tallest short man on the planet. When he walked into a room, he owned the space with his kindness, power, and strength.

Maybe it has something to do with the fact that he holds black belts in five different types of martial arts. Movie-star handsome with the most gorgeous wavy dark hair, big blue eyes that look like cracked marbles, and a deep dimple in his right cheek, Mikey has always loved me for exactly who I am. He has been my biggest cheerleader and confidant through all of it. If only he were straight, I would have convinced him to marry me and make babies years ago.

The moment he pulled up into the driveway, I ran out the door and jumped in the passenger seat. He gingerly kissed me on the cheek and said, "Okay, Princess, where to?"

"The boardwalk in Mission Beach, and thank you, thank you, for coming to rescue me! I've been going crazy sitting in that house by myself, day after day, drowning in my misery. Now, tell me everything about what you've been up to, and don't leave out any juicy details," I thanked and demanded at the same time.

"No way! I can fill you in later on my fabulous, party-filled life of debauchery and luxury," he joked. "Right now, I need you to tell me, in that oh-so-sexy British voice of yours, how you are healing physically and, especially, what's going on with that beautiful heart."

"Well, the good news is that the doctors say I am healing as predicted and will soon be free to talk and eat and write and cook and get back to life. If only I could figure out what life to have. The bad news is that I feel stuck in an endless nightmare of depression, despair, and hopelessness," I said.

I felt hot tears surging out of my eyes and dropping like little water bombs onto my chest.

I had promised myself I wouldn't get all weepy with Mikey, and now in less than ten minutes, my eyes were gushing like water fountains. I was having a big old, ugly cry in his front seat. Thankfully, I had stuffed my pockets with tissues and began gingerly blowing my nose with foghornlike noises.

Once the salty wave of grief had passed, I then told him my dream about Barry burning alive in a boiling vat of oil and how satisfying the idea of revenge was. I expected him to launch into a lecture about the importance of forgiveness and that revenge wouldn't heal me. Yada, yada, yada.

"Oh my God! Holly! Revenge, that is exactly what you need right now! That asshole needs a taste of his own medicine, but I think we should limit it to something that won't get you twenty-five to life," Mikey said with a lopsided grin. "Tell me about the things he most hates or the things that scare him or drive him crazy. I will personally make it my mission to torture him."

"That's easy. Snakes, rats, and crickets. He shrieks like a little girl around rodents, and the sound of crickets is like nails on a chalkboard for him."

Mikey was quiet for a minute and then asked, "Do you still have the security camera app to his house on your phone?"

Before I answered, I pulled out my phone, and there it was. Somehow, it had never occurred to me to dump it. But I thought, by now Barry had most likely deleted my access to it. I clicked on the button, and voila! I was now looking into our—no, his—home with a wide-angle view.

I showed Mikey the camera view, and an evil gleam came into his eyes.

"Holly, how can you tell if Barry's home or away?"

I thought about it for a moment and said, "He's a man who loves routine. He's obsessive that way. Give me a day and time, and I can most likely tell you where he is and what he's doing."

"Perfect. Today is Tuesday. Where will he be this evening, and for how long?"

"It's poker night at Larry's. He'll be there from eight till eleven or midnight," I explained.

"Are you sure?"

"Ninety-nine percent sure. Why? What are you thinking, Mikey?"

"Better you don't know. Plausible deniability and all of that. Let's go for a walk, catch an early dinner, then I will go 'run my errand' and take care of business, okay?"

We walked the full length of the boardwalk, all the way to the volleyball nets at the end of Mission Beach and back. Mikey grabbed fish tacos for dinner while I resentfully slurped a smoothie, secretly hoping for a bite. I couldn't chew because of the wires in my mouth. Mikey dropped me off at home around 7:30 P.M. He asked for my phone, so he could check the camera before he began his mission. We decided that he would return it to me later that night, along with a full revenge report.

Here's what happened. Mikey called his old friend Frank, who has a collection of pet snakes and reptiles, and asked him where to buy small snakes, a few rats, and several thousand crickets. Frank turned him on to his supplier at Sports Arena, which was just a few miles from Mom's house. For a hundred bucks, Mikey bought three thousand live crickets, four rats, and four small snakes. Then, he drove to Barry's and parked down the street.

Before getting out of the car with his three brown paper bags of miniterrorists, Mikey checked the security camera on my phone and found the house was mostly dark and empty. Fortunately, it was a moonless night, and the suburban street was very quiet as he walked to Barry's.

Mikey had been to Barry's house more than once and knew that, off the master bedroom, there was a walled-in private patio, easily accessible by walking along the east side of the house. Inside one of the brown bags, he had three ziplock plastic bags of crickets—a thousand or so in each.

He grabbed one bag, unzipped it, and poured the critters over the wall onto the patio. Then, he walked further along the east side until he came upon a large outflow vent, and he carefully deposited a snake and a rat into the vent along with the second bag of crickets. Finally, he made his way up onto the roof, where he found a very large vent and funneled the final bag of crickets, snakes, and rats into the house.

Mikey arrived back at Mom's at 9:15 P.M. with a slightly crazed look in his eyes and a big goofy grin on his face.

"That was the most fun I've had in years," he said, cheeks flushed, offering me a high-five. Since he was as tall as me, our hands slapped together in perfect unison as we did a happy dance around the kitchen. My jaw throbbed from the movement, but at that moment, my desire for payback overrode everything else. In all our years of friendship, I had never seen Mikey so excited.

Pushing aside a dark curl from his gorgeous blue eyes, he continued, "What an adrenaline rush! I can't wait to see what happens when the monster gets home." Mikey's obvious delight had me buzzing with excitement as well.

"Oh yes! I'm turning on the security app," I screeched, speaking louder than I meant to. I grabbed my phone from Mikey's well-manicured hand. "Let's see what's going on. Barry always leaves lights on, so we should get a clear view."

The house appeared still, but I could hear an unidentifiable clicking sound. Were those the bugs climbing the curtains? I suppressed a smile through my gated mouth.

Barry usually returned from his poker game around 11 P.M., so we prepared to settle in for the next two hours. I poured Mikey a generous glass of his favorite Austin Hope Cabernet, from which I planned to steal tiny sips through my wired jaw. We sat down on the bar stools around the kitchen island and began peering into the phone's screen, looking for human movement as we turned up my phone volume and added more interior lights.

"Can you hear that? Or am I imagining things?" I whispered, trying to quiet my pulse that surged in anticipation.

"Yes. We're safe here, Holly. You don't have to whisper." Mikey laughed. He placed a gentle hand on my shoulder. A waft of his delicious cologne reached my nostrils. His scent always calmed me somehow. It was both reassuring and promise-filled, as if everything was going to be okay, even when it wasn't.

A faint chirping sound on the video emanated from some corner of the room.

"Three thousand crickets should be enough to drive him crazy. I can't wait to see what happens when he sees the rats and snakes," I said, my heart racing as I bounced in my seat in rhythm with the drumming of my heart. Jubilation mixed with a big dose of vindication overcame my senses.

For a second, I thought I might faint, so I focused on Mikey's chatter about his latest crush, a handsome man named David, who was a celebrity personal assistant for an aging film star known for her excessive drug use. Unfortunately, David's work schedule often interfered with their dating plans, and Mikey wanted advice.

"Should I tell him that I love him, but he needs to get a new job? Should I keep him as a fuck buddy, or maybe I should marry him, and he can be my trophy wife? Well, what do you think?" he pressed me impatiently.

This is what I loved most about Mikey. He was fun-loving, zany, rarely serious, adventurous, and very intense.

"I can't help you there, Mikey," I told him, poking a straw into his wine glass and slurping up the last drop. The red liquid soothed my pulsating jaw. "Having never met David and knowing your propensity for flirting and playing the field, I'm not sure any of these options make sense right now. Why don't you bring him down here for a weekend, and we can hang out and see if he's a fit for our family?" I suggested this with as much sisterly warmth as I could muster.

As I got up to pour Mikey another glass of wine, he picked up the phone and immediately began yelling. "Oh my God, oh my God! Holly! Holly, look at this!"

A long slick reptile swished across the screen. Another big black slithering snake gracefully slid down the wall toward the front door.

Two more snakes joined the first, each weaving its tail along the walls. One landed on the high-end lightly stained, beige travertine floor as it headed toward the kitchen.

And then, several rats scurried past the snake on the floor to get out of harm's way. One snake took off after them at lightning speed. It was like watching a televised nature show. Only this was happening in the place I once lived. My mouth filled with bile at the thought.

Suddenly things sprung to the next level. Snakes slithered after the rats running rampant in every direction possible. It was a full-blown scene straight out of a segment on National Geographic TV! The evil part of my mind began worrying that the snakes and rats would finish their show and disappear before Barry got home. I furrowed my brow, lifting my fingers to my mouth to bite my nails, then realized I couldn't open my mouth wide enough. I wanted to spit fire.

As if the Goddess of Karma herself heard my concern, the front door opened. And there he was, Mr. Barry Tavers, phone in his left hand, keys in his right, oblivious to the depths of hell he was about to step into.

We held our breath as he walked over to the side table to place his keys in the Murano millefiori glass bowl. The keys dropped with a ping against the glass as Barry suddenly froze, both hands raised slightly at his sides.

The crickets! As if on cue, they decided to begin singing in unison, offering a spontaneous chorus of chirping. One of the snakes slithered across the top of his loafer. Jumping back in panic, he screamed.

"Fuck! What the fuck is this?"

Mikey held his sides, kicking his head back as he howled with laughter. My stomach did a gleeful backflip as Barry hopped from one foot to the other, shuddering and shrieking as if he were being eaten by a crocodile. It looked like he might pee his pants any second. I joined Mikey in laughter as we did another high five.

The video was too dark to see his exact facial expression, but the snakes that crossed his path were clearly visible. A donut-sized rat scampered underneath the wraparound sectional sofa.

Barry stood paralyzed in the foyer. I could almost hear his brain trying to process what was happening when three more rats came scurrying from the kitchen toward the front door. Unfortunately for the rats, a snake managed to make a snack out of one of them.

With a rapid movement, Barry grabbed the keys from the glass bowl. "Jesus fucking Christ!"

His shout echoed down the hallway as he ran with legs spread wide out to the front door.

"I declare this mission successful and complete!" Mikey announced as he wrapped me in a warm brotherly hug. I sank into his arms, exhaling more deeply than I had in weeks.

Revenge was a dish best served with creepy-crawlies. Little did I know then that one day my revenge would take on even more dire proportions.

CHAPTER SIX

Destination India

Six weeks after my accident, I was free of wires in my mouth, the cast on my wrist, and the scar over my eye was barely noticeable. I was pleased and grateful for the healing progress of my physical wounds, yet my internal, emotional injuries remained in critical condition. I was able to walk and talk, but inside I carried deep, weeping, bleeding wounds for which there were no pills, lasers, stitches, or miracle cures.

To acknowledge the milestone in my healing, my precious Auntie Geeta sent me a beautifully wrapped gift. The box contained a gorgeous coffee-table-sized cookbook of vegetarian recipes from India and a large, round, stainless steel spice box filled with smaller round containers of colorful Indian spices. The gift was deeply meaningful to me. After all, it was Geeta who had instilled in me a curiosity about all things Indian, and her early cooking lessons had paved the way for my career as a chef.

A red envelope floated out along with the gift and that included a handwritten letter and a surprise: a check for ten thousand dollars! Auntie Geeta had always been exceptionally generous with me, but this was above and beyond. I took a moment to acknowledge how much gratitude I felt for this woman, who showered me with love like a second mother, perhaps because she had never had children of her own.

In a beautiful looping script, Auntie Geeta wrote:

Dear Holly,

It's time to rescue yourself and give yourself the space to discover what you are going to do "with your one wild and precious life," to use the words of the late poet Mary Oliver.

I know how traumatizing this time has been for you. I also know that pain is the fuel for change and that you will come out the other side of this. While it doesn't feel like it now, there will come a day when you will be happy again.

I had planned to give you this money as a wedding gift and now would like for you to have it as a "restart and reboot your life" gift. It comes with an idea: I will soon be bringing my parents from Michigan to San Diego to live in my guesthouse, and I will need someone to cook their favorite Indian comfort foods for them a few days each week. My cousin Divya lives in Rishikesh, India, a beautiful place on the Ganges in the foothills of the Himalayas, and she runs a cooking school there.

Given your love of cooking, if it feels right, I think a few weeks with her would be perfect for you. And then, you can bring your new Indian culinary skills back to San Diego to share with my parents and all of us. What do you think?

Love, Auntie Geeta

P.S. Hopefully, by the time you return home, I will have gotten your money back from Barry.

P.P.S.—A quick joke: Did you hear about the zoo with only one dog? It was a Shih Tzu!

I laughed out loud for the first time in a zillion years. In my head, I made a mental note to call Auntie in the morning and tell her how much I loved her and how much I appreciated her lifetime of care and support.

Then I picked up the check for ten thousand and began talking to it. "Okay, beautiful windfall gift. What shall I do with you? Yes, India is enticing but also very scary. You know, I've never traveled alone, and I'm not sure a country like India, with over a billion people, is for a beginner like me. What do you think? Do you think this money might be better used extracting my rapidly aging eggs just in case I manage to find my soulmate before my system shuts down and I am consumed with hot flashes? You probably don't know this, but thirty-eight is two years past the recommended age for extracting eggs, with any real hope of eventually having a live birth. So, Mr. Check, what do I do: India or potential babies?"

Unfortunately, Mr. Check was not forthcoming with any sage advice, so I dug out a notebook and pen from my bag and drew a line down the middle of a page to make a good, old-fashioned pro-con list.

On the plus side of the column, I wrote the following:

Might be a life-changing adventure.

Learn new, useful career-enhancing recipes and dishes.

Cooking school in India will look great on my résumé.

Auntie Geeta's cousin is extended family, so I wouldn't be totally alone.

No possibility of running into Barry.

Then, on the minus side of the page:

Risk of getting deathly ill and miserable from Delhi Belly.

Twenty-one hours of flying time to a strange land.

What if I get kidnapped and disappear, never to be found?

I may fall into even deeper despair and loneliness.

I sat for a few minutes studying both sides of the page, then in a rare instant of clarity, I thought, "Oh, Holly, don't be such a chickenshit. You've got nothing to lose and everything to gain. This is an incredible, once-in-a-lifetime gift. Just do it!"

I left for India on November 1 with one wheeled carry-on bag stuffed with my favorite and most comfy clothes for layering, along with an extra pair of walking shoes. Auntie Geeta assured me I wouldn't need my usual hair and makeup supplies or fancy clothes. Whatever I needed could be purchased there, including an extra suitcase for the trip home, should I decide to indulge in retail therapy.

She gave me strict instructions on how to avoid the dreaded Delhi Belly, which included me raising my newly mended and now pain-free right hand and taking an oath swearing that I would not, under any circumstances, eat street food or salads, or anything that wasn't cooked within an inch of its life. And the only fruit allowed was fruit that I personally peeled myself. I also promised that I would always use bottled water to brush my teeth and would keep my mouth shut in the shower.

Mom put together for me a backpack of everything I could possibly need to stay healthy, including antibiotics, over-the-counter stomach remedies, an assortment of strange-to-me medicines, and Bach flower remedies. She included my favorite go-to protein bars, instant oatmeal packets, and several one-serving packages of my favorite gluten-free chocolate chip cookies.

At 4:30 A.M., Mom drove me through the inky black early morning to San Diego International Airport, and we both cried as we said goodbye. My flight to Newark departed at 6:30 A.M. with a connection in Paris before landing in Delhi and catching the short one-hour flight to Dehradun.

After twenty-three hours of flying time and countless layovers, I was grateful that, with Auntie's generous gift, I had splurged and bought business class tickets. When I reached my final destination, I was exhausted, dazed, jet-lagged, and confused. Thankfully, I easily spotted the driver holding the sign with my name waiting just outside the small terminal.

The weather forecast for Rishikesh was sunny skies with a high of 72 and a low of 55 for every day in the foreseeable future. Too bad they were wrong. A curtain of light rain fell as we drove along the winding road through forests and small roadside stands into Rishikesh, giving the landscape a dreary glow. While there wasn't a lot of auto traffic, we encountered all kinds of unusual things on the road: We barely missed hitting a family of five on a scooter, passed an oxen-pulled cart loaded ten feet high with hay, and avoided dirty skinny cows wandering in every direction. I noticed my driver often putting two fingers to his lips in a kiss and then touching his heart. I was uncertain if he was giving thanks for narrowly avoiding an accident or doing another kind of worship.

Soon we barely moved at all. We hit a traffic jam. I could see (and hear) what seemed to be a parade. The driver explained, in his singsong, broken English, that it was the first day of *wedding season.* This parade was composed of a colorful group of musicians playing drums and brass instruments that sounded a lot like a New Orleans second line.

As we slowly inched forward, I could see the parade was leading a handsome groom wearing a bejeweled turban, riding a white horse draped in brightly colored silks embroidered in gold. The surreal sight felt like a bad omen, a visual reminder of the death of my wedding dreams. This wasn't the *Welcome to India! We're glad you're here!* I had imagined. A wedding season? Really? After I had just canceled my lifetime subscription to happiness forever? Misery level: 10+++.

When Mom had delivered my backpack for this trip, I had emptied it to check out all the goodies she had packed for me. In addition to all the pills, potions, and tasty treats, she had included a "gratitude journal." Ever the self-help junkie that she is, inside the journal, I found a photo of the two of us along with a note:

> *Dear Holly,*
>
> *I am hoping you will take a few moments at the end of each day to write down the things for which you are grateful, things you found beautiful or made you smile, and to rate your misery level so you can begin to see the lessening of the pain you have suffered. By doing this you will have a reference for your healing process.*
>
> *Love, Mom*

Despite the wedding parade traffic slowdown, I arrived at my hotel in less than thirty minutes. Divya knew the owner of the place and had arranged for a forty-dollars-a-night rate for three weeks that included breakfast and promised a Ganges view.

As I walked into the lobby, the young Indian man behind the desk smiled and put his hands into prayer position over his chest as he greeted me. "Namaste, welcome, Miss Holly."

I couldn't *namaste* back as both hands were busy with my various travel bags, but I did my best to put a pleasant smile on my face.

The Ganges view from the lobby was beautiful, picturesque, like something out of a fairy tale with majestic hills in the distance. Two ultrasleek dark red sofas featuring gold-embroidered, multicolored silk sari pillows were perfectly positioned to look out upon the flowing river two stories below.

Gentle Indian tabla music was playing, and large copper bowls on the floor were filled with small, fresh flowers arranged in the shape of a mandala floating in water. Through the floor-to-ceiling glass windows I could see, less than a football field away, a colorful reddish-orange suspension bridge that spanned the river. From the window, I could see layers of ancient-looking fairy-tale pink-and-peach-colored buildings stacked up a hillside. I later learned that this area was filled with mostly small shops and ashrams. It all looked and felt a bit otherworldly.

The few moments of enchantment ended abruptly when I arrived at my room on the third and top floor just before sunset. I was instantly disappointed. It was basically four walls, and a tiled floor, completely lacking in personality, charm, or beauty. I'm not sure what I was expecting for forty bucks a night, but this clearly wasn't it. For a moment, a scene in the plush Budapest hotel with Barry flashed before my eyes. Only, I was no longer in Budapest.

And I was no longer with Barry, for that matter.

I opened the drapes to discover a small balcony with a plastic chair and a view mostly of a crumbling building across the alleyway. My view to the far left was what a New York realtor would generously call a "pocket view" on the river. Too tired to think about unpacking, I took a quick hot shower with my mouth sealed shut, fell into bed (which was surprisingly comfortable) with my favorite travel pillow, and was asleep in seconds.

I fell asleep around 6 P.M., exhausted from the more than 23 hours of flight time, only to be abruptly awoken four hours later by banging noises. Someone was pounding on a shared wall with a hammer! Then I heard what sounded like people moving furniture around. For an hour, it was one big noise after another. I finally got back to sleep around midnight, hoping that 7 A.M., when I was told breakfast would be available, would come quickly. By 6:55 A.M. I was dressed and headed to the lobby to find the dining room, only to discover that the floor I was on had a locked wrought iron gate, keeping me from the staircase.

Oh my God! I was locked in. Trapped. Hungry. Frightened. If there had been a fire, I could have been burned alive! Now I was furious—and did I mention also very hungry? Me at my worst . . . *hangry*.

How could they do this? I went back to my room and called the front desk and gave the young man an earful. He promised to come get me immediately.

I met him at the gate, which was now open, and he tried to convince me that while a padlock had been in place, it wasn't locked, and it was there to keep out intruders. It was a completely unbelievable story, but at least I was free. That is when I discovered the dining room wouldn't open until 8:30 A.M.

Desperate for a caffeine fix, I decided to take a walk just as the sun was beginning to rise in a sky of mist and clouds.

As I stepped outside in the faint morning light, I stopped at the front door to take a good look around in order to be able to find my way back. Across the street was a mini-billboard that appeared to be a political poster of a middle-aged man in a turban wearing garlands of flowers around his neck. Excellent, a landmark. My hotel was on a main road and the road traffic was light. Somehow I found the beep beeps of the three-wheeled auto-rickshaws, some emitting a surprising "Land of Dixie" theme, oddly comforting.

I knew that if I turned right, I would be headed toward the bridge I had seen earlier from the lobby. As I began walking, I could faintly hear the sounds of chanting but couldn't determine where it was coming from. *How perfect*, I thought in my recently missing feeling of optimism.

"My first morning in India, and holy music is welcoming me."

I was thinking about the few people I had met so far and how kind, gentle, and caring they seemed to be. There was a sweetness to them, and an unhurried way of being that was a new experience for me. I loved how they greeted me with *namaste*, a gesture I made fun of when my mother dragged me to her yoga classes. Here in Rishikesh, that simple act meant "the divine in me bows to the divine in you." For the first time, I saw it as a truly authentic greeting.

Except for a few skinny cows and two mangy dogs, I seemed to be the only one walking around. Within the first hundred yards, I came to a small village market area with a collection of clothing, jewelry, and snack shops on both sides of the street. Even though everything was shuttered and closed, most of the shops sported colorful window displays that I planned to check out later in the day.

The chanting was now getting louder and was coming from behind me and toward me. I saw a dozen chanting men, some in orange robes, some in white robes, all wearing turbans, walking briskly and carrying what looked to be a stretcher with a dead man on it—his face covered in ashes and his torso wrapped in an orange sheet. I stepped aside. The only witness to the procession.

What the hell have I gotten myself into? I thought.

There was a break in the shops to my right and a wide asphalt pathway down to the Ganges. I could see a two-story building with "The Bliss Café and Spiritual Bookshop" painted on one side of the building with a steep, narrow wooden staircase leading to the entrance.

At the top of the stairs was a window-paned door with light shining through, and a sign above the door proclaiming to have the best coffee in Rishikesh.

Excited, I flew up the stairs and tried the door. It was locked, but through the glass, I saw a sixty-something Indian man wearing a navy and yellow University of Michigan sweatshirt. When he noticed me standing at the top of the stairs, he walked toward me. He had a mane of salt-and-pepper-colored curly hair and a warm smile. As he unlocked and opened the door with his left hand, he used his right hand to gently cover his heart as he bowed slightly, saying, "Welcome! We are not quite open yet, but please, come in." He was fatherly and kind. *If only Auntie Geeta could meet someone like this,* I mused to myself.

Floor-to-ceiling bookshelves covered the walls, with most of the shelves sagging from the weight of the books. It was impossible to tell if the volumes were new or used, but I assumed they were a bit of both. Behind the front desk, I saw a big pass-through window that appeared to be the still-dark café.

"My name is Deepak. What has you up so early this morning?"

"Thanks for allowing me in, Deepak. My name is Holly. I just arrived late yesterday from San Diego, California, and I am desperate for some coffee," I said without taking a breath.

As Deepak slowly turned toward me, I could immediately sense a warmth wrapping around me. It felt both foreign and familiar at the same time, and I sensed it wasn't merely the heat pushing the morning air through. I felt at peace.

"Regrettably, the coffee won't be ready for a bit," Deepak replied. "But I just made a fresh pot of masala chai. Would you like a cup?"

"Thank you." I smiled, suddenly regretting my boldness for storming into his place in my typical tsunami-like fashion. "I'd love it."

Deepak walked back into the darkened café area, presumably to find a cup for me.

When I first walked in, I noticed he had been standing in front of a small, framed photo of himself, surrounded by what looked like a holy woman and a holy man, both in orange robes. I couldn't help but stare at his Michigan sweatshirt, a familiar item in America juxtaposed with a new and foreign place. Auntie Geeta owned more than one of them herself. An ironic sense of synchronicity appeared at the edges of my imagination.

Holly, you've been in India for less than twenty-four hours. I chastised myself for being so foolish. *You cannot expect a miracle the minute you arrive. Why do you always want so much? The familiar voice of self-doubt and loathing flooded my brain.*

Deepak interrupted my thoughts as he handed me a steaming cup of chai. I breathed deeply, turning my attention to the kind man before me. "Does it contain sugar?" I asked him as politely as I could. Standing in front of this stranger felt like wearing a new pair of shoes. It was both pleasant and unusual. I shifted my weight from one leg to the other.

His face read that "crazy American" reaction I imagined he was thinking. I chewed my bottom lip, inwardly kicking myself for making such a fuss.

"Don't worry. I always make it with honey." He laughed, quickly putting me at ease. "Are you a diabetic?"

"No," I replied. "But sugar is a form of poison I avoid like the plague."

"Well," he started slowly. "Honey represents the sweetness of life. A cup of masala chai with honey in the morning is like a prayerful blessing for a good day and a good life."

Okay, then Deepak, I'm in. In one sip, it became one of the most delicious things in a cup I had ever tasted. This fragrant, satisfying cup of deliciousness was warming my tattered soul.

"Have you come to Rishikesh to attend a yoga teacher training?" Deepak asked casually as he sorted the cups before him.

"Definitely not," I blurted, my face immediately turning red. "Um, I mean, I realize this is the 'Yoga Capital of the World,' but I don't particularly enjoy the practice. Besides, I recently broke my wrist, so I don't see any downward dogs happening in the near future."

Deepak laughed heartily, which gave me the confidence to continue my story. In my usual TMI mode, I told him about the accident and my other injuries, but I left out the Barry part. It was humiliating enough to share what happened with a good friend, let alone a stranger I had just met in India.

I was slightly nervous about prying, but my curiosity was piqued, and I finally asked him how he came to have a Michigan sweatshirt. He gave me a giant smile and said, "It's my alma mater."

Before he could say more, the door opened with the sound of clinking bells, and in walked one of the café workers. Deepak introduced me to the young man and told me that if I wanted to wait fifteen minutes, I'd finally be able to have that cup of coffee. The chai had worked its caffeine magic on me, and I decided to continue for a little more walk and then head back to the hotel for breakfast. Before I left, I noticed his business card in the little container next to the cash register. It read "Deepak Kumar, Ph.D., Purveyor of Fine Books." I took one as I walked out the door.

At exactly 8:30 A.M., I arrived back at the hotel and found my way downstairs to the dining room. I was surprised to see that I was the only guest. A server greeted me with a menu and asked if I would like coffee or chai to start. I ordered coffee and scanned the menu, hoping for eggs. The menu was a hodgepodge of Asian-like dishes, most with rice or noodles with veggies but no eggs in sight. I asked my server about the possibility of eggs, and he explained to me that Rishikesh is 100 percent a vegetarian city and eggs were not possible.

How did I not know this? Three weeks, no eggs? No chicken? No *anything* I usually eat? He quickly suggested his own favorite item on the menu, the masala breakfast dosa. He described something that sounded like a crepe, so I agreed to just go for it.

Minutes later, a gigantic crispy crepe arrived—overhanging both sides of the plate by several inches—filled with lumpy mashed potatoes and some bits of green veggies I didn't recognize. A few side sauces and yogurt came with it. From the first bite, I was hooked. I later discovered the dosa shell/wrap was created from ground rice and lentils. I finished every delicious bit of it and nearly asked for another order, but decided to see how I digested this one, first. It certainly felt good in my mouth and tummy. I made a mental note to ask to learn this dish in cooking school. After breakfast, I headed back to my room and was shocked to discover a family of monkeys on my balcony. Ridiculously loud and bouncing around, as monkeys are known to do, the biggest one pressed up against the glass window and seemed to dare me to engage with him. Not my idea of fun. After the noisy night of banging, the now chattering monkeys, and the discovery that I had been locked into my floor and could have died if there had been a fire, exhaustion began to cover me like a wet blanket.

In the midmorning light, the view from my room was a bit depressing. It overlooked a string of old weathered buildings with peeling paint and old-fashioned antennas on the roof. My "pocket view" of the Ganges was too narrow to be inspiring or enchanting. I began to think I should ask for a different room or even move to another hotel.

Perhaps for lack of attention, the monkeys didn't stay long, and with the combination of interrupted sleep and jetlag, I crawled under the covers and took a nap.

CHAPTER SEVEN

Does God Make Mistakes?

The next day I again woke up before dawn and strolled over to the Bliss Café and Spiritual Bookshop, hoping to find my caffeine fix. Through the window, I saw Deepak sitting in the one worn-in, torn, big cozy recliner with a book in his lap. When he saw me peering through the glass window of the Dutch door, he quickly got up and welcomed me in with a big smile that felt like the sun warming my frozen heart just the tiniest bit. Like a lighthouse of love, he radiated waves of compassion and care, and it felt good to be on the receiving end.

It was a bit crazy that I was noticing such things as generally I thought all this "energy" talk was just a bunch of nonsense Mom and her friends liked to speculate about. I was here to attend cooking school and get my life back, not philosophize. I didn't know whether it was karma, dharma, or drama that drew me back into Deepak's place, or maybe it's true that we all grow up to become our mothers. After arguing back and forth with myself for a few silent moments, I finally concluded that if, when in Rome we do as the Romans, then when in India, I might as well have a conversation with a man named Deepak about the nature of the Universe.

As Deepak prepared my cup of chai, I picked up his book, *Conversations with God*, and flipped through it randomly. It seemed to be a dialogue between a man named Neale and God, and suddenly I had an idea. . . maybe Deepak knew the answer to my question from *Heaven Can Wait* and, if I were lucky, maybe he would know the answers to some of my biggest questions about life. As always, I was anxious to know just when I would find my one true love and get married.

"Deepak, may I tell you a story about a movie I recently saw?"

"Yes, of course, Holly. Tell me anything and everything. You have my full attention!" he said with a delighted smile.

I proceeded to share with him Joe Pendleton's story of mistakenly being carried off to heaven at the wrong time. When I finished recounting the film's story, I asked him, "Do you think God makes mistakes?"

"You know, Holly, you and I have something in common. One of the reasons I have been reading this book over and over again is because, after my wife died, I had the same question."

"Your wife died?" I asked sympathetically. Hot tears shot to the outer rims of my eyelids. The idea of losing a beloved spouse seemed utterly unbearable. I silently nodded as he continued.

"Yes, she passed a little more than ten years ago. Pancreatic cancer. She was just fifty-five. We were living in Ann Arbor, where I was a professor of psychology at Michigan. We had a beautiful life together, three kids, all grown now, and after she passed, I moved home, here, to Rishikesh." He told me this with a very wistful look on his face.

"I became driven to understand why God would take the love of my life from me. I know it wasn't my fault that she had gotten sick, but the deeply irrational part of me wondered what I could have done differently. I was filled with grief, guilt, and at times rage at God," he continued.

"This book is among the many things that helped me to make peace with the situation and to know God again. So, in answer to your question: No, God does not make mistakes. Mistakes are impossible in the Kingdom of God and impossible in the experience of God.

Therefore, mistakes are impossible in your life because you are an individuation of God. Me, you, everyone: we are all God.

"Difficult as this may be for you to believe, you have never made a mistake in your life. Nor has anyone else."

Who was he kidding? I thought. *I made the biggest mistake of my life getting involved with Barry, a mistake that not only broke my heart and took my money but nearly cost me my life.*

"Think about it like this," Deepak began. "We came into a body with temporary amnesia about who we really are. There is a gift in forgetting. It allows you to ultimately remember who you are and re-create yourself. We must first forget in order to re-create and remember. I discovered that instead of wondering why what happened *happened,* it became essential and useful to be in a state of gratitude for what IS right now. Right now, you are here. Your feet are here. Your understanding is what it *is* right now."

I looked down at my feet, understanding absolutely nothing about what he had just said. My mother might understand this kind of language, but I sure didn't.

As if he had heard my thoughts, Deepak continued while uncrossing his legs and leaning farther back into his old chair. "Everything that has ever happened is happening now, and the only question is what to make of it. And knowing that, you can remember into being that which you most desire."

We sat in silence for a while, me clueless and him in contemplation, sipping our chai. While I heard what he had to say, and I had a vague feeling it might be true, I didn't fully understand. I really wanted to get what he meant, but it felt like I had cotton in my ears, which distorted everything.

The confusion on my face must have been evident because Deepak motioned me to join him at the window overlooking the Ganges. In the faint early morning light, Deepak pointed to the bridge on our left and the little ferry boat below, and then across the river to an ashram that had a large Shiva statue on a platform in the river. He suggested that just before sundown, I cross the river, either by walking over the pedestrian bridge or taking the two-minute tiny ferryboat and attend the Ganga Aarti Ceremony at Parmarth Niketan

Ashram. He explained that aarti is a sacred ceremony performed at sundown, in which prayers, chanting, bells, incense, and flaming lamps dispel darkness. Often people made offerings to Ganga in small palm-woven baskets filled with candles and flower petals. He told me all I had to do was to sit quietly and let the love of Mother Ganga and the prayers fill my soul. It sounded like a promising proposition, but I wondered if my soul, with all its punctures and holes, could be filled with anything but grief.

Deepak told me that after the ceremony, I could attend the satsang, and I would have the opportunity to ask questions of the American-born holy woman, Sadhvi Bhagawati Saraswati. I wondered, *What the heck is a* satsang*?* I made a mental note to google its meaning later. (According to the internet, *satsang* is a Sanskrit word that means "gathering together for the truth" or, more simply, "being with the truth.") I wasn't sure if I was ready to be with the truth just yet, but I had a sinking feeling I wouldn't be able to ignore it forever.

CHAPTER EIGHT

The Future in the Palm of Her Hand

The next morning, as I walked down the stairs in my hotel to the dining room for breakfast, I noticed a sign with an illustration of a deeply lined palm and a photograph of a pleasant-looking man. The sign said, "Vedic Palm Readings with Master Sanjiv Wednesdays, 10 A.M. to 1 P.M. *Your Future Awaits in the Palm of Your Hand.*"

Hmm, I ruminated, *it's Wednesday and while normally this would be more like my mother's thing, not mine, I don't need to be at cooking class till eleven. And given my current state of loss and confusion, maybe the answers are no further than the palm of my hand.* So, with some curiosity and a little optimism, I decided, *What the hell! Let's go meet Sanjiv after breakfast!*

I sat down at Master Sanjiv's small table in the lobby. It was adorned with a purple-and-gold silk runner and a small sandalwood Ganesha statue that sat next to a pot of marigolds holding one slender stick of incense wafting into the air. I looked into the deep, dark brown eyes of the palm reader, who gave me a lopsided smile as he told me that his fee was 600 rupees (Rs 600) for thirty minutes (less than ten dollars). With strings of prayer beads hanging from his neck, and dressed in a gold silk kurta (a collarless shirt) embroidered with a red-and-black design, the man appeared to be no more than thirty. His professional demeanor put me at ease.

"Great, let's do it," I said, smiling.

Sanjiv slowly took my hands into his and, with great intention, examined my palms. Both sides of my hand, all my fingers, and he pressed on my skin in various places, noticing the thickness of my hand, the shape of my fingers, the lines across my palm, the various fleshy mounds. His face was mostly expressionless. After a few minutes, he asked me, "Are you ready?"

I nodded slowly, uncertain if I would ever be authentically ready for anything ever again.

His brown eyes met mine as he spoke. "You are currently in the most painful time of your life." He exhaled as if to underscore his words. I sat motionless, thinking to myself, *Well, I know that! But what line of my hand is telling you that?*

Blowing air through my tightened lips, I waited for him to continue.

"But upon your arrival to Rishikesh, you have officially entered the spring of the soul. A time of rebirth. Who you are meant to become will begin to blossom," he said brightly.

"Ah yes, I see too that this time of emotional and physical wounding is a crucial part of your growth. It is your karma. It is what brought you to Rishikesh so that you can discover your true dharma."

Dharma? Karma? Schmarma!

His voice interrupted my thoughts. "You reside too much in the mind. Here you will discover your heart." He grew silent.

Just when it was getting interesting! My heart? That was the last place I wanted to be! Damn. Would I ever love again? I had so many questions. I wanted to ask him about my love life, children, and happiness, but I didn't want to interrupt him.

He inhaled slowly, then continued. "One of the most important lessons you are about to discover is that God never makes mistakes."

My eyes widened as a shiver raced from my tailbone to my cranium. Hadn't I just discussed this very thing with Deepak?

"Mother Ganga will teach you what real love is. She will wash away the wounds in your heart from the false love you once thought was real."

Everything about him seemed real and genuine. My shoulders dropped an inch and my breathing evened.

He then took my right hand again and looked at the side leading up to my pinky finger. Closing his eyes, he said, "It is unclear what your future is as to whether or not a child will come into your life."

My shoulders lifted toward my ears. So much for soothing.

My lifelong resistance to all Mom's woo-woo bullshit kicked into full gear. I suddenly felt like a loser with a growing sense of regret for having even sat down for this crap. My mouth stayed shut, but my mind screamed, *Who the fuck are you to tell me that I may or may not have children? You have no right to destroy my dream and expect to get paid for it, too!* I considered running out the door, but I thought better of it. My inner good girl scolded me for being so foolish. For a moment, I struggled with myself before finally pulling out my wallet.

If only he had properly played his role and indulged my fantasy by telling me the date, time, and place I would meet my one true love, along with the birthdates of my children, I might have considered sending him referrals. I slapped down the Rs 600 in front of him and went off to cooking school, feeling angry and stupid for wasting time and money, thinking that someone could gaze at my hand and tell me my future. Apparently, my life wasn't going to be fixed in a thirty-minute reading. No, it was going to take a turn of events so surprising I would have no idea it was coming.

CHAPTER NINE

The Big Island

That night, I tossed and turned in bed, unable to stop thinking about everything the palm reader had told me. It sure felt to me like God had made some mistakes. For the umpteenth time, my mind drifted back to what a mistake I had made by so blindly trusting Barry.

Only a month after Barry and I returned from Budapest, he had surprised me with a four-day whirlwind trip to the Big Island of Hawaii—complete with a detailed packing list of what I should bring: sexy lingerie, bikinis, a hat, SPF, a few cute sundresses, and a notebook. I asked him what the notebook was for, and he gave me a mysterious smile and said he was sure I would want to take some notes along the way.

We'd landed in Hilo and then taken a short drive to the beautiful tropical Balinese-themed home he'd rented for us in the Puna district, which I discovered was home to a colorful community of artists, writers, farmers, and free spirits. The house was surrounded by a plethora of papaya, banana, and mango trees, as well as plumeria, orchids, and other exotic flowers. Standing in the garden, I felt as if I were wrapped in the arms of Mother Nature's abundant lusciousness. The bright, rich colors, the sweet perfume of the flowers, and the gentle, sensual touch of the sea breeze were beyond delicious.

The master bedroom was round with a wooden vaulted ceiling. The king-size bed was on a raised platform—and, once in bed, I could see that the 280-degree ocean view was spectacular. It was clear to me why this was a favorite place for Barry. Everything about it was yummy.

Barry arranged for a local chef, Bhakti, a beautiful Hawaiian woman with full hips and long wavy black hair, to prepare a romantic dinner for the two of us in the garden next to the koi pond. She was a delight and explained where each organic ingredient came from, including the delicate opah fish that her husband had caught that afternoon.

Dessert was a delicate Hawaiian version of an English trifle, which was light, creamy, and filled with a variety of fruity tastes that were new to me. Barry was quick to tell me that he knew I was going to love the dessert and that one of the surprises he had in store would occur the next morning, and it involved an exotic fruit tutorial. He and Bhakti exchanged a quick look as he winked at her, and then he brazenly suggested we head to the bedroom for a second "dessert."

Around 10 A.M. the next morning, Bhakti arrived with fruit-filled platters containing whole and cut dragon fruit, rambutan, cherimoya, lilikoi, rollinia, starfruit, and good ol' papaya, too. The platters were skillfully decorated with local blossoms, and she had placed several gorgeous arrangements of local flowers around the open-concept kitchen. It was a true visual feast for the eyes and a treat for the tummy.

Barry came out to the kitchen, handed me my journal and a pen, and then posed us for a variety of selfies in the kitchen, bursting with color, light, and sweetness. Exotic Fruit 101 class was now in session. Bhakti and I spent the morning tasting and sampling the bountiful collection of fruit as she demonstrated myriad ways to create exotic cocktails, sauces, and desserts.

I grew fond of the strange and wonderful dragon fruit that looks like an alien egg from outer space and tastes a little bit like kiwi. My favorite preparation of the day was the Orange Dragon Fruit Cocktail, which was super easy to make (and gave me a lovely little buzz):

ORANGE DRAGON FRUIT COCKTAIL

dragon fruit
orange juice
honey
rum

- Slice the top off a dragon fruit and set aside.
- Using a spoon, carefully scoop out the flesh of the fruit and put it into a blender. Be extra careful not to damage the exterior of the fruit.
- Blend dragon fruit, orange juice, and honey until smooth. Fill a shaker and use a 1.5-ounce shot glass to measure 1 part rum and 3 parts of the dragon fruit puree per cocktail. Shake well with ice and then pour back into the shells and enjoy.

Barry had been excited to take me to Kehena Beach, a black sand lava beach across the road from our romantic hideaway. I was wearing my cutest, skimpiest bikini and matching sarong and a pair of delicate jewel-encrusted sandals with paper-thin soles. Had I been thinking straight, I would have worn sneakers to walk on the uneven and sharp-edged lava rocks that led to the black sand beach. *Too bad Barry hadn't bothered to send me the Excel spreadsheet on what kind of shoes to pack for this adventure, I thought a bit resentfully.*

It became apparent that I was struggling and would end up ruining my sandals and almost cutting my feet, so Barry, ever attentive and creative, doubled up the beach towel and laid it on top of the rocks so I could take a few painless steps. He repeated this gallant process many, many times until he finally decided to pick me up and carry me the rest of the way. On that day, he truly became my Prince Charming, and I even felt a bit guilty for judging him so quickly.

Moment by moment, I was falling deeper in love with Barry. I had never had anyone spend so much time focused on me and my happiness by creating memorable and meaningful experiences. It felt as if I was the center of his universe. He knew my wants, needs, and desires even better than I knew myself. He orchestrated the most perfect experiences. If only I had known that his wealth and entire existence were based on a total lie.

CHAPTER TEN

Cooking School

A few days after my arrival in India, my one-on-one cooking class with Auntie's cousin Divya was scheduled to begin. She lived a short walk from my hotel in a gated compound of modern-looking three-story apartment buildings.

While the directions for the walk were simple, the walk was not what I expected. Once I crossed the busy street in front of my hotel, I found myself on a quiet, tree-lined, uphill dirt road. All along the path up to the complex were warning signs that read: "Beware of the Monkeys." I was familiar with "Beware of the dog" signs from home, but monkeys? After the minor encounter with them on my hotel balcony, I worried if they might attack me now that there was no hotel window to protect me against them.

What would I do if I got attacked by a monkey? What would the monkeys want with me? A bit fearful (I could hear but not see them), I headed quickly up the uneven dirt path, keeping my head down and praying to have a monkey-free journey. Fortunately, I did.

As I approached Divya's front door, I could smell incense and hear faint chanting. I knocked and a beautiful fifty-something woman wearing a sky-blue-and-lime-printed cotton kurta and sporting a big red bindi on her third eye opened the door and welcomed me in.

"Namaste, you must be Holly," she said as she placed her hands in prayer position over her chest. "Welcome, I'm so happy to meet you. Please come in, you can leave your shoes there," she said, pointing to the outdoor shoe rack.

Divya explained that she was just finishing her morning puja, a form of worship, and to please come and join her. We walked into a small alcove with an altar featuring a large mango and a coconut, several small Hindu Gods and Goddesses carved in sandalwood standing next to a large bronze statue draped with a garland of flowers. Divya handed me a smoking stick of incense and motioned to me to begin a clockwise movement of passing the smoke around the Goddess as she chanted:

"Om Annapurnayai Namaha Om Sadapurnayai Namaha

Om Hrim Namo Bhagavati Maheswari Annapurna Swaha Om Hreem Shreem Kleem Namo Bhagwatye Maheshwari Annapurna Swaha"

When the ritual was complete, Divya explained to me that the Goddess Annapurna oversees food and cooks, and she was also known as Parvati, wife of Shiva. The term *anna* means "food" and *purna* means "filled completely."

"It is believed that when food is cooked with the spirit of holiness, it becomes alchemy. When you honor Annapurna, she blesses the food and turns it into *Amrita*—the Sanskrit word for healthy and nutritious food, which gives immortality. Now, isn't that something we all want and need?" asked Divya.

I wondered if praying to her and eating the food she blessed would also heal a broken heart.

Divya walked me into her kitchen and told me that today I would be her only student. She wanted to hear about my journey with cooking and food while she showed me the proper way to make classic masala chai.

The kitchen was surprisingly large with light wood floor-to-ceiling cabinets on one side and more cabinets above and below the black granite countertops. In the middle of the room was a large black island with a white countertop.

When she opened a drawer filled with small round stainless steel spice containers like the ones Auntie had gifted me, I noticed Divya had dozens more than I had. She slowly pulled eight of the spices from the drawer and named them all, then carefully measured them in different amounts into a small bowl for mixing. She then brewed loose black tea and added a pinch of the just-mixed masala, plus another pinch of shredded fresh ginger. She strained it, poured it into a cup, and then added honey and a little milk.

It smelled amazing and tasted just like Deepak's masala chai. We sat down on padded stools around her kitchen island and I began to tell her about my love of all things food. I began by describing my custom-made dollhouse, complete with its Easy Bake Oven and about the first time I successfully made slice-and-bake chocolate chip cookies.

"Mom was so proud of me and we had a beautiful tea party with sparkling cider in delicate cups alongside the cookies. As a teen, I began watching the Food Network every day after school, as well as reading recipe books for fun. My mom was never much of a cook, but my grandma was and she taught me the classic American dishes . . . everything from meatloaf with mashed potatoes and peas to fried chicken, spaghetti and meatballs with homemade marinara sauce, and macaroni and cheese."

I rambled on, telling her that I considered the stars on the Food Network to be my personal chef tutors, and I kept a notebook filled with recipes and ideas that I cooked up for dinner several times a week. I fantasized that I would grow up to be as beautiful, sexy, and talented as Nigella Lawson with her cooking skills along with the enviable marriage of Ina Garten, the Barefoot Contessa.

"I dreamed of having a Jeffrey, a husband just like hers, who gushes over every dish I serve and plans wonderful surprises for me from time to time," I confided to Divya. "Eventually I went to college for a liberal arts degree but after two years dropped out and attended CIA—not the spy office in James Bond movies but the Culinary Institute of America, which is one of the best culinary schools in the States. It was the only time in my life that I ever got straight A's. I worked in hotel catering for a while and then for a private catering firm. I almost had my own catering firm, but it's now on hold," I said, finally taking a big breath after delivering the short version of my life with food.

Divya refilled my teacup and shared some of her fond memories of learning to cook.

"Our stories are a bit similar, Holly. I also learned to cook from my grandmother. One day, Dadi, my mother's father, was sick in bed. Nani told me we had to cook a special dish for him that would make him all better. It's called khichri and it's classic Indian comfort food. Today, I will teach you Geeta's parents' favorite version of it. So, Nani taught me that the secret healing ingredient was something every cook had to master and she asked me if I was big enough to learn how to do it. Of course, I said yes. I think I was maybe six or seven years old. I was thrilled to be learning a secret that would help heal my grampa."

"Of course, who wouldn't want to know the secret sauce to cooking and healing. Please tell me!" I implored.

Being with Divya in her kitchen and watching the reverence of her morning ritual and blessings created a new sense of purpose to cooking and food I had never experienced before. Preparing food was a vehicle toward a spiritual life. In fact, it was a sacred act of love.

"As you are cooking, stand in front of the bubbling pot of rice and veggies and spices or whatever you are cooking, and place your hands in namaste over your heart. Close your eyes and send strong intentions of infusing the food with all of your love. Focus your attention on your heart and see a giant wave of love emanate out and then land into the pot to combine with your food," Divya said.

She passed me a plate of a crisp and tasty snack that looked a bit like party mix made with dry Rice Chex and Wheat Chex cereals, pretzels, and peanuts that Carly's parents used to serve. It was delicious and I made a mental note to get the recipe later.

Reliving my food history for Divya filled me with warm, tender memories and I noticed that my misery level had plunged to about a 5 from my usual 9 or 10.

Divya decided that my first real cooking lesson would be how to make khichri.

She first gave me a tour of her kitchen cabinets and refrigerator, showing me the variety of basic ingredients she used most. Everything was homemade and organic, including her yogurt, ghee, even her special spice blends. As she walked me through each of the items, she explained the healing benefits of the various spices, foods, and condiments, frequently pointing out their digestive qualities.

For instance, cardamom is good for indigestion, gas, and constipation. Ghee is also good for digestion and contains brain-boosting nutrients that stave off dementia. Yogurt is filled with B2 and B12 vitamins, and one cup a day provides 50 percent of your protein requirements. She was definitely a devotee of the "food as medicine" school of cooking. I was her eager apprentice.

BASIC KHICHRI

½ cup moong dal (split mung beans)

½ cup basmati rice

1 tablespoon avocado oil

1 teaspoon cumin seeds

½ teaspoon fresh ginger
(or a pinch of ground ginger powder)

¼ teaspoon ground turmeric

1 teaspoon sea salt

¼ teaspoon black pepper

4 cups water

For garnish:

½ cup chopped fresh cilantro

a few slices of lime or lemon

INSTRUCTIONS

- Combine the rice and moong dal in a medium bowl. Soak the mixture in water for about 15 to 20 minutes. Rinse well until the water runs clear and drain.
- Add oil to a medium pot on medium to low heat. Once the oil starts to warm up, add the cumin seeds and stir for a minute until the seeds start to brown and become fragrant.
- Add the ginger and ground turmeric. Stir and add the rice and moong dal mixture. Season with sea salt and black pepper. Stir and add the 4 cups of water.
- Increase the heat to medium-high to bring the water to a boil. When the water comes to a boil, turn the heat down to a gentle simmer. Let the khichri simmer for about 30 minutes, stirring occasionally, until you get a porridge-like consistency. It should be soft and creamy.
- Carefully (as it will be hot) taste the khichri to make sure the rice and dal are fully cooked. If not, you may need to let it cook a little longer.
- Turn off the heat. Adjust the garnish, if needed, and stir again.
- Serve and enjoy.

MASALA SPICE MIX

10 tablespoons cinnamon
7 tablespoons cardamom powder
7 tablespoons ganthoda powder
7 tablespoons ginger powder
7 tablespoons ground black peppercorn
7 tablespoons ground cloves
3 tablespoons ground nutmeg

MASALA CHAI

¾ cup boiling water
½ cup milk
2 tablespoons loose black tea
½ teaspoon masala spice mix
a pinch of fresh shredded ginger

- Brew for two minutes then strain.
- Add sweetener of choice and drink.

CHAPTER ELEVEN

On the Banks of the Ganges

After leaving Divya's with a belly full of the delicious khichri we'd made, I was feeling both peaceful and energized. I completely understood why khichri is known as a panacea. It's kind of like calling chicken soup the Jewish penicillin. And, I thought to myself, *Maybe there really is something to this infusing food with love concept!*

It was just after 4 P.M. and, rather than go back to the hotel, I decided to take Deepak's suggestion to cross the river, explore the ashram side, and then attend the sundown aarti ceremony.

As I walked toward the river, the dusty ground crunched beneath my feet and reflected the light of the sun towering above me. The occasional breeze cooled my face before sweat could form on my forehead. Equally grateful for the sun's piercing radiance and the gentle breeze, I breathed deeply at the polarity of nature.

When I reached the water's edge, I decided I would try taking the small ferryboat across and purchased my ten-rupee ticket. There were a few Western faces on the boat, but mostly it was extended Indian families. The Ganga River was flowing swiftly and, in the afternoon light, it was the most gorgeous celadon color, a color I didn't think Crayola had yet created for their big box. It also reminded me of my favorite ring that featured a large oval chrysoprase gemstone.

The entire ride lasted less than two minutes. An unusually healthy-looking brown-and-white cow greeted me at the dock. I sidestepped her and quickly walked up a flight of stairs, passing a variety of vendors hawking unusual-looking edibles or small woven baskets with flowers called puja baskets. At the top of the stairs, I had two choices: I could turn right and head toward the ashram and the site for aarti, or I could turn left.

Since I had extra time, I decided to turn left and explore the area. I found myself walking a shady tree-lined path along the river. There were few people, it was mostly quiet, and I could hear the rushing of the water, birds singing, and faint chanting off in the distance. There was a palpable serenity and beauty, and I began thinking about what the palm reader had said to me, suggesting that Ganga would provide me with healing.

Although this sounded strange, I began to wonder if that was possible and, if so, how would it happen? He never mentioned that I needed to actually go into the water, so how would I get healed unless I soaked in the river with its healing properties? Maybe this was different from an Epsom salt bath for sore muscles. Or, maybe this was a question for Deepak in the morning.

Eventually, I turned around and headed in the other direction. This path merged up and to the left, and I made a hard right turn onto a small paved lane with a variety of shops, street food vendors, cows, and some of the most unusual-looking people I had ever seen.

One man in faded robes had dreadlocks nearly brushing the top of his feet. With a dazed, possibly crazed, look on his face, he stood perfectly still with his palms outstretched, seeking donations. Another holyman type wearing a colorful turban had set up shop on an equally bright blanket under a shade tree with a big sign that read, "Meditation Man, Enlightenment Lessons."

Hmm, I wonder if he has a "blue light special" for instant access to Shangri-La or if there is a package deal to reach Nirvana, my snarky self mused.

I took my time strolling through the area and ducked into a few of the better-looking jewelry stores. When I exited the nicest of the shops, I realized that I was standing exactly where I needed to be, right in front of the Parmarth Niketan Ashram, the site of the aarti ceremony. There was a large seating area directly on the river, facing a huge Shiva statue on a platform placed in the middle of the Ganges. A few hundred people were already sitting on the steps, or what they call the *ghat*. Everyone was barefoot or in socks, so I placed my shoes alongside the others before walking down the shallow steps and sitting down in the middle of it all.

A few minutes later, I began to hear the music behind me, and when I turned around, I saw two boys, maybe ten or twelve years old, in marigold robes. One was playing the tabla, and the other the harmonium, a cross between an accordion and a child-size piano. Then a procession of more than a hundred boys just like them came walking down the steps. They passed me and then formed two groups with a fire pit separating them. Behind the boys, I saw the holy woman and the holy man from Deepak's photograph arrive.

They walked straight toward me and then sat down next to me. Holy shit! Had I inadvertently placed myself in the middle of their place of honor? The woman seemed to have read my mind. She reached out, smiled at me, grabbed my hand, and simply said, "Stay."

The holy woman, who appeared to be around my age and definitely American, in spite of the orange robes, spoke into her microphone and welcomed us all in English, and then the holy man spoke in Hindi and began chanting, and pretty much everyone joined in. Even though I didn't know the words, I began to feel as if the music and the words were pulsating inside me. The sun was now low in the pink-and-red-tinged sky, the river was flowing past, and the fire pit was shooting orange-and-yellow flames.

I felt transported back into a magical and mystical place and yet I was aware that I was fully present in a way I had never experienced before. There were several more chants, and at one point, about a dozen people were given brass lanterns emitting a flame that they moved in large clockwise motions. The entire aarti ritual lasted about thirty minutes and, before it ended, the holy woman invited everyone into the ashram to attend a satsang in English, where she would answer any and all of our spiritual questions.

I picked up my shoes off the rack and followed the holy woman, and several dozen other people, through the entry gates to the ashram that spilled into a large rectangular garden peppered with statues of deities and was surrounded by two- and three-story buildings. We were guided into a large, carpeted meeting room that offered seating on the floor and a few chairs for the older devotees. The musician boys had quickly relocated from the aarti ceremony location and were softly playing their instruments here. As I scanned the room for a place to sit, a tall African American man with a friendly face, probably in his late fifties, approached me. "The floor can be pretty hard." He smiled, offering me his jacket as a cushion. I craned my neck upward, taking in his lean six-foot frame. His dark glistening eyes emanated a kindness much like Deepak's.

For a second, I froze, not knowing what to say. After all, the last time a man had made such a gesture, I had gotten into a heap of trouble, falling head over heels in an instant. Pushing Barry's memory out of my mind, I inhaled deeply, returning the man's polite smile, and gratefully accepted. "That's very kind of you," I said quietly.

"The mind can only absorb what the backside can endure," he said, then clasped his hands in a namaste and made his way toward the back of the room, where a group of younger people each offered him a warm embrace. He then settled onto the floor next to me.

When the room filled to capacity, the holy woman arrived and sat on a slightly raised platform in the front. She was friendly and cheery and introduced herself as Sadhvi Bhagawati Saraswati and, in a warm, friendly voice, directed us to close our eyes for a few minutes of meditation before taking our questions.

Fortunately for me and my uncooperative monkey mind, the meditation lasted just a few minutes. Sadhviji then told us she had received a few questions from the ashram's Facebook page, but before she would answer them, she asked if anyone had a question to begin the session. I quickly raised my hand and, as if anticipating I would be the first one to ask, her assistant handed me a microphone.

"Hi," I said a bit shyly. "Thank you for the lovely aarti ceremony and for this opportunity to meet with you. My name is Holly. I am new to all of this." I turned my head toward the kind man who had approached me before the ceremony began as if to gather some assurance that I wasn't making a fool of myself. He smiled broadly at me, giving me an encouraging wink. I smiled back before continuing.

"In the few days since I arrived in Rishikesh, I've been told a few times that the Ganges River will be my healer. Can you help me understand this?" I could feel the blood racing to my cheeks in a blend of anxiety and desperation.

She laughed and said, "This is one of my favorite questions. Let me begin by telling you the story of Mother Ganga. She is the most sacred riverbed in the world and cuts through the foothills of the Himalayas, originating at a glacier that is more than thirteen thousand feet above sea level. The Goddess Ganga is the daughter of King Himavat, the king of the Himalayas, and Queen Meru, and is the sister of Uma, Bhagawan Shiva's divine consort. It is said that the Goddess Ganga gracefully departed from Her Heavenly abode and took the form of a flowing river that has descended upon Earth, an act of grace and compassion to bring healing and liberation to Earth rather than decimation."

Oh geez, I thought. *This sounds like the equivalent of a Hindu fairy tale. A river is a Goddess who came down from heaven to be born from a glacier?* Despite the makeshift pillow, my butt was going numb from the very hard floor. I shifted my weight to find a more comfortable position and turned my attention back to Sadhviji.

She stopped for a moment as if to give me time to take it all in. I could feel my chest relax at the thought of the river's healing powers. Could she really wash away my sorrows as Sadhviji promised? Before I could fantasize further about jumping headfirst into the Ganga, she continued, "Her riverbanks are lined with rocks, softened and smoothed by Her waters, large ones upon which one can sit for hours, medium-sized ones that fit perfectly in the palm of one's hand, for holding and meditating upon, and small pebbles, one or two collected by the pious so that Mother Ganga may flow through their home as well.

"Where the river ends and people's lives begin is impossible to discern. Ganga is as inextricable from the lives of Indians as the very blood flowing through their veins. Whether She is a source of tangible water for daily drinking, bathing, and cooking, or whether She is a source of intangible inspiration and liberation prayed to with each morning's bath in innumerable cities across the world, She is fundamental to the lives of more than one-seventh of the world's population.

"When I first arrived in Rishikesh, in 1996, at the tail end of the monsoon season, Her waters were still high, but the mesmerizing fury of Her flow at its peak had subsided. She was full but gentle. Rushing, flowing, tumbling off rocks and high riverbanks but clear again in the autumn after months of carrying high mountain silt.

"I do not remember whether I had even removed my shoes and put my feet into Her waters when She swept up my soul. Instantaneously, my life was Hers. Tears of having come home, tears of being in the presence of Truth, tears of witnessing the divinity, it all poured from my eyes the moment I beheld Her. 'Please heal me of all of my pain and suffering. Just let me stay here on Your banks forever,' I had whispered, and I knew the prayer had been granted even before I asked. She carried my life in Her waters and bestowed it upon me the moment I arrived."

OMG. Did she just say the river healed her pain? Did I hear that or imagine it? And what kind of pain is she talking about anyway?

My mind raced with possibilities, and I barely listened to what came next.

"She has gifted me with waters in which to bathe my body, waters in which to rinse stale thoughts and patterns from my mind, and waters in which my soul has tastes of reuniting with the Source. I have heard from *She who is within me,* answering questions I've asked and questions I have not yet asked. As a mother, She provides for all life and livelihood for those who depend upon Her as their source of existence; inspiration and liberation for those who meditate upon Her; and spiritual connection to those who invoke Her name in their daily bath across the world."

Sadhviji took a sip of water from her metal cup.

The room was quiet as we all pondered the birth of the Ganga story. As if reading my mind, Sadhviji then looked directly at me and said, "Holly, and all of you, if you desire to have the healing and blessings of Mother Ganga, remember that She is the divine purifier who washes away the ignorance, the illusions, and the chains that bind us to our false identities. But She can only do that if we let Her! So, find time each day to sit by Her banks and give yourself permission to let go.

"Let go of that which is holding you back and binding you to your suffering. The highest goal of the spiritual path is freedom. Mother Ganga gives us this ultimate liberation, ultimate freedom *if* we are prepared to let go of our attachment to our drama, to our stories, to our temporary, finite identities. Holly, the chains that bind you are in your own mind. Sit in Mother Ganga's lap and give yourself permission to let them go. You, and everyone who is here, have been called here to Rishikesh, to Mother Ganga's holy banks, to accept the invitation of the divine universe to wake up, to open your petals to the light, to experience the true freedom of yourself.

"As you sit on Her banks, allow yourself with each exhalation to just let go, breathe out the pain, the grudges, the history, and identity. Let Mother Ganga wash over you and through you. Thank you for coming," she said as she joined her hands together in a namaste and gracefully left the room.

I stood up, stretched, and gathered my things, helplessly holding the jacket the kind man had given me without knowing how to return it. He seemed to have disappeared without a trace. My stomach growled loudly as I felt a tap on my shoulder.

"My name is Kurt." He smiled, gently taking his jacket out of my arms.

"I'm Holly." I smiled weakly, suddenly distracted by my hunger pangs.

"Are you hungry?" he asked.

A chill ran down my spine. Was it that obvious? Before I could answer, he continued. "Sometimes the participants are invited to enjoy dinner there and tonight is one of those nights," he said enthusiastically. "It is by far the best food in all of Rishikesh! They grow all their products organically at the ashram's local farm."

"I'm in!" I nearly shouted, hoping it was as good as he said it would be. *Did I just manifest a free dinner?* I wondered to myself. *Or did this man somehow intuit I was in need of food and then make this kind offer? Or was this just a coincidence, or maybe synchronicity?* Once again, I found myself thinking of my mom and her influence on me after all. Perhaps, she was right, and there was something to believing in a power larger than ourselves.

Kurt led me into the dining hall, where he seemed to know everybody. Dinner was served from big pots and ladled onto a round silver plate divided into several sections. I could identify the rice, dahl, and chapatis, but the two other veggie-looking dishes were a mystery. Kurt dug out a saltshaker from his backpack and offered it to me.

"It's the world's best Himalayan pink salt and has magical healing properties in it," Kurt explained. I wasn't sure if he was serious, but I used a few shakes anyway. Healing properties or not, the food was surprisingly tasty and felt nourishing.

Kurt told me he was an explorer, blogger, author, and a seeker of wisdom, and that he spent six weeks each year in Rishikesh taking various yoga trainings. Attending aarti and satsang were part of his daily program.

Using his chapati as a little food shovel, he asked me what type of yoga I did before stuffing food in his mouth.

"I'm more of a hiking or running or stand-up paddleboarding girl than a yoga type," I explained. "It's not that I am against spiritual practices like yoga or meditation. In fact, I once tried meditation, but it made me anxious. I discovered at some point that my true form of meditation is dreaming up new recipes and testing them out!"

"How did you end up in Rishikesh?" he asked innocently.

I inhaled slowly, then explained my trip was research for my career as a chef with my recent focus on Indian comfort food. I left out details about Barry and the car accident, but I told him enough to satisfy his curiosity. Besides, it might have been difficult for him to understand why someone like me could have come to Rishikesh of all places.

"Kurt, thank you for letting me sit on your jacket during the satsang. The moment before you handed it to me, I was thinking about how sore my skinny butt was getting and finding it hard to concentrate," I said to him with a grateful smile.

"Well, Holly, welcome to Rishikesh. This is what is 'normal' here. The power of manifestation is amplified in Rishikesh. It's literally manifestation on steroids! The Universe grants your wishes and desires, sometimes even before you know you have them," he explained with a wink.

"Last year I arrived in Rishikesh after flying for twenty hours and I was totally exhausted. I went to my hotel room, which was a big disappointment, and fell dead asleep. The next morning I was debating whether or not to change hotels but couldn't decide. On my way to a café for breakfast, I ran into a woman I had once met in a local yoga class. She excitedly told me that she had just bought a hotel with rooms that had great views of the river. She asked if I'd like to see it and consider staying there.

"The moment she took me into a room on the third floor, I was hooked. It was perfect for me, with an expansive view of the Ganges and a super comfortable bed. In fact, I became a certified yoga instructor and now consider this my home away from home."

He made it all sound so easy. Feeling a familiar sense of impatience, I tried to imagine what it must have felt like for him to find his passion. I, too, yearned to feel at home. Somewhere. Anywhere. As Kurt took a step toward me, a warm sensation overcame me as if he were bathing me in some kind of energetic wave of unconditional love. I had noticed that same vibe at the satsang. It felt unfamiliar and yet comforting at the same time. "Meditation is something I have been doing since I was in the ninth grade," he said casually. "My mom suggested that it would help me with my game. Never did make it to the NBA, but it has helped me in so many ways to live the life of my dreams." Kurt paused for a moment as I tried to absorb what he was saying.

"Some things you can't change, like your height. In my case, I couldn't compete with the taller basketball players, so I shifted gears, went to college, got an MBA, and even worked successfully on Wall Street for a while. Sounds like a picture-perfect life, right?" Kurt tossed his head back as he laughed heartily. Before I could respond, he continued, "At some point, I realized nothing would make me happy until I was willing to take a chance. India taught me that."

Willing to take a chance? Hadn't I done that with Barry? The lump in my throat swelled as I tried to finish my food. Kurt smiled warmly as he turned his attention to his plate. We ate the rest of our meal in silence.

After dinner, Kurt volunteered to walk me over the bridge and back to my hotel. He explained that while Rishikesh was relatively safe, his mama had taught him to be a true gentleman, and he was happy to escort me and provide any protection necessary. Secretly, I was glad. I didn't tell him I had been worried about walking home alone under a moonless sky dodging random cows, stray dogs, chattering monkeys, and potentially scary street people. I was beginning to think that maybe, just maybe, someone up there was looking out for me. I even had this crazy random thought that perhaps I could fix Kurt up with Mom someday. They would, at the very least, be kindred spirits.

Before I got into bed, I decided to pull out the journal Mom had given me and make a few notes about what had been my best day in a very long time. I was grateful for the time spent with Divya and the beauty and serenity of my walk along the Ganga under the warm sun. The aarti ceremony was surprisingly moving and meaningful, and I realized that Sadhviji's Satsang, and the meal with Kurt, had me feeling something close to hopeful. *Everyone struggles in some way.* It wasn't as if I was the only one who had had to overcome disappointment in this world.

My ongoing feelings of anger, despair, and fear of the future, at least for this day, had nearly abated. Perhaps it was because all of my senses were engaged, I had spent the day taking in new information, sights, sounds, smells, tastes, and experiences, and there just hadn't been room for me to dwell in the pity party that had become my new normal.

I decided in the morning, I would figure out a daily routine that would have me up and out of bed with a sense of purpose and passion instead of just hoping to randomly figure out how to fill the time when I wasn't in cooking school.

Misery level: 3. Progress!

CHAPTER TWELVE

One Step Forward, Two Steps Back

The next morning I stumbled into the bathroom, where my cell phone was charging, after hearing my text alert ping. Still half asleep, I squinted to figure out what 212 area code number was messaging me.

The text read, "Kleinfeld is excited to remind you that your wedding gown appointment is tomorrow at 10 A.M. We look forward to meeting you and your entourage. If for any reason you need to reschedule, please call us ASAP at 212-555-1212."

In an instant, I was back at the bottom of the pit. *No fiancé. No wedding. No best friend. Nothing but broken dreams.*

Fuck. Fuck. Fuck.

I had made the appointment two weeks after we got engaged. Watching the TV program *Say Yes to the Dress* was my guilty pleasure, and often Carly and I would watch at the same time, texting our snarky comments back and forth as the various small-town girls with small-town budgets and wealthy Bridezillas with unlimited budgets (drooling over fifteen-thousand-dollar Pnina gowns) all suffered dramatically over whether or not they would ever find the perfect dress. Corny, I know, but also fun. Now, it was just one more reminder of what a first-class loser I had become. Mom, Auntie, Carly, and I had planned a girls' trip to New York to shop for my dress at Kleinfeld, the ultimate paradise for wedding gowns. I know Mom had canceled the flights and the hotel, but I had never thought to cancel the appointment at Kleinfeld itself. I crawled back into bed, texted back to the store that the wedding was off, and cried until I couldn't breathe.

Just the night before, I had felt hope for the first time in forever, and now, once again, the rug felt as though it had been pulled out from under me. The ceiling spiraled above my head. Even closing my eyes didn't help. In fact, it made it worse. My fragile world of hope had toppled in an instant. *Damn phone. Damn dress. Damn Barry!* The blood drained to my feet, pulling me down with a heaviness I couldn't seem to offload. Sighing deeply, I lay back down on the bed and didn't even bother to rate my renewed off-the-charts misery level.

An hour later, I pulled back the drapes and saw it was going to be a beautiful, sunny, and cloudless day when I would have welcomed a heavy, dark gray sky to match my mood. I pulled on my clothes, didn't bother to brush my hair, stuffed a pants pocket full of tissues, and headed out the door to get my caffeine fix.

"Holly, who died?" Deepak asked when I walked into the bookstore. I started crying again, and he led me to his big recliner chair, sat me down, handed me his handkerchief, and then said he would be right back with my masala chai.

I felt stupid and embarrassed for sobbing, loudly, I might add, with someone I barely knew, and yet he knew me well enough to identify the pain I walked in with.

Deepak handed me the steaming mug of chai and sat down on the small stool next to me, and said, in the most loving and gentle voice, "Cry as much and as long as you need to. It is just us here. It's a safe place."

After a few sips, I calmed down enough to speak coherently. I explained to him that no one had physically perished but that all of my lifelong dreams had died recently, and that this morning I had been reminded again of all I'd lost and that I felt like I would rather be dead.

He looked at me and said, "I understand. I felt that way myself many times the first few years after my wife died. I know it does no good to be told that it will get better." He paused for a moment, then added, "Do you want to tell me what happened?"

I had googled my new friend, Deepak Kumar, Ph.D., and discovered he was a former professor of counseling psychology at the University of Michigan. I had already spent enough time with him to feel that I was in a "safe place," plus I knew that he was a good, and even professional, listener. I wanted to tell him everything, and yet I felt ashamed and scared that talking would lead to more ugly crying. What if he had customers walking in?

Deepak sat quietly next to me. He seemed comfortable in the silence. I didn't feel any pressure coming from him. Finally, I took a deep breath. "All I ever wanted was the white picket fence," I said. "A normal life with a loving husband and a few kids, a golden retriever, living in a good neighborhood, where I could be a stay-at-home mom, making life beautiful for my family. I thought I was finally on my way to having my dream turn into reality when it all blew up. The man of my dreams crushed my heart, murdered my soul, and I nearly died. In the blink of an eye, my lifelong dreams were blasted into a million, billion, zillion bits," I somehow managed to whisper.

I took another sip of my chai, blew my nose, and continued: "Now I'm lost. He broke my heart, stole my money, cheated on me with my best friend, and ruined my business. I'm essentially homeless now, and I no longer want to live, and even if I did want to live, I have nothing to live for."

Deepak looked at me with the sweetest eyes and gently said, "Tell me more."

"I never knew my father," I said somewhat dramatically.

Deepak sat motionless, waiting for me to continue and for this detail to make sense. Obviously, drama wasn't going to get me out of telling him the whole truth. I took a deep breath, collecting myself.

"I never knew my dad," I explained weakly. "For thirty-eight years, I have pretended it was okay to grow up in a single-mom household, but secretly I wanted the perfect, intact family that all my friends seemed to have. I wanted a dad. By the time I was seven, I had begun concocting an imaginary family with my dollhouse and dedicated my entire life to creating the ultimate life and home for them, believing that my desire would make it so."

In a flow of snot and tears, I witnessed myself convey the whole dreadful saga as it poured out of me, oozing between the slits of Deepak's old recliner and landing with a plop on the floor.

"Let's be honest," I said after sniffling some more. "All I ever wanted was to be the center of somebody's universe. More than anything, I wanted a loving husband and adorable kids. I truly thought that when Barry and I got together, my prayers had been answered, and my 'real' life was about to begin.

"Geez, even my fantasy of being kissed beneath the fireworks came true with him! He really had me fooled. He not only told me he loved me but he actually showed me through so many loving acts. I fell for all of it. The worst part is that I now feel tortured by what I can never 'un-know and un-see' in him. I don't know how to stop obsessing over and missing the Barry I thought I knew and the love and life I had. I thought I would enjoy it for the rest of my life."

When I came up for air, we just sat quietly together for a minute. I felt lightheaded and buzzing as if I was out of my body, and at the same time, it felt like I had massive amounts of adrenaline running through me.

"Thank you for trusting me and sharing your pain with me," Deepak said. He drew slightly closer. "You don't know it yet, but you are going to have a life that will make all of this pain worthwhile, and someday you will look back and think to yourself, 'Thank God I experienced this suffering.' But, of course, right now, you can't imagine that. You are grieving a loss of unfathomable betrayal, the loss of all of your biggest dreams, and the trauma of almost losing your life. Your heart, your soul, and your physical body need intensive care now. It needs self-love, self-care, and support as you embark on your healing journey."

He was right. I was knee-deep in the grieving process and much of what he had said made sense, although it was still unimaginable that I would ever find this was all worthwhile. I mean, *Honestly. How much can a woman take?* Then I remembered Deepak had a story, too, one that was arguably sadder than mine. I suddenly felt less alone, so I dared to ask him.

"If it's not too personal, can you tell me how you got through the loss of your wife?"

Deepak was quiet for a few moments, and then he looked at me.

"I had the white picket fence, but we faced incredible obstacles to get there. Nancy was a blonde-haired, blue-eyed Minnesota girl. I was a dark-skinned immigrant with a funny name from a faraway place. She was a senior, and I was a graduate student when we met at Michigan. We literally bumped into each other walking through the Quad, and I caught her as she was about to fall." He smiled as he remembered. "One of the books she dropped was *Autobiography of a Yogi*. I picked it up and handed it to her. I told her I had just finished reading it, and that started a conversation that lasted for five hours at the student union.

"We had read many of the same books and shared the same sense of humor and taste in movies, including an obsession with Monty Python. I never for a moment thought she would be interested in me, but luckily for me, she was. During that time, my parents had been actively consulting with matchmakers back home to seek a suitable wife for me. On my weekly telephone calls with them, they would always ask when I was coming back for a visit so they could arrange the meetings. I didn't dare tell them about Nancy. Nancy's parents came to Ann Arbor for a visit and arranged for us to go out to dinner.

"Her parents were polite, and her father asked me very specific questions about 'my future' and when I planned to go home to India. It was obvious I was not what they had planned for their darling daughter. I tried to be as friendly and vague as possible. Nancy and I were so well matched that we really believed we were soulmates. We were madly, happily in love, and we were sure we had been together many lifetimes."

Lifetimes. The notion jumped out at me again as I concentrated on what Deepak was saying. *Was there more than one? Didn't Auntie Geeta quote Mary Oliver in her going away letter to me, saying we only had this one life to live? Or maybe we had specific lessons in this one life that we had yet to live out.*

"In the spring," Deepak continued, "I completed my master's degree and was offered a junior teaching position at the university. Nancy was still working on getting a degree in social work. When I accepted the teaching position, I wrote my parents a long letter telling them of my plans to stay in America. And that I had met the love of my life. I included a photograph of the two of us, letting them know that they could tell the matchmakers to give up on me as I planned to propose to Nancy.

"You can't imagine the reaction my parents had, because she was not Indian. They called and told me that she would not fit into our family since she is not a Hindu, that they were very disappointed with me, as were my grandparents and that, as a Westerner, she would never be a good mother and would put herself and her career before family, and we would end up getting divorced.

"As painful as hearing all that was, I proposed to her the next week and she said yes. Her parents' reaction wasn't much better—it was the American version of what I got from my family—we ended up eloping.

"Eventually, after our first child was born, both sets of parents relented and ended up becoming wonderful grandparents and loving in-laws. But defying them initially was one of the scarier things I've ever done.

"When our oldest was nearly two, Nancy insisted that we bring him to India to meet my family. She said that even if my family didn't want to meet her, she wanted our son to receive the blessings of his grandparents and extended family. Fortunately, my father wanted to meet 'the mother of his grandchild,' and Nancy being Nancy, her kind, caring, loving self won their hearts."

Deepak beamed with pride as he recounted Nancy's courage to face their intercultural differences head-on. Without even trying, I began to like Nancy, too.

"We had nearly thirty-one amazing years together until she got sick. It all happened rather quickly . . . she had been losing weight and feeling tired for a few months and finally went for a checkup only to be given shocking news. She had stage four pancreatic cancer. She died at home, just four months later, surrounded by me and the kids."

I thought Deepak might cry at this point. I sure felt like starting up again, but I tried to sit as still as possible as he continued. I could not imagine suffering such a loss. My heartbreak suddenly seemed less agonizing than his. Death, after all, is an irretrievable loss. You never get the person back. And even though I never wanted Barry in my life again, a part of me was starting to believe that I might be able to get a piece of myself back in the process of letting the idea of him go.

"I don't really remember much about that first year after she passed. I was in a constant state of agony, disbelief, and unspeakable pain. My grad students were covering most of my classes for me and, when I had to show up to work, I pulled myself together for a few hours and powered through. Many days I had to convince myself to survive just for the next five minutes and would find something, anything, to distract me. I even went to some support groups, but being in the presence of other widows and widowers didn't help me.

"There were nights when I literally shouted obscenities out loud to whatever God or gods exist. My kids were really afraid I was going to take my own life, so they held an intervention, just the three of them and me. They asked me what the one thing was that I had always been passionate about. Or what was the one thing I had always dreamed of doing. I couldn't think of anything, especially since Nancy wasn't going to be by my side. Then my daughter said to me, 'Daddy, look at all the books you have, you must have thousands, and you've always cherished books and reading. Why don't you open a bookstore?'"

I looked around the bookshelves surrounding us like wise guardians and tried to imagine his daughter envisioning what I now saw before me.

Hmm, I thought, *she's right about that.*

"But instead of agreeing with her, I told her that bookstores seemed to be the worst business in the world right now.

"We didn't come up with any solutions that night, but she had planted a seed. I began looking over my huge book collection, many of which are spiritual classics, books on metaphysics, meditation, mindfulness, and all types of religions, and I wondered if there was some connection between me and the world of books."

A new picture of Deepak started to emerge in my mind. He had fulfilled a lifelong dream despite his pain. *Or perhaps,* I thought, *because of it.*

"On a trip home a few months later to visit my mother, who was still going strong, almost ninety-six, I decided to take a few days to attend the aarti ceremonies in Haridwar and Rishikesh," Deepak said. "As I was walking around Rishikesh, I stopped at this bookstore and café for lunch and spent an hour browsing the collection. The elderly owner and I had a long conversation about Krishnamurti, and then he shared with me that he was getting too old to run the business. He needed to find a buyer and told me he thought my love of books made me the perfect candidate.

"My first reaction was 'That's crazy!' so I graciously thanked him and told him I would soon head back to Michigan.

"He stared into my eyes and said to me, 'That is your past. Your future and your healing are here next to Ma Ganga.' And with that, he walked away."

Deepak picked up the framed photograph of himself with Swamiji and Sadhviji.

"This was taken that very evening, after the aarti ceremony at Parmarth Niketan Ashram. It was my first time there, and Swamiji walked over to me and said, 'Welcome home' and then Sadhviji invited me to the private puja area to spend more time with them. There were about thirty of us seated on rugs, and we were told to ask anything we wanted. I asked, 'How do you go on living when you don't have a reason to live?'

"Swamiji signaled to Sadhviji to answer, and I still remember she looked straight at me and said, 'the things, the people, the goals, the enjoyments of our lives—whatever they may be—these are not what we live for. If you've been living for something or someone that you've failed at or lost, then you haven't understood life.'

"She explained to me that we are not here on Planet Earth with the gift of a human body to be the perfect wife or husband or mother or father. We are not here to be successful in our careers or anything like that, even though that's what most of us think. I had always thought that my whole reason for living was Nancy, and she *had* been. But, that wasn't really right nor my true purpose, even if Nancy had still been alive.

"Ultimately, Sadhviji reminded me we all lose our relationships either through death or divorce. Nothing is permanent. It's a fallacy and a misdirection to live for someone or something or even for the whole fantasy drama of a white-picket-fence life. We are here on Earth in this precious human form to experience the divinity of our own selves and to connect with the divinity of the Universe, which ultimately isn't separate from our own true self. That's the purpose of our life."

I inhaled deeply, attempting to digest what he had said, not certain I really wanted to understand because if I accepted this as the truth, then I had to come to terms with the fact that, up until now, I had had it all wrong. I had spent my entire life waiting for the one person who would give me the life of my dreams.

"But if the purpose is to experience our own divinity," I asked, "why is it so hard to do? What's the point of all this suffering?"

"Sadhviji explained that the relationships we have and the tasks we perform are not supposed to be our reason for living," Deepak said softly, "but rather, they are a vehicle for our awakening to the truth of our own divinity. The highest goal of a relationship or a job or any goal is not how long I can hold on to it, or how much joy I can get from it, or how much I can make from it. It is rather, how can it bring me closer to the Divine? How can it bring me closer to the Truth? How can it help me expand and open to grace?

"Sometimes that happens in health and success. Sometimes that happens in sickness, death, and loss. She gave examples of so many of the sages or prophets of all religions and how they *all* struggled. They were all, in our way of looking at things, victimized and betrayed. They all lost so much. If God had wanted us to model our lives based on only happiness, gain, and success, surely His incarnations, prophets, and sages would have lived those lives. But they didn't.

"From Lord Krishna and Lord Ram to Jesus Christ and Lord Buddha—look at their lives. Would you want to live any of the lives they did? They showed us, through lives of loss and struggle, that the point of life is not to just get through it as easily and perfectly as possible, with your white picket fence, but to allow your heart to break open and let in the light of the Divine.

"So, Sadhviji helped me understand that Nancy was a wonderful, divine part of my own life's journey of realization, and that beyond Nancy, I had a purpose. A purpose of realizing my connection to the Divine. Nancy and I believed that we were more than soulmates, that we are twin flames, and that we have been together before and will be together again. So, you see, Holly, you did not take birth just to have a nice, easy, well-to-do life with Barry and a white picket fence. You were born to be cracked open to the light of the Divine who lives within you and connects you to the Universe."

It was a lot to take in. I sighed deeply. "Is there even a chance in hell that I will find my twin flame?" I asked, feeling the lump in my throat growing.

"Holly, you took birth to realize who *you* really are, and what I know for sure is that your real, true soulmate is out there. And he is looking for you, just as you are seeking him. In time you will heal from this horrific heartbreak. One day, at the right time, which will be in divine timing, you and your beloved will meet."

His reassuring words soothed my pain in a way I hadn't experienced before. I felt a flicker of hope dance in my heart.

"It is very fortunate that you are here in Rishikesh. There is a reason why it is one of the holiest cities on Earth. The veils between the worlds are thinner here. Magic and miracles occur here on a regular basis. I want you to know that I am holding the sacred space for your healing, your transformation, and ultimately the coming together of you and your beloved."

When he had finished, Deepak inhaled deeply, then smiled at me and said, "Are you hungry? I have something special in the kitchen for you."

"Yes," I told him. "In fact, as usual, I am starving." A few minutes later, he returned from the café's kitchen and brought me a tray with a delicious cheese omelet, Indian spiced potatoes, and a hot cup of chai. I devoured every bit of it.

It turns out there is a black market for nonvegetarian food in Rishikesh, and I was truly touched that he remembered that I mentioned missing having eggs for breakfast. That, plus feeling Deepak's compassion for my story, hearing his story of losing Nancy, and my happy, full belly, brought about a level of comfort I couldn't quite name. The food and his story soothed me on such a deep level that I could feel the pain begin to peel off my skin and slip to the floor, drop by drop, like a dripping faucet.

I don't know whether it was the spicy food, Deepak's history, or the rising heat outside, but I began to feel slightly feverish as if my sorrow needed to incinerate from the inside out. What had started out as a morning misery level of 10+ now barely ranked a 2.

CHAPTER THIRTEEN

To Dip or Not to Dip?

When I left Deepak's place, I headed down to the pathway along Ganga for a walk. With a million little reflective crystals, sunlight lit up the river flowing past. I remembered what Sadhviji had suggested about giving my problems to Mother Ganga and letting her wash away my pain, but I really didn't know how to do that.

I was thinking that maybe I should sit at the edge of the pathway and just let the water run over my feet when I suddenly heard a man calling my name. Shielding my eyes from the bright sun, I turned around and saw Kurt wildly waving, and then he broke into a trot to catch up with me.

"How auspicious to see you here, Holly," he grinned as he gave me a big bear hug.

"Auspicious? Why is that?" I asked.

"Well, I was just thinking about you and hoping I would run into you at aarti later because I want to take you on a little field trip less than an hour from here where there is a special meditation spot, Vashistha's Cave, and also a beach area near it where you can easily get into the Ganga. I figured you would want to try out some of Sadhviji's suggestions about letting Ganga heal you, and Ganga at this location is very calm and gentle. What do you think? Do you want to come with me tomorrow?" he asked, with a ton of enthusiasm.

My mother would call this unexpected invitation an act of grace or synchronicity. For a moment, I reflected on my first encounter with Deepak. Perhaps instead of expecting it, synchronicity happens just when you think it won't. A warm feeling rushed through me as I enthusiastically agreed to meet Kurt at the taxi stand near my hotel the next afternoon. Kurt advised me to buy an inexpensive long-sleeved kurta to wear into the water and to bring a towel, so I wouldn't return home wet and cold.

I ended up buying two kurtas to wear on top of each other so that I could graciously be prepared for this big adventure. I also picked up several extra pairs of socks to keep my feet warm during aarti, satsang, and all the other many events in places where I couldn't wear shoes.

The next day Kurt and I found a brand-new, clean taxi and headed out on a stomach-churning curvy road. The views of the river were breathtaking, and on this day, the color of its waters ranged from electric turquoise to a deep blue. Kurt entertained me with myths about Sage Vashistha, whose cave we would soon be entering. It's believed that Vashistha was the human son of Lord Brahma and that after his children died, he tried to commit suicide in the Ganga, but the Goddess Ganga threw him out. Legend has it that his grateful wife fell in love with this particular location, and so they moved to spend the rest of their lives by the river and the cave.

The old Sage spent many years meditating in the cave. Now the public is invited to sit in complete darkness and complete silence and meditate in this ancient, special place that vibrates at a very high frequency. Kurt remembered that I was not a meditator and explained that if at any time I became uncomfortable or bored, I could quietly leave and wait for him down by the river.

When we arrived at the entrance to the cave, I told Kurt that I was going to walk behind him and hold on to his waist. If there is a word for darker than black, that is what we walked into initially, but once we got into the main part of the cave, it was slightly illuminated by a single candle, and I could make out the outlines of a few other people, most sitting in the lotus position.

Fortunately, this time I brought my towel with me to sit on and made myself as comfortable as possible. I then closed my eyes, wondering what to do next. I decided to focus on my breathing for ten breaths. Then I would know if I wanted to stay longer. I took a deep breath in counting to four, held it for four, and exhaled for four. I had done this once in a yoga class Mom had dragged me to. As I exhaled on the tenth breath, I decided to sit just a little while longer. I figured a few thousand years of meditation vibration couldn't hurt me and knowing that Kurt was right next to me was comforting.

I decided to try to align my breath with his, since I could clearly hear when he exhaled and did that for a little while until it seemed as if I was in a place of relative peace and barely having any thoughts.

Eventually, I felt Kurt nudge me as he took my hand to help me up, and we left the cave. I was surprised when he looked at his watch and then announced that we had been in the cave for nearly forty-five minutes. *Hmm*, I thought, *maybe I could be a meditator after all.*

We walked down the rock-strewn beach, and as we prepared to enter Ganga, I was happy to see we were the only ones there.

Kurt pointed down the shore, indicating a spot for me to go into the water. "The Ganga is calmer near the caves, so it's a good place to commune with the water," he said as he pointed to the river. "You'll be safe. Let Ma Ganga take care of the rest."

The thought of letting Mother Nature take over made my eyes widen, but Kurt seemed so trusting. I wanted to feel that trust, too.

The sun was already blazing, and I could feel my scalp begin to pucker under the heat. There was no breeze, but I knew the river came from a melted glacier high in the Himalayas, and I wasn't sure if I would be able to handle the cold water. I shimmied out of my yoga pants and took off my top kurta, and then tested the water with my right foot and was surprised that it wasn't as cold as I'd expected. Kurt, already seated in the river, appeared to be meditating again. I decided to find a place to sit in the water away from him and figure out how to give my problems to Ganga.

I walked a little way down the beach to the spot Kurt had pointed out, found a shallow area with a sandy bottom, slowly eased into the water, and sat. It was a great choice because the water was mostly still, and I was only wet from the waist down. Once I was sitting comfortably, I closed my eyes and raised my face to the sun, and made up a simple prayer of gratitude.

"Dear Ma Ganga, thank you for the beauty of this place. Thank you for being willing to wash away my pain and sorrow. Thank you for the healing of my heart, the healing of my spirit, and the healing of my physical body. Thank you to Mom and Auntie Geeta for supporting me in this journey, thank you for bringing Deepak, Divya, Sadhviji, Swamiji, and Kurt into my life to guide me toward wholeness and healing. Oh, and one more thing, I am willing to let go of my suffering."

Sitting in the cool, clear, calm water, I couldn't think of anything else to do or say, so I just sat, hoping that Ganga really did possess curative healing powers. I wondered when and how I would "know" that Ganga had healed me. After a short time, I heard the crunch of sandals nearby. "Are you up for another adventure?" Kurt's voice lifted me out of my prayer. When I opened my eyes, I saw him winking at me. "I would like to take you to the Beatles' ashram." And with that, he offered me his hand as I rose to stand before him.

Our taxi driver was patiently waiting for us, parked underneath a large fig tree. As we headed to the ashram in Rishikesh, the driver turned up the radio for us. Repeating the words, "Beatles! Beatles!" as he wildly flailed his non-driving hand in a wave-like motion, I finally realized he wanted to make us aware of the song playing. It was my all-time favorite Beatles tune, "Blackbird," which I used to listen to while playing with my dollhouse.

I had never really understood the lyrics, but I knew every word. As if on cue, Kurt, the driver, and I sang along, doing our best to stay in tune. The music helped distract me from the man's erratic driving style. Our trip to the cave had taught me that not all roads were paved in India. A cow lazily crossed the lane about a hundred yards ahead.

"Holly, did you know that this beautiful song was written right here in Rishikesh?" Kurt asked, holding on to the back of the driver's seat as the car swerved to the middle of the dusty road to miss both the cow and a nearby pothole. His head nearly hit the roof during the maneuver, but he seemed unfazed. I turned my attention to Kurt as much as to distract myself as to learn about the song's history.

"That's so random. How do you even know that?" I asked with more than a bit of skepticism. My hands gripped the side door handle for good measure.

"You are too young to remember, but in 1968, when the Beatles were at the height of their global popularity, George Harrison began practicing Transcendental Meditation. He convinced John Lennon, Paul McCartney, and Ringo Starr to join him at the Maharishi Mahesh Yogi's ashram. They had recently decided to give up drugs and were actively seeking a spiritual replacement. It was George who was really looking for the meaning of life. I guess you could say their souls were looking for something more," Kurt explained with a knowing look in his eyes as he took a deep breath.

"My mom still has several Beatles albums from her teenage days. Do you think meditating helped them write 'Blackbird'?" I asked, curious to discover if there is a connection between creativity and meditation. An ox pulling a cart of firewood skulked steadily in our direction. The driver veered deftly out of its path in time for a tuk-tuk to pass us, blowing gas fumes into our open windows. I exhaled heartily to expel the carbon monoxide that was filling the car's interior.

"The Beatles wrote most of *The White Album* during their ashram days. They even used a tiger shooting as inspiration for the song 'The Continuing Story of Bungalow Bill,'" Kurt said before launching into a few of its verses to jog my memory.

Our driver slammed on the brakes as another ox cart piled with eight-foot-high cotton bags towering precariously behind the driver holding the reins merged in front of us.

"You seem to be quite the Beatles expert, Kurt." I smiled, trying not to reveal the mounting terror rising from my chest. "Perhaps you can get a side gig as a Rishikesh tour guide," I teased while eyeing the cart before us. I wondered how the ox cart driver remained so calm despite the load he was carrying. *Maybe he meditates, too,* I mused.

"Kurt, does meditating make *you* happy?" I asked.

"You know, Holly, I would say it does. I have discovered something better than happiness. There is a place inside of our soul that seeks inner joy, a place that in Sanskrit is called *santosha*, which means "utter contentment." This is a state where I can be at peace regardless of the things that make me happy or unhappy. For me, I reach santosha by meditating, but it isn't the only way to get there. It's just what works for me."

A good dose of utter contentment sounded like something I could use at that moment. The chaotic drive was everything but relaxing, yet somehow Kurt remained balanced and trusting throughout the entire process. *Could I have that, too?* Santosha seemed just the thing, but I had no idea how to get there. As we bounced our way back to Rishikesh, I wondered if the day would ever come when I could feel that sense of peace again.

CHAPTER FOURTEEN

OMG, the Fucking FBI!

Happy to still be alive after the grueling taxi ride, I got back to my hotel room around 5 P.M. and decided to skip the aarti ceremony after my exploration in the meditation cave and sitting in the Ganga River. I planned to have an early dinner and then watch movies on Romedy Now, a fun India TV network specializing in American romantic comedies. I was ready for a bit of silly, mindless entertainment.

After my shower, I sat down to check WhatsApp and found a voice message from Mom.

"Holly, Auntie and I need to set up a time to talk. Don't worry, but we need to talk to you about the FBI agent who came by the office looking for you. He wouldn't give us any details except to say he has an active investigation and that you may have been a witness to a crime and he needs to interview you. Please don't worry, just let me know when you can get on a call with us. I love you."

My first thought was that this had something to do with Barry and then I pushed that away. Even though he is a completely nasty, evil creep, what in the world would the FBI want him for? I looked at the time. It was now 6 P.M., which meant it was 5:30 A.M. in San Diego. I typed Mom a quick note that I was in my room, and she could reach me at any time. In less than a minute, my phone lit up with the WhatsApp game show–sounding alert.

Just seeing Mom's face made me want to cry. I hadn't realized how homesick I was and how much I missed her! I could see she was sitting up in bed, her biggest reading glasses perched on her nose, and her hair was her usual wild morning bedhead mess. And, for a second, I swear I could smell her grapefruit-scented body lotion.

Mom didn't have much more information than what she'd said in her original message. She said she had told the agent I was "out of the country," on an extended trip but nothing more than that.

He had asked for more details, but Mom smartly didn't tell him a thing so he had asked her to please contact me, and ask if I would be willing to get on a call with him. He insisted I was not in any trouble, but that I may have pertinent information for an international case he was working on.

"Did you see his badge?" I asked cautiously. A string of bile inched up my throat.

"Yes," Mom said quietly. "He said his name is Special Agent Jackson Turner. In his forties, average height, all-American-looking, very polite, thinning light brown hair, dressed in beige khakis and a blue button-down oxford shirt." I marveled at Mom's observation skills when it suddenly hit me who I'd inherited my skills from.

"Is it possible you captured an image of him on Auntie's security system?" I asked.

"Most likely. Once I get to the office, I'll find out and send you what I have."

"Thanks." I exhaled, grateful she didn't ask why I wanted the picture. "I don't see any reason why not to talk to him. Unless Auntie thinks it's a bad idea."

"I will ask her and let you know." Mom's voice sounded full of worry.

We spoke for a while longer. I told her about my adventures and how much I loved cooking school. Neither of us mentioned Barry.

As soon as we disconnected, my hand automatically went to text Carly and tell her about the FBI development. Then I remembered Carly was no longer in my life and I felt a confusing wave of sadness.

I was shocked to discover that there was still a part of me that missed her. This woman who had betrayed me so greatly had been my sister for more than twenty years. Now I had this gaping hole in me that was sad, angry, and feeling all alone in the world.

As my BFF and then business partner, Carly was my "go-to person," as they say. While I had many casual friends, no one came close to having the depth of my connection to Carly.

After my near-fatal car accident and hospitalization, many of my friends had reached out to me, but because I could neither open my mouth to physically speak nor type with my broken wrist, it was nearly impossible to respond to them. Before I left for India, I sent out a group email explaining why they hadn't heard from me and gave them a progress report. It was just hitting me now that I really didn't have anyone I could confide in with details of my life that were so scary to me now.

As I fell asleep, I heard a voice in my head say, "Ask Ma Ganga to send you a new best friend."

As soon as I woke up the next morning, I checked my messages and found one from Mom that simply said, "Here's a fuzzy image of the FBI agent."

I opened up the file and there he was: the mystery man I had seen in Budapest, the one I mistook for someone familiar! I wrote to Mom and said I would certainly talk with him. I had nothing to hide. I hadn't done anything wrong and was curious about what he wanted from me. I asked her to give him all my contact info and to let him know he should contact me as soon as possible.

CHAPTER FIFTEEN

My Foodie Soulmate

One night after satsang, Sadhviji invited me to join some of her nonprofit board members for dinner. These were some of her most devout donors to the Global Interfaith WASH Alliance, an international organization dedicated to clean water, sanitation, and hygiene, which she headed. She was very passionate about it.

I was seated next to a beautiful thirty-something woman named Maya, who literally radiated positive energy. Dressed in a bright red, blingy kurta and shredded, faded, stylish skinny jeans, Maya was a fun blend of East meets West with a Fitbit on one wrist and about a dozen gorgeous gold bangles on the other. Maya told me she was in Rishikesh for the quarterly board meeting and was staying at the Ananda Spa, which I had heard was a super fancy retreat for the rich and famous. Even Oprah had been a guest there.

This was my third post-satsang dinner, and while the food was tastily vegetarian, when the server plopped a dollop of dahl on my plate, a thought ran through my mind, *I would kill for a Hodad's cheeseburger.*

Maya burst out laughing and said, "Me, too!"

Which is when I realized that I'd actually said this out loud. As my face turned red, I asked Maya how in the world she knew about

Hodad's. Maya said with a hungry look in her eyes, "This might surprise you, but I went to San Diego State University for my master's degree in hospitality. The cheeseburgers at Hodad's are my all-time favorite burgers.

I'm also addicted to the onion rings at Burger Lounge, the fish tacos at Oscars, and the guacamole at the Taco Stand in La Jolla."

We spent the next hour lusting over our favorite San Diego foods, including a shared passion for Cardiff Crack, the best marinated tri-tip steak in the world today. We compared notes on everything from best pizza to cupcakes, tying on the best guilty pleasure dessert (either the Pizookie at BJ's or the to-die-for Super Messy Sundae at Sammy's), and best BBQ (from Phil's BBQ, of course), and more.

"Y'know, Maya, I think we just might be foodie soulmates, but explain to me how a Hindu justifies eating burgers and steak?" I asked.

"Well, I am only a good Hindu while in India, but outside of my home country, I indulge in all my favorite forbidden foods. Even though I was raised a vegetarian, I now consider myself a 'chegan,' a cheating vegetarian." She laughed.

After this deeply bonding conversation, Maya offered me a ride back to my hotel. I discovered there are cars and roads in the back of the ashram for getting back to the other side of the river. She invited me to come to Ananda the next day for lunch and a swim, and then insisted that I accept a gift of an ancient Ayurvedic treatment at the spa.

Of course, I said, "Yes!" I mean, *who wouldn't want a spa day in a holy city, no less?* Rishikesh, one of the four most holy cities in India, seemed to have something for everyone. From ashrams to a luxurious spa. I was excited to explore it all.

When I got back to my room, I decided it was time to create a daily schedule for myself. The Virgo part of me was craving routine, consistency, and a new sense of purpose. In the ten days since I had arrived in India, so much had happened. For someone who had resisted all talk of fate, destiny, synchronicity, and the like, it appeared (or was starting to feel like) I might have to rethink my thinking.

Could it just be a coincidence that on my first day, I had met a kindred spirit like Deepak offering me his wisdom and unconditional love, not to mention a daily dose of much-needed, caffeine-laden chai? And it was Deepak who showed me the way to aarti and Swamiji and Sadhviji.

And through them, I met Kurt and now Maya, all of whom generously offered me friendship, insight, solace, and—dare I say it?—a spiritual connection?

After more than six weeks of post-op recovery, mostly home alone at Mom's, it felt good to be back out in the world and connecting with people, even though I was still on an emotional roller coaster with no end in sight.

Several times a day, I experienced overwhelming feelings of worthlessness, hurt, and despair, or worse, intense anger, and I hit 10+ misery levels. Yet, there were also moments when I found myself humming that seventies disco tune, "I Will Survive" by Gloria Gaynor, feeling nearly upbeat, with something akin to hope for brighter days. As the saying goes, "If there's horseshit in your backyard, there's a pony out there somewhere."

I was grateful that I had accepted Auntie's plan and agreed to come to Rishikesh. And even though thinking about my recent past and my future still filled me with dread, I could feel a stirring of possibility inside. Maybe Deepak's morning chats about how we don't really make mistakes, and the importance of having gratitude for right now, for what *is*, were beginning to have an impact on me.

And yet, having spent most of my life focused on the dream of marriage, motherhood, and the white-picket-fence fantasy, I now deeply grieved the loss of this dream. It seemed as if my entire identity, my reason for being, was gone, and I needed to accept this. But with *what* would *I replace it*?

Never a "deep thinker" and also an admitted psychotic optimist, I now saw that I had to figure out who I was, what I wanted, and what new dream I could dream for myself. I was a natural-born lemonade maker; in the past, I would take whatever difficulties came my way and find their silver lining. Until now.

Did I want a pony or a unicorn or something else entirely?

Somehow I was now hoping that it was possible to find these answers here in this beautiful holy city of Rishikesh . . . especially if I could figure out how to be patient and just sit with the "not knowing" of it all.

CHAPTER SIXTEEN

Ananda!

"Oh, oh, aah, OH! Aahhhhhh, mmmmmmm, oh yes."

These moans of pleasure slipped out of me as I fell into a state of transcendent ecstasy as four synchronized hands massaged fragrant sesame seed oil up, down, and around my limbs and torso. I was in the midst of a sensory-rich ballet designed to heal and balance my out-of-whack *doshas*, a term I didn't understand, nor did I need to. I knew that it had been forever since I had experienced pure pleasure . . . something I'd forgotten was even an option.

Maya had arranged for us to have Abyhanga Shirodhara treatments, which may sound like a form of torture, but is a sensuous, soul-stirring healing experience.

This was the Abyhanga part. A blissful massage to enliven all of my senses while also calming me into a state of being I had never visited before. What came next was the Shirodhara treatment that has warm sesame oil drizzled back and forth across your forehead, specifically targeted to the third eye, in a rhythmic sequence designed to quiet mental chatter and encourage sound sleep.

The petite massage therapist gently asked me to turn over. Looking closely at my face, she felt my pulse, then nodded.

"Hmmm . . . your Vata, which is *your* dosha, is nestled too deeply in the mind," she said. I wrinkled my forehead as I looked at her inquisitively.

"That can't be good," I mused. "What's a dosha?"

The therapist smiled warmly. "It is the energy that circulates in your body."

Wasn't energy a good thing? She seemed to sense that I didn't understand. "You think too much. We need to get your Vata in balance." She asked me to close my eyes as she began to drizzle oil slightly back and forth across my forehead. Shirodhara was supposed to bring deep relaxation, inner calm, and peace. Whatever state that was, I wanted more of it. I melted into the table and quietly drifted off into a soft slumber.

After the treatment, I could feel myself yearning not just for a sense of equilibrium but for a return to my previous happy-go-lucky self. My morning chats with Deepak were beginning to loosen the grip of my despair. I noticed that my depression and sadness had become a bad habit, akin to wearing a favorite, ugly old bathrobe every day. It wasn't a good look, yet I felt stuck in its familiarity.

Deepak had described the metamorphosis a caterpillar goes through to become a butterfly and how the magic occurs through the development of imaginal cells. Was that what the Shirodhara treatment was for me? Was it perhaps the beginning of my transformation?

A few hours before, I had taken the scenic half-hour drive up a treelined mountain road to the luxurious Ananda in the Himalayas. We entered the massive grounds through tall majestic gates, home to a former palace, now a very posh hotel and spa. Located on the top of a mountain and surrounded by a verdant mix of pine, cedar, and palm trees, Ananda was surrounded by a fine mist hanging in the air, infusing the setting with a magical, mystical vibe.

Maya was waiting for me in the lobby, looking like a regal yogini. Her dark hair secured in a messy bun atop her head, and wearing the sexiest peek-a-boo cutout leggings and matching tank top I'd ever seen, she wrapped me in a fragrant, joy-filled hug of indeterminable florals and spices. The leggings were a woven crisscross pattern that ran a vertical path down her warm brown-skinned legs, pretty but perhaps a bit provocative as it wasn't yet 10 A.M.

"Holly, we are going to have the best day ever!" Maya enthusiastically informed me. "The plan is first we take a yoga class, followed by a swim, then lunch on the veranda where I swear to you it will be safe for you to eat the world's best salad, and then our spa treatments."

On our way to yoga class, we walked on rich colorful tapestry carpets, marble floors, and hardwoods as we passed beautiful art-filled walls. Maya filled me in on the history of Ananda. Once the summer palace of a prince, it had been transformed into one of the world's premier healing spa destinations. Finally, Oprah and I had something in common: we'd both been pampered at India's finest resort.

Given that my wrist was barely healed, I wasn't sure how much of the class I could actually do, but I was determined to give it a try. The first sequence was a round of Sun Salutations, where I quickly discovered that the downward facing dog was not this girl's best friend. Fortunately a bit later in the class, we moved into *shavasana*, a pose I easily excelled in. I simply lay on my back, arms at my side, palms up, and breathed. Above me was a domed ceiling with a stunning Mughal-influenced blue-and-white-tile mosaic. *I could get used to this.*

After yoga, we went to the pool and bobbed in the shallow end while I spewed out my horror story of Barry and the accident. My crushed dreams of being a happily married mom. The loss of my best friend and business. All of it just came rushing out of me, and surprisingly I didn't cry. Not even once. Maya was a compassionate listener, and even though I barely knew her from our short time together at the ashram, I intuitively felt I could trust her.

When I came up for air, she said, "Here's what I know for sure, Holly. Karma is karma. That monster will be punished and whatever past karma brought him into your life, you are now complete and finished with. While you may feel uncertain about your future, I know that amazing things are happening right now; things are lining up that will birth you into an unimaginable life of joy and fulfillment."

"But what and when, Maya? I am so scared that I will never be happy again."

"Well, let's focus on what we can do today, which is to go have a fabulous lunch and then a spa treatment that I promise will put you into a state of profound bliss," Maya said. With that, we dried off and went to lunch.

After ordering, Maya shared with me her own tragic love story. Married off at twenty-five in a somewhat arranged union to the heir of another hotel family, Maya and Shekhar had known each other most of their lives.

"The first time I noticed him was at my cousin's wedding. I was about seven, and he was around ten, and it was love at first sight for me. I can still see him in his turquoise blue-and-gold raw silk Bandhgala suit with brass buttons, looking like the handsome young prince he was. I was wearing a pink chiffon big girl sari, and while we never actually spoke, we threw shy glances at each other all day," Maya recalled with a wistful smile on her face. "We didn't attend the same schools and only occasionally saw each other at large events, and I admit I often fantasized about him as my possible Prince Charming.

"Over the years, Shekhar developed a reputation as the king of the local nightclub and party scene. Even though we didn't run in the same social circles, I was always aware of him. Handsome. Charismatic. Fun. I was more than delighted when the matchmaker, and our parents, decided to arrange an official meeting. As per tradition, he came to our home with his family.

"We had a beautiful meal together, and then Shekhar and I sat in the garden the rest of the afternoon talking. It was a magical day, the conversation flowed effortlessly, and we laughed a lot.

"We decided to be 'modern' and told our parents that we wanted to date for a few months before deciding if we would marry. I have to admit to you I was ready to say yes that day," Maya explained.

She told me their wedding was seven days of decadence, including more than a few Bollywood stars, supermodels, and global VIPs. Her wedding planner said it was the most expensive wedding he had ever organized. She explained what happened at each of the seven events, including one party that lasted until 6 A.M. and required that the dinner buffet be opened and fully serviced for ten hours.

"It was a spectacle, even by Indian standards. He arrived on a painted elephant to a crowd of more than three thousand. Our guests entered the grounds through a long, winding tunnel made entirely of imported flowers. If you saw the movie *Crazy Rich Asians*, that will give you some idea of just how elaborate my wedding was."

I couldn't wrap my head around a buffet to feed three thousand for ten hours. *Just how rich was her family?* I wondered.

"Holly, you were brought up with Disney's idea of a princess. On my wedding day, I was a mini-Maharani. I wore more than a million dollars of antique jewelry with my red sari, which weighed a ton because of all the encrusted jewels. And after the actual wedding ceremony, I was carried off in a litter by six strong and beautiful men and handed off to my new in-laws, as is the custom in India. I now 'belonged' to my husband's family."

"Wow, sounds like an amazing spectacle, Maya. What went wrong with the marriage?"

"My Prince Charming was a drug addict and an alcoholic. His family knew all along. They had sent him to a rehab center and thought he was healed, but he was a terrific actor and fooled everyone, pretending to be sober and all. His parents purposely selected me, thinking that I was such a good girl that once we had a few kids, he would mature and all would be well in the end. Since I didn't know he had a problem, I didn't think anything of it when we drank champagne on our honeymoon.

"At first, I was completely unaware of the drug use, but within months he started going out at night by himself, coming home really late, and clearly not in his right mind. One night I confronted him and he slapped me and knocked me down. I locked myself in the bathroom and called my parents, who came and picked me up immediately, and that was the beginning of the end. A year later, after him promising countless times to be better and do better and completing stays in two more treatment centers, I had to get out, and that was that."

Maya told me that getting a divorce in India was still a big deal. The divorce rate hovers around two percent because there is still so much social stigma around it.

I asked her if she had been in love with Shekhar. Maya said she was mostly in love with the idea of being part of a hotel dynasty with a handsome man who seemed to be so together. The hardest part was getting over her wounded ego and thinking that she had failed because now she was a young divorcée. Now she wasn't even sure she *wanted* to marry again.

Later, we ate our garden salads that were dressed with a creamy, savory turmeric dressing. "So, Holly, enough of this talk about my tragic marriage. I have a proposition for you," Maya announced, changing the subject as we dug into our leafy meal.

"As I've told you, my parents own several five-star hotels, and my current role involves dreaming up new, innovative ways to keep our current hotel clientele excited, as well as maintaining and growing our reputation as a modern cool and chic hub for locals. They can come, enjoy, and fill our restaurants and bars.

"I've got this idea to open a California-style restaurant in our hotel in Delhi, one that features cheeseburgers and . . . everything from beef and turkey to total vegan. We'll also serve hotdogs, fish tacos, french fries, onion rings, milkshakes, and pizza. I see the décor as a 1950s-style diner with a long counter, bar stools, and cozy red leather booths. We'll have Beach Boys music and all kinds of American pop music playing and maybe even add singing servers.

"To make all of this happen, Holly, I need you. I need you to come and be my consultant, to design the menu and train my cooks. And then, when we are up and running and a huge success, I want you to re-create it on our other properties. What do you think?" she asked before taking a long sip of her green iced tea.

Before I could answer, Maya added, "If you say yes, we will pay you ten thousand USD a month plus give you your own suite in the hotel, unlimited room service, and have a car and driver available for you. See, it's a relatively short-term gig because after the grand opening, your work—at least for the time being—would be done. Please seriously consider it."

I tried to shut my gaping mouth at the level of trust Maya had placed in me so spontaneously. I wondered if I would ever again be able to be so decisively sure about anyone I had just met. It showed, because somehow my mouth wouldn't close.

Maya laughed, looking completely amused by my reaction, saying, "I think I know you more than you know yourself. You can shut your mouth now!"

"It's an incredible offer, Maya," I said, finally, "but it's just so sudden. Are you always so quick to jump into a big project with a virtual stranger?"

"It's true," Maya admitted. "I'm impulsive, but I have great instincts, and I trust my inner radar." And then, flashing a million-watt full-on thirty-two-teeth smile, she added, "Besides, I googled you! According to the *La Jolla Light*, you're 'San Diego's Hottest New Chef.' I believe we've been divinely guided to make some serious foodie magic together."

Sitting on that outdoor terrace, under the banyan tree, eating the delicious, healthy lunch, I felt a shift in my energy, as if a tremendous weight of worry about my currently nonexistent career had been lifted and replaced with a sense of relief and excitement. I sensed I was about to step into a new world. A world that would enliven and challenge my creativity and sense of purpose. And begin to refill my empty bank account.

And maybe the instincts my new friends in India seemed to have might rub off on me.

I knew I had to pay more attention to their intuitive skills. *Well, I do have a ten-year visa*, I thought excitedly. When planning to come to India, Auntie had suggested that I buy the ten-year visa for $150, just in case I fell in love with her homeland and wanted to make many more visits.

"This is just the start of what I suspect will become a lifelong love affair with India for you," she had said. "This way, you are free to extend your stay or to return as often as you wish."

At the time, I thought it was a silly added expense, but now I knew having the extended visa was already fortuitous. A rush of excitement filled my chest and shoulders as I absorbed the enormity of the offer. Perhaps, Maya was my Fairy Godmother, and rather than provide Prince Charming, she waved her magic wand to open up a whole new career path for me. I knew I would learn a lot just by working closely with her on a daily basis.

"Maya, I don't quite know what to say. It's the most mind-blowing and wonderful offer I've ever gotten. It sounds like a perfect project for me, especially at this very moment in my life. But, give me some time to think it through. From what you described, I can completely envision it. I would put up screens and show reruns of an old TV show called *Happy Days* and movies like *Gidget* and *The Endless Summer.* We'll transport the customers straight to the heart of Malibu!"

We brainstormed ideas through the rest of our lunch. It sounded like an amazing opportunity, but because my biggest disappointment and the reason I was here in India were the result of my big impulsive decision, I told her I wanted to slow down to think it through to its logical end. We agreed that I would give her my answer after we met in Delhi and I saw the location. That gave me ten days remaining in Rishikesh before my return flight home from Delhi to LAX. My options were to take a day or two to spend with Maya before my flight home, or to stay in Delhi and take her up on her generous and astoundingly fun-sounding offer.

Kurt was right. Instant manifestation in Rishikesh was on steroids! Not only had I asked for a new best friend, but she came with a possible solution to the beginning of my future. Where would this opportunity take me?

CHAPTER SEVENTEEN

Tasty Healing Treat

At today's cooking class, I asked Divya if it was possible to design a dish with the intention to go beyond infusing the food with love, and add ingredients that would help heal a broken heart.

Kind, talented Divya read right through me. Standing in the kitchen in an orange paisley tunic and solid orange dhoti pants, she had the perfect sweet treat. She called it "Healing the Heart Halwa."

We whipped it up in less than twenty minutes and it was incredibly delicious. Fortunately, we made more than enough, and I put some into a little package that I planned to share with Deepak. Although Nancy had passed away ten years earlier, I figured a little more healing in the form of a tasty treat never hurts.

The next morning, walking to Deepak's, I continued thinking about my future and how to know best what to do. The more I ruminated, the faster my heart beat as my mind started to race between possibilities. Cooking Indian comfort food a few days a week for Divya's parents was a basic and temporary option for my return home, but I had to face that it was certainly not a plan to get excited about. But maybe Maya's offer was?

Confused, I began spiraling downward with depressing thoughts.

Was the best part of my life now over? Would I ever feel real joy again? How would I recover from this swamp of negativity? Was my baby clock about to strike midnight?

Did I really want kids or was it all some juvenile fantasy to rewrite my history of no dad, no siblings?

At times I felt so much fear running through my body I thought I might pass out. My arms would get weak and waves of dizziness forced me to sit down to take deep breaths until I collected myself and calmed down.

Would I ever be whole again? And perhaps even worse, was I ever whole before?

Two mangy, short-haired brown mutts walked up from behind me and snapped me out of my pity party. Tails wagging, they appeared to be harmless, but I wasn't taking any chances of being mistaken for breakfast.

"Okay, puppies, while I'm sure you are both enlightened masters that have reincarnated to protect this holy city of Rishikesh, I don't have any offerings for you right now, and I'm late for a very important date," I said in a soothing Alice-in-Wonderland voice while I picked up my pace. The dogs stopped in their tracks and looked at me almost dumbfounded. *They had obviously never met Alice in Wonderland before*, I joked to myself.

When I arrived at the bookstore, Deepak had my masala chai waiting for me on the worn wood counter. In the short time we had known each other, we had already established a pattern for our mornings, and I felt a wave of gratitude for his warm, welcoming smile. When I walked through his door, I could feel and see the love and care emanating from his beautiful dark brown eyes. In a strange, wonderful, and inexplicable way, he felt like "home" to me.

We sat together using our hands to enjoy the sticky sweet halwa I'd brought with me, and I told him all about my exciting offer from Maya, and how much fun it was to find another foodie. And how it was significant to me that Maya also shared our *being single* issue. It felt special that Maya told me about the pressure she was under from her family to accept one of the endless streams of men offered by the matchmaker. Her grandmother said she needed to become a "homely girl." I told Deepak I thought that was a cruel thing for her grandmother to say, especially because Maya is very beautiful.

Deepak burst out laughing and then explained that in American culture, *homely* means "unattractive." In India, on the other hand, many men were seeking a "homely" girl because it meant that they were good at cooking, cleaning, and creating a presentable home.

"Ha, Deepak! And to think all along, it's been my life's dream to be a 'homely girl.' Maybe I should be the one meeting with the matchmaker! I wonder if she would know what I meant once I described a home with a 'white picket fence.'"

Deepak laughed. "No, even if you brought a picture of a home with a white picket fence, she probably wouldn't understand your desire. You may have noticed there aren't any here."

Now he was making me smile, too.

"Holly, I promise you there is a wonderful plan for your life. Something better than your imagination can conceive of. Can you accept the idea you are in a time of transformation? Think of now as winter. Spring will come, the snow will melt and your new budding life will start to blossom. You are discovering what your soul is yearning for. You can't rush it any more than you can force your hair to grow faster by tugging at it. You cannot force the process, can you?"

He paused while looking deep into my eyes. I sat very still, hanging on his every word. "No, you can't," he continued, "because you know and trust that Mother Nature is doing her job in the proper divine time."

"Crap," I whined. "I never thought it would take so long. So, are you saying there isn't anything I can do to speed up the process of figuring out my life?"

Deepak's answer totally surprised me.

"Actually there is, Holly. You can start enjoying the life you have right now, today. It begins with gratitude. Would you allow me to take you through a little process?"

Deepak appeared to be going into therapist mode. I wiggled in my seat, feeling sweat forming on my palms.

Deepak continued, "In this very short process, know that there is no way you can do it wrong.

"Just listen to my voice and follow along, okay?" I nodded in agreement.

"Holly, sink into this big old recliner and just relax as much as you can. Begin by closing your eyes and take a big, deep breath, in through your nose and out through your mouth."

I did that, and then he said, "Now, take another long, slow deep breath in, count to four . . . and hold for a count of four. Now, release your breath to the count of four."

I followed his directions and noticed something inside me was beginning to feel different.

Deepak's words guided my thoughts. "Okay, now let your attention flow from your head down to your heart space. Imagine you are sitting inside your own heart, and you feel warm, safe, and protected. Remember something for which you are most grateful. Stay focused on your heart space and let whatever or whoever shows up show up."

I was surprised when it was Deepak's face that popped into my mind. I heard his voice encouraging me to let feelings of gratitude wash over me. I could actually feel this sweet feeling of gratitude for having found him and receiving his friendship and guidance.

"As you experience these feelings of gratitude, shift to something about *yourself* for which you feel grateful."

I was surprised when the thought, *I am grateful to be alive*, came to me. Followed by the thought, *I am grateful for the EMTs who found me and put me safely into their ambulance and delivered me to the capable doctors who saved my life. For those who put the parts of my mouth together and took such good care of my head, face, hands, and body. Now I can talk, walk, and hold things effortlessly.*

"Okay, Holly," Deepak said. "Now let go of the feelings of gratitude and see the face of someone you love that you know loves you back, and allow yourself to experience that love now."

Instantly, I saw my mother's face, and I experienced so much love from her and for her. I could also sense all the lifelong love she had for me. I heard Deepak reminding me to keep my attention focused on my heart space while I was holding the feeling of that love.

Then he urged me to see myself being filled with love from the top of my head to the bottom of my feet. I was now in a cocoon of loving feelings. Then he asked me to bring up someone else for whom I felt love, and I saw Auntie Geeta's face. Then images flashed before me from my childhood of times spent with Auntie. By now, I was floating in an ocean of love.

"From your heart space of gratitude and love, you have just arrived in a magical frequency where you can make a wish to the Universe. I will be silent now for a minute to give you time to decide what you most want to wish for," Deepak whispered.

My eyes still closed, I asked myself, *What is my deepest desire?* I swear I heard a voice whisper to me, "Ask to be healed of anything that will stop you from having a full and happy life." *Yes,* I agreed, *that will be my wish.*

"Holly, just nod your head when you have made your wish."

With eyes still closed, I nodded gently, and Deepak then said, "Know that what you have asked for is already yours. Trust that, on the unseen plane, it has already occurred, and soon it will manifest in the physical world. There is nothing more for you to do. Nothing to stress about. Remember to trust that a grand, divine plan is already in motion for you.

"As you sit here, you are wrapped in the arms of God. You are exactly where you need to be. You are loved. You are safe. You are whole. You are complete. Your wish has been fulfilled.

"Now take a long, slow deep breath and let all the feelings and images go.

"Begin to feel your feet resting on the floor. Notice the temperature of the room . . . and when you are ready, simply open your eyes."

At once, my arms and legs felt very light, as if I had fasted for days on end, but without my usual hunger pangs. I had never felt like this before—completely satisfied, not wanting or needing anything else than being right there, in the moment.

Deepak's face lit up. "That, dear Holly, is the effect of Santosha, a state of utter contentment. Do this exercise daily until it is a part of your daily routine. You can see that it will help you feel lighter and lighter until your soul elevates to where it should be."

"Thank you so much," I said quietly. "I could feel a real shift happening."

Deepak smiled warmly. "And thank you, dear Holly, for the sweet treat. Your halwa tastes very similar to my mother's."

HEALING THE HEART HALWA

¼ cup ghee

⅛ teaspoon cinnamon

1 inch vanilla bean (finely chopped)

a pinch mineral salt

1 cup grated carrots

½ cup pitted dates, mashed

20 sprigs saffron, gently ground in warm water

1 cup water

- Heat the ghee in a pan.
- Add the cinnamon, vanilla bean, and a pinch of mineral salt.
- Simmer until you can smell the aroma.
- Stir in the carrots, saffron, dates, and half of the water. Simmer for 8 to 10 minutes, adding more water as needed to make a thick paste.
- Place in a bowl and let cool for about 5 minutes. If you want a smooth consistency, let cool and blend in a blender.
- Serve lightly warm. Yum!

CHAPTER EIGHTEEN

My Three-Thousand-Year-Old Prophecy

"Madam, we are so sorry to inform you that you are not in your right mind," my translator said.

"What the fuck?" I responded, and then hoped like hell no one else in the room understood what I had just said.

I was seated in a hard, wooden chair facing a large table that had bundles of old palm leaves filled with tiny hieroglyphic-like writing on them, and held together with some form of string. For more than two hours, I had been slowly going through the process of finding the leaf on which my past, present, and future had been written more than three thousand years earlier by enlightened sages, assisted by Lord Shiva, creating predictions to help people find their destiny.

"Madam, the leaf says that you are not currently in your right mind." *Okay,* I thought, *I know that, but how does the leaf know that?* I haven't been in my right mind for the last two months, probably longer. So how did I end up here? In the very south of South India? In a small, cement block room with a young priest reading Old Tamil predictions off a palm leaf that were being interpreted by a *Hinglish*-speaking man named Babu?

Upon learning the gory details of my recent past, while we were having a spa day at Ananda, my new best friend Maya had decided that what I most needed, to get my life back on track, was a Nadi reading.

Which is how I found myself a few hours outside of Pondicherry in a room framed by large, colorful portraits of Hindu Gods and Goddesses illuminated by a single flickering, buzzing fluorescent light bulb as I listened to details about my life, most of which weren't even available on the internet.

Fortunately, Maya had arranged for Dr. Q, the dapper European scholar who oversees the Nadi reading service, to sit next to me specifically to interpret the interpreter. After a bit of back and forth between Dr. Q and Babu, with a lot of head-bobbing happening on both sides, Dr. Q laughed out loud.

"Madam Holly," he explained. "What he means is that you are in a period of your life where you do not know your life's purpose and you are not supposed to know this at this time."

Learning that "you are not in your right mind" really meant "you don't know your purpose" was a big relief to me. Good that Dr. Q translated for me; it was definitely a true statement, but then I was saddened to hear that the leaves weren't about to fill me in on what's coming next for me career-wise. Maybe the leaves were not that familiar with American girls who work but would like to become "homely girls."

My itinerary that day had been decided at Ananda when Maya borrowed an inkpad from the front desk and made an imprint of my left thumb on a notecard to send off to Dr. Q. She initiated the search for my "bundle" with the details of my life.

Maya explained that she'd had a spectacular reading a few years earlier, where she was given in-depth information on her most recent past life (and the bad karma she had accrued, and how to do a special puja to erase it).

She was literally giddy recalling the details they gave her about the coming decades related to money, health, career, and her love life, along with pertinent information on her parents, including their names, social status, health issues, and more. At the end of her reading, she was asked if she was willing to hear the date, time, and circumstance of her death, which she agreed to, but didn't share that with me. Whew!

This Nadi reading sounded like exactly the kind of information to reboot my life and I bellowed out a huge, resounding, "YES! Maya, please! ASAP!"

Maya went back to New Delhi, and a week later, she sent me a text message that my bundle had been found. She added that it was very auspicious that this happened so quickly. "Very unusual," she said. She was so excited that she offered to escort me to Tamil Nadu for the reading.

I did a quick google search and discovered that Pondicherry is a charming, former French colony on the Bay of Bengal. It was described as having a New Orleans look and vibe to it. Half the town was a mixture of restored and decaying early-twentieth-century colonial architecture that still retained its strong French influence, while the other half was very much Indian.

"Yes, Maya," I texted. "I would love that!"

She quickly wrote back saying she would make all the arrangements, be my personal escort, and I was to be her guest as a way to further entice me to accept her consulting offer. Maya had arranged a car to meet us the morning after we arrived in Pondicherry, to drive the nearly three hours for my reading in the small village of Vaitheeswarankoil, population ten thousand. Now, that's an extraordinary true friend!

Unlike California freeways, this part of the world is knitted together through two-lane roads (mostly paved), with rice paddy fields on either side. Seeing farmers wearing broad-brimmed straw hats, leaning on hoes while chatting on their mobiles was something that, I admit, surprised me.

We passed many small square blockhouses and small snack shops offering dozens of varieties of chips with crazy hot spices. Brightly clad sari-wearing women were bent over in the space directly leading to the front entryway of their blockhouse homes. Maya explained that they were performing their morning ritual of pouring colored sand into intricate geometric yantras placed where a welcome mat would normally go. Known as rangoli, these yantras are a sacred form of art in India. Each yantra offered a diagram of a particular frequency's vibration to provide another day of protection and blessings on their families, and their dogs, goats, and chickens, many of which lived in the house with them. Before we stepped through the door of Dr. Q's establishment, we smelled the inviting incense. He warmly greeted us and offered us freshly made masala chai, which we gladly accepted after the long journey. He and Maya had a quick catch-up talk before she explained she was going out for a few hours with the driver to do a puja at the Vaidyanathaswamy Temple where it is believed the Hindu Gods of healing reside. Her favorite auntie was suffering from gout. Maya planned to send her some ancient healing energy since it was believed that you could be cured by giving away crystal salt and black pepper in this temple.

"Holly," she said softly as she wrapped me in her bangle-filled arms. "Today will change your life in a good way. It is likely your session could take up to three hours. Take lots of notes and I promise to return for you before your session is complete."

As Dr. Q walked me into the next room, he said, "Holly, it's so wonderful to put a name and a face to your thumbprint."

The look on my face must have been one of utter confusion, which made him laugh.

"Until just now the only thing I knew about you was that you were a female friend of Maya's. As part of our process, we only have the seeker's thumbprint . . . never a name, gender, or vital information. This is how we keep the process pure," he said with an obvious sense of much pride.

While the priest (the reader) and his translator were doing a prayer and ritual to prepare for our session, Dr. Q went on to explain how things would proceed. First, he asked that I write down my first name, my mother's first name, and my father's first name, then write beside each name the number of letters in each. I shared with Dr. Q that I didn't know the name of my father, and he said that was okay; we would discover his name in the reading. *That is a heart-stopper!*

It had never occurred to me that I would learn something—anything—about my father from this reading. He told me that they would begin by asking me a series of "yes" or "no" questions. As long as I answered "Yes," they would go on to the next question. If I answered

"No," that meant they needed to move on to the next leaf. He also said I was never to offer any additional information except "Yes" or "No," and that the reader did not know anything about me—not my name, age, birthday, or country of origin. Nothing. Zip. Nada. Once my leaf was found, they would provide the information on the leaf and when they finished, at that point, I could ask specific questions if they hadn't already been answered.

Dr. Q walked me to the reading room and introduced me to Guruji, the reader, and the translator, who both slightly smiled and welcomed me with their palms pressed together in front their chests in a traditional namaste.

The priest, who couldn't have been more than twenty-five, picked up the first bundle, looked at the top leaf and spoke in a language I have never heard. Then Babu translated what the priest had said into English, in a heavy accent, which I strained to comprehend.

And so, we began.

"You work as an artist, painter, or writer?"

"No," I said as I also shook my head from side to side. New leaf.

"You were born in November or December?" "No."

New leaf.

"You are a college graduate?" "Yes."

"You are an employee of a large enterprise?" "No."

New leaf.

"You work as a healer?" "No."

New leaf.

"Your mother has three children." "No."

New leaf

"Your mother is named after a saint?" "No."

New leaf.

You were born in March or April?" "No."

New leaf.

This process went on for more than a half hour. Sometimes there would be five yeses in a row, and then, the dreaded "No" would come and Guruji was on to the next leaf. I was beginning to think that there was no leaf for me.

Dr. Q had warned there was no guarantee that everyone had a leaf, or that the correct bundle with my leaf would be found and that, if that happened, it meant this wasn't the correct time to have a reading.

Leaf after leaf was discarded, and with it, feelings of despair arose.

My misery level was creeping upward as each leaf was discarded.

Finally, at around forty-minutes into the reading, with leaf number thirty-eight, this happened:

"Your mother's name begins with *L* or *G*?" "Yes."

"Mother's first name is *L*?" "Yes."

"Mother's name has five letters?" "Yes."

"Mother's name ends in A?" "Yes."

"Mother's name is Laura?" "Yes."

"Mother has high blood pressure?" "Yes."

"You were born in September or October?" "Yes."

"You were born in September?"

"Yes."

"You were born September twenty?" "Yes."

"You were born early morning, four or six A.M.?" "Yes."

"Maternal grandmother taught you skills you use for a career?" "Yes."

"You are a graduate?" "Yes."

"Your work is food?" "Yes."

"You had recent head injuries?" "Yes."

"Your name is Holly." "Yes!"

"Your father is named after a saint?"

Shit.

We were so close to having my leaf. What if this makes them go to another leaf?

Dr. Q piped up and told Babu to tell Guruji to continue.

"Madam Holly doesn't know the father's name. What name does the leaf give? What further information does it have about the father?" he asked.

As Babu explained the situation to Guruji, he carefully studied the leaf that I was hoping was *my* life history. Guruji and Babu then appeared to have a debate as to what they would or could share with me. Eventually, Babu said, "Father's name is Thomas. Father has three daughters. You are youngest daughter."

Holy shit! I have a dad. I have sisters. Does that skinny old leaf have their mobile numbers? I wondered.

At this point, the three men were all in agreement that they had now found my leaf. The actual reading would now begin.

"We want to advise you that you must manage your hunger, or serious health issue will befall you," said Babu.

"Huh? I have never missed a meal in my life," I said.

"No, madam, we said you must manage your hunger."

"Yes, I heard you and I'm telling you I have never missed a meal. I do not have any hunger issues."

That's when Dr. Q tapped me lightly on the shoulder and said, "Holly, they are saying *anger*, they aren't saying *hunger*. They say you have anger issues, and if you don't manage them, you might get sick."

Oh. I let that sink in for a moment. *Anger issues . . . me?* Generally, anger was never my problem, but since my multiple betrayal fiasco, the truth is that in between feeling lonely, broken, and depressed, I had to admit I'd also felt intense anger and rage. I wrote down in my journal, "Find healthy ways to release anger and get to forgiveness." Remembering the dream about Barry's demise in the boiling vat of hot oil, I made a mental note to address my anger issues.

I began to squirm in my seat as they revealed that I had just come out of the most difficult period of my life, which was when they told me, "Madam, you are not in your right mind." Meaning that I didn't know my true life purpose. It was amazing that they were able to describe details of my physical and emotional trauma by reading a tattered ancient palm leaf. Plus, in that leaf, they said it was predicted I would have this difficult experience because this suffering was karmic debt from my past life.

For the next two hours, they slowly described in detail both my past and a year-by-year highlight of my future that ranged from years where my health would be strong, to when Mom would have challenging health issues. They told me my good year for buying clothes and jewelry, and a great year for me to buy property. And the year to avoid having a business partner who would cheat me, and named several years of positive reputation and potential fame. All in all, they seemed assured that I would lead a good and happy life.

I asked them both if they could explain why I had suffered so much and why my lifelong dreams of a family were not coming true.

Guruji and Babu had a lengthy conversation with much head nodding up and down and side to side going on, when finally Babu asked, “Madam, would you like to know about the past life in which you incurred this karma?”

“Please tell me everything!”

“In your most recent past life, you lived here in Tamil Nadu. Your name was Arti Nataraj. You were the only daughter of good parents, and you had a mostly happy life with one much older brother who worshipped you as if you were his own child. You had a better education than most, and you were trained as a healer.

“Unfortunately, you had relations with another man, not your husband. You broke your husband’s heart, and he left you alone and childless. To redeem yourself, you became a devotee of the Goddess Parvati, wife of Shiva, known as the Goddess of Love, fertility, and family. You devoted yourself to creating an orphanage for girls that became well known throughout the country. You are recognized in the history books on this subject as you provided the little girls with love, affection, healthcare, and education,” Babu explained as he looked at me with respect shining through his deep brown eyes.

I managed to *not* take in this monumental aspect of my past life history and narrowed my questions to one. I asked, “So, are you saying that I won’t marry, and I won’t have children?”

Again Babu and Guruji had a long chat, pointing to various symbols on my leaf, and finally, I was told, “It is not the correct time for this information to be revealed to you. And we suggest that to remove the karmic blocks from your past life, you do the remedy of a Guru Puja,” Babu said.

Dr. Q saw the disappointment as my shoulders slumped and my smile drooped. He asked Guruji when I should come back for the next reading, and they did some calculations and said that in two years’ time, this information could be revealed.

More disappointing news. I would be just past forty in two years.

Was it time to seriously consider freezing some eggs?

My final question for the day was, "Can you explain how to do a Guru Puja?"

"Madam, you shall go to the Thiruvenkadu Temple and bring the following offerings to the priest for the puja: clothing for two ladies and clothing for two men, nine coconuts, and fifty-two kilos of rice," Babu explained.

Dr. Q furiously scribbled down notes, then, looking up at me, said, "Holly, you are in luck. That temple is less than a half hour from here. I will take you and Maya to the temple and assist you with this."

A few minutes after my reading was complete, Maya arrived. We jumped into Dr. Q's sapphire blue Tata Hexa XT SUV and went to a local market to buy two red saris, two men's dhoti sets, several giant bags of rice totaling over a hundred pounds, an assortment of fresh fruit, flowers, and nine coconuts.

She was anxious to hear all about my reading, so I leaned forward to get closer to Maya, who was in the front passenger seat.

"Maya, the reading was crazy amazing! I don't know how they figured it all out with just a thumbprint. Much of what they knew isn't available on the internet, even if they tried to search for me. I was hoping to find out when I would have kids and with whom, but instead, they gave me dreadful news. According to my palm leaf, I have been childless up until now as punishment for my past life as an unfaithful wife. While they didn't say I was a slut, that's certainly what they inferred. And that's why we are headed to the temple now to try to rectify my situation with a Guru Puja," I said before I screamed as Dr. Q swerved to avoid hitting a cow in the road.

Dr. Q apologized profusely for the near miss as I continued to share with Maya. "The most startling news was learning that my father's name is Thomas and I have two half sisters."

"Oh, Holly, that's amazing! I bet you can find them with a DNA test and discover your biological family and ancestors," Maya encouraged.

A few kilometers later, Dr. Q slowed his car down and pulled onto an adjacent dirt road, stopping in front of a ramshackle stand with a roof covered with faded palm fronds and held up by four wooden posts adorned with faded painted lotus flowers.

Several locals mingled in front, sipping out of small metal cups. As we jumped out of the car, Dr. Q told us this was his favorite coffee walla, and we were in for the tastiest treat in South India. He ordered for us (no special orders taken here!), and we watched as the man, clad only in his dhoti, quickly and artfully poured the steaming hot brew from cup to cup in a giant wet arc of coffee, milk, and who knows what else.

With my first sip, I fully understood addiction. I've never smoked opium or crack, but I imagine this comes close to the same euphoria one experiences. This was simply the most delicious cup of coffee I'd ever had. It tasted like hot, melted Häagen-Dazs coffee ice cream and I didn't dare think about the sugar or calorie count.

"Why do you call this place your coffee walla?" I asked Dr. Q.

He and Maya both laughed, and Dr. Q explained. "A walla is not a place or a thing, it's a *person* who is the best at what they do or offers a great product or service. So there are chai wallas, ghee wallas, and rickshaw wallas. You have just experienced the world's greatest coffee walla."

As we got back in the car, Maya explained. "Holly, think of it this way, a walla is what you might call your 'go-to' person."

"So, based on what you are saying, I could call Deepak my love walla, right?"

Maya gave me her ten-thousand-watt smile.

"Well, I've never heard it used that way, but yes, Deepak is truly your love walla. You may have invented a new expression! Love walla, what a beautiful explanation for your personal guru."

A smile filled my heart and face. I had never thought of Deepak as a guru. Given his humility, he probably would have objected to the term. But deep down, I knew he had become my personal spiritual guide, teaching me important lessons about love and life.

Without any conscious consent on my part, this peaceful thought triggered a place in my heart that had still been holding a lot of pain. *If Deepak is my Love Walla*, I thought to myself, *then surely he's come into my life to help me restore everything that Barry, that heartless love thief, has stolen from me.*

My internal tangent was interrupted as we arrived at the temple, and I experienced a moment of déjà vu when I saw the nine-story structure that looked like an ancient Hindu wedding cake. Built somewhere between one and two thousand years ago, I imagined that its architect was an Indian version of Walt Disney's creative genius. Painted in shades of coral, baby blue, and pale green, the temple was dedicated to Lord Shiva, the "auspicious one," famous for his love and devotion to his wife, Parvati.

"Time to let go of our monkey minds," Dr. Q reminded us. "Take a few deep breaths, and remember that we have come here to participate in a sacred ceremony. One of the 'boons' of this particular temple is the ability to pray for a special wish."

Before I could rationally think about this, I heard a small voice inside me say, "I wish to know my daddy."

CHAPTER NINETEEN

Blacker Than Black at 3 A.M.

I forced myself to wake up from a nightmare . . . I had been attempting to walk through a dark forest, my feet were encased in deep mud, I tripped over vines and fallen trees, and was being eaten alive by mosquitoes, lost, dazed, confused. I was desperately trying to figure out where I was, how I got there, and how I was ever going to get out. Every breath was a struggle and there was a part of me that was simply ready to give up.

My situation was so horrific that some part of my brain said, *This isn't real, this can't be happening . . . force yourself awake*. And I did.

I sat up, still not certain of where I was, and reached for my phone. It was 3 A.M. My room was unusually silent, and as I glanced over at the curtains, I noticed that no lights were shining through. Must be a power outage. Not an uncommon occurrence.

My chest felt constricted, heavy, as if a two-hundred-pound boulder were pressing down hard on my heart. Relieved to be awake and terrified about my life.

My brain was stuck in a negative feedback loop of persistent fearful thoughts and questions.

How could I have been that stupid? Why did they do this to me? What did I ever do to deserve this? What will I do now? Where will I live? Will I ping-pong between depressed and angry for the rest of my life?

Should I get out of bed and go jump into the swift current of the Ganga River and just let her sweep me away in the inky darkness?

As I contemplated whether or not I was serious about suicide, indulging these dark thoughts and allowing myself to attend my own pity party, I realized it was never anything I could seriously consider.

Holly, stop this right now! Haven't you learned anything from all of your adventures thus far? I challenged myself. *Who cares if you don't know where you will live or what you will do? What you do know is that right now, at this moment, you have everything that you need.* And with that, I heard the hum of electrical things sparking back to life and took it as a sign of confirmation that even though I didn't know my future, I could trust that good things were coming.

Misery level: 10+++.

CHAPTER TWENTY

Make Mine Simple

When I was little, upset and complaining about one thing or another, my mother would often laugh and say to me, "Hey, kid, keep up that whining, and I will be forced to call the Whambulance."

I was a teenager before I understood what sarcasm really is, and my mother's words were an introduction to it.

On my first visit to see Deepak after returning from Pondicherry, I thought of this as I heard myself say to him, "Geez, I just want to be happy. Why is that so hard? What's it going to take? It's not like I'm asking for something unreasonable. Ninety percent of the world already has this. I'm a simple girl. I want a husband and some kids. Now. In. That. Order. I just want to be happy," tumbled out of my mouth like bitter lemon rinds, leaving me feeling like I was still seven years old.

Deepak looked at me with a raised left eyebrow and softly said, "No."

Nothing else. Just "No." A big, fat "No" just hanging in midair like a loud, stinky, unacknowledged fart.

"What do you mean, 'No'?" I asked quietly.

"Holly, here's the problem with *happy*," he began. "Yes, happy feels good. It seems like the goal to shoot for, but happy isn't where you want to land. Happy is a state of being that is contingent upon someone or something. You were happy in the beginning with Barry because you thought all your dreams were coming true. And then you were unhappy because all your dreams came crashing down.

"Your happiness was tied to both a person and a goal. The secret sauce to a great life is not about happiness. It's about *santosha*. Remember that term from the heart exercise we did? It is an ancient Sanskrit word that means contentment, utter contentment. When you find and ultimately live santosha, you are in a satisfying state of contentment that is not dependent on anything or anyone.

"Contentment is being willing to accept both your happiness and your lack of it at any given moment. This is the practice of the spiritual warrior, to love what is, the good, the bad, the ugly, and to remain centered in appreciation and gratitude," he explained.

"But Deepak," I whined, hearing my mother's sarcasm swell within my brain, "what about my goals, my dreams, my desires? Do I just throw up my hands and hope for the best?"

"Yes and no. It's a paradox. Your desires and dreams are important, and I believe they come with a promise of potential fulfillment. So, yes, dream big. And at the same time that you are moving forward to co-create your dreams with the Universe, stay detached and surrendered from the outcome itself. Be content with where you are. Have an appreciation for where you are and allow yourself to deeply feel how good life is right now as the wiser, trusting part of you knows that what you've asked for is already yours on some unseen plane. We must be patient to see when, how, or if it manifests on the physical plane."

My head was beginning to melt. In my mind's eye, I could see my brain matter swirling down the drain, liquefied by the hot mess my life had become. This all sounded like the kind of conversation Mom and Auntie Geeta would have when they returned from an Esther Hicks Law of Attraction cruise. The last thing I wanted to do was become part of the "Woo-woo weirdness, ask and you shall receive," crowd. Even my teeth began to hurt.

And yet, hearing it from Deepak, some part of me was getting it. I swallowed my reluctance as I leaned forward to absorb his words more intently.

"You've spent nearly your entire life focused on a goal based on a decision of a young girl. Holly, what if God has a better plan for you? What if your imagination isn't vast enough to dream up the people and things that will bring you more love, joy, satisfaction, and contentment than you could ever imagine?" Deepak asked this with a knowing, compassionate smile on his face.

"But if I give up this dream," I whined, "and I don't know what it is I really want, how will I ever make anything happen? I am really good at making stuff happen, but I totally suck at throwing up my hands and hoping for the best."

Deepak put his right hand to his heart and beamed waves of the most loving look at me as he said, "*Learning to be with not knowing is perhaps one of the hardest things to master in this life.* This means that we allow ourselves to be *okay* with what is happening and stop ourselves from endlessly worrying about an unpredictable future. It requires a big act of faith that something larger, grander, than us is at play here. It requires paying attention to the whispers and callings of our own souls. And we must be willing to sit patiently in the sea of uncertainty, certain that the Universe always has our back."

The tingling of the bells on the front door announced the first customer of the day, which I took as my cue to take my wildly out-of-control monkey mind for a walk along Ma Ganga.

The sunbeams danced upon the surface of the river like gleaming diamonds. As I started along the path, part of me wanted to figure out the answer to my "what the fuck am I going to do with my life" drama with an instant solution, and the other part of me wanted to see if I could find a way to stop freaking out and lean back into the arms of God and take my chances. This last option did not feel good at all. It felt unsafe, wrong, and scary. And yet, some rational part of my mind now acknowledged that my approach to life has not been working for me.

CHAPTER TWENTY-ONE

What's Love Got to Do with It?

The first thing I noticed when I walked into Divya's was the beautiful swirling, intricate Mehndi (henna) designs on her hands and feet. "Whose wedding did you go to?" I asked.

Divya smiled and then presented me with the full view of her palms. "We didn't go to a wedding. This is for tomorrow when my sisters and I celebrate Karwa Chauth. It's an ancient Hindu festival that happens once a year where we dress up as brides and fast for an entire day as we pray for our husbands' continued good health and prosperity.

"It's a traditional ritual that begins before sunrise by eating fruit, provided to us by our mothers-in-law, and we fast until we see the moon. Then the fun begins as we have a celebratory break-the-fast meal together. It's how we show our love, devotion, and respect to our husbands."

Somehow the idea of this pissed me off. "And, when does he fast and pray for you?" I asked a bit more snarkily than intended.

Divya smiled, ignoring my attitude.

"Actually, many of the younger men in the bigger cities are now realizing just how important their wives are to their good health and prosperity so they, too, are participating in Karwa Chauth. I enjoy the traditions of my faith and I believe that sending out good energy returns good energy. I don't feel there is any downside in spending a day focused on my beloved husband. If you had asked me about this the first time I did this, I would have given you a completely different answer. Now, let's go do some cooking."

We walked into her immaculate kitchen and she handed me a bunch of greens to rinse and chop. "This is methi," she said as she swiftly moved about the kitchen. "You might also know it as fenugreek leaves, and here are two bunches of spinach leaves. It's not only spellbindingly delicious, it's a very healthy dish that is rich in fiber and good for diabetics."

I was half listening, dying to hear more about the early days of her marriage. I had shared some of my secrets with her, but would she be willing to do the same?

"Divya, is it too personal to ask you how you and Ravi met?"

I could see Divya's mind working to decide if or what she would share with me. As she poured us both more hot water into our nearly empty teacups, she smiled.

"Well, this probably is not the story you might expect," she began. "As you know, our culture still mostly prefers arranged marriages, with the parents actively seeking the man and his family that is a fit for ours. It's not about what the daughter wants, although we do have the ability to say no. My parents were always very clear that I would attend and graduate from college and that marriage would not be an impediment to that. At nearly eighteen, I was deep into my studies of botany and chemistry, and marriage was the last thing on my mind.

"One evening, my father came home from a night out with my Uncle Krishan, Geeta's father, with news that Uncle believed he had found the perfect husband for me. Uncle had been very persuasive that this man, Ravi, came from an excellent family and that I would be lucky to have such a husband. And time was of the essence because Ravi, an engineer with a very prestigious position in a big company, was visiting family in India from London for the next month.

"In typical Indian matchmaking style, it was quickly decided that Uncle and Auntie would invite the twenty-six-year-old 'catch,' along with his parents, sister, and another aunt, for a visit at Uncle's house. When they arrived, all of us sat awkwardly in the sitting room for fifteen minutes, and then Ravi and I were given permission to go off on our own to get to know each other a little bit. He was surprisingly open right from the start and did almost all of the talking. He told me that his bride would have to be willing to move to London and be willing to travel and take care of his parents when they needed help.

"He also explained that he had already met more than fifty women through various matchmakers and that he was getting a lot of pressure from his parents to find a bride and settle down. I thought he was a nice guy, but honestly didn't feel any kind of attraction to him, and couldn't imagine that my father seriously wanted me to marry so soon, especially to a man nearly ten years older than me. And yet, that is what happened. Three weeks later, with just six days of planning, Ravi and I had more than a thousand guests at our wedding.

"We spent five days together, and I had sex for the first time, and then Ravi went back to work in London, and I remained at home with my parents for the next eighteen months to complete my education. During that time, Ravi and I saw each other a couple of times when he came to visit me and the rest of his family, but we were still virtually strangers.

"Back then, there was no internet, and no Skype or WhatsApp, and overseas calls were expensive, so we wrote letters, which took ten days or more to send and receive. When I was finally ready to move to London, I was terrified to begin this new life, in a new country, with a man who was my husband yet also a stranger.

"Our first five years together were a nightmare. We never made love, even though I tried everything I could think of to seduce him. My self-esteem was nonexistent, and I thought I was the ugliest woman on the planet. On top of that, his mother had grown very cold toward me, and neither Ravi nor I could figure out why. One day, in our third year together, I picked up the phone and heard Ravi talking to a woman . . . I listened and realized he was talking to our neighbor and friend, a single woman everyone called Baby, and they were making plans to get together. I quickly suspected he was having an affair, but I didn't say anything. I thought Baby was my friend. She had always been so warm and friendly to me. Now I began to wonder if she was the reason my husband never touched me."

I was both riveted and a bit taken aback by how matter-of-fact Divya was in the delivery of her story. I was also somewhat triggered by her cool and seemingly casual acceptance of such a deep betrayal. *Were cheating husbands more accepted in her culture?*

"A few months later, Ravi discovered that Baby was cheating on him and, when he confronted her, she broke it off with him, saying she preferred the other man who was single and wanted to marry her. Ravi confessed everything to me, and while I was packing to go home to my parents in India, he swore to me he would never do it again. He said that if I gave him another chance, he would devote the rest of his life to making me happy. The next two years were the roughest period of my life. I found out that my father and Ravi's mother had arranged for my father to pay a dowry of a thousand grams of gold. That's about fifty thousand dollars in today's money. And somehow, a misunderstanding occurred, and Ravi's mother began demanding an additional thirty grams of gold, which my father wouldn't pay, and all of this caused unspoken tension among the family.

"During this time, I constantly considered divorcing Ravi, even though that is rarely done in our culture. I could see that he was trying to be a loving, attentive husband, but it just wasn't enough for me. Eventually, I told him that the only way we could stay together is if we moved back to India. I have always been very stubborn, and he knew it was either take me home or let me go. Smart man that he is, we went home.

"Once we got back to India, our life as a couple really began to take form. We had two sons, we both had work that we loved, and over the past forty-four years, we have learned to love each other deeply. Today we are best friends and partners, and even though it was not predictable we would have a happy ending, once Baby was out of the picture, he chased me as if I were Mandakini under the waterfall . . . she's the Bollywood version of Elizabeth Taylor," Divya said with a satisfied smile.

We sat in silence for a long moment as I felt the sweetness of Divya's love story wash through me. "You have no idea how much I needed to hear this," I said finally, surprised by the emotion in my voice. Inspired by how much this woman had been through, I gave her hand a hard squeeze. "Your story restores my faith that love can, and will, find a way."

After a lunch of the delicious methi, rice, and red lentil soup (dahl), Divya asked if I had seen Tapovan yet, a village area to the north in Rishikesh that was bustling with cafés, markets, and pharmacies. I jumped at the chance for a little shopping and a new adventure.

"My husband has the car today, so we will walk down the hill and take a tuk-tuk," she said with a laugh. "I promise you it will be a true Indian experience."

The walk down the hill from her home was thankfully monkey free and we quickly found a brightly painted yellow-and-green "Tuk-tuk limo," an open-air vehicle with two wooden bench seats facing each other. I quickly began to pull myself into a seat when Divya stopped me and said that we first had to negotiate the fee. She and the driver got into a very spirited conversation in Hindi, which involved much hand and head gesturing. From what I could see, it appeared a bit hostile until Divya handed him some rupees. At once, they both smiled, and she motioned me into a seat.

"What was that all about?" I asked, genuinely curious.

"That rascal wanted to charge us three hundred rupees when the normal rate for the two of us should be sixty rupees. Because you are an obvious foreigner, he thought I might have been as well and he was trying to take advantage of us," she explained.

I quickly did the math in my head; three hundred rupees was around four dollars, and Divya had negotiated a grand total of eighty cents. It seemed rather odd to haggle over such a low price, but I trusted her instinct and hopped onto the backseat nearest the driver. The plume of fumes emanating from the back was nauseating at best. At that moment, I wished I had brought a scarf to cover my nose from the smell.

After traveling no more than a kilometer, the tuk-tuk driver pulled over and stopped.

"Oh, Holly. I meant to warn you; this ride will soon get very crowded." I gave her a puzzled look. For a second, I thought there might be a chance that a family of monkeys might jump in for a free ride.

"It is best you move over here and sit next to me," Divya said, patting the seat closest to her. I grabbed the back of the driver's seat to push my way toward her. Suddenly, a mother and four small children filled the bench I had just vacated. I was beginning to get a flavor for India in a new way. Things happen and you have to adjust. I filed the thought away in the "how to be flexible" drawer in my mind.

The tuk-tuk took a hard left turn, which had the kids squealing to hold on while I reached out to make sure none of them fell out. The mother smiled at me benevolently as if to signal the kids had mastered the art of Indian travel in a way I had not yet.

We began winding up a paved road with tall trees on both sides. The dark green foliage was filtering the sunlight, giving the surroundings a mystical, dreamy appearance. Despite the tight space, I couldn't resist feeling a bit mystical and dreamy myself. I inhaled the scents of the street food vendors and nearly forgot about the fumes trailing behind us.

A little voice inside my head whispered a word of encouragement. "Well, look at you now, Holly." A sense of pride swelled within me as I melded with the jolting movements of the tuk-tuk. Just a few weeks ago, I could not have imagined actually enjoying a ride like this. India, this exotic and chaotic country, had somehow entered my bloodstream.

The dreamy, peaceful feeling didn't last long. The tuk-tuk picked up three more passengers who squeezed in next to Divya and me, literally forcing Divya's legs on top of mine. The situation became both hilarious and uncomfortable. After a brief spell of bliss, I now began to wonder if eighty cents was too much for this crazy ride.

Within fifteen minutes, we arrived at a corner of the two main streets in Tapovan. Divya and I hopped out and spent the next hour wandering in and out of the various stores. She bought spices, vegetables, and a few homeopathic remedies from the pharmacy, while I picked up a few sandalwood statues.

Walking past a large temple, Divya pointed out a young man dressed as the half human–half monkey Hindu god Hanuman. He was wrapping a red string around another man's wrist.

"Holly, would you like to receive a blessing that will stay on your arm for many months?" Divya asked.

"Sure, why not," I said. I offered my right arm to the young man.

The monkey god man proceeded to tie a long piece of red string around my wrist, and as he did so, he spoke in near-perfect English:

"This will provide you blessings for success in the near future and will also assist in the healing of your wrist."

And then, he walked away. My mouth widened ever so slightly. *How in the world did he know the wrist he just wrapped the string on was still healing from a fracture?* I thought.

Seeing the question on my face, I explained to Divya that my wrist had recently healed after I broke it. I was dumbstruck that this stranger in a crazy costume wearing a gold-and-green headdress and a monkey-face mask while draped in robes of red and gold *knew* about my injury.

"Holly, this is India. You are in Rishikesh, one of the holy cities where blessings occur naturally," Divya said to me rather solemnly, looking me straight in the eyes. "The veils between worlds are thinner here on Ma Ganga, and accessing the divine is to be expected rather than a surprise. What just happened for you was a rather blatant experience of this, but if you stay in the present moment and stay aware, you will find that these things are happening all the time." Divya smiled as she took my hand.

"Now, let's go have some tea at my favorite café with the world's most spectacular view."

METHI

1 bunch methi (fenugreek leaves)

2 bunches spinach leaves

3 red chili peppers
(or more, as needed for spiciness)

6 to 8 garlic cloves

1 tablespoon rice flour

1 teaspoon dried ginger

4 tablespoons oil

2 tablespoons cumin seeds

¾ teaspoon sea salt

1 teaspoon coriander powder

- Wash and chop methi and spinach.
- Chop chilies and garlic, add cumin and ginger, and make paste.
- Boil spinach and methi for 5 minutes and drain completely. Then strain and blend.
- Heat oil, add paste, and mix for 30 seconds. Add everything else, mix well, then blend.
- Add salt and pepper to taste. Garnish with yogurt.

CHAPTER TWENTY-TWO

All You Need Is Love?

Hearing Divya's story of growing into love with her husband opened a vein of curiosity in me to delve deeper into my own thoughts and beliefs about love.

I thought Barry loved me. I thought I loved him. And if what we had was love, I was done.

In my thirty-eight years on Planet Earth, I had never questioned what love was. I had assumed it was a feeling, a warm, fuzzy sensation of light, laughter, and complete acceptance. Of course, when you're in love, it's obvious that love is the best feeling on earth. Until it's not.

I decided to google "love," and among the many definitions I found, this one was particularly compelling on ThoughtCatalog.com:

A widespread incurable disease that is known to affect the mind and sometimes the body. Symptoms may include affected judgment, lightheadedness, watering eyes, chest pains, and an increased need to be with the person who infected you. Is highly contagious and can be deadly.

As I walked through the front door of the Bliss Café and Spiritual Bookstore the next morning, Deepak blasted me awake with his usual sweet smile and sparkling eyes.

This was what unconditional love felt like . . . a face that lights up and nearly screams *I'm so happy to see you.* I imagined that is what a father's love would be like. An unexpected wave of happiness washed through me.

Suddenly I noticed I could breathe deeper as I felt my soul sink into the truth of this very safe person and safe place for me to land.

During our morning chai-and-chat fests, as I called them, Deepak had learned more than he probably cared to about my relationship with Barry. In his kind and nonjudgmental way, he had allowed me to vent without ever pointing out the many red flags that had surfaced from the very beginning.

"Deepak, given everything I've told you about Barry, I have a couple of professional questions I'd like to ask you, if that's okay?"

His expression turned serious, and he nodded yes.

"Do you think Barry ever loved me?" I asked in barely a whisper, not at all confident I was ready to hear the answer.

Deepak let out a long sigh.

"Holly, a man like this is not capable of love. Technically, he could be diagnosed as a toxic narcissist, maybe even a sociopath. From everything you've told me about him, he displays that classic profile: arrogance, a sense of entitlement, little if any respect for boundaries, selfishness, self-importance, haughty and belittling behavior, and grandiosity. Expecting him to love you would be like asking a man with no arms to hold you.

"Simply impossible and not your fault."

"Did I love him? It sure felt like love to me, and it was more intense and wonderful than anything I've ever experienced in the past. I thought we were soulmates . . . if that wasn't love . . . what is?"

Deepak looked into my eyes.

"Love is many things. It's more than just feelings. Most importantly, love is a behavior. It's a practice, a decision, a way of being, and while it does come with good feelings, over a lifetime, the feelings come and go. To maintain lasting love, the behavior must always be loving. A long-lasting marriage requires a combination of trust and connection and friendship, and good communication. We humans need to feel emotionally and physically safe in order to thrive together.

"Narcissists tend to be very smart, and Barry knew just what to say to you and how to say it so that you could feel like finally there was someone who totally gets you. Someone who knows your innermost thoughts, needs, and desires. Unfortunately, Barry *love-bombed* you, and you fell into a state known as 'being in love.' This set off cascades of feel-good hormones in your brain, things like dopamine, oxytocin, and adrenaline. You went into the state I like to call 'the socially acceptable form of insanity.'

"It's nature's trick to get us to pair up and mate and procreate to keep the species going. If you are lucky, this state lasts as long as three years, and then you move into a state of more mature, deeper love that isn't as intense but is, in its own way, sweeter and more satisfying."

I let that sink in. He was right. I had been *love-bombed.* And I had lost the war. A hot chill trickled down my spine, landing in my pelvis and burning my dreams of happily ever after. Wringing my sweaty hands together, I exhaled what felt like a plume of ash.

"So, Deepak, now what do I do? As much as I hate him, despise him for what he did to me, there is a part of me that wants to go back to all of our good times together, to hear all the beautiful things he said to me, all of the promises of a life and family together, all the romantic gestures that made me feel so loved and adored. It feels like inside the bad Barry, there is a good Barry, and I want him back," I said as a flood of tears slid down my cheeks. For a moment, it felt like I could drown there in a puddle of tears.

"I understand, Holly, I really do. On a certain level, you are going through a severe withdrawal. Some researchers say that getting over heartbreak is more difficult than overcoming cocaine addiction. It's going to take time and your acceptance that you are in a state of grieving. You are suffering the loss of love and the loss of your lifelong dream.

"I promise you will recover from this with patience and by being gentle with yourself. I have said this to you before, and I want to again remind you that God has a wonderful plan for you, one filled with authentic love, true joy, and a lifetime of goodness.

"Now that the worst is over with Barry, there is a vacuum. You now have plenty of room in your life for your next wondrous adventure," he concluded.

CHAPTER TWENTY-THREE

More Bad News

Email from Auntie Geeta (Mom was cc'd):

My darling Holly,

Your mom has been keeping me up to date with your adventures in Rishikesh. I am happy to hear that you are enjoying Divya's cooking classes and making some new friends. I look forward to sampling your creative play on Khichri when you return home.

Now, regarding your $100,000 investment in Barry's home: I wish I had better news to share, but unfortunately, I discovered that he never added you to the deed as he said he would. No surprise there. It turns out that the house is owned by his parents' trust. So, technically he never had the right to add you. He did send me a copy of the agreement you signed, and there is a clause in it that states that if you are the one to leave the relationship, you forfeit your investment. It also states that if you decide to sue him and lose, you are responsible for his legal fees and trial costs.

Given that his career (and main source of income) appears to be filing nuisance suits, surprisingly quite successfully, most of his victims opt to settle and get away from him rather than risk a lengthy and expensive court battle. While we might be able to sue and potentially win, if he does prevail, it could cost you all of his legal fees, which could be substantial (and of course I would never charge you for my time).

From what I have learned about him, he has plenty of time to keep these fights going for years and years. And, even when he has lost a lawsuit, no one has ever been able to collect from him.

Your mom thought one way for you to recoup your money would be to sell your engagement ring. She took it in for appraisal, and it turned out to be a fake diamond. It's called a Moissanite, one of the best faux diamonds made, and at 5 carats, it is worth around $4,000.

Sorry to be the bearer of so much bad news, but under California law, if you call off the wedding, you legally have to return the ring. With your okay, I will arrange to have the ring returned to that monster.

If you want to discuss any of this, let me know when you are free to talk. Holly, please try not to let all of this keep you down. You've been through so much, I promise you, the worst is really over.

As the brilliant, wise woman Maya Angelou said, "My wish for you is that you continue. Continue to be who and how you are, to astonish a mean world with your acts of kindness. Continue to allow humor to lighten the burden of your tender heart."

Love and miss you, Auntie Geeta

P.S.: I know how much your current situation sucks. Please remember that the beautiful lotus flower blooms from mud.

I shook my head in utter disbelief. The disaster known as Barry Tavers was less like mud and more like an endless pit of quicksand. I wondered if I would ever get free.

Suddenly I was haunted by the words that Barry had spoken to me with such confidence on our first date: *Holly*, he had said, *I am a master strategist and I always win.*

My whole body shuddered at the memory. I closed my laptop, walked back to bed, and pulled the covers up tight.

CHAPTER TWENTY-FOUR

The Interview

As much as I didn't want to crawl out of the safety of my cocoon at the hotel, I had to. Today was the day of my FBI interview, and even though a big part of me felt down and out and full of dread, I resisted indulging in my pity party du jour.

Knowing that Barry had once again screwed me over, I began to feel a sense of excitement and anticipation about the interview. Perhaps this was my one chance for revenge. I was anxious to finally discover what this was all about, especially since learning the FBI had followed us in Budapest. If the agent was willing to come all the way to India to interview me, this was no small-time investigation. Hopefully it would end with Barry's head on a stick—and I was up for it!

Agent Turner had sent me a short, polite email asking when I planned to be back in San Diego and if we could arrange to meet in person. Not a word about why he needed to speak with me. I copied Auntie Geeta and Mom on my reply and explained that I was currently studying in India, and I was not certain when I would be returning home.

The next email from him asked if I would be available to meet with him in India.

What?

That message spoke volumes!

Before I responded, I called Mom and Auntie. "You are never going to believe this, but I've been offered an amazing, high-paying job consulting for a hotel chain in Delhi that wants to build a California diner," I told them with unsuppressed excitement. I downloaded the details about the consulting job offer from Maya and explained that I wasn't exactly certain when I would be coming back to San Diego.

"Holly, honey! That sounds like a fabulous opportunity, and you should take it for sure. But please, let's discuss this FBI situation first," said Auntie Geeta, quickly shifting into her very businessy-lawyer voice. "Well, I just got an email from the agent, and he is offering to come to Rishikesh to meet with me," I shared.

Auntie was insistent that I not speak or meet with the FBI alone. She told me that if I were to meet with the agent, ideally, it would be at her office, but since the agent was willing to go to Rishikesh, she would arrange to have her brother Sumant, an attorney in New Delhi, accompany me in the meeting.

Now, five days later, wide awake and highly energized, I showered, shaved my legs, and put on makeup for the first time in months. Our interview was going to be videotaped, and I planned on looking like the innocent woman I knew myself to be. Having never intentionally committed a crime, I felt certain that I was not in any trouble. And, just in case that rat Barry someday saw this interview, I was determined to look as good as possible.

After years of indulging my guilty pleasure of reading true crime books and watching hundreds of episodes of *Law & Order*, I knew that sometimes innocent people get into bad situations. The defense lawyers seemed to always want their witnesses to portray a girl-next-door look. I then slipped into the only dress I'd brought with me, just in case I managed to find my way into a gourmet restaurant or party.

It was a simple, conservative, high-necked, navy-blue A-line dress with three-quarter sleeves and a thin gold belt. Standing in front of the mirror, I had two thoughts: *I look like someone's first-grade teacher. And too bad I forgot to pack a string of pearls.*

Auntie's younger brother, Sumant, and I had had dinner the previous night. Although his specialty was contract and business law,

Auntie had briefed him on how to best protect me in the interview. Like Auntie, he was in his sixties, warm, friendly, and very talkative. He shared with me funny stories of their childhood in New Delhi, including their sibling rivalry in the debate club. Highly competitive and verbose, they were lawyers-in-training by high school. Being with Sumant felt like family, and even though this was his first FBI interview, I felt safe knowing he would be there with me.

Sumant and I met in the lobby of my hotel and jumped into an auto rickshaw for the quick ten-minute ride to Agent Turner's hotel, where we found our way to a small, windowless conference room. We arrived promptly at 9 A.M., when Agent Turner greeted us in a navy-blue blazer, blue oxford shirt, and khaki pants. He was taller than I remembered with his short brownish hair and grayish eyes, and I found him to be rather handsome. Without meaning to, I glanced at his left hand, searching for a wedding band, which he did not have. I quickly suppressed a smile, realizing that even at the most absurd times, I was still a romantic girl at heart.

He offered us coffee, tea, or water before he seated me in front of a small but professional-looking video camera. Sumant sat directly across from me, and Agent Turner was to my right at the head of the conference table. As he flipped on the video camera, Agent Turner asked us to call him Jackson. He then explained that everything that would be discussed was highly confidential and then swore me in with an oath—just like on TV. He then looked me straight in the eyes.

"Holly, it's absolutely essential that you be one hundred percent truthful with me today. Do you understand?"

I nodded in the affirmative.

"For the record, please state your full legal name."

"Holly Louise Grant."

"Please take your time and tell us how you know Barry Tavers and the nature of your relationship."

My neck and cheeks flushed as a tightness gripped my heart, and a pang of anxiety shot through me, knowing that I would now have to admit my foolishness to a complete stranger. Who knew how many other FBI agents would eventually see this!

Sumant gave me a slight smile and an encouraging nod of support from across the table.

I slowly took a sip of water and launched into the story. In as neutral a tone as I could muster, I started with the night we met at his mother's gala, the whirlwind romance, the trip to Budapest two weeks after we met, the marriage proposal in Petco Park, and the embarrassing engagement gift of a boob job, which I delivered while shifting in my seat and praying to suppress the red-hot shame I could feel on my face.

"Take your time, Holly. You're doing great," Agent Jackson encouraged.

I took another sip of water and went on to explain how he insisted we move in together in order for me to have a little time to get to know his twin girls before they left for college. My stomach began churning when I realized it was time to describe that night of my near-death car accident.

I gave myself a quick pep talk to boost what little courage I had and spilled it all: the betrayal I discovered on my phone, the pain and horror of watching my dreams disintegrate, my waking up in the hospital, the six weeks of painful recovery at my mom's house, and the reason I came to Rishikesh.

Agent Turner never interrupted me and listened as intently as anyone I had ever sat with. As I spoke, he jotted down some notes on a yellow legal pad.

When I finished, he gave me a warm, kind look. "Thank you, Holly," he said in a soft voice. "I imagine this has been difficult for you to recall, and I appreciate your candor and willingness to share your story. What is the nature of your relationship with Mr. Tavers today?"

"I haven't spoken to him since I left the hospital, and have not had any communication of any kind with him. I don't plan to speak to him ever again."

"You said that the purpose of the trip to Budapest was for Mr. Tavers to buy art for his parents' private collection. Can you tell me what you recall about the art dealer, his name, and the nature of his relationship with Mr. Tavers?"

"On the drive to have the lunch meeting, Barry told me he came to Budapest at least once a year to catch up with his dear friend, and to see what new acquisitions he might pick up for his parents. He may have mentioned that there was a family connection between Mrs. Tavers and Lassie's mother, but I'm not quite sure about that. He did seem to think that there was royal blood somewhere with one of the parents.

"I think the art dealer's real name is Laszlo Varga, and his mother, Ilona, might have been a cousin to Mrs. Tavers. She died quite a while ago. When we arrived, Barry and Lassie embraced like long-lost brothers. . . they even looked like they could be related. They were very excited to see each other and immediately jumped into a conversation about family and shared friends while Lassie gave me a short tour of his castle-like home. Lassie was very charming, accommodating, and friendly."

I could feel the sweat dripping down my back. After a short pause, I looked up at Agent Turner. "What else do you want to know?"

"What kind of questions did Lassie ask you?"

"Well, he complimented me on my shoes and the scarf I was wearing, and he asked me who my favorite designers were. It wasn't a very deep conversation," I said.

"Any other questions you can remember?"

"He wanted to know who my favorite artists were, and I misunderstood and told him I was a big Beatles fan but currently had a playlist filled with Ed Sheeran, Shawn Mendes, John Legend, and Taylor Swift, which he found very funny because he was asking me about art artists, not pop artists," I explained.

I was happy to see that Agent Turner was amused by this.

"I told Lassie I wasn't very knowledgeable about fine art, but I was interested in learning more from both him and Barry. He did ask me what I was most passionate about, which was easy because I think about food and cooking nearly all the time. That conversation was interrupted when it was time for us to be seated for lunch," I recalled.

At that point, Agent Turner took out a folder and placed an eight-by-ten-inch color photo of Lassie in front of me and said, "Holly, do you recognize this man?"

"Yes, that's Lassie," I said.

"What can you tell me about the art you saw on display in his home?"

"I know there were a few names I recognized, like Pissarro and Rauschenberg. There were sculptures and some large Chinese vases, and I just assumed it was all expensive, high-quality stuff, but I'm not an expert. Every room was filled with art, including the guest bathroom that had some beautiful oil miniatures," I recalled.

Agent Turner nodded, made a few notes, and then asked, "Did you happen to notice anything about a security system in the house?"

I closed my eyes and imagined standing in the grand entrance and then remembered there were small high-tech-looking stainless steel cameras beaming down from every corner of the ceiling. I remembered wondering if they were also in the guest bathroom, but they were not. I explained this to Agent Turner, who then asked if I noticed any security people in or around the house and, if there were, did they have weapons.

"I didn't see any. I met the butler, and I saw a few women in uniforms who appeared to work in the kitchen and also a woman who served us lunch, but I was not introduced to any of them. I'm not sure if the women spoke English."

"What was discussed at lunch? Did you hear any talk about previous business transactions?"

"Lunch was mostly a discussion about food. Lassie told us we were having a typical meal of what he called 'highly elevated peasant food,' which was pretty tasty but not anything I wanted recipes for."

"What happened after lunch?"

"After we finished our cappuccinos, Lassie suggested that I relax on a lounge chair by the pool while he and Barry conducted some business. Barry grabbed my hand and told Lassie that he wanted me to see the art, and then, while they negotiated, I could hang out on the covered terrace and wait for him. I did catch a glimmer of disapproval in Lassie's face, but he smiled and said we should follow him.

"So, we went down a spiral staircase, off the main entrance, into a large, ultra-modern-looking home office with beautiful French doors leading to the garden. The floor was a shiny black marble surface; the desk and other furniture were contemporary, with a sleek, shiny white design; the walls were bare. The modern look was a surprising contrast to the rest of the house, which was formal and filled with antiques.

"We sat in two matching black leather chairs, possibly Eames chairs, that had these funny red leather things on the legs that appeared to be leg warmers. Lassie walked into a back room and came out with an easel on which he placed an oil painting that even I recognized was a Monet. Not a Monet I had ever seen, but clearly a Monet . . . plus he showed us where it was signed.

"He told us that he had recently acquired it from a family that had found it in the back of an attic after a relative had died. He said this was a painting that hadn't been seen for at least fifty years, and the family had asked that it not be sold to a museum or go to auction but to find a family that would love it just for its beauty."

"Holly, can you describe the painting for me?" Agent Turner interrupted.

"Yes, it was a scene of the painter standing in a garden painting a canvas."

"Thank you. Please continue."

"Well, Barry was as excited as can be, even though I could tell he was trying to stay cool. He told Lassie he was a true friend for giving his family first dibs on acquiring a painting of this stature. Lassie seemed very pleased with himself and, as if pretending to be an infomercial salesman, he said to Barry, 'But wait, there's more!' and brought out a slightly smaller painting and placed it on the easel.

"This work was not as beautiful. Lassie said it was a pastel, but it was mostly tones of a sepia-like brown of a woman combing her hair. It was signed up near the top by Degas. It wasn't anything I would want to hang in my home, but clearly, anything by Degas is probably worth a small or even large fortune.

"I don't remember what story he told us about where this painting came from," I offered as an uninformed opinion about it all while I took a moment for a long drink of water. I explained to Agent Turner that Lassie then opened the French doors, pointed to the alcove with the lounge chairs, and told me to go and relax and enjoy his garden while he and Barry finished up.

"A while later, they came to get me. Barry was carrying a long white tube with a shoulder strap attached, and I assumed the art was in the tube. We thanked Lassie for his hospitality, and when he led us out the front door, a car and driver were waiting to take us back to our hotel."

"Did Mr. Tavers have a briefcase or anything with him that might have held a lot of cash, and do you have any idea of how much Mr. Tavers paid for the art?" asked Agent Turner.

"No. He didn't have anything with him besides his wallet and cell phone, and I didn't dare ask what he paid for the art. Remember, at this point, I had only known him for two weeks. I still didn't even know his middle name."

"Do you recall Barry ever mentioning to you visits to Switzerland or the Cayman Islands?"

"No."

"What do you know about how he earns a living?"

"Well, he told me he works as an attorney and also oversees his family trust and investments, and he acquires art for his parents' private collection," I said. Then I shared everything I could remember that Mom had told me the investigator had uncovered about his one-hundred-plus nuisance lawsuits.

Agent Turner then took out another eight-by-ten-inch color photo and placed it in front of me.

Fuck. A sickening wave of shock rushed through me, and I sucked in a very deep breath while trying not to pass out or puke. Threatening me was a crisp and clear photo of us at U.S. Customs at LAX with the art tube slung over my shoulder.

"Holly, can you tell me what is in the art tube?"

The memory of Barry handing me the tube as we took our luggage off the carousel at LAX came flashing back, and I remembered Barry saying to me, 'Let me wheel our luggage through customs while you carry the art.'"

"Did you see him put the art in the tube?"

"Yes," I say in a defeated, tiny voice. "I watched Barry take the paintings out of the tube and admire them before he took out three charcoal sketches and carefully rolled the two paintings into them, and put it all back in the art tube."

"What happened to the art once you returned home?"

"I never saw it again, and we didn't discuss it."

"Where do you think the art went?"

"I would imagine he brought it to his parents' home in Rancho Santa Fe. I know they have a very sophisticated security system with cameras everywhere. I saw them when I catered their event," I recalled.

"What is the security system like at Barry's home?" he asked.

I described it to him, including giving him the passcode to turn it off, which, when I was living there, was his mother's birthday, 7/2/29.

"I remember this date because Barry, oddly and proudly, told me his mom shared a birthday with Imelda Marcos," I said. I watched Agent Turner trying to suppress a grin.

"Barry liked to make passcodes by using a family member's first name followed by another family member's date of birth. His PayPal password was Holly7229# when we were still together. I once watched him enter it on his laptop."

Agent Turner then gave me a very serious look. "Holly, I will now explain to you why we are here and what is going on. I must remind you that everything I am about to say is highly confidential, and you cannot speak of this to anyone except your legal counsel. Do you understand?"

I nodded gravely.

"Interpol and the FBI have been working closely together for a long time investigating the Tavers family and Laszlo Varga. We believe they are trafficking in stolen art. By carrying the art into the U.S., you became an accessory to a major international crime. We don't believe you knowingly participated in a crime, but we can indict you if you don't cooperate with us. Are you willing to testify if need be?"

I swallowed hard. The moment of truth had come in a way I hadn't expected. It was better than ordinary revenge. It was an even more powerful way out of the personal hell Barry had put me in. I sat up straight in the chair and looked Agent Turner straight in the eye.

I looked at Sumant, who nodded.

"Yes, of course, I will assist in all ways possible." My heart raced, and a rare wave of euphoria washed through me. Just thinking about Barry and his despicable mother being in big trouble was starting to make me happy and excited. I was definitely having a delicious moment of schadenfreude.

"Yes, sir. I will testify."

CHAPTER TWENTY-FIVE

Mount Vesuvius Had Nothing on Me

"Holly, you are a very lucky girl," Sumant said with a weighty, serious look. "I think Barry set you up by giving you the art to carry through customs without declaring it. Had you been caught, it would have been your word against his, and you would be facing ten years or more in U.S. federal prison . . . or worse."

Sumant and I were halfway through our lunch at the Bliss Café. As I absorbed his assessment, my appetite immediately disintegrated. Sumant was right. I had been set up and used by that despicable lowlife.

A wave of anger rushed through me, and my brain exploded with sky-high plumes of flame and smoke and rocks from middle-earth.

Barry did this to me. On purpose. With intent. He targeted me.

He used me as the everyday, nice, all-American girl next door who could walk through customs carrying priceless works of art and get away with it. If I had gotten caught, he would have denied it all and sacrificed my life to save his own.

I wanted to annihilate him, destroy him, make him suffer until he begged for mercy. Then I would shoot him point-blank in that over-Botoxed forehead of his.

In my overheated mind, I concocted a revenge plan while not letting Sumant see or feel my rage. This was a whole new level of anger for me. It felt nuclear. I stopped myself from wanting to take my arm and sweep everything off the table and then go kick out the floor-to-ceiling windows until everything around me fell to the ground.

Then I broke down crying.

Hot tears escaped from the corners of my eyes, and within seconds I was a heaving mess in a big, heaving, out-of-control, ugly cry.

Poor Sumant. I had learned from Auntie Geeta that public displays of emotion were not kosher in India, and it was clear he didn't know what to do.

Fortunately, Deepak could see (and hear) me via the pass-through window from the bookshop. He rushed over, sat down next to me, and instantly handed me his clean, white linen handkerchief.

"It's gonna be okay, Holly," Deepak said in his inimitable, deeply loving way. "Just let it all out." He looked at Sumant. "You must be Holly's lawyer. I'm Deepak. What happened? Did the FBI interview go badly?"

"Nice to meet you, Deepak. I'm Sumant. The FBI interview went very well. I'm sure you will understand that we can't discuss the details. Our Madam Holly isn't in any trouble, just a bit overwhelmed at the moment," he said as he glanced down at his watch.

"Holly, I must go and catch my flight to Delhi. I will update Geeta and let you know the next steps. You did a great job today. You should be very proud of yourself. Please call me if you have any questions," Sumant said quickly as he put a handful of rupees on the table. And then he was gone.

I couldn't blame him for wanting to make a quick escape. I managed to squeak out a quick thank-you as he headed for the door.

As I loudly blew my nose, my sobs began to subside. The anger still swelled heavily in my chest. *How could I have been so foolish to fall for Barry's scheme?* I righted my frame and inhaled deeply. On the exhale, I turned to Deepak.

"Technically, you are still a therapist, right? So technically, anything I say to you is confidential, right?" I asked him. Before he could respond, I added, "So I am not breaking any rules if I want to tell you what happened today?" It was more a statement than a question.

In a gentle, loving voice, he looked at me and said, "Whatever you say to me, Holly, will be in the vault. Just between you and me. You know I will help you in any way I can."

I breathed a deep sigh of relief and launched into a lengthy recap of the FBI interview, including the evidence and photos Agent Turner had shown me, and concluded with how unbelievably angry I was that Barry had set me up.

"Holly, your anger is justified, and anyone hearing your story would understand. Betrayal may be the hardest emotion to recover from because, most of the time, we are betrayed by someone very close to us. Someone we love. Someone we believe loves us. Someone we trust. Suddenly, we are blindsided by them as if the rug has been ripped out from under us, and we are left in a state of grief, disbelief, fear, confusion, and loss. There is no pill or mantra to fix this quickly, but with time, there is a recovery path that will heal your heart and soul. You have also lost your faith and trust in everything, including yourself. And there is a way back," Deepak assured me.

Sitting next to the floor-to-ceiling windows of the café, I let the sight of the flowing Ganga capture my attention while I absorbed what Deepak was saying. What possible way could I go to restore faith and trust in men? The feelings of betrayal ripped through my soul like a machete. As I peered across the river, I imagined my anger gushing through a big red hose from my chest to the water, cleansing the toxicity from my body.

Deepak's voice pulled me back as he continued his explanation.

"I'm sure you have heard of the five stages of grief? Well, there are also stages of healing from betrayal, and right now, you are in the beginning. It is the scariest stage, where your world as you knew it has been shattered, and you are terrified because you don't yet have a new worldview of your life. Discovering Barry and Carly's betrayal followed by the near-death car accident threw you into a fight-or-flight stress response, thereby lighting up the reptilian part of your brain."

I immediately imagined the snakes slithering across Barry's floors. Reptilian brain? It seemed plausible that I had something in common with those creatures. But weren't we humans more than that? I worried that part of my brain would hold me hostage for the rest of my life. Deepak softly lifted my chin and stared into my eyes.

"Part of you is now in the next stage, survival mode, where you look for a way to heal. For many, this is the stage in which they get stuck," he said. "Right now, you are in a negative feedback loop of focusing on blaming Barry and Carly, and making them a target of your anger. When you keep repeating your story of how right you are that they wronged you, it prevents you from relearning how to trust. You don't want to get stuck there, but many people do."

The doorbell rang at that moment. Deepak got up from his chair.

Stuck? I don't want to get stuck. I've flown halfway around the world to get unstuck, for God's sake.

But the anger was so overwhelming I had no clue how to jump off the roller coaster I was on.

As I watched Deepak help a customer pay for his book, I suddenly felt so tired, without a fiber of strength in my body, threadbare and exhausted like a muddy carpet that had been trampled on by careless feet. Deepak returned to the chair across from me with a smile. He paused for a moment, granting me some time to collect myself. I could tell he had more to say, so I calmed myself enough to tune in to his wisdom.

"To continue your healing, you need to be willing to ask yourself and discover, what was the gift of this? What did I learn? What do I know now that I wouldn't have known if I hadn't lived through this exact experience? How have I grown? These are not easy questions, but they help you adjust to the present as you make new rules for yourself and become more discerning about who you allow into your life."

He had that right. There was no way I would ever let this happen to me again. The thought surprised me, causing a flicker of hope in my heart. Had I really learned something from this? I could feel a seed being planted somewhere inside me. Of what I did not know, but I sensed a nearly imperceptible shift like slow-flowing lava marking the landscape for future fertile ground.

Deepak shuffled his feet quietly in his chair to prepare me for the final blow of reality.

"The final stage of your healing is like a rebirth filled with self-love and self-care; you have new beliefs, your mind heals, and you have a new worldview. This is where you now become the strongest, wisest version of yourself and where you get to forgiveness. You never forget, but you can learn to forgive," he said.

I knew it! So, I would have to practice forgiveness, after all. Something I was not ready for. Deep down, I knew he was right, but I wasn't ready to hear it fully just yet. Letting go of my rage, getting to forgiveness? It all felt like an impossible mountain to climb and not one I had the will or energy or willingness to tackle.

We sat in silence together as I took it all in.

"I'll never forgive him. Or Carly. Especially Carly. She, more than anyone, knew my lifelong dream was finally coming true and then she willingly, knowingly blew it all up. I hate them both so much," I said, knowing how immature I must have sounded to this special, kind man.

Deepak went to a nearby bookshelf and came back with a book written by Emmet Fox, its cover worn thin from years of use. He turned to one of many dog-eared pages. "Close your eyes, Holly, and take a deep breath. I want to read you something."

I did as instructed and Deepak began:

"When you hold resentment against anyone, you are bound to that person by a cosmic link, a real, tough mental chain. You are tied by a cosmic tie to the thing that you hate. The one person perhaps in the whole world whom you most dislike is the very one to whom you are attaching yourself by a hook that is stronger than steel." Deepak stopped reading and looked up at me. Fresh, hot tears poured down my cheeks.

"Holly, you may not realize it," he said gently, "but hating someone binds you just as tightly to that person as longing does. Hate is a poison that gets into your bloodstream. Before we can heal, we have to release any hurt and upset we're still holding on to. Forgiving helps you to let go of the pain and all the destructive emotions of anger, bitterness, and resentment. Forgiving is for your sake. It's for your well-being and healing, and it's a slow process that happens in layers and stages."

"I don't want to be bound to Carly by anything, much less some cosmic link or mental chain," I said, blinking the tears from my eyes. "I just want to be free from the whole ugly experience."

"Then consider that Carly's actions were ultimately the greatest gift she could have given you," Deepak suggested gently.

Before I could protest, he continued. "It wasn't Carly's fault that you were targeted and manipulated by a sociopath. Her seeming betrayal that day saved you from embroiling yourself in a life of unimaginable darkness and pain. With that one act, she exposed Barry for what he really was and opened the door for you to reclaim your freedom."

Maybe it was Deepak's power of suggestion, but I suddenly felt lighter, as if that mental chain of resentment had been broken by the realization that, in part because of Carly's actions, I was actually free.

Deepak must have noticed the softening of my face. As if wanting to leave me to soak in this transformation for a few minutes, he gave me a loving nod before walking back into the bookstore.

I slowly dove back into my mostly uneaten lunch of veggie tofu and fried rice (which would have been better with some grilled chicken or shrimp in it) and Diet Coke. My appetite was suddenly back. I could always gauge my emotional state by my ability to eat. Clearly, I was feeling a bit better in the aftermath of this raging eruption of tears.

CHAPTER TWENTY-SIX

Busted!

Three days after my FBI interview, my phone pinged at 8 P.M., with a message from Mom that read: "Urgent. Check your email, watch, and then call me!"

Seconds later, I clicked on the link Mom sent. A red-hot banner announcing breaking news flashed onto CNN as the announcer began reporting: "Fifteen FBI agents arrived close to 5 A.M. this morning at the home of Rancho Santa Fe, California, art collector and socialite Phyllis Tavers." A wave of disgust rippled through me as the camera panned to a glam shot of Phyllis and Donald. "Under a moonless sky," the reporter continued, "a tactical team wearing full body armor and carrying assault weapons pounded on the front door yelling, 'FBI! Open the door.'"

I watched in disbelief as the video showed a haggard-looking Phyllis, who had her plastic surgeon on speed dial and never went anywhere without a full face, wearing a faded housedress, glasses, and matted hair. She looked confused and every bit her age as she was escorted to a waiting vehicle, her hands handcuffed in front of her.

"A source tells us that Tavers was arrested and charged with trafficking in near-priceless art, allegedly stolen from the Jews by the Nazis. This investigation is part of a multiyear effort initiated by Interpol. It is believed that Barry Tavers, the eldest son, was also arrested at his La Jolla home around the same time this morning. It is not known whether his father, Mr. Donald Tavers, is considered a suspect. It is reported that Mr. Donald Tavers has late-stage dementia and is wheelchair-bound with round-the-clock care nurses at his home."

I watched as the segment then cut to an interview with a woman claiming to be the Tavers's neighbor, identified as Lois Davis, who approached TV reporters with her matching standard poodles in tow. She was a fifty-something, perky-looking woman clad in a Gucci tracksuit, sporting long blonde I-still-think-I'm-in-my-thirties hair, and puffer fish lips slathered in glossy coral lipstick. "I have lived on this street for thirty years and have never seen anything like this. It's shocking to discover we are residing near criminals," the woman gushed with a little too much relish. "We were never close to them, just waved as we passed by. The Tavers are known for their fancy galas and fundraisers, and I've always heard that Phyllis never met a camera she didn't like . . . but that may have changed today."

Behind Lois Davis and the young, handsome CNN reporter, I could see at least four TV news vans, all with lights and cameras pointed at the Tavers's grand circular driveway. The anchor continued. "The FBI agents, armed with a search warrant, are still on-site and it is not yet known what they have recovered.

"We have additional reports that an accomplice of the Tavers's, an art dealer based in Budapest, was also arrested. Our CNN International crew is working on this developing story at this very moment. News has just confirmed that the Tavers's son, Barry, was also arrested in a similar fashion a few minutes ago at his home in La Jolla. Back to you in the studio."

I quickly dialed Mom's number.

"Mom, hi, what the fuck? This is so totally crazy, I knew this was something about art but I had no idea . . . Oh my God, this is such a nightmare!"

"Holly, take a breath. You're going to be okay. Auntie just called to tell me that Agent Turner has assured her that as long as you testify, you are safe. And he and Auntie and I want to tell you that you must not speak to the media. It's likely they will want to interview you, especially since all the local TV outlets have that footage of Barry proposing to you at Petco Park," Mom said.

Mom and I talked for a while longer, discussing the pros and cons of extending my stay in India to avoid the media.

After we hung up, I made myself a cup of peppermint tea and sat out on the balcony. The lights of the ashram across the river danced on the reflection of the water, and I could faintly hear chanting along with the whoosh of the current. Barry and his evil mother in handcuffs . . . the thought of this had me smiling. Maybe there was something to all this karma stuff after all.

Before I could indulge and enjoy the pleasure of Barry's pain and humiliation, I heard my phone ping again. Another link from Mom, this time with a photo from the *Union-Trib* online site of Barry in handcuffs and, in the background a tall, beautiful blonde (wearing Barry's bathrobe). I recognized her as a local La Jolla realtor who claimed to be number one in the state in overall sales. It was not clear if she had also been arrested, but it seemed that I had already been replaced. Replaced! And just like that, I dropped from my current tolerable misery level of 2 or 3, up to 10+++. I was filled with hate, rage, and immense self-loathing.

It was late. I knew I couldn't sleep with this massive, intolerable anger and adrenaline running through me, so I pulled out my journal to purge my feelings through words I'm sure Deepak might wince at.

With a red pen, I wrote:

Asshole Barry:

Fuck you for pretending to be my Prince Charming. Fuck you for manipulating me.

Fuck you for killing my dreams. Fuck you for taking me to Budapest.

Fuck you for telling me I need plastic surgery. Fuck you for being a sick, sociopathic narcissist.

Fuck you for stealing my money.

Fuck you for giving me a fake diamond engagement ring. Fuck you for being a lying piece of shit.

Fuck you for setting me up and nearly getting me

arrested in your art fraud shit.

Fuck you for fucking Carly. Fuck you for ruining my life.

Fuck you for nearly throwing me under the bus at customs. Fuck you for making me feel so stupid.

Fuck you for being a predator.

Fuck you for all the phony romantic gestures. Fuck you for betraying my trust.

Fuck you for casting a spell on me.

Fuck you for all the false promises of having a happy family. Fuck you for spreading lies about me on the internet.

Fuck you for plunging a knife into my heart and ripping out all hope for love.

I knew there were more fuck you's inside me, but for now, I had emptied out the most painful ones. I closed my eyes and attempted to assess where I was on my misery scale. The intensity of my anger had subsided, leaving me with predominant feelings of hopelessness and exhaustion. Not bothering to change from my clothes to my nightgown, I turned off the light, slid under the comforter, and prayed for the deepest sleep possible.

What is that fragrance? Hmm, sniff, sniff.

Smells like plumeria married to honeysuckle, yet different. I open my eyes and discover I am lying in a mosaic of flowers. I turn my head to the right, and the buds are tiny yellow-and-white blossoms, most likely the ones I can now smell. I push myself up onto my elbows and see that I am in a gigantic flower field. My legs and feet are entwined with green leaves sprouting magenta-and-orange flowers that are pulsating and puffing out small plumes of different aromas, some of which I don't think I've ever smelled before. Some of the flowers are colors I didn't know existed. Where am I? What is this place?

"Why, Holly, you are home of course," explains a throaty, sexy voice. I see a woman standing over me. Or rather, I see her, and I see through her.

Where did she come from? She might be an angel. If I believed in angels, but I don't detect any wings.

"No, Holly, I am not an angel."

Shit. She is also a mind reader, whatever she is.

"Holly, I am here to help you. Actually, I am you. I am your future self. A very long time ago, you asked me to come to you at this time in your life. So here I am. I hope you are happy to see me again."

Oh crap. More of this wacko New Age, woo-woo stuff, *I think, but instead, I say to her, "Okay, how are you going to help me?"*

"It's okay if you call me woo-woo weird stuff, Holly. I don't take it personally."

She sits down beside me, a shimmering and pulsing Goddess-like vision but thankfully not scary. I've never done LSD, but I imagine this might be what it's like.

"First, I want to congratulate you on the marvelous Fuck You list you made last night. Brava, bella. It was pitch-perfect. I'm very proud of you. Now I just want to help you complete the exercise. If you allow yourself to continuously let your anger trigger you, it will be detrimental to your health and happiness. As you discovered in your journaling, it's great to give yourself a few minutes to lean in to the anger, but then you must refill and replenish your soul with self-love, self-compassion, and self-care. Are you willing to do that?"

"Maybe. What do you mean exactly?"

"Holly, you've been through a war with a sick soul who traumatized and exploited you. You are healing, and you will continue to heal, and the truth is there will always be a small part of you that never fully gets over this. You will live with a piece of this wound for the rest of your life. Some call it a 'living loss.'

"The good news is that you will soon begin to find that this pain, this loss, comes with gifts, and there will come a day when you may even find yourself grateful for the experience. I don't expect you to believe this now, so just tuck it away for another day.

"For today, I am here to help you heal as much as possible, to help manage your anger and resentment, and most importantly, to get to forgiveness."

"What's your name?"

"You can give me any name that delights you. And, in the future, you are free to change my name to something else."

Okay, not the response I had hoped for. *"Grace. For now, I will call you Grace."*

"Let's make a little plan for when your anger bubbles up. And unfortunately, it will continue to bubble up but not as frequently and with much less intensity. When you feel this anger, imagine you have your fingers laced around Barry's throat.

"Resist the urge to crush him, take your fingers off his throat, and place your hand over your own heart as you see his image disappear. At this moment, say to yourself, 'This is no longer about him. It's now about me, and I know and trust that I am becoming a healed and whole woman ready and available for real love with a partner who has the capacity for true love, devotion, and reciprocity.'

"This is what self-care and self-compassion are about. Are you willing to do that?"

"Grace, I'm too broken. And I'm now too old. It's too late for me to have the kind of love that I have dreamed of my entire life," I say, and with that, the tears slide down my face and onto the flowers, causing some of them to turn black and white and wither.

"Yes, Holly, you are right. God decided that out of the eight billion people alive on the planet, you are the only one who doesn't deserve love," Grace says with a serious look.

And then we both laugh.

We laugh that my "future self" is a smart-ass just like me.

We laugh because we both know that God has not singled me out for a lifetime of loneliness. We laugh because it is just so damn funny!

And then, I wake up.

TWENTY-SEVEN

Blessings and Bracelets

My dreamtime visitation with my "future self" catapulted me into some long-lost feelings of optimism and, dare I say, happ— Well, maybe not exactly *happiness*, but definitely more peace. In fact, I could barely locate my misery level to measure it.

With just a few days left of cooking school in Rishikesh and no solid plan of when I would be leaving India, I decided to stop trying to figure out whether or not to use my return ticket home or accept Maya's amazing offer to consult on her dream California-style diner for the New Delhi property.

Auntie sent me a message that Agent Turner had called to say it would be at least nine months before the trial and possibly longer since Barry's MO was to stall and complicate all the legal actions he was involved in. And, she implored me to stay off social media since it was likely that Barry would try to pull some shenanigans to stop me from testifying. I already had my Instagram privacy settings arranged so that just a few friends and family could follow my sporadic posts and, even if he knew I was in India, a country of more than one billion people, I would be very hard to find.

Knowing that I wanted to bring home some small special gifts for Mom, Auntie, and Mikey, I decided to do a little shopping to find each of them a gemstone bracelet or necklace, and then ask if Swamiji would bless them. While I still wasn't a "believer" per se, I knew my dearest loved ones would just love knowing the gifts had Swamiji's powerful, healing energy infused in them.

Nearly every day, I had been walking the small streets of Rishikesh on my side of the river, and had passed a little jewelry shop that appeared to be a bit more elegant than the other more touristy stalls located near the ashram.

Pushing through the glass-and-wood front door, a delightful blast of air conditioning welcomed me in. The long glass cabinets, trimmed in dark wood and brightly lit from within, seemed to be calling my name. A dazzling array of gemstone bracelets sparkled and next to each bracelet was a short description of the stones and the spiritual gifts they brought. I was instantly drawn to a pretty peridot and pearl bracelet. The yellowish-green color of the peridot stones combined with whitish seed pearls was nestled on a piece of black velvet with a little card that said, "Peridot alleviates jealousy, resentment, spite, bitterness, irritation, hatred, and greed. It reduces stress, anger, and guilt, and opens the heart to joy and new relationships. Pearls attract wealth and luck."

If this wasn't a sign that I was in the right place, then what would be? Imagine discovering healing jewelry specifically for my biggest challenge, anger! The young, handsome salesman noticed my interest and, within seconds, had secured the bracelet on my right wrist while he said to me, "Madam, today's special price for you, Rs 1,200."

Wow, not even twenty bucks! Of course, I said yes and then asked him what stones were good for women seeking enlightenment.

He reached into the display case and presented me with a bracelet of round beads of malachite with small inserts of gold between the stones. "These are known to be gems of transformation and also good for opening the heart to the Divine."

"Do you have another one just like it?"

As he handed me the second one, he took out his small hand calculator and punched in some numbers.

"Madam, special price for taking two of these is Rs 3,200."

"I want to buy a bracelet for a man that will increase his wealth. What do you have for that?"

He walked over to another cabinet and came back with a bracelet of unevenly cut gold-looking stones that was interspersed with black lava beads.

"The pyrite is for luck and good fortune, and the lava is for strength and courage. Very auspicious for a man."

In the back of the store, hanging on a well-lit wall, were dozens of long Rudraksha Mala beads. Nearly everyone in Rishikesh wore at least one of these. I knew they were used in meditation and consisted of 108 beads for the 108 names of God with one extra bead, and often a tassel. I picked out several with different-colored tassels. Beneath the mala wall was a cabinet that featured a variety of gold charms of the various Hindu Gods and Goddesses, but what really caught my eye was a large double Rudraksha seed set in gold. The description read:

"Wearing this powerful seed can create a space within you that never gets disturbed, which is never in any kind of turmoil, and which outside situations cannot touch. It assists in bringing you to high peaks of consciousness."

My friendly helper smiled knowingly as he handed it to me. "Madam, this is a very special and powerful piece. Very rare, and we don't always have them. This one is priced at Rs 10,500. Today, I can offer it to you with a ten percent discount."

Without me asking, he did the calculation and revealed the price in dollars to be around $138. I said yes to this as well. It would be my gift to Deepak, my personal Love Walla, for all of his loving care, advice, support, friendship, and countless cups of masala chai. As my purchases were tallied, I remembered that haggling over price was a respected part of the retail culture in India.

"Oh, and I would so appreciate it if you would give me an extra 10 percent friends and family discount, okay?"

Surprisingly that seemed to work! Each item was placed in a small velvet pouch, along with the description card of what it was. All the small pouches were then placed in one large drawstring velvet pouch with my receipt.

I saluted my kind salesman with my pressed palms over my heart in a namaste before stepping out into the bright sunshine. My feet automatically headed toward the Lakshman Juhla Bridge to cross the river and head over to the ashram.

I planned to grab some lunch at the canteen and also find Sadhviji to ask her the best way to approach Swamiji to bless the newly purchased gifts.

As I walked underneath the ragtag canopy covering the jumble of small stalls, shops, and cafés, I began to feel a bit of melancholy, knowing that I would soon be leaving this place that was slowly feeling like home to me.

I had come to love Rishikesh, where my senses were always enlivened, the water looked wetter, the air sparkled brighter, the scents were a crazy blend of incense, cow dung, and tangy spices. My ears were tickled and entertained by the sing-song voices of languages I couldn't understand, and always, always, in the background was a soundtrack of soul-stirring chanting. I was never a fan of Disneyland and the artificial, over-manicured everything; Rishikesh had become my amusement park of choice.

Simply standing still and observing everything around me was often mesmerizing. There was a magical, otherworldly quality to this place that filled me up in a way I had never thought about before. As a lifelong "anti-seeker," I sometimes wondered if this was the experience Mom and Auntie had been searching for.

Divine timing was definitely at work when I walked through the arches of the ashram and immediately bumped into Sadhviji. She opened her arms to embrace me and instantly knew why I was there.

She laughed and said, "Great timing," as she took the velvet sack of goodies from my hand.

"Let's have Pujya Swamiji bless these for you right now," she said. "Follow me to the garden. He will soon be there to meet with some devotees."

We walked into a sweet garden and sat under the little hut-like structure on neatly arranged rugs. When we saw Swamiji approaching, we all began to rise, and he quickly motioned for us to sit down. As he sat down, he waved for me to come forward. I scooted toward him on my knees. He looked into my eyes and presented me with a delicate, sacred Rudraksha Mala and placed it over my head. I was beyond surprised to be receiving such a precious gift. Sadhviji then handed him my velvet pouch. While he held it, eyes closed with a serene look on his face, he chanted, in his clear, pitch-perfect voice, before giving it back to me. In my mind, I took a snapshot of the moment and placed it in my heart.

Being in the presence of Swamiji felt like standing in front of a spiritual furnace. He just radiated love and goodness, kindness and wisdom, and I was hopeful that the blessings he bestowed on those gifts would be transported back to my friends and family as they wore their beads.

As Sadhviji and I walked back to her office, she invited me in, motioned to me to sit on the couch, and asked if I was hungry.

"Starving."

She picked up her phone and, in Hindi, placed an order. Ten minutes later, two trays arrived with steaming plates of rice, dal, veggies, and chapatis.

As we ate, I timidly asked Sadhviji if she would share with me exactly what kind of healing she received when she first entered Ma Ganga. I really wanted to understand what kind of pain and suffering she had experienced. I had, of course, googled her and discovered that she had grown up Jewish in Los Angeles, graduated from Stanford, earned a Ph.D. in psychology, and was now a revered holy woman who spent much of her time speaking at the UN and major conferences around the world. She also ran the largest ashram in Rishikesh capable of hosting a thousand people and caring for hundreds of orphans. She, Swamiji, and the Dalai Lama worked closely on environmental and conservation projects. And she did all this with a smile on her face and immense humility.

"Holly, it's a long story, but I am happy to tell you a very short version." Sadhviji lifted the tray of food off her lap and placed it on the dark lacquered coffee table in front of us. She closed her eyes for more than a second while gently placing her hand on her heart and then said, "As a child, I was sexually, physically, and emotionally abused by my birth father. And, even though my stepfather came along and was loving and kind and adopted me, the damage was done. I suffered for many years from eating disorders, addiction, and depression. I was placed in hospitals and treatment centers many times, sometimes for as long as four months. From the outside, my life looked pretty good. My parents gave me everything, including summers at an exclusive camp in the Swiss Alps. I was a great student and had plenty of friends, but mostly as a teen and young adult, I was tortured by my addictions and obsessions."

She stopped to take a few bites of food. I reminded myself to breathe.

This was not the story I was expecting to hear.

"My essential nature is one of a scientist, which led me to study psychology to try to get a handle on my behavior. I would discover ways to manage and control myself that would work for a while, but eventually, I would spiral back down into a pit of pain and self-loathing. The only reason I came to India was to accompany my then husband who was on a mission to find his guru.

"At that time in my life, I had no interest in spirituality, I was not a 'seeker' and honestly, the only thing about India that intrigued me was the access to interesting vegetarian food. One day while my husband was out on his guru search, I took a wrong turn heading back to my hotel and ended up at this very ashram.

"A series of very wild and unusual things happened to me, which I will share with you at a later time, but once I met Swamiji, I quickly knew, in every cell of my body, that I had found my true home here in Rishikesh at the Parmarth Niketan Ashram. It was Swamiji who advised me to give my pain to Ma Ganga. It's hard to describe in words what happened on that day twenty-three years ago when I surrendered my pain to her. In many ways, I experienced her as an actual Goddess, and I merged with her essence and became one with All That Is. I felt the waves outside of me and inside of me, and I lost track of time, my mind became nonverbal, and I was a part of an undulating divine canvas of color and energy and serenity," she concluded with a long sigh.

We sat in silence for a bit. My food grew cold. My arms were buzzing as I absorbed her story. I wanted to say something, the right something, but words evaded me.

"Holly, what happened to me is also possible for you. While you are now experiencing suffering, in time, you will discover that life is like the ocean. There are days when the sea is calm and we are happy, and there are days when the waves knock us about and we are sad. The spiritual path is to anchor yourself in the depth of the ocean, where life is continuously calm and stable despite what's happening on the surface. It's an expansive state of joy, an experience of life in all of its-all-okay-ness. In Sanskrit, we call it *santosha*. It's the state of utter contentment where you remain satisfied and at ease in spite of the storm."

There was that word again, *santosha*, the term Kurt and Deepak described to me before. I was beginning to believe I was on to something.

But what?

CHAPTER TWENTY-EIGHT

Last Visit with Deepak

After leaving Sadhviji, I took my time walking back to the bridge, breathing in the sights and sounds of this crazy yet very sacred place. Even though my normal routine was to see Deepak in the early mornings, with just one day left in Rishikesh, I found myself wanting to drop by and give him the now-blessed gift.

The bookstore was empty, and there were just a few travelers with backpacks sitting in the café at a booth overlooking the river.

Deepak was both happy and surprised to see me walk through the door in the middle of the afternoon, and like always, his face lit up as if I were his favorite person in the world. Every time he looked at me that way, my heart popped open with bursts of joy and waves of gratitude.

In my few short weeks with him, Deepak helped me change my perspective about what real love is and what it feels like when it's authentic. A little wave of sadness crept into my chest as I realized it might be a long time before I saw him again and experienced the force of his waves of unconditional love.

"Holly, are you having a chai deficiency moment?" he joked.

"I just realized that I am leaving late tomorrow afternoon, and I need a selfie or two of us. Are you up for that?"

We quickly positioned ourselves in front of the tallest bookshelf to take the first few and then walked into the café to get a few more with the bridge and river in the background. Mission accomplished, Deepak motioned for us to sit at the corner booth.

"You are looking very radiant today, Holly. Rather serene and peaceful."

"I have you to thank for most of it, Deepak. Your love and kindness and advice pulled me out of the bottomless pit of despair that I arrived in."

I handed him the small black velvet pouch. "I can never really repay you for all that you have given me."

His eyes widened as he held the gold-encased double Rudraksha between his thumb and forefinger. He was silent for a few moments, then reached under his kurta and pulled out a long gold chain that had a few gold, sacred charms on it.

"Holly, this is beautiful. I have long wanted one of these, and I will wear this around my neck, close to my heart, every day and always think of you when I do."

"I'm so happy you like it." I could feel tears beginning to gather in the corners of my eyes, so I quickly tried to lighten the mood.

"I'm sure that the first morning I walked in here, you would have never guessed that a crazy girl from Southern California would pull you out of retirement to piece her heart and soul back together."

In his humble style, Deepak looked down. "You can't begin to imagine what a blessing you are in my life, Holly. Because of you, my life has changed for the better. For the past ten years since I lost Nancy, I have been sleepwalking through life, resigned that I was now in my fourth and final stage of life, destined to strictly study spirituality until it was my time to leave.

"All of the conversations we had, all of the ways you so openly and with great vulnerability shared your pain with me, gave me the courage to look at my own pain. I realized the advice I shared with you was really me talking to myself."

I felt like my brain was melting a little bit. I could feel his sincerity, and what he said made sense, but I never thought about how my pain and healing would also be a catalyst for his. Part of me didn't believe it, and another part hoped it was true.

"One of Nancy's favorite authors and teachers was Marianne Williamson, and there was a time when Marianne was a reverend at a church in Michigan, where we lived. We went to one of her Sunday services, and she said something I have never forgotten. It's a line from *A Course in Miracles*: 'the only thing missing in any situation is that which you are not giving.'

"Sadhviji once invited me to do seva, what you would call volunteer service, at the ashram's free medical clinic. They have medical doctors, dentists, and even a vet for the animals, but no one to help with emotional and psychological issues. At the time, I declined. I was certain that stage of my life was over. Thanks to you, Holly, I see now that is what has been missing in me for such a long time. It is the sense of purpose that I have truly missed, my counseling days and the joy of helping others. I am going to start volunteering at both the ashram clinic and their outreach to local villages."

He smiled his warm Deepak smile, and I could feel another wave undulate beneath my solar plexus.

And then it began . . . hot, salty tears were streaming down my face. I felt such gratitude for this person who had only been in my life for three short weeks. This kind, gentle man had nurtured me on every level and somehow put me on a healing path to restore my heart and soul.

Deepak walked me back into the bookstore. The afternoon light was streaming through the open front door, illuminating the tears on both of our faces. As I traced my fingers over the old recliner one last time, a thought flashed through my mind. This is what it feels like to have a *dad.* Then, for the first time ever, Deepak hugged me.

"You have become like a daughter to me. You will always have a place in my heart."

"And you have become the father I never knew . . . thank you for loving me," I whispered. I lowered my head with a newfound sense of humility.

"Thank you, Deepak, for helping me heal."

CHAPTER TWENTY-NINE

Washed in Grace

For my last full day in Rishikesh, I decided to go back to Vashistha's Cave to take a final dip into Ma Ganga to surrender the remainder of my pain, and perhaps to receive healing for my heart.

Once in the water, my hair fanned out around me like a halo of hungry tendrils soaking in the loving, pulsing energy of Mother Ganga. Arms and legs akimbo, I became a floating angel immersed in this river of love and mercy. The midday sunbeams warmed my face as I gave Her the last of my pain and suffering.

"Take me, Mother, take all of me. Release me from my past, from my fury, my suffering, and my need for answers. Let me surrender and merge into the safety of your arms," I prayed.

Within me, I could feel my heartbeat and see the water turning to streams of light in my veins. I felt as if I was floating in a sea of love and mercy, wrapped in the arms of the Divine, cradled in pure joy and happiness. My heart was wide open and I had entered a dimension beyond thought.

Euphoric waves coursed through me and the current whispered words of love into my soul, and then a gentle voice spoke to me. "Holly, this is how it happens. This is who you really are. This is who you have always been. Who you are is more than enough, as you are everything. You are safe, you are love, and you are loved."

For the first time ever, I was finally me. The real me. And I also knew there was no just "me," but that I am part of this loving, pulsing, "*is*-ness" and there is nothing for me to do, nowhere for me to go, just a way for me to be . . . *santosha*.

Misery Level: Zero.

CHAPTER THIRTY

Delhi, Here I Come

As far as airports go, Dehradun is considered an oasis of calm. A rectangle of tall floor-to-ceiling glass walls surrounding a handful of gates, it is clean, modern, and highly organized by Indian standards. My fellow travelers, many sporting wrists and necks adorned in prayer beads, emitted an essence of sandalwood-scented chill as we lined up to pass through the relatively short security line.

It seemed like a year had passed since I arrived in India, a tired, confused, and lost woman terrified of the future. Now, just twenty-two days later, the future was still a big mystery, but I was no longer frightened. In fact, I was actually feeling excited, having finally accepted Maya's incredible offer.

As I sat in the boarding area for my Jet Airways flight to Delhi to meet Maya, I checked my watch. Was it possible that only five hours ago I had floated in the Ganges and had an experience for which I have no name? Transcendence? Bliss? A combination of both?

I had consciously stepped into the river to surrender my pain to Ma Ganga, hoping that Sadhviji was right. That I would be healed of my suffering. What happened transported me to a place of knowing and feeling utter contentment. My desire to be free of suffering was fulfilled.

I was finally at a misery level of zero and I went deep inside myself, hunting, trying to figure out where my pain was lurking. When I peered fiercely into that space where it was once housed, I saw a tingling light, a pulsation of unspeakable love. Gone were the sticky feelings of despair along with the fearful, sloshing queasiness that cropped up every time I thought about the future.

When I tried to tap into the searing heat of my rage at Carly's betrayal, I found stillness where a stinging sensation had existed. And when I thought of Barry, my heart no longer ached. My time of simultaneously hating him and longing for him had vanished.

What I had never anticipated was that I would miss my pain.

I had heard about veterans who had lost limbs in battle but continued to experience pain from an arm or leg that was no longer there. It was as if I had allowed my suffering and misery to become such a part of me physically and emotionally that I found myself searching for it. I had created a deeply held identity as a victim of love.

For the past three months I had been so wrapped in storm clouds of despair that, without the heaviness of my anguish, I now felt naked. Surprisingly, a new me was emerging and I found myself smiling for no apparent reason. I was feeling sunny and optimistic, even though I was no closer to having a game plan for the rest of my life than before my trip to India.

Despite this newfound serenity, my rational mind, always in practical mode, was filled with questions:

Was this real? Would the experience of santosha wear off like novocaine? Who am I? What will become of me? Where do I belong? Should I stay in India or should I go home? If I go home, where would I live?

And, while my mind was skipping through these possibilities, I noticed that my body wasn't responding with the usual feelings of dread in the pit of my stomach. The questions arose and lightly floated by, and somehow, I had faith—and trust—that it would all work out. Even better, I realized that I didn't need to know the outcome right now.

What exactly happened to me in the river? And more importantly, will this new state of contentment last? If so, for how long?

Maya sent her driver to pick me up at the Delhi airport. My evening flight from Dehradun was less than an hour, about the same length of time it took to crawl through the tangled mess of typical Delhi traffic as we headed to her family's five-star hotel.

We pulled into the brightly lit porte cochere where my car door was instantly opened by a tall gentleman sporting a striped turban, a huge handlebar mustache, and a cummerbund cinching his long white dress coat with brass buttons. I felt like Cinderella arriving at the ball as he helped me out onto the red carpet.

"Welcome, Madame Holly! We have been expecting you. My name is Mohan, and if you need anything at all, I will take care of you. Madam Maya has arranged for you to stay in our Gayatri Devi Suite. It is her favorite. We will have your bags sent up momentarily. Now, please follow me."

The noise of the Delhi traffic was noticeably absent as I stepped through the double brass doors of the suite into a large foyer of the most luxurious room I had ever seen. Several steps into the center of the foyer was a big circular copper pot floating with an array of fresh flowers, including lotus blossoms, rose petals, and marigolds.

Mohan handed me an old-fashioned brass room key, and took me on a tour of the suite, which included a living room, dining room, and two master suites, both with king-size beds. The hardwood floors were a warm almond color, the walls a muted pale pink. There were two raspberry-colored velvet couches perched on a Mughal-design rug of various shades of beige and copper. An ornately carved wooden dining room table was surrounded by eight large throne-like chairs upholstered in shiny red silk with gold threads running through it.

I had no idea what or who Gayatri Devi was, but this suite was clearly designed to house a queen.

A delicate chime announced the arrival of a porter with my small suitcase and backpack. A short, younger man in a less impressive white uniform walked in and asked if he could unpack my bags for me. I suppressed a laugh as I thanked him and declined. He walked backward to the door and left. Mohan gave me a card with his direct line and the Wi-Fi code, and made me promise that if I needed anything at all, anytime, day or night, to please let him know.

Since both bedrooms were the same size and equally beautiful, one with hues of dark purple and gold and the other a bit more masculine in shades of beige, taupe, and chocolate, I chose the purple one. In the center of the bed was a square, ivory envelope. The notecard read:

Dear Holly,

I am so happy you are here with me, and I knew you would choose the purple bedroom!

I will come to see you tomorrow morning.

Whenever you are hungry or want anything at all, pick up the phone and call room service.

You are my guest. There is no charge, just go easy on the Dom Pérignon.

See you at 9 A.M.! Maya

P.S. Check out the closet. I selected a few things for you from our lobby boutique.

I was definitely hungry. It had been nearly twelve hours since my last meal. The room service menu, encased in a rich leather cover, was on the bedside table, and I quickly found the twenty-four-hour dining page. The moment I spotted the French toast made from brioche with real maple syrup and blueberry puree, I began to salivate. I ordered it with a side of chocolate ice cream. I was ready for a trayful of all-American comfort food.

While waiting for my late supper, I went to the closet to see what goodies Maya had gotten for me. Expecting to find just a few items, I discovered at least a dozen hangers containing several colorful tunics, a few skinny pants in matching colors, a pair of American jeans, and some really cute and fun tunics and T-shirts. If Maya was trying to bribe me into staying, she was doing everything right.

I had seventy-two hours to decide whether to stay or rebook my return ticket for a later, unspecified date. I would think about that later. For now, I sank happily into the purple king-size bed and hungrily waited for my meal.

CHAPTER THIRTY-ONE

Stay or Go?

Maya was the Queen of Seduction. Her desire to keep me in Delhi as her creative muse and project manager on her dream California-inspired diner was impressive. She blatantly appealed to my badly damaged ego, telling me that I was the singular person on Earth who could create the newest, trendiest eatery in India, and also promised me massive amounts of publicity. Maya wasn't just a pretty, young rich heir to a hotel dynasty; it turned out she was also a social media influencer with one and a half million followers.

Under her social media handle, @mayafoodiegirl, Maya transported her Anthony Bourdain–like approach to food to her followers. Her postings covered both the food and the culture, along with mouth-watering photos. She favored out-of-the-way mom-and-pop joints all over Delhi, ones that served authentic and exotic international cuisine.

Fearless about the food she covered, Maya featured Ethiopian, Moroccan, Portuguese, Chinese, Lebanese, Burmese, and just about everything that wasn't the usual samosas or dosas.

She offered me full use of the hotel's PR firm to garner coverage in India's largest newspapers and magazines, TV interviews, as well as introductions to Bollywood stars who would all show up for the Grand Opening party.

I was mesmerized by the thought of it all. It really wasn't a hard decision. My choices were to go back to San Diego and look for a new career (since my reputation in the local food business had been trashed through Barry's bullshit) and spend the upcoming holidays with Mom, or I could stay in Delhi making magic with Maya and her seemingly unlimited supply of money and imagination.

I decided to stay.

I was taking a long, hot, jasmine-scented bath when I heard Maya calling my name as she walked in on me.

Note to self: hotel owners have passkeys to all rooms.

"Good morning, Pari," she sang out.

"Oh geez, Maya, have you forgotten already? My name is Holly."
"Yes, my personal Pari! *Pari* means 'fairy,' and you, dear girl, are mine for making dreams come true." She laughed.

Maya was dressed in a sorbet-colored confection of silk layers that managed to seem both traditional and fashion-forward chic at the same time.

After six weeks of living in pajamas and sweats while recuperating at Mom's, followed by three weeks rotating a few pairs of yoga pants with cheaply made local tunics, I was excited to think about wearing clothes that looked good and reflected my newfound blissful state.

"Holly, something's different about you," Maya said suddenly, a quizzical look on her face. "You're glowing, and your eyes are all sparkly. You seem so peaceful. Did you meet someone?"

Feeling somewhat shy and hesitant, I nodded my head yes. "Yes, I met myself," I said, my cheeks flushing. "I know that probably sounds strange, and it is a bit strange, but I had this amazing experience in the Ganga. Sadhviji had told me to give my troubles and pain to the river, so on my last day in Rishikesh, I went into the water next to Vashistha's Cave. As I was floating and remembering her advice to surrender, I was filled with a sense of unconditional love for myself and everyone. It was like a miraculous healing.

"My suffering disappeared, and since then, I have been in a state of something I would call bliss."

"Oh, Holly! What a blessing! How wonderful!" Maya exclaimed. "It sounds like you experienced a state called *nirvana*."

"How long do you think it will last?" I quipped back.

Maya closed her eyes as if searching for the right words. I watched, wondering what her answer would be.

"It's not something that fades with time. You've been touched by grace; you've seen the face of the Divine, and this experience will always be with you. Even though there will be difficult days during the course of your life, as there are for all of us, you will carry this knowledge in your heart as a touchstone of who you really are," Maya said, channeling her inner Goddess Saraswati. I took a deep breath and savored the idea for a moment.

And then, changing gears and summoning my best Valley Girl accent, I rallied back. "Awesome, Dudette! Let's go enjoy every minute of this probably temporary bliss. Besides, I'm dying to see the rest of this amazing property."

With its five-star rating, the Four Seasons Gresham Palace in Budapest had been the most luxurious hotel I had ever stayed in up to that point. As Maya guided me through its lobby, she proudly explained that her hotel had been ranked a rare seven stars, thanks to the spectacular level of experience and service they offered their well-heeled guests.

We began with a stroll through the lush gardens filled with majestic ancient banyan trees whose twisted and gnarled trunks, resembling elephants' knees, reached deep into the earth. The large, leathery leaves of the stately banyans provided a dark green canopy of shade against the bright sun. Palm trees and flowering trees I had never seen before peppered the wooden path we walked. Small benches beckoned one to sit, meditate, and breathe in the intoxicatingly sweet frangipani. Despite the incessant traffic around the hotel, the garden was a relatively quiet sea of tranquility in a city of twenty million.

Maya guided me through the pool area, the outdoor dining patio, the Ayurvedic spa replete with a fresh juice bar, and a gym filled with every high-tech piece of equipment available. She introduced me to the spa manager as "the new VIP consultant who will be creating the hottest new foodie place in Delhi," and directed her to make sure I had a private trainer and a daily massage since she planned to work me hard, and I would need to "keep my chin up and my nervous system chilled."

We then walked outside to Maya's favorite offering, an outdoor yoga deck built at the base of a gigantic shade tree where live music accompanied the asanas. A small group of international yoginis in their requisite lululemons were in warrior pose while a young, Bollywood-level-gorgeous man played the sitar and his beautiful wife provided the rhythmic, resonant bass of the tabla. They both broke into big smiles when they saw Maya, who was enthusiastically blowing them kisses. Never a fan of yoga, I started to reconsider giving it another try in this serene and enticing environment. While my wrist may never again support me in downward dog, I had enough strength to fake my way through a basic spinal twist. It was easy to imagine myself doing some simple flow yoga to the live soundtrack provided.

Now that I had seen the best of the pool, gardens, spa, and yoga offerings, we headed into a gallery near the lobby, where Maya introduced me to her ancestors in their museum-quality portraits. Her paternal great-grandfather had built this hotel in the 1930s, leaning on the Maharaja's palaces of Jaipur, Udaipur, and Mysore for inspiration. The gallery, with its museum-like hushed stillness, held happy memories for Maya. When she was a young girl, her father would often bring her to view these portraits while recounting stories of his youth growing up in the hotel and learning the trade at the foot of his beloved "Dada."

"My father once told me, 'Someday you will be the queen of this hotel, Maya. You and your children to come will continue the family dynasty,'" Maya recounted solemnly.

"I really do love everything about this business. When I step inside each day, even when the world around me is chaotic and crazy, I feel like I've entered my own beautiful and elegant world. A world where I am safe and loved."

We basked for a long moment in the bliss of each other's company before continuing on our tour.

Our final stop was a café that had been shut down for a few years. This was the site of Maya's current passion project. The café, once a jazz club open to the public, had its own driveway with a valet stand in front of the restaurant entrance. Hotel guests, however, could use their key cards to access the café through a secret passageway just off the lobby. It was easy to visualize transforming it into a cool, chic California-style diner. With different flooring, a paint job, and new furniture, the dining area could easily be designed to look and feel like Malibu. Maya was lit up like the Fourth of July, chattering away about where the flat-screen TVs would go, and about the slick, bleached-wood-plank flooring it would have, and creating a signature line of flip-flops. The small stage upon which the hottest, coolest musicians had been featured would become a dance floor with a big old-fashioned jukebox to twist the night away to the surfer tunes of the sixties and seventies. She was unleashing a creative orgasm of ideas that felt like we were on a tandem hang ten on a "surf's up" kind of day. I was getting a contact high from her enthusiasm.

Unlike many hotels where there was one large shared kitchen for all the food operations, the café had its own well-sized kitchen that was in pretty good shape. With a slight remodel and some new equipment, a frying station, and three new grills—one for beef, lamb, and turkey burgers, one for veggie burgers and all things vegan, and one for everything else—this kitchen would be an easy project.

It was now the end of November. Maya explained to me that November through March is high season for tourism in India, mostly because of the more temperate weather. She fully expected we could do a red carpet opening for both the locals and the jet-setters on March 1. According to my math, we had roughly 120 days to design, renovate, build, create a menu, train the chefs, and hire the staff, while also teaching them how to speak like San Fernando Valley girls and guys. Thereafter, we would have to beta test everything.

"Maya, where in this hotel are you hiding your magic wand and your genie in a bottle? Just how are you going to make all this happen?" I asked, furrowing my brow. Having watched countless hours of the Property Brothers, I knew just enough about remodeling to know it always took longer than expected, and there was always a sagging, mold-filled ceiling lurking somewhere.

"Oh, Holly," she laughed. "It's easy. We have an entire construction department here filled with lightning-fast electricians, carpenters, designers, installers, and bricklayers. I don't need a magic wand: just a plan, a deadline, a big smile on my face . . . and," she said in a whisper, "a few well-placed rupees to get things done on time."

The morning had flown by. As we went back up to my suite, we ordered room service for lunch. Maya was thinking about naming the diner "California Dreamin'," after the song by the Mamas and the Papas. We asked Siri to play it for us, and while we sang along, it became clear to me that this was not the best possible name. The lyrics had a dark, dreary quality that did not match the vibe we were going for. Something more like "Surfin' Safari" by the Beach Boys or "Surf City" by Jan and Dean.

I then asked Siri to play "Wipeout." Maya had never heard it before, but she instantly fell for the Beach Boys' driving percussion. We bounced around the room, drumming on every solid surface. Despite our love for the song, we quickly decided "Wipeout" was not a great restaurant name; however, we decided it was the perfect name for a signature drink. All thoughts about naming the restaurant vanished as we latched on to the possibilities of a signature drink.

My suite didn't just have a small minibar; it had a fully stocked bar of top-shelf liquor, including Gran Patrón Platinum Silver Tequila, a blender, and anything else a mixologist would need. We began brainstorming the "signature" drink and agreed that it should be a hybrid India-style margarita: fresh mango juice with the potency of a Long Island iced tea. We called room service and amended our lunch order to include fresh mango, orange juice, and limes.

Just as I was putting the tequila in the freezer and checking to make sure we had plenty of ice, room service arrived with our pizza. Maya had insisted I try it as the crust was made from traditional Indian garlic naan, homemade tomato sauce, and authentic mozzarella cheese from Italy. It was exceptionally delicious, and the texture and crunchiness of the naan, with the yummy cheese on top and in the crevices, was about as good as anything I had ever tasted. Clearly, this was going on the menu for the diner. With full tummies, we applied—some could say, sacrificed—ourselves to the roles of beach bunny alchemists. Neither of us had ever made a margarita, but fortunately, google supplied a ton of recipes.

We pulled out the blender and began experimenting with the mango and orange juices, while figuring out if we both preferred Cointreau, Grand Marnier, or Triple Sec with the tequila and lime. We even tried one version with all three liquors, which was too much of a good thing. In less than an hour, we had to give up. We were totally wasted and had forgotten to take notes on which drink had which ingredients and how much.

As I plunked down on the silk-covered couch adjacent to the kitchenette, a thought permeated my tequila-saturated haze.

"Moondoggie."

"Holly, what did you say?"

"Moondoggie. Oh. My. God! That's it. That's the name. Don't you remember him from the movie *Gidget*? He was so dreamy. He saved Gidget's life and fell in love with her," I explained in my woozy state.

"Who is Gidget? What in the world are you talking about?" Maya's speech sloshed into the air fiercely.

"The best beachy surf movie ever! *Gidget*—it stands for "girl midget." Sandra Dee played this young, adorable girl who loved to surf in Malibu, and Moondoggie was this gorgeous, super cool dude. Let's call the diner Moondoggie's."

"But what does Moondoggie mean?" Maya asked. She suddenly sounded sober. "I mean it sounds cool, but also very strange."

"Moondoggie is someone who loves to surf at night under the moon," I explained.

Maya grabbed the tablet off the coffee table and punched the keypad a few times. Within seconds, we were transported to the shores of Malibu, watching *Gidget* on the flat screen.

"I must meet this Moondoggie now!" she laughed.

In our mutual state of tequila-fueled giddy dreaminess, we regressed to teenagers sighing over the hunky love interest, James Darren, a.k.a. Moondoggie. We were rooting for darling Gidget to get the guy, to win over Moondoggie, and to fall in love.

The rest of the afternoon was spent time traveling to the mythical good old days of surfing as we watched several of the old "beach party" genre films, including *Beach Blanket Bingo.*

Maya was captivated and shared with me it might be possible that, in her last past life, she was a Malibu surfer girl, thus explaining her current passion for the beach lifestyle.

Immersing ourselves in the films, along with the tequila and the divine slices of pizza, we had opened a creative vein and unleashed rockets of creativity. We were in sync as we downloaded the vision and the future of Moondoggie's.

Fortunately, Maya had the presence of mind to record our conversation because we were sparking ideas too fast to write them down and, in our inebriated state, most of it would likely soon be forgotten.

We decided the color theme for the diner interior would reflect the sandy beaches, the myriad shades of blue of the sky and the Pacific Ocean, the vertical racing stripes of the surfboards, and the yellow and red bikinis. The serving staff would be known as Beach Bunnies and Beach Bums, all wearing branded board shorts and the girls sporting bikini tops. We would create name tags for them, our very own surf club, with names like Gidget, Annette, Frankie, Kahuna, Loverboy, Lorelai, Baywatch Mitch, The Dude, and Spicoli.

We also designed a piece of performance theater around the delivery of our signature drink, "the Wipeout." A giant gong would be struck to announce it as two servers would hand-carry an oversized coconut husk filled with the delicious custom-made margarita topped with sparklers and four long straws as the song "Wipeout" was being blasted through the sound system.

By 7 P.M., we were feeling a bit wiped out and ready to call it quits. I had only been at the hotel for less than twenty-four hours, and so much had happened. I needed to stay awake long enough to call Mom and to also call the airlines and change my flight home. I was tired, but mostly I was excited—excited and elated to feel alive again, on purpose and optimistic.

The next 120 days were going to be a luxury-wrapped adventure, and if I had had the energy, I would have gotten up to do a happy dance, except I couldn't move. At that moment, the phone rang. It was Mom calling. I had so much to share.

"Holly, are you packed and headed for the airport? Should I plan to pick you up? I can't wait to see you! It's been so long!" Mom said without coming up for air.

"Hey, how is the best mother in the entire Universe," I asked. "Have you had your coffee yet?"

I could see her right now, in her tattered pink chenille robe and matching slippers, leaning on the counter watching the slow drip, drip, drip of her Mr. Coffee.

"I'm making it right now. Are you okay? You sound so . . . different," she said with a slight tone of trepidation.

"I've never been better, and I need to tell you about the most amazing, life-changing things that have happened in the past few days. But I'm not coming home just yet; I probably won't be home until mid-March."

Mom went silent as I launched into a long and detailed recap of the past twenty-four hours with Maya and her five-star hotel, beginning with a quick video tour of my two-bedroom, three-bath Gayatri Devi suite.

The words erupted out of me like Old Faithful in Yellowstone as I explained the plans for the diner and the massive amount of work in front of me, the crazy, generous consulting fee of ten thousand a month plus my complimentary suite, room service, the spa, and a driver and car.

"You sound so . . . happy?" Mom said as both a statement and a question.

I took a deep breath and whispered, "Yeah, I am. I am happy, but it's really something better than happy. You know how miserable I've been, and I was pretty sure I'd never feel like this again, but something has changed, and it's not just the job. It's . . . well . . . it's deeper than that," I said, trying to decide if I wanted to attempt to explain my water-borne blessing of sorts while fumbling for the right words to try to explain what happened to me on my last day in Rishikesh.

Then I knew that if anyone wanted to hear about my experience it would be Mom. She lived for this stuff.

"Well, Mom, this may sound a bit, or even a lot, crazy, the short version is I gave my pain to the Goddess, to Ma Ganga, and she took it, and healed me. At one of Sadhviji's talks," I continued to ramble, barely coming up for air, "she told us about surrendering our fears and problems to the Ganges and the miraculous healing that could happen. The first time I tried it, nothing happened. And nothing happened a few other times, but two days ago, I walked into the Ganga and leaned back, and as I floated, I offered up all my pain and anger and resentment.

"I had this experience that I can barely comprehend, let alone put into words. I was filled with bliss and self-acceptance and a knowing that I was okay, and everything was going to be okay, and my body, my being, was filled with warm golden light as if I was lit from within. I guess this is what *nirvana* is like, only I think the Sanskrit word for it is *santosha*, which means "contentment." Since then, I have been content and feel healed. I no longer feel like the walking wounded."

For the first time ever, Mom had nothing to say. And it was okay. I mean, what can you say when your daughter, the lifelong skeptic, shares her profound mystical experience? The one you yourself have been chasing your whole life? It took me a few seconds, but I finally realized Mom was quiet because she was crying.

"At this moment, I have never been happier for you. I feel like I've just witnessed your birth all over again," she said, and loudly blew her nose. I laughed at the cosmic joke of how quickly life returned to ordinariness, and then she laughed. Then we couldn't stop laughing until it was time to hang up.

CHAPTER THIRTY-TWO

Burger Bingeing

Cows are sacred in India. And they are mostly skinny, very dirty, and left to roam through traffic as if they owned the place. That said, they are also very tasty when properly prepared with cheese, pickles, bacon, and special sauces on a super tasty bun. Maya and I decided that Moondoggie's would have the very best burger in Delhi, which meant we had to take a deep dive into the Delhi burger scene and sample the competition. We found a list online of the top ten burgers and created a twenty-day plan to visit each joint for either lunch or dinner, taking a day off in between each "burger binge," since we also had to taste test the fries and onion rings. Our R&D included a massively expensive burger at the Leela Palace Hotel (more than Rs 2,000—twenty-six dollars). It was called the New York Angus Burger. While it was indeed delicious, I knew I could create something even more scrumptious.

Several places fell into the "fast food" category: decent burgers with zero ambiance or excitement. There were also classic American franchises like Hard Rock Cafe and Johnny Rockets, places I once loved as a teen. We were committed to creating a unique foodie experience that was delicious, sexy, and fun, a place the local cool millennials would flock to, along with the international hotel guests.

While Maya was very passionate about life, she was also a freespirited soul with a short attention span, having been born with both a silver spoon in her mouth and a magic wand in her hand. She never felt the need to create hard deadlines. I was her total opposite. I lived for to-do lists to check off every day. I loved schedules and deadlines, and ways to measure success on a daily basis. Fortunately, Maya was happy to let me take over as project manager and create the timeline. We jointly conjured up everything from the staff uniforms and communal sinks in between the unisex bathrooms, to planning the red-carpet grand opening.

My days were full yet peaceful and fun. Weekends were reserved for sightseeing, from manic pedicab rides through Old Delhi and visits to ancient forts and temples to shopping excursions in Hauz Khas Village or the super-high-end DLF Emporio, a luxury mall. It was at the mall where I had an unexpected mystical moment. DLF Emporio housed some of the most expensive and elegant stores on the planet.

Home to the usual prestigious names like Gucci, Prada, Vuitton, Chanel, and so on, the stars of this modern gilded spending palace were several designer bridal boutiques. Brides with deep pockets shop for handcrafted saris made with real gold thread, Swarovski crystals, seed pearls, and every other imaginable gem and silk combination.

Even though I couldn't do the math in my head, converting rupees to dollars, I could tell the outfits cost tens of thousands of dollars. Maya explained to me that Indian brides often bought seven outfits for seven days of wedding celebrations. As she was explaining how each of the various celebrations differed, I began thinking out my own destroyed wedding plans and the missed Princess Day at Kleinfeld I didn't get to experience.

I could see Maya's mouth moving but I could no longer hear anything she was saying. I felt myself hovering over my body and watching it all as if in a dream. I had become a witness to the scene and heard my inner-self whisper: "Okay, kid, admit it. Aren't you happy now that you didn't end up marrying that creep, Barry? Don't you feel like you dodged a bullet?"

Huh? What's happening to me? Did Maya hear that, too?

I was feeling a bit giddy, and I was also searching for my pain. Where were those waves of loss and despair?

I looked for that yearning feeling of "I just want to go back to the way things were. Where's that guy who doted on me and promised me the sun, the stars, and the moon?"

I heard my inner voice say, *Oh geez, Holly. You gave it all to Ma Ganga, remember? That pity party has sailed. You no longer need to drown in a sea of sadness.*

And then I snapped back to reality. At least, I thought it was reality.

It was becoming hard to tell what was real and what wasn't. Somewhere deep in the recesses of my memory, I saw Mom and Auntie Geeta debating something from *A Course in Miracles* that said everything we saw was an illusion. Auntie was smiling and totally agreeing, but in my mind's eye, Mom wasn't going for it. Realist that I was, I decided that as long as I could see and feel my feet, that would be the reality I would live in.

"Holly, you have a little lost-in-space look on your face. What are you thinking about?" Maya inquired.

"Oh, sorry. I was having an existential moment with myself, trying to figure out if life is an illusion."

Maya smiled, and I felt a shower of gratitude roll over me. This was one of the things I liked best about Maya. I could say shit like this, and she didn't think I was the least bit strange.

"Well, I'm the perfect person to ask," Maya teased. "Did you know that my name *Maya* literally means 'illusion'? My parents named me Maya because it also means 'magic,' and they wanted me to have a magical, whimsical, and mystical life. They wanted me to be able to comfortably walk between all the worlds," she said with the confidence of a queen. "Enough deep talk for today! Let's go find some burgers," she said as we headed for the elevator.

Christmas came and went. My one sole Christmassy event was a celebratory Zoom visit with Mom and Auntie Geeta while I was eating a room service dinner of spicy chicken tikka masala, and they were having their annual donut binge. The sight of the chocolate-covered, cream-filled donuts made me a tiny bit homesick. My sweet tooth was hard to satisfy in India. The desserts offered were not my idea of a good time.

I answered their endless questions about my new life, new job, and new everything in New Delhi, including my newfound interest in yoga. My bias toward yoga as a trendy New Age way to exercise your way to God was replaced when Maya introduced me to a soothing, healing form of yoga that didn't require turning myself into a human pretzel.

My weekly routine had expanded to include restorative yoga classes with Ritaji, who was my favorite instructor. An elegant, older British woman with long white hair and a curvy, flexible body, Ritaji taught yoga as a way to rest, heal, and restore balance to the body, and my body absolutely loved it. As the obvious newbie in the class, I would watch her float over to my mat and often readjust my position with her soft, graceful hands.

Raised in both Delhi and London, Ritaji had a delightful accent and an endearing manner of speaking. Clearly wise and experienced, she was also intuitive and compassionate. She looked and sounded European, yet when speaking, she nodded her head left and right like Indians were known to do. After all this time, I still couldn't figure out if it meant they were agreeing or disagreeing, but it did seem they were making an effort to be friendly.

The best part of every class was the end, in which Ritaji would recite a word of the day while we positioned in my favorite pose, Shavasana. Lying on my back, eyes closed, listening to the lovely, lilting voice of Ritaji was my idea of heaven. My body was motionless, gently relaxing into the mat as the sounds of birds chirping and singing filled the space. The air temperature felt like a warm, comforting blanket, calming my monkey mind to a pleasant stillness. I felt my heart beating slowly as I filled with gratitude. The experience of the river, of santosha, was palpable.

Yesterday's class had been especially enlightening.

She began in her warm silky voice. "Allow yourself to sink into your mat, relaxing your body as you also open your mind and listen with both your ears and your heart. Sukha," Ritaji said as if chanting. "Su Kha," she slowly repeated with crisp enunciation. "Sukha," she continued, "is a brilliant state of great happiness."

Lying in corpse pose, my chest slowly rising and falling, I noticed my ears were buzzing, beckoning Ritaji's wisdom, anticipating hearing how to have my own piece of sukha.

"The first Noble Truth of Buddhism is Dukkha, which means suffering, and many believe that Buddha said that Life Is Suffering, period, but this is a Western misinterpretation. The Buddha said life contains suffering, not that all of life is suffering. The study of Buddhism offers a path to be free of suffering," Ritaji continued as she slowly walked around the room.

Yes, I thought, *my understanding was that the major tenet of Buddhism was based on life equaling suffering. I mean, who would be willing to hang out in that belief system?*

"I'm sure all of you have a lot of experience with suffering. Today, I invite you to embrace the opposite of dukkha, which is sukha. *Sukha* means 'freedom, liberation, joy, ease, and pleasure.' Sukha is a deep and lasting state of happiness. There is a path to sukha with a yoga practice that focuses on the joy of life, living in harmony and balance with the cycles of nature and your body, by taking nourishment that soothes body, mind, and soul.

"You also know that even when you are not in the experience of suffering, you aren't automatically in the state of sukha. As you move through this life, notice what and when you may be experiencing sukha, when you might be in the sweet state of freedom or joy. Begin to consciously choose to have more of those experiences," Ritaji ended. Her eyes were closed as she kneeled on her mat, hands in a namaste over her heart, and a small smile on her lips.

On most days, I was the first one off my mat at the end of class, anxious to get on to whatever was next on my to-do list. Intrigued by the word of the day, I remained flat on my back, closed-eyed in Shavasana, wondering how *sukha* was different from *santosha,* and if santosha was a higher or a lower level of being. Sukha sounded a lot more enticing than santosha, even though, so far, santosha certainly had eliminated my suffering or what I now know is also called dukkha.

I felt someone hovering over me and was happy to see it was Ritaji. "Holly, everything okay?" she asked.

"Oh yes, thanks. I loved today's class. I guess I am so relaxed and restored I forgot to get up," I said, trying to make light of my dawdling.

"Good, don't get up. Stay where you are." And in a flash, she was seated on the floor beside me.

"I hear you will be with us for a bit, working with Maya on the new café. I'm happy you are finding value in this class. If there is anything else that I can provide for you, please feel free to ask me." She said this in a kind voice that felt like a warm grandmotherly hug.

"Well, actually, there is something I'd like to learn from you. I'd like to know more about sukha. Do you think I could take you to tea and drive you crazy with a bunch of newbie questions?" I asked hopefully.

"Thank you, Holly, what a brilliant idea! I would love that. The hotel does a proper British high tea service in the Atrium beginning at 4 p.m. Should we meet there and indulge in some scones, strawberries with clotted cream, and the world's most delicious lemon tarts?"

After yoga, I took a quick shower and headed to Maya's office for a series of meetings, discussing everything from the color and fabric of the serving staff uniforms to checking out images of several classic Wurlitzer jukeboxes for sale on eBay. We were trying to decide between one big jukebox near the dance floor or several small coin-operated ones that we would place at each booth. Ultimately, we decided on the one large one that lit up in a multicolored wonder of primary colors and was filled with the hit tunes of the sixties.

One of the things I loved about working with Maya was that she had someone for every aspect of our enterprise, from architects, carpenters, designers, and printers to cooks, servers, and a team of concierges who knew how to procure almost anything we asked for.

Whatever we dreamed up for Moondoggie's, Maya had an employee on speed dial who could make it all happen. Maya picked up the phone on her desk, punched in a few numbers, and told "Rohan" that she had just emailed him the photo and specs of the jukebox she needed with a few suggested delivery dates. All I heard her say was, "Yes, yes, that is all, thank you." Voila. Done. From what I had observed so far, no one ever said no to Maya, and things mostly seemed to go her way. I found it comforting to be hanging out in her privileged bubble.

"The sixties-era surfboard was actually known as a longboard about ten feet in length. It was placed in a forward motion on a small wave," I explained to Maya's branding and social media team. We were gathered around a shiny white oblong-shaped conference table in the conference room next to Maya's office. The task at hand was the designing of a Moondoggie's billboard to plaster around Delhi as part of a teaser campaign.

I had a clear vision for it. The feel and colors of the photo-realistic illustration would evoke a mid-sixties vibe with a surfer who looked a bit like Frankie Avalon with an Annette Funicello type in a red polka-dot swimsuit on his shoulders confidently riding the waves in a classic tandem surfing pose.

The headline would be simple: Meet Us at Moondoggie's!

I had collected a series of old movie posters from the era to demonstrate to the team members the style and tone I was going for.

"For the two months leading up to opening day, we want this image everywhere: billboards, social media, on fences, the sides of buildings and buses, wherever we can place it. We want to create intrigue and have people guessing and asking 'Just what in the world is this Moondoggie's?'" I explained. I took a sip of sparkling water and waited for a response.

The small team, mouths closed, all looked directly at Varun, their young hipster leader. Dressed in the skinniest bright red pants with a green-and-red Gucci Hawaiian-style floral shirt, Varun walked over to the young woman illustrator who had done the initial attempt at a surfer on a wave. He looked at her sketch page as he slowly stroked his Vandyke goatee. He then politely asked her if he could take over the drawing. She nodded and offered him her seat. Varun opened a box of stubby chubby colored pencils and pulled out two shades of blue, a mustard color, a red, a green, a dark brown, and, with the speed of Edward Scissorhands, he began working. In under two minutes, he had created a rough outline drawing of the image that was in my head.

I studied Varun's illustration, which appeared a bit too contemporary for my taste. I suggested he go for the more retro style of the movie posters I had shown them, explaining that we wanted to create an authentic California diner with a sixties vibe.

Nodding his head enthusiastically, he agreed and promised us that his team would have several comps for us to see in a few days and would size them to fit billboards, use as posters, and on social media. They were also going to get started on a website simply called Moondoggie, where we would eventually sell branded items, including beach towels, caps, and T-shirts.

Maya quietly beamed as she observed the camaraderie of the creative team. Watching her vision manifest was deeply satisfying for both of us. When Maya and I returned to the hotel, she had a meeting with her father to review some budget items unrelated to Moondoggie's. I had a few hours of kitchen design to figure out with the construction project manager until my 4 P.M. high tea date with Ritaji.

The Atrium had become one of my favorite places in the hotel that was quickly beginning to feel like home. Its floors were covered in deep, rich Mogul-designed carpets, the walls were carved antique chestnut, and the ceiling was clear-paned glass, allowing sunlight to flood the rectangle-shaped room. I spotted Ritaji sitting in the right back corner and told the sari-clad hostess I'd be happy to seat myself.

With a big smile, Ritaji waved to me. Dressed in a long silk tunic and loose trousers, known as a shalwar kameez, she embraced me lightly and leaned in to kiss me on both cheeks. The table was set with beautiful, Victorian gold-trimmed porcelain crockery painted with delicate flowers. As she poured tea into my dainty cup, she said, "Holly, what a brilliant idea this is. I've ordered us a full three-tier stand of goodies, and we are starting with my favorite rose tea, which, by the way, is made with real rose petals."

I had spent my childhood playing with my dollhouse, imagining tea parties just like this, but I realized this was my first real "tea party." My afternoon tea parties were often just me with my dolls and plastic tea set, pretending to be fancy and regal. I felt unexpected tears forming in the corners of my eyes as a wave of nostalgia washed over me.

I quickly moved my eyes to look up to the ceiling, a brain hack I had learned to stop myself from crying, and I managed to prevent my voice from cracking as I smiled brightly and thanked Ritaji for making the time to meet with me. I put on a brave face, something I had done all my life to make sure no one else around me felt uncomfortable. But my efforts were in vain because Ritaji noticed right away.

"Holly, where are you right now? How can I help you?" Ritaji asked quietly.

I took a sip of tea, reached for a small smoked salmon and cucumber sandwich, and gave her a wistful shrug.

"The last couple of months have been the most painful and confusing time of my life," I said, not knowing really where to begin. "And then I went to Rishikesh and had a series of unexplainable, mystical experiences that have been wonderful and healing, but I don't trust that the feeling will last once I leave India. Like the magic will one day wear off. Does that make sense?"

I took a bite of the crustless sandwich.

"Tell me more. Tell me everything. Tell me whatever you feel comfortable sharing," Ritaji encouraged.

I condensed a lifetime, mostly the last nine months of my life, into a stream-of-consciousness TMI recap of dreaming of the happily-ever-after life, the meeting of Prince Charming under the fireworks-filled sky, the proposal, Budapest, Hawaii, the discovery of his and Carly's betrayal and the truth of who he really was. I shared the near-death car accident, the FBI, going to Rishikesh, learning from Deepak and Sadhviji, meeting Maya, the Nadi reading, and ended with my experience in the Ganga River. My chest heaved as I recounted the story to my new friend.

Ritaji refilled my teacup. I sliced a scone and took a generous helping of fig jam. Before Ritaji could speak, I recounted my conversation with Deepak about what happiness was and wasn't, and what santosha was. I noted how this was helping me understand how to be in life, how to have a life that didn't look like the life I had planned, and learning to trust that somehow my life would be great anyway.

"At the end of the last class, when you spoke about sukha, I wanted to understand more about what it is, and how to get it. I mean, is sukha the same or different from santosha?" I asked. All these new concepts swirled in my mind. It was hard to keep them all straight. I hoped my new friend could help me place them in a context I could understand.

"For me, sukha is about happiness, pleasure, and ease," Ritaji began. She radiated a calm that drew me in like the waning tide on an ocean shoreline. For a moment, I thought I saw a soft halo of white light encompassing her entire head down to her shoulders. I blinked hard, thinking I might be hallucinating. *What is in this tea?* I thought. India had certainly gotten under my skin. I sat up straighter, forcing myself to focus as she continued.

"Santosha is a powerful practice to bring your full attention into the moment in a way that brings clarity, contentment, and peace. Both sukha and santosha are equally wonderful states of being to strive for," Ritaji shared. "Your friend Deepak is a very wise teacher."

She paused to let her words sink in. A warm feeling washed over me as I thought about Deepak. Lifting my teacup, I allowed myself to feel an overwhelming wave of love wrapping me like a cozy sweater on a cool autumn morning.

"Holly, how are you feeling right now?" she asked.

"I feel light. Weightless. I feel kind of like my moment with Ma Ganga but different. I also feel happy." I paused, then looked at my plate.

"Must be the scones," I quipped, once again eyeing my teacup to detect any mysterious contents that might have magically slipped in there.

"Yes, the scones do add sweetness to our lives. That is another indicator of sukha. Sweetness, the sweetness of life, and it is a bit different from santosha. With santosha, we are in a place of equanimity, a place of balance between the mind and body and bliss. Holly, you can have both sukha and santosha," she said as she handed me an elegant lemon tart wrapped in gold foil.

I was truly beginning to believe it. Santosha was a place of bliss. I prayed I could hold on to it or at least remember what it felt like when life would inevitably spin off the rails again. But this time, I would be more prepared. Of that, I was certain.

CHAPTER THIRTY-THREE

Queen for a Day

Clicking on my iPad, I needed to know what it meant to be a queen, if not for a lifetime, then at least for a day. That's what Agent Jackson had told me I would be. It seemed like a strange phrase to use in such a formal situation. Scrolling through my internet search, I found this definition: "Proffer or 'Queen for a Day' letters are written agreements between federal prosecutors and those under criminal investigation. They permit these individuals to inform the government about their knowledge of crimes, and supposedly assured that their words won't be used against them at any later proceedings."

Agent Jackson contacted me to update me on my role in Barry's case and let me know I would soon be needed in San Diego for a meeting with an assistant United States attorney (an AUSA), the lead prosecutor in Barry's case, a woman named Susan Karson. In his professional and serious way, Jackson actually said very little except that *things were progressing better than expected.*

He then dropped a bit of an unexpected bomb.

"Holly, it's critical that you sit down and meet with Ms. Karson. She needs to hear your story and be able to ask you questions before deciding whether or not to indict you.

"As a federal agent, I strongly recommended she not do that. I explained to her that you are, in my opinion, an innocent victim in all of this. But it's not within my purview to make any enforceable promises to you. However, I'm nintety-nine percent certain that once she hears your story, there will not be any charges against you," he said in a very long-winded explanation.

My heart dropped to the bottom of my stomach, and I felt lightheaded. My arms were tingling, and not in a good way. *Holy shit.* Somehow in my newfound states of santosha and sukha, I had been riding a wave that never included the possibility of prison time.

What I was now feeling didn't even remotely resemble contentment or happiness. This was a variety of visceral fear I had never experienced before. I had never imagined I would be in a position that might land me in prison. I was a rule-follower. I was always the good girl. The fear-induced adrenaline rush was making me lightheaded.

"Is there really a chance I am going to be charged in this?" I asked politely.

"There is always a chance, of course, but quite honestly, I don't see that happening. Ms. Karson is a very smart and very fair woman who lives for putting bad guys away. Holly, you are definitely not one of the bad guys. You, unfortunately, got hooked up with a very bad guy and this is your blowback. She's offering you what the prosecutor calls a Queen for a Day letter. This means you sit down for a no-holds-barred interview. She can ask you anything and your job is to be completely forthcoming, direct, and to answer everything one hundred percent honestly. Nothing you say can be used against you. I'll be there, your lawyer will be there, and you simply tell the truth," he explained.

"Will Barry be at this Queen for a Day meeting?"

"No. Definitely not, and he won't be privy to any of what is discussed. If things progress down the path that I think they will, you will never have to interact with him again, unless you choose to," he said, somewhat mysteriously.

That made me feel a bit safer. I felt like Agent Jackson was a trustworthy guy, even though I barely knew him. Then I remembered that I had once trusted Barry, too.

What if my trust meter was permanently damaged?

Auntie Geeta had told me that following Barry's and Mrs. Tavers's publicly humiliating arrests, Barry had immediately hired Marc Russell, a high-profile criminal defense attorney and a regular expert on Fox News, to defend his mother. True to his brand, Auntie explained that Barry intended to represent himself but was smart enough to know that it would be seen as a conflict of interest to represent his mother. Knowing that Russell's sky-high fees would come out of his parents' pocket, Auntie assumed that Barry was securing the absolute best representation to make sure they all walked away free and clear. At the arraignment, both mother and son had pled not guilty and were released on a million-dollar bail, each, after surrendering their passports.

After learning that Barry planned to be his own lawyer for the trial, I asked Auntie Geeta if he would be the one to question me when I was on the witness stand. She replied that he likely would, then quickly assured me that I would receive plenty of witness prep to get me ready for the grilling. Even so, I knew it would likely be one of the more unpleasant experiences of my life. Whenever I imagined this scenario, I would also indulge my dark side and see my testimony putting that asshole behind bars for a very long time.

Barry hated places that were dark, cold, and damp. And he certainly hated critters of all kinds. For a moment, I recalled that night watching him squirm at the snakes, rats, and crickets Mikey had deposited at his house. I imagined him now in a cell with big roaches scurrying across the floor while he spent sleepless nights trying to cover his head under a stiff, smelly pillow to drown out the endless noise of other inmates, his body on constant alert for his fellow inmates, some of whom wanted to beat him up. Barry deserved all of that and more.

It was now the beginning of February. Agent Jackson said that they would like to meet with me right away and that the absolute latest I could show up would be March 10. Knowing that Moondoggie's red carpet opening was set for March 1, I figured the earliest I could leave Delhi would be on March 3. I would then need a few days to adjust to the twelve-and-a-half-hour time difference, so I told Agent Jackson

I would be ready to meet on Friday, March 6. He was fine with that and said he would make sure Auntie Geeta and I received an email confirmation with the Queen for a Day letter attached.

Sitting in my regal hotel suite in New Delhi, I found it hard to accept the dire predicament I now found myself in. Somehow, I had always thought of my "Queen for a Day" as one in which I would be trying on wedding gowns at Kleinfeld, not sitting in a stuffy room with lawyers and law enforcement praying I wasn't going to end up in an orange jumpsuit. The irony weighed heavily in the pit of my stomach. Nothing in my time with Deepak had prepared me for a situation like this.

Rather than allowing my mind to spiral down into a cyclone of negativity and scary thoughts, I decided to play with my imagination. I sat down, closed my eyes, and envisioned myself sitting in the bookstore with Deepak. I saw us each holding steaming cups of chai as I gave him an update on my FBI situation. I visualized him, being as he was privy to this very confidential part of my life, listening carefully as I confessed to him that I had no idea how to feel or be with this news.

With the image of wise Deepak in my mind's eye, I practiced the meditation techniques I had learned, following the inflow and outflow of my breath, and allowing thoughts and sensations to move through me like leaves floating down a stream. After a few minutes, I felt chills as I began receiving a download of information as if Deepak were, in fact, sitting right in front of me.

"Remember when you were a little girl, and you had just lost a tooth, and you would run your tongue over and over again in the empty space where your tooth had just been? This is what you are doing now as you are searching for your recently lost misery. A part of you really misses the pain, but it is a phantom pain. You no longer need to suffer. You have matured, and you are fully capable of dealing with a little discomfort and even some fear about the potentiality of this situation. You need not suffer unless you choose to. You'll be okay, Holly, whatever happens," I heard Deepak say in his most paternal and loving tone of voice.

I opened my eyes, feeling peaceful and centered, and smiled with a deep sigh of relief. I walked over to the large, ornate gold Chippendale mirror hanging in the foyer and blew myself a kiss as I walked out the door for a three-hour meeting with the head chef and his team.

Today's session would be a hands-on class in the preparation and presentation of a paneer-stuffed masala cheeseburger, served open-faced on naan with sweet mango chutney—my American take on India's famous street-style sandwich. A perfectionist when it came to burgers, fries, and guacamole, I knew the kitchen crew needed to be carefully coached on the ABC's of Californian cuisine. Fortunately, neither the head chef nor the sous chef were vegetarian. Cows are sacred in India, so I was surprised at how willing and open the younger Indians were to American food.

My cooking demo was followed by my weekly spa appointment. Today I had planned one of my favorite Ayurvedic treatments, written in Sanskrit as *Pizhichil* but pronounced like "pizza chili." It happened on a long table designed as a shallow bath filled with warm sesame seed oil. Moving the liquid across my body, the therapist washed oil over me in a gentle wave-like motion, which, combined with simultaneous massage, triggered a state of bliss that easily rivaled eating a chocolate soufflé with vanilla ice cream. The treatment, and my imaginary visit with Deepak, averted any need to indulge in cyclonic negativity.

PANEER-STUFFED MASALA CHEESEBURGERS

1.25 pounds ground beef (80% lean, 20% fat)

¼ cup cilantro, finely chopped

¼ cup diced red pepper

⅓ cup panko crumbs

1 tablespoon curry powder

½ teaspoon garlic powder

1 teaspoon sweet chili sauce

8 pieces store-bought naan (sandwich size)

1 package store-bought paneer cheese, cut into ½-inch cubes

Salt and pepper to taste

Mango chutney for garnish

Curry Sauce (mix all together in small bowl)

½ cup plain yogurt

2 tablespoon mayonnaise

1 tablespoon curry powder

½ teaspoon cumin

½ teaspoon garlic powder

½ teaspoon onion powder

- In a large mixing bowl, combine ground beef, cilantro, red bell pepper, panko, curry powder, garlic powder, chili sauce, salt and pepper. Form into 4 patties. Press 5, small ½-inch cubes of paneer into each patty.
- Heat a large nonstick skillet over medium heat. Add patties and cook 3–5 minutes on each side until fully cooked.
- Toast naan (in toaster oven or in oven) with thin slices of paneer on bread. Place one patty on each bun and add Curry Sauce. Serve with a side of mango chutney.
- Note, this is a spicy dish. If you prefer mild, cut all the dry seasonings and cilantro in half.

CHAPTER THIRTY-FOUR

The Queen of Vegan Goes Down

I was snuggled under the covers, blissed out from my Ayurvedic massage, and just about to turn off the lamp when my phone pinged with a message from Mom.

"Holly, you won't believe what he's done now," it said. Below it was a link to an article entitled, "The Queen of Vegan Loves Bacon." Feeling a jolt of adrenaline, I clicked on it and began reading.

> "Rachel Rosenberg, owner/chef of North Park's wildly popular Queen of Vegan Café, has long touted the health benefits of a vegan lifestyle, but her fans and patrons are abandoning her in droves, driven by a recent viral video that features the animal rights advocate eating bacon."

In the video, Rosenberg is seen explaining that while she mostly eats vegan, bacon has always been her favorite food. She then goes on to list a dozen of her most popular recipes, from pizza to cupcakes, which feature bacon as a key ingredient.

"In response, the James Beard award winner and cookbook author claims the video is a deepfake, maliciously spread by her former business partner and former boyfriend, Barry Tavers, whom she is suing for breach of contract after he failed to fulfill his commitment to funding a restaurant the two were planning.

"In a recent podcast, Tavers made a further claim that Rosenberg deceives her patrons by using lard in her refried beans and that the dishes presented as 'nut-free' on her menu nearly harmed one of his daughters.

"'After eating Rosenberg's Thai Chicken Bowl with Faux Peanut Sauce, my daughter, who has a severe nut allergy, began swelling up and choking. Thank God she had her emergency epinephrine injection in her purse, or she might have died,' he told the audience.

"Rosenberg has released the following statement on all of her social media channels: 'This video is a deepfake. It's appalling that technology exists in which my image and voice have been manipulated to spread these lies. As someone who was raised in a kosher home and who has never eaten or even tasted bacon, it's horrifying to have my reputation slandered in this way. These allegations are wholly untrue and deeply painful.

"'My commitment has always been and remains to serve guests the highest quality organic, vegan food. And for the record, I have a nut allergy myself, which is one of the reasons I became a vegan chef dedicated to creating delicious food. My food is prepared with the highest levels of safety, integrity, and love.'"

"An employee of Queen of Vegan, who has asked to not be identified, reports that business has declined by 70 percent since the video surfaced and that it's believed that PETA (People for the Ethical Treatment of Animals) has asked Rosenberg to resign from its board of directors."

My eyes lingered on a very pretty headshot of Rachel, broadly smiling and posing in her kitchen and wearing a large crystal crown and an apron sporting her Queen of Vegan logo.

After reading the article for a second time, I had to remind myself to breathe. Barry knew full well that Rachel was someone I greatly admired in the small circle of hot young San Diego chefs. He also knew that, like Rachel, I aspired to open my own restaurant someday. I clearly remember introducing the two of them when I took him there for lunch soon after we got engaged.

Even though my heart broke for Rachel, for having to deal with a possible career-ending nightmare that Barry had dumped on her, I was also shocked that in the few months we had been apart, he had managed to connect with her as both a lover and a business partner. I wondered, *If he can take down the Queen of Vegan, how much damage is he capable of inflicting on me?*

My phone pinged again. "Well, what do you think?" Mom asked. "Mostly, I feel so sad for Rachel," I texted back. "She doesn't deserve this. How can one person be so totally evil? And I also feel a little guilty. I introduced them."

"Oh, Holly, you know this is totally not on you. Barry Tavers is a virus. A black mold. Hurting everything and everyone in his path. Let's be grateful he will soon be in the rearview mirror. When you get back, we can go for lunch and give Rachel some support. In the meantime, I'll write a super positive Yelp review."

"Thanks, Mom. I love you. Going to sleep now." But sleep was not to come. It had been a while since I had felt anything close to sadness.

My santosha experience and the excitement of co-creating Moondoggie's had me in a near-constant state of fulfillment and satisfaction with a good dose of optimism. While my broken heart no longer felt that broken or consciously yearned for Barry, I was filled with conflicting emotions and questions:

Just how long has Barry been flirting with Rachel? Was he secretly seeing her when we were together?

What retaliation was he planning for me once I got home to San Diego?

Will it ever be safe for me to return to the food business? Can I ever trust a man again?

CHAPTER THIRTY-FIVE

May We Be Blessed

We were just days away from our red-carpet opening for Moondoggie's, and both Maya and I were surprisingly and serenely chill. Whichever Hindu Gods or Goddesses Maya was praying to every morning were continuously blessing our project. Despite the short timeline, all deadlines were being met and all the pieces were falling into place.

The only thing that took longer than expected was designing our signature margarita, Wipeout. We realized we were both amateur drinkers and unable to properly conduct taste tests of our concoctions while keeping track of the ingredients. We proudly admitted defeat and outsourced the job to a professional mixologist in America, my college friend Ashley who ran a bar on the bay in Long Beach, California.

Ashley decided that we actually needed two signature drinks, neither of which was a margarita. We now had recipes for a very exotic purple gin and tonic and a knock-your-sari-off Long Island iced tea to give our bartender, Ruhan. He was an Oxford dropout who had fled his studious life and become a Bollywood wanna-be in Mumbai for a year before joining the hotel staff. He arranged a taste test for us.

The drinks were delicious and had a beautiful purple tinge to them from the special gin used in both. Since both cocktails were best served in individual glasses, we gave up on the idea of the dramatic presentation with the "Wipeout" music we had originally planned. At one point, we considered the possibility of offering these super potent drinks with a free Uber ride home but, in the end, decided against it.

Between Maya's frequent social media postings, Varun's team of expert marketers armed with teaser posters and billboards, and several mentions in the Delhi equivalent of Page Six, we were deluged with invitation requests from the young and the restless who lived in a constant state of FOMO.

One gossip columnist quipped that Moondoggie's was the hottest invitation since the hundred-million-dollar wedding of Isha Ambani and Anand Piramal! We had confirmation that four of Maya's favorite Bollywood stars—Vivek Oberoi, Deepika Padukone, Dia Mirza, and Shilpa Shetty—had RSVP'd positively along with several other well-known faces.

The fashionista bloggers were busy debating what our dress code of "Malibu Chic" meant. And our PR team was still working on confirming a lifestyle reporter from *The Times of India* along with several local TV news teams. If we didn't have to compete with a lot of breaking news on opening night, we just might luck out and have a gaggle of news crews covering us.

Unlike most red-carpet openings where a "step and repeat" backdrop was used for all the interviews and still photos, Maya decided to create a very cool beach tableau by the entrance. She arranged for a half-ton of white beach sand to be trucked in, built an authentic-looking lifeguard stand with a bold Moondoggie's sign on it, and hired a young David Hasselhoff look-alike to wear a red Speedo and pose with the VIP arrivals. Always the planner, I made sure we had a pair of board shorts for him to put on in case Maya's parents threw a fit when they saw this nearly nude man on their property.

Bollywood rivaled Hollywood for its worship of all things celebrity, and this grand opening was almost certain to garner a ton of coverage.

To ensure that our project was indeed blessed, Maya had arranged for Sadhviji to leave her ashram in Rishikesh and come to Delhi to perform a special blessing that would occur at 8 A.M., the day before the opening. As a surprise to me, Maya, true friend that she was, asked Sadhviji to bring Deepak with her.

Maya and I, along with her parents and a valet, were waiting on the red carpet with garlands of red and white roses, jasmines, and marigolds to welcome our guests, when Sadhviji and Deepak arrived at the hotel in their Mercedes limousine. Maya placed a tilak made of vermillion powder on Sadhviji's forehead. Dressed in a sleeveless blue-and-gray tweed-like Modi jacket with its fashionable stand-up collar worn over a steel-gray kurta, Deepak approached me with a million-watt smile. I felt a rush of love for my dear friend and teacher, and ran into his arms, causing him to drop his small overnight bag.

Wiping away the tears streaming down my face, I hugged him tightly.

I was mindful not to smother him with my enthusiastic embrace.

"I am so glad to see you, my dear friend," Deepak said. "You look so happy and beautiful! Big city life must be agreeing with you."

"You look rather handsome yourself in your Modi jacket!" I quipped. "And for the first time ever, you've seen me crying happy tears instead of those my former pitiful, heartbroken self cried." I took a step back to survey my friend once again.

"I have a million details to attend to," I said. "But we'll be seated next to each other at dinner tonight. I can't wait to tell you everything!"

That evening, Maya's parents arranged a small, intimate vegan dinner in the garden for all of us. Longtime supporters of Sadhviji's many philanthropic efforts, especially the Divine Shakti Foundation to help women and children, Maya's parents were excited and honored to have Sadhviji at their hotel.

Our dinner table was perfectly placed under a giant banyan tree peppered with tiny twinkle lights. The two antique candelabra on the round table provided the only real light. Maya's mother was dressed in a stunning black-and-red sari dotted with crystals, while her father wore a black silk Nehru jacket. While soft sitar music played in the background, it was easy to imagine that it was a hundred years earlier, and we were having dinner with a Maharaja and Maharani.

"I miss our morning chai chats, Deepak."

"Me, too. I think about you every day now, wondering how you are. How are you *really,* Holly?"

Sitting side by side at the beautifully appointed round table, we talked as if we hadn't been apart for three months. The flowing ease of our conversation was natural, comfortable, and familial. He was happy to learn that I had finally committed to a yoga practice, and I sang praises of Ritaji and how she was teaching me more than how to attain a flexible body. Her words of wisdom expanded all the lessons I had learned from him. In the midst of our conversation, I remembered I needed to invite Ritaji to the blessing ceremony. My ever-romantic side was musing that perhaps Deepak and Ritaji would be a match. They had both lost their soulmates. Perhaps they could grow old together.

The next morning, we gathered in the café along with our entire staff of forty-four—the cooks, servers, senior hotel management, and everyone who was directly involved with Moondoggie's. When I walked into the room, Maya was busy placing brightly colored pillows on the wooden dance floor in a half-moon pattern around a small indoor firepit.

As the staff walked in, they quietly sat down and only spoke in whispers while we waited for the Homa fire ritual to begin. Off to one side of the room, a young woman seated on a colorful rug was playing a harmonium, setting the tone for the soon-to-begin sacred ritual.

Punditji, a small, thin man dressed in baggie white dhoti pants and a long collarless kurta, was arranging a series of items on a low table serving as an altar. I recognized the two silver deities in the center. The elephant God, Ganesha, known to be the remover of obstacles, was next to Lakshmi, the Goddess of good fortune and prosperity. Both were adorned with garlands of bright flowers. A whole coconut sat in a simple brass bowl half filled with water and surrounded by mango leaves. Dots of red kumkum, a ceremonial powder made from saffron and turmeric, were strategically placed on the deities and the coconut. Small squares of sweets and more flowers were also on the altar.

As I was about to sit down in the back row, Maya came and took me by the hand and said, "Holly, you will be sitting next to Punditji as you will have the honor of assisting him with today's puja. Don't worry. He speaks English and will show you the few things you need to do. It's very easy."

In plain view of everyone as the only American in the room, I felt a little conspicuous in my seat near the altar. I knew nearly everyone in the room, and I could see that Deepak and Ritaji were sitting next to each other. Both had their eyes closed. The vibe in the room was both calm and crackling with anticipation. My heart was racing even though I didn't know why. This was different from anything I'd ever participated in, and I didn't know what to expect.

Soon most of the staff had taken their seats on the pillows. Maya escorted her parents to the right of the priest and then sat down next to them. Sadhviji then walked in and sat down in a chair near me that was a position of honor. Punditji came and bowed to her, reverently touching her feet. After they exchanged a few words in Hindi, he turned his attention to the altar and began lighting a brass wick lamp. He picked up an ornate brass bell and rang it several times as he began chanting mantras. His voice filled the room, and the chants had a divine quality to them. I felt as if I could feel the vibration of the words awakening ancient primal memories. The chanting was both foreign and now familiar to me as well as comforting, and while this only lasted perhaps five minutes, it felt timeless.

Next, he lit the fire and chanted different mantras as he tossed something granular into the fire that I later found out is called *samagri*, a mix of cow dung and herbs to purify the air and create positive energy. Punditji motioned to me to take some of the mixture to feed to the fire before having Sadhviji, Maya, and her parents do the same.

A few minutes later, Punditji stopped chanting and said something to the harmonium player. She instantly began to play her mini organ-like instrument as everyone stood up and sang *bhajans*, the devotional songs they all seemed to know. Chants for Ganesha and Lakshmi were sung while a lamp was passed as we each took turns moving the lit instrument in a circular motion.

I recognized this part of the ceremony as similar to the aartis I had attended at the ashram. While I didn't know the words, I hummed along and let the sacred sounds fill my soul as they blessed our new creation, Moondoggie's.

When the chanting was complete, Punditji broke the coconut on the floor and put the many pieces, along with the sweets and fruit from the altar, onto a platter. This was passed around to offer everyone who wanted a piece of the *prasad*, the blessed food, to eat and ingest the blessings.

As the flames of the fire subsided, Sadhviji began to speak.

"It's so beautiful to be with you all on this special day as you open this new restaurant," she said, looking around the room with her sweet smile and sparkling eyes. "Typically, people come into a restaurant to nourish their bodies, and we ask that this place, through your devotion and your dedication, be a place that nourishes not only people's bodies but also their hearts and their minds and their souls.

"May you fill people not only with food, but also with an experience of abundance and joy. May not only their cup runneth over, but may people feel so full, touched, and fed on every level that they are inspired to then go out to help and serve others." Sadhviji then turned to look at Maya and her parents and continued.

"May this business be a great success on every level, and may that success ripple out not only into your pocket but may it also ripple out into the families of all those who work for you and to the families of all those who are part of the whole supply chain. May your success ripple out to every aspect of the economy. May it be a success for everyone involved, and may that prosperity ripple out and impact everyone," Sadhviji concluded, pressing her hands in a namaśte over her heart.

A line quickly formed, and Sadhviji began blessing and anointing the third eye of each person with the red kumkum. When she pressed the red powder onto my forehead, she looked into my eyes and said, "Deepak shared with me your healing experience with Ma Ganga. Please know that what happened was just as real as standing here in this room is. You received the Mother's grace. You are always, always welcome at the ashram, and I am always here for you. Please think of us as your Indian home," she said in a voice filled with love and tenderness.

The atmosphere quickly shifted into a more festive mode. Servers began passing out champagne glasses containing a nonalcoholic mango spritzer, and Maya's father gave a beautiful short and sweet toast to Maya and me. Maya's mother, a force of nature in her own right, chimed in and offered her blessing and ended by profusely thanking Sadhviji for her gracious presence and good wishes.

Knowing I soon had to go back to San Diego, I felt a mixture of joy and sadness for having to leave Maya and the restaurant we had created together. I would miss so many of the people I had met in India. As I drifted off to sleep that night, I could hear Kurt's voice whispering to me in my dreams: "You will be safe. Let Ma Ganga take care of the rest."

WIPEOUT GIN AND TONIC

4 tablespoons Empress 1908 Gin
4 tablespoons Cruzan Mango Rum
tonic water (or diet tonic water)
lime juice
garam masala
sugar

- Mix gin, rum, and tonic water
- Dip the rim of each glass in lime juice (on a plate) and then dip in equal parts garam masala and sugar.

WIPEOUT LONG ISLAND ICED TEA

2 tablespoons white tequila

2 tablespoons Cruzan Mango Rum

2 tablespoons vodka

2 tablespoons triple sec

2 tablespoons lime juice

4 tablespoons ginger syrup
(substitute simple syrup or agave nectar, if necessary)

sugar

garam masala

2 tablespoons Empress 1908 Gin

sparkling water

- Dip the rim of each glass in lime juice to coat, then dip in equal parts garam masala and sugar.
- Mix the white tequila, Cruzan Mango Rum, vodka, triple sec, lime juice, and ginger syrup in a shaker.
- Pour over four glasses filed with ice and add ⅔ cup of sparkling water to each cocktail.
- Float a tablespoon of Empress 1908 Gin on each.

CHAPTER THIRTY-SIX

Ruby Red Slippers

"Girl, you've got to tap into your clothing superpower for this meeting," Mikey pleaded through the speakerphone. It was great to hear his voice after *so long*. Because of the time difference and his crazy schedule, we didn't have a chance to talk while I was in India. Standing in front of my closet at Mom's house in San Diego now, I called him in a panic over what to wear.

"Power shoes. That is what you need."

"Mikey, you are a lifesaver. Thank you!" As we hung up, I considered my options.

Mikey was right. Power pumps were just the thing to both ground and elevate me. A few years earlier I had bought a gorgeous pair of cherry-red patent leather heels to wear to important functions. My fantasy was that the shoes would evoke my inner Wonder Woman, and wearing them would remind me that I am capable of anything and everything.

If I ever needed to channel her, it would be today, as I faced the prosecutor who would decide whether or not to indict me. I figured since my footwear was a bit edgy, the rest of my outfit should scream conservative, so I chose a simple black pantsuit and a delicate white silk shirt with a Peter Pan collar. Seated at an interrogation table, I would hopefully appear to be a picture of innocence.

"Holly, dear, you look like a very proper, honest woman," said Auntie as if reading my mind. I slid into her idling brand-new steel-gray S-class Mercedes. She put her hand on mine and smiled.

"No need to be nervous. I'm certain all will go as planned. I've heard the assistant United States attorney, Susan Karson, is a decent woman with a reputation for being sharp and fair," Auntie said comfortingly as she backed the car out of the driveway.

My outward appearance was deceiving. Internally, I was a roiling mess of dark, anxious thoughts. Technically, although inadvertently, I now knew I had committed a crime. They had video footage of me walking through customs carrying stolen art. How had I never thought to question him about bringing in the art? My thoughts ranged from practical to absurd as my breathing became ragged and my chest felt tight.

What if they decided that I was "in on it"? What if I'm found guilty?

How much time would I get? What kind of prison would I be in?

Would I have to join a prison gang and get a tattoo?

I pushed these thoughts away as we motored toward my fate. Using the breathing techniques I had learned in India, I consciously chose to calm and center myself. Breathe in for four counts, hold for four counts, and breathe out through my mouth for four counts.

In less than fifteen minutes, we arrived downtown at 880 Front Street, a very drab, unadorned government building. After parking in a nearby outdoor public lot, we went through security and took the elevator to the fifth floor. There, we were escorted to a stuffy meeting room with white walls and a stained blue carpet. I could feel myself fantasizing about how many other people had been interrogated in this room, their lives ripped apart by the truth of their crimes.

Once again, I gave my negative thoughts a shove, trying to visualize the blissful flow of Ma Ganga running through my veins instead. We sat down at an old and well-used conference table that had a projector in the center and pointed at a screen that was next to a whiteboard with markers.

Auntie, acting as my attorney, handed me a bottle of water and mouthed the words "breathe" as the double doors opened. Agent Jackson held the door for a forty-something woman with auburn hair in a totally cute pixie cut, wearing big, black smart-girl glasses. She was dressed in a black sheath and black leather pumps. She looked a bit like a saucy Audrey Hepburn, but her face expressed a seriousness and focus that terrified me.

Agent Jackson gave me a friendly smile as he formally shook my hand and introduced us to Susan Karson, who also firmly shook my hand before placing her briefcase on the table and opening it. She then motioned for us to sit. She and Agent Jackson walked around the table and sat opposite us.

Susan eyed me carefully for a long moment before asking if we were ready to get started. I searched her face for a trace of warmth or empathy but found only a cold stare. I nodded nervously.

Without another word, Susan clicked on an audio recorder. After stating the date and time and naming everyone in the room, she began.

"I'm only interested in getting the truth, Ms. Grant. Your only job here today is to speak to me honestly. Not how you wish it had been, but how it actually was. And I'll let you in on something: I already know the answers to some of the questions I'm asking. I'm not asking them to find out what happened. I'm asking them to find out if you'll tell me what happened. If you don't understand something I ask or aren't sure what I mean, please ask me to clarify. This is a very important point, and I don't want you assuming what I mean. Now is the time for clarification. Do you have any questions whatsoever?"

"No, I understand."

"Good. Let's begin with your telling us in as much detail as possible the following: how, when, and where you first met Mr. Tavers. What he told you about how he earns a living. How you came to accompany him to Budapest. Then describe everything you remember about the art acquisition and the return trip to the U.S. You can take your time, and please be as specific as possible. I will try not to interrupt you and may ask for more details when you have finished," Susan explained.

Palms sweating, I looked down at my hands and began. "It all started on a warm summer night at the gala . . ." and then I stopped and shuddered as I remembered it was exactly one year ago today that we had met, one year to the day since my world had been turned upside down.

Auntie gently placed her hand on my back. I sat up straight and began again. "One year ago today, I catered, which was then the biggest event of my career, at the Tavers estate in the Rancho Santa Fe . . ."

For the next forty minutes, I carefully gave a chronological recounting of my relationship with Barry. Susan occasionally wrote something on her yellow legal pad, but her expression remained neutral.

When I was finished, I took a sip of water and looked at Auntie, who mouthed "Well done!" to me.

Susan asked a dozen or more questions, most of which I thought I had already answered, but I answered again. When she seemed to be out of questions, she smiled for the first time and said, "Please excuse Agent Turner and me for a few minutes." They got up and walked out of the room.

"Great job, Holly! You were the perfect witness, very believable," Auntie said. "And, after hearing your story in one sitting, I'm so sorry for all that you have gone through this past year."

"What happens now?" I asked.

"We'll find out soon, Honey."

Auntie's phone buzzed. She checked it and then furiously began texting someone.

Susan and Agent Jackson walked back into the room a few minutes later. They were smiling and Jackson actually winked at me.

"Holly, I want to thank you for your candor and your cooperation today. I appreciate how difficult and painful this situation has been for you. Having met the defendant, I am aware of his talents as a liar and a con artist. Your ex-fiancé is a real piece of work. I've met a lot of shady criminals in my career, but he is among the most cunning and slick. Your testimony at trial will be a significant contribution to our case," Susan said with a compassionate, knowing look.

"While we almost never do this during the first interview, I've heard enough today to feel confident that you are an innocent victim in this, and therefore we will not be bringing any charges against you."

I felt like a giant bunch of helium balloons released from my chest. As I inhaled, I could feel my lungs expand deeper and wider while a river of relief coursed through my veins. For a second, I thought I could hear Ma Ganga whisper a blessing in my ear. I resisted jumping out of my seat to hug Susan and thank her profusely. Instead I said, "Thank you for believing me. What happens now?"

"We'll be in touch as soon as we have a trial date."

Susan stood up, signaling the end of the meeting, and handed me her card before collecting the audio recorder and snapping her briefcase shut.

Agent Jackson walked us out, praising me for handling my "Queen for a Day" with such grace and poise.

Meanwhile Auntie Geeta was busy texting away. "Holly, I'm so sorry. Something has come up, I've gotta go. Can you take an Uber home?" Auntie hectically looked up from her phone.

I gave her a quick hug and told her it wasn't a problem. "Don't worry," Jackson chimed in. "I'll drive her home." Auntie busted out the door in a hurry.

Jackson insisted on driving me to Mom's house before heading back to his office in Sorrento Valley about twenty minutes away. I asked him if his car, a black Jeep Cherokee, was an official FBI vehicle and he laughed, saying it was a government issue, and mostly for official business. He glanced at me and grinned, assuring me that, so far, I qualified as official business. When we pulled into Mom's driveway, I instantly spotted a gigantic bouquet of roses at the front door.

"Oh shit," I said under my breath.

"That's an unexpected reaction to roses. Looks like someone has an admirer," Jackson said plainly.

"I'll bet they're from Barry. Today is the one-year anniversary of our first meeting."

"Stay in the car," Jackson commanded. I noticed a slight shiver of pleasure run down my spine at his take-charge demeanor. Something stirred inside me as I watched him get out of the car. As he approached the front door, Jackson grabbed the card sticking out of the arrangement. Without asking, he opened the sealed envelope and began reading.

I could see the concern on his face as he walked back toward the car. He handed me the card. "Given what I know about him," Jackson commented, "I'm not surprised."

> *My darling Holly,*
>
> *The best part of my life began a year ago today when we met underneath the firework-filled sky. While the fireworks of the past six months have torn us apart, I know that we can move past it all and begin again. We are perfect for each other.*
>
> *Let's forgive and forget and create a love-filled life together with our future children.*
>
> *Please call me.*
>
> *I love you with all my heart, Barry*

As I read the note and took in his obviously manipulative words, I tasted bile creeping up in the back of my throat. The familiar feelings of betrayal and despair tried to fight their way back into my internal dialogue. I pushed them away as hard as I could, remembering that I could choose not to suffer and struggle. Handing the card back to Jackson, I spoke with a sudden surge of confidence.

"Would you mind disposing of these flowers for me, please?"

"Yes, happy to. And Holly, you should know that recently Susan and I had a meeting with Barry to review the evidence and witnesses lined up against him. That includes you. And there are other details I can't share with you right now. It's likely he is going to do his best to dissuade you from testifying, which in our book is witness tampering. So you need to be vigilant and steer clear of him," Jackson stated.

"No need to worry about me. I've got my high school softball bat next to the front door," I joked.

"Very cute. Listen, I'm not kidding. Keep your doors locked, install a Ring camera if you don't already have one, and when you go out, be cognizant of your surroundings, okay?" Jackson took out his business card and underlined his cell phone number. As I slid off the passenger seat and onto solid ground, Jackson gave me a caring smile.

"You can call me anytime, for any reason, whether you hear from Barry or not." He walked back to the front door, grabbed the roses, put them on the floor of the back seat, and drove away.

Seeing that ostentatious bouquet permanently ended my love affair with the color red. They would forever remind me of Barry and the heart blood I'd shed to get over him. Looking down at my red power heels, I considered tossing them as well. Who needs red ruby slippers when you have a real live FBI agent to take a bullet for you?

At that moment, I was extremely grateful that the anguish and betrayal I had once felt had been replaced with a newfound serenity, with the occasional resurfacing of disgust and disbelief that someone like Barry really existed. The contrast between the two men was so stark. There was no part of me that was even remotely interested in connecting with Barry ever again.

But Agent Jackson was certainly a person who restored my belief in men.

Thanks to my experience in the Ganges River and all of Deepak's sage advice, I had full clarity now that what happened with Barry was not love. I had been played by a master manipulator and just as the gash on my head and my broken jaw and wrist had healed, so had my heart. Waves of santosha rocked me into my now familiar calm as my soul filled with gratitude for all I had learned from the experience.

It felt reassuring to have someone like Jackson so obviously concerned for me, even if it was technically his job. So far, my "Queen for a Day" was going really well: no indictment and now my own Kevin Costner–like bodyguard. He certainly didn't look like the knight in shining armor I ever imagined, dressed instead in his own uniform: a blue button-down oxford shirt and khaki pants. That was just fine with me, I mused as I walked into the house.

After changing into my daytime outfit—black yoga pants, my favorite pink T-shirt featuring caricatures of RBG and the ladies of the Supreme Court emblazoned across my chest, along with a baseball cap—I collapsed on the sofa and pulled out my phone. It had been an entire day without checking texts or emails, and my inbox was exploding with messages. Three texts were from Mom, each more urgent, wanting to know why I wasn't responding. I got back to Mom and told her all was well. I promised I would give her a complete download when she got home.

I listened to a lengthy voice message on WhatsApp from Maya. She was positively giddy with an array of great news, including a big and positive review in *The Times of India* with a picture of long lines of chic-looking, hungry millennials queuing up, wanting to be seen eating at Moondoggie's. She shared a bunch of statistics about social media impressions, new followers, and stats that didn't make much sense to me, but they were clearly a home run in her mind! In simple terms, Moondoggie's was a smash hit.

I sent her a quick note to connect with me when she was awake, knowing she was currently in deep REM sleep since it was the middle of the night for her.

"Hey, sleepyhead, wake up."

I rolled over, trying to pretend that Mom wasn't trying to wake me out of the deep sleep I had fallen into. Jetlag was wreaking havoc on my internal clock, and the last thing I wanted to do was open my eyes.

"C'mon, Holly. Get up! If you don't get up now, you'll be wide awake at 1 A.M. Come on, uppy, uppy," Mom implored while she massaged my hands as if I were eight years old, not thirty-eight.

"Oh, all right. What time is it?" I asked with my eyes still tightly closed.

"A little after 5:30 P.M. Let's go grab a Frappuccino and go for a walk before it gets any darker," Mom suggested.

We walked over to Starbucks for our drinks and then headed south on Fifth Avenue to the main entrance to Balboa Park. We walked across the iconic multi-arched cantilever Cabrillo Bridge toward the Plaza de Panama. The inky twilight framed my mom's face as she gave me the news that Auntie's dad had fallen this morning and had been taken to the ER.

Fortunately, he hadn't broken anything, but it was a big scare for all of them. Auntie Geeta was finally solidifying plans to move them both into her guesthouse, which likely meant I would soon have a part-time job cooking Indian comfort food for them. I sleepily smiled at the thought of finally being able to work in a kitchen again, even if it was at home.

I gave Mom a short version of my "Queen for a Day" ordeal and about finding the roses by the front door when the special chime tone for my WhatsApp began ringing. A notice informing me that this was from a number not in my contact list sent chills down my spine because I could clearly see that the number was Barry's cell. Having previously blocked him, this was the only way he could now reach me since I only added WhatsApp after arriving in India.

"Oh, shit, it's him," I cursed to myself as I hit the ignore button.

"Barry?"

"Yep. I guess I'd better let Jackson know Barry tried to call," I said with a sly smile, putting the phone down for a moment to collect my thoughts.

"This is so like Barry to try to find a way to win me back before I become his worst nightmare," I laughed and said to Mom, who didn't seem to find the humor in this at all.

"Holly, we're putting in a Ring security system tomorrow."

CHAPTER THIRTY-SEVEN

But I Need You

The long walk in Balboa Park with Mom was exactly what I needed to sort out a day filled with too many highs and lows. I was relieved that I was now free of any threat of prosecution or prison.

I even allowed myself a fantasy about Jackson and began to feel the possibility that maybe someday I would love again. Just knowing that I felt some interest—and maybe he felt it, too—had my romance meter up and running.

And, at the same time, I felt confused and conflicted about the roses Barry sent and his attempt to call me. Even though I was no longer suffering over the loss, the memories of the good times with him still taunted me. I found myself indulging in illusory moments of wishing I *had* found my Prince Charming and that we were going to live the life of my dreams. Ever practical, I would talk myself back down to reality, down to Planet Earth, where my Prince Charming was a lousy scumbag that made black mold look like gold.

When did life get so fucking complicated?

Jetlag was overtaking me like a June gloom fog rolling onto the shoreline. I decided I would tell Jackson tomorrow about Barry. Minutes later I was deep into a ten-hour peaceful, dreamless sleep.

The chiming sound of my WhatsApp notifications began begging for my attention. I wasn't yet conscious enough to figure out where my phone was and fought the impulse to wake up. It didn't matter what time it was, or who might be calling, more sleep was the only appetite to surrender to.

Or so I thought.

A minute later the chiming sound happened again, only this time it was very brief, which meant that I had a message, not a caller.

Rolling over required energy I didn't have, but eventually, my hand groped the nightstand and found the phone. I hit play for the voice message, anticipating Maya's sweet voice. What I heard sent a rocket of adrenaline through me.

"Holly, baby," Barry crooned. "This is your long-lost soulmate, the one who loves you unconditionally and forever. I know now that you were the best thing that ever happened to me and I promise I can make you happy beyond your wildest dreams," he said enthusiastically like a cheerleader's chant.

"Holly, I need you. I need your sunshine, your light, your warmth upon my body. It's a beautiful, warm spring day. Why don't we get together for a walk on the beach? Let me tell you, let me show you, all the reasons why we are meant to be together," he begged.

"Can you believe it was a year ago today that we took our first beach walk? Remember how amazing that was? Holly, just give me one hour of your time. I promise you won't regret it, and then someday we will look back on this day as the start of our true love destiny. Call me, okay?"

Thankfully I was lying down or the dizziness I was feeling would have knocked me to the floor. I felt like I was in an emotional spin cycle of anger, disbelief, and disgust with a tinge of fear.

After lightly tapping on the door, Mom walked in carrying a tray with a mocha almond latte and two glutinous chocolate croissants.

"Good morning, sugar, don't get used to this, but I made your favorite double trouble caffeine fix," she said as she placed the tray next to me and began nibbling one end of the flaky, yummy pastry.

I smiled at her and reached for the coffee cup with one hand while pushing play on my phone so she could hear for herself what the monster had to say.

Mom's smile sagged into a grimace and her eyes narrowed as she listened to Barry's pitch for a do-over.

"Fuck," she said in a sad voice. "Now what? You're not going to call him back, are you?" Mom's face looked contorted with fear.

"No way, Mom, but I am going to turn this lemon into lemonade," I said with a sly grin.

"Agent Jackson made me promise to let him know if anything like this happens. He sort of predicted Shithead would try to weasel his way back into my life."

I forwarded the voice message to Jackson with a note that read: "You were right!! Listen to this message that came through today on WhatsApp. If you think it would strengthen your case, you can put a wire on me and I will go meet with him and see what he offers me to not testify against him. WDYT?"

A few minutes later, Jackson responded.

"Someone has been watching too many crime TV shows. Thanks for letting me know. The case is strong enough. No need for you to see him. For now, don't answer back and save the message. BTW, I gave the roses to a friend who runs a nursing home in Mission Hills to distribute to her patients. I'm leaving for Sacramento in the morning, but here's my cell phone number. You can call or text me anytime."

I was relieved that he wasn't going to wire me up and put me undercover. Just thinking about seeing Barry in court made me queasy. Thinking about Jackson also affected my stomach but, interestingly enough, in a more exciting, butterflies kind of way.

"You can call or text me anytime," he had written. I allowed my insides to swoon for a moment.

Okay, I thought. *Now how exactly should I interpret that? A simple statement of fact? A cryptic way to say 'I want to hear from you again'? Am I imagining something that isn't there?*

If I had a daisy, I would have pulled the petals, "He loves me?" "He loves me not." *God, I am still such a starry-eyed, juvenile, romantic,* I thought as I reached for the croissant Mom had left on the plate.

The days flew by. I couldn't think of any good pretense or reason to call or text Jackson since I didn't get any further messages from Barry. I felt a little disappointed, not because Barry went silent, but because Jackson wasn't here. A sense of missing him tugged at my heart.

Luckily, Auntie Geeta kept me busy by sending me dozens of texts from Michigan and hiring me to prepare her guesthouse for the arrival of her parents. She was helping them pack up and downsize a lifetime of stuff into a few suitcases to move them in. They would be coming in a week. Although the guesthouse had a kitchen full of the best appliances, the cabinets, fridge, and pantry were bare. My instructions were to shop and fill everything. From pots and pans, dishes and glasses to food, spices, teas, and alcohol.

Dada, as he preferred to be called, had a daily whisky straight up every afternoon at 4 P.M., while Nani drank Earl Grey tea with a little milk and biscuits.

I found a handyman to install safety bars in the hallways, in the shower, and next to the toilet. I stocked the hall closet with fresh towels and created a little altar space, complete with Hindu icons, incense, and candles in an alcove for morning rituals. I also got in a little practice time, cooking the comfort foods I had learned from Divya for Mom every night. I completed the project with an hour to spare, and a big pot of khichri on the stove to greet them.

The next morning my WhatsApp chimes went berserk. I saw it was Barry and ignored it. A minute later, I heard a single chime letting me know I had a message.

Hearing Mom in the kitchen and smelling the freshly brewed coffee, I grabbed my phone and stumbled into the kitchen.

"I've made you some avocado toast with yellow heirloom tomatoes, crispy bacon, and toasted sesame seeds," Mom said brightly. I watched her bustle behind the butcher block island before handing me the plate full of goodies.

As I chewed each delicious morsel, I could literally taste my mom's love. Thinking back to Divya's cooking class, I was reminded of the sanctity of preparing meals. *Food really can transport emotions,* I thought, closing my eyes as I swallowed.

I soaked up the brief moment of santosha in the midst of the escalating chaos that was my life. Snapping back to reality, I carefully placed my phone on the counter in front of Mom. "Get a load of Barry's latest message," I said, pressing the play arrow.

"Hey, babe, you can't stay mad at me forever," whined Barry's voice. "You know I am beyond sorry and will spend the rest of my life proving to you how much I love you and making sure you have everything you have ever dreamed of. Why don't we meet at George's Rooftop today for an early lunch, say 11:45 A.M., before the crowds hit? We can even talk about when I can return your $100,000 if you'd like. Just meet me there, Holly, okay? I promise you will be glad you did," the sleazy, creepy bastard said in a cheerful, optimistic tone.

"Did he just say what I think he did? Did he really admit he owes you a hundred thousand?" Mom asked with a gleeful look in her eyes.

I took a step backward. Mom was right. He had admitted that! She always knew how to cheer me up. A wave of glee encompassed me as I considered what she had said.

"Yes, he did say that, didn't he?" I grabbed my mug and took a long sip of coffee, brain cells perking up and thanking me for the kick start.

"You know, we should talk to Geeta. Perhaps, if you sue him in a civil suit, we can use this message as evidence to get your money back," Mom suggested.

"Well, it couldn't hurt to ask Auntie, but I'm not going to meet him for lunch. I would really, really love to get that money back. But let's face it: if I meet him, he's just going to try to use that as leverage so I won't testify against him," I said, feeling a bit ashamed that I had been dumb enough to have given him the money without reading the document. I used to say that love is blind. Now I say that gullibility is.

My shame quickly receded and transformed into excitement when I realized I had the perfect excuse to reach out to Jackson. He had insisted that I let him know any time Barry contacts me, and this one was particularly juicy.

I took another big bite of my avocado toast and then texted Jackson: "Got another voice message from you-know-who offering me a type of bribe! I'm not falling for it."

Jackson replied: "Are you free for lunch? I have to be downtown this morning. Want to meet somewhere in Little Italy at noon? I can take a look at your phone then, and we can discuss it?"

"Sounds good. Should we meet at Burger Lounge? It has the best onion rings."

"Yes, they do, and they also have the best quinoa burger. See you there. PS: Don't forget your phone."

Trying to focus, I tucked the phone in my back pocket and turned my attention back to the breakfast Mom had lovingly prepared for me.

"OMG, Mom! This is the best avocado bacon toast ever, and you are the best barista ever and just the best mom ever!" I gushed, snapping a piece of bacon in half before stuffing it into my mouth.

"I know that, and thank you, and I don't remember putting any catnip in your coffee. What's up with you?"

Talking nonstop, at two-hundred words per minute, and lacking all editing and restraint, I downloaded the details of my lunch plans with Jackson for the day.

Mom was genuinely happy to see me happy, and of course, she gave me her "he seems like a good guy, BUT please take it slow," advice. She made me promise to maintain a professional relationship until after the sentencing so as to reduce any chances of impropriety.

"Just be careful. And when this is all over, make sure you don't get yourself into a rebound relationship," she said. She vigorously wiped down the sink with a cloth before continuing. "And, just because he has a gun, doesn't mean he can protect your heart," she warned.

"Oh, Mom, don't worry! I'm not rushing into anything, and honestly, I don't really know if we will ever get beyond the agent-and-witness zone," I assured her. I knew this was a lie because I was really hoping this *was* going somewhere. But Mom didn't need to know *everything*, even if she pretended she did.

When I got to Burger Lounge, Jackson was already seated on the patio. He stood up to greet me with a warm, inviting smile, which was unexpected but most welcomed.

"I'll go up to the counter and order. I'm getting the quinoa burger with white cheddar cheese and onion rings. What would you like?"

"Wow, that's perfect! I'd like the exact same thing. We might be foodie soulmates," I said with my biggest smile. The last time I had said that was to Maya. I sighed for a moment, wondering how she was doing and making a mental note of just how much I needed to fill her in on the next time we talked.

My train of thought was broken by the gorgeous man who was approaching me with two plates of burgers. He looked handsome in a conservative navy suit, rep-striped tie, and lace-up shoes. I felt a bit underdressed in torn jeans, old, faded yellow Converse sneakers, and a pale, yellow slouchy sweater.

"Let's eat first before it all gets cold, and then we can talk about the defendant," Jackson suggested. He gently placed the food in front of me, swinging his tie back over his shoulder with his free hand before onion grease got onto the silk. Again, I noticed his smooth left ring finger was not wearing a wedding band. I snapped myself out of my reverie as I dove into my burger.

Reflecting on Jackson's professional manner, I particularly loved that he never called Barry by his name. He just referred to him as "the defendant." Although it would also be fun if he called him "the perp"!

Once the onion rings, fries, and burgers were consumed, I pulled out my phone and played Barry's message for him. He wanted to listen to it twice.

Then he asked, "What hundred thousand is he talking about?"

I realized he didn't know this part of my saga. It hadn't come up because when we did my first interview in Rishikesh, I had never thought to mention it. Then again, during the interrogation with Susan Karson, it didn't occur to me to talk about it. I guess once I finally realized I'd never see that money again, I completely suppressed the memory of it.

With a deep breath and a big sigh, I explained the whole dreadful, embarrassing mess to him. Seeing his eyes fill with care and compassion as he listened made me realize that he was a trustworthy man. With him, I felt seen and heard and, most importantly, safe. A sense of warmth and contentment enveloped me inside and out.

When I finished my story, he put his hand on top of mine, looked deep into my eyes, and gently said, "I'm so sorry this happened to you, Holly. You were played by a sociopath, so please don't blame yourself. Men like that target smart, successful women and you were scammed by a master. If I may say so, it's actually proof of how special you are. Guys like that only target great women.

"Unfortunately, this happens more often than you would think. He will get his, probably sooner than you think. There are no federal prisons that are like country clubs for white-collar criminals. Stories about tennis courts filled with hedge fund traders are greatly exaggerated. He will have nightmarish experiences in prison," Jackson promised.

Jackson wanted to send the voicemail to Susan to see what she thought, but his initial response was simply that he didn't think it was necessary to make the case. As soon as he heard from Susan, he would let me know her decision. He reminded me that I was not to have any contact with the defendant.

Lunch flew by, and 90 minutes later, Jackson announced he had to leave for a meeting at his office. As we started to get up from the table, he looked at me intently. "I'll be traveling for the next few weeks, Holly," he said. "But if you need anything, I'm available anytime by phone, text, or video chat, okay?" Not knowing what else to do, I clumsily saluted him as we parted ways.

On the way back to my car, I called Auntie to see if there was anything Nani and Dada needed while I was out. She told me Nani was craving masala chai, and most of the ingredients Auntie needed to make her special secret recipe were not in the pantry.

"There is an Indian market out on Convoy. If you have time to go, I will text you the address and the list of spices."

"Of course, Auntie. Somehow at cooking school, we never got around to learning how to make the spice mix. Happy to bring everything to Nani in a little while, and I could use a good cup of chai myself." I laughed.

When I turned the corner onto Mom's wide, tree-lined street, I was still floating on cloud nine after my time with Agent Jackson.

I was so lost in thought when I pulled into the driveway that I never noticed Barry's beige Escalade idling a few houses away on the same street. I gathered my things from the car and was making my way toward the house when it happened. Barry quickly pulled his car into Mom's driveway, blocking me in from behind.

I stumbled backward toward the house, instinctively locating my phone in my bag and calibrating the distance between my body and the front door. Then, as if this were some joyful reunion, Barry stood up, flashing his best used-car salesman smile and holding what appeared to be a small gift bag from Tiffany. *Christ, what now,* I thought to myself.

As he stepped out of the car and I saw him for the first time in nearly a year, I was shocked at his appearance. He looked older and much more haggard in the midday sun. His sports coat draped loosely on his tall frame, and his skin looked thin and sallow. Then I noticed something on his face I had never seen before: those suspicious protruding lumps that betray a poorly constructed cheek implant. *Eesh.*

I also noticed my reaction. I was neither flooded by oxytocin nor racked with adrenaline. If I had to describe my primary emotion, I'd have to call it pity—although not quite.

"What do you want?" I asked coldly, surprising myself with the confidence in my voice.

"Holly," he began. "I know how hard all of this has been on you, but I can help you," he said, slowly inching his way closer to me. "I can help you rebuild your business. I can make your dreams of summers by the lake and winters skiing in Lake Tahoe come true. I can give you the children you've always wanted.

"I've never loved anyone the way I love you, and hurting you was the biggest mistake I've ever made in my life. If only you could forgive me."

All I could think about was how pathetic he looked.

My attention was drawn to the light reflecting off the small blue Tiffany's bag that Barry had been holding by his side. Seeing this, Barry smiled like the cat who just ate the canary.

"Holly, this is indisputable proof that you can trust me again," he said, handing me the bag. I could see it was filled with an enormous pile of cash. "This is the hundred thousand you invested in the house. I'm returning every penny of it to you, just like I said I would. In this bag are a thousand one-hundred-dollar bills. Please take it. It's yours."

I steadied myself on the front porch railing, caught off balance by this grand gesture. And then, as if I had a devil on one shoulder and an angel on the other, a moral argument broke out within me.

On the one hand, this *was* my money—in fact, it was all the money I had had in the world at the time I gave it to him. I thought about the security this could bring me and the possibilities it would open up. I looked at the neatly stacked piles of one-hundred-dollar bills that represented my life's savings up to that point. The fair and logical conclusion to this ugly mess would be for Barry to return this money to me.

This is the argument my mind was making. My gut was telling me a different story.

In my gut, I knew Barry was a liar and a con man and a thief. I knew he must have an ulterior motive for returning my money now, or he would have done it months earlier. My gut was telling me not to trust him and that he was somehow trying to lure me back into some kind of a trap.

Was Barry trying to implicate me into accepting a payoff not to testify against him? I stood there, looking down at the money, mentally trying to put the pieces together when Barry spoke again.

"Holly, I'm returning this money with no strings attached. This is proof of my love for you and my desire to be with you.

"You have to believe me," he continued. "I had no idea about the origins of that art. This was all my mother's doing. You know what an evil witch she can be. She is the one who used me! Give me another chance, and we can send her to prison and live the life we always talked about."

I took a deep breath, trying to steady my body and refocus my mind, both of which felt completely destabilized.

As if sensing my weakness, Barry's tone changed, now growing more firm.

"Holly, even if you can't love me again, even if we can't be together, you don't want it on your conscience to send an innocent man to prison when you know my mother is the one who's guilty. Not even you could be so selfish." And then he added, "You know I could never do what they're accusing me of. *You know me.*"

Something about those words, *You know me*, hit me like a sharp slap in the face. Suddenly I was jolted awake from the hypnotic dream state Barry had been trying to lull me into. As I thought about all the things I did, in fact, know about Barry Randal Tavers, a flood of words erupted from me like lava and, with them, all the pent-up rage from the months of hell he had put me through.

"That's right, Barry," I snapped. "I *do* know you.

"I know that you are nothing like the man you represent yourself to be. I know you didn't go to Harvard Law and that you were disbarred three years after you graduated from whatever overpriced, no-name law school your family bought your way into. I know that your only source of income—other than selling precious art stolen from the Jews by the Nazis—is filing lawsuits in which you name yourself the plaintiff against anyone with deep pockets.

"I know that you've been married not once but three times and that you have a disabled child whom you abandoned and disowned. I know that you're not forty-two like you told me, but forty-nine. I know that you have exceptionally gaudy taste and zero class. Who in the hell 'gifts' their fiancée a boob job months before the wedding? With all your physical and moral imperfections, did you think it was a good idea to cast that stone? And did you really think I'd go through with it?

"What I know about you, Barry Tavers, is that you are nothing but a coward and a parasite. You've gotten away with it all these years, slithering under the radar by using your corrupt knowledge of the law. But this time, you're up against people smarter than you. And my career? Better than ever. Thanks for asking."

I was practically panting at the end of my tirade, feeling a huge wave of relief followed by an intense fear of Barry's response.

To my surprise, Barry looked completely unmoved, his right lip curled up in a sick half-grin. Taking a condescending tone, he said quietly, "Holly, I don't know who's been filling your head with these lies," as he approached me with a sympathetic, outstretched hand.

"My mother, Barry. That's who," I said, pushing his hand away. "My mother always sensed you were a total and complete scumbag, so she hired a private investigator to find out who you really are. I read the report, every word of it. You are nothing but a sick, twisted, sadistic motherfucker. And you're also an idiot if you think you just show up here with a bag full of *my* money, and buy my love or my silence. I'm not like you, Barry. I can't be bought."

With a deep breath, I crumpled up the Tiffany's bag and threw it at him, sending a dozen loose one-hundred-dollar bills blowing down the driveway.

Barry looked at me with raw, unveiled rage before turning to retrieve the money. Without meaning to, I had just bought myself enough time to plan an escape.

With a shaky hand, I scrolled through my phone and located the home security app, my finger hovering above the "sound alarm" button. As Barry shoved the last of my crumpled money into his tasteless Tiffany's bag and started to lunge toward me, I pressed the button on my phone, filling the neighborhood with a loud, piercing siren.

"You have about ninety seconds to crawl back under your rock before the San Diego police arrive," I said, before turning on my heel and walking inside, feigning a lot more confidence than I actually felt.

I collapsed face-first onto the couch and seconds later my phone rang, an emergency response woman asking if I needed assistance. I quickly explained that my would-be intruder had run away. She kindly suggested she send someone out anyway, just in case he came back, but I told a white lie and said my boyfriend was on his way over and I didn't feel I needed a visit from the cops.

With shaking hands, a pounding heart, and adrenaline buzzing through me, I checked to see if the Ring had captured the drama.

Sure enough, in high-def Technicolor, there was Barry holding the Tiffany bag with the money, all of it, clearly visible.

Strangely, it was nearly impossible to hear anything he was saying, but my tirade, f-bombs, and all was fully audible.

I texted Jackson, "Please call me soonest."

"Call you in two minutes."

As I waited for his call, I thought about doing some deep breathing but opted instead to head for the freezer to pour myself a double shot of ice-cold tequila. The smooth, smoky golden elixir was exactly what I needed to calm myself down.

The phone rang, and I gave Jackson a fast, detailed rendition of what happened, including that I had taken his advice and installed the security camera doorbell, which had captured all the drama. He listened carefully, asked me if I was unharmed, and then said, "Showing up at your door with a hundred thousand dollars in cash sure sounds like witness tampering to me. Best to lay low for a while, Holly. Make sure all the doors and windows are locked and call me immediately if he tries to make contact with you again."

I agreed, feeling relieved but still shaken by what had happened. Hoping to keep him on the phone a bit longer, I tried to think of something more to say, but Agent Turner was all business. "I've gotta run now, Holly," he said, somewhat abruptly. "I'll be back in touch when I know something more."

"How's my favorite witness?"

A text from Jackson, finally. It had been more than a month since the Barry-with-money fiasco. Seeing his name light up my phone, my heart skipped a beat.

Hmm, favorite witness . . . that's kinda cute, I thought, as a variety of feelings began to surface from joy (he made contact!) to confusion. How should I answer this?

"Well, favorite FBI agent," I responded playfully. "I'm currently mastering the art of making South Indian dosas, a savory crepe filled with curried potatoes and spices."

"Sounds delicious. I have some very good news to share. Can I stop by in a few hours?"

My monkey mind rapidly jumped from "Oh my God, finally! Thank God!" to "Oh no . . . I've got to wash my hair."

"Does 5 P.M. work?"

"Yep, see you then."

After a rapid shower and blow-dry, a little mascara and lipstick, I put on my Moondoggie's branded T-shirt and a pair of leggings and placed the fragrant dosas, plated on a bright-red-and-orange serving tray, in plain sight on the kitchen counter.

Whew. Ready. Now, what in the world is the good news? I wondered. Right on time, he knocked on the door, a huge smile on his face.

Skipping all the usual pleasantries, I nearly shrieked as he walked into the living room. "Please don't keep me waiting!" I begged.

"Good news number one: you don't need to testify. Barry has accepted a plea deal. He is definitely going to prison. I can't give you the details yet, but I thought you'd be excited to know the end is in sight," he said with a big smile.

Without thinking, I jumped up, threw my hands in the air, and started to shake and shimmy while shouting, "Yes, yes, yes!"

"Whoa, Holly! Holly, settle down! I'm going to get seasick watching this," Jackson jokingly complained.

"OMG, I can't believe it! This is just . . . yes! I'll never have to see or hear from that monster again," I said gleefully. Jackson knew just how much this meant to me, particularly in light of Barry's latest ambush.

"Well, that's up to you of course, but here's good news number two: the sentencing hearing has been set for Monday, July 20. And, if you want to, you can attend the hearing. You can be there when the judge sentences him, and he is walked out in handcuffs. How would you like that?" I took a moment to consider what that would be like. To actually bear witness to justice in action. I felt a rush of adrenaline that was partly fear at being in the same room with Barry and partly the excitement of knowing he was being punished for his crimes in the real world.

And for his crimes of betrayal and the theft of my heart and my money.

"I wouldn't miss it for the world." A wave of gratitude engulfed me as I became present to the reality that all of this could have turned out far differently.

"Jackson, thank you for everything you've done to make this happen! Thank you for believing me and for making sure Susan believed me. You have restored my trust and faith, and I now know there really are white knights out there."

After he left, I instantly called Deepak. Even though it was a little after 6 A.M. his time, I knew he'd be up, and I pictured him walking about his café, preparing for the day. I wanted him to be the first to know my nightmare was over and had a happy ending.

During our hour-long chat, we talked as if we had never been apart. He shared that he was deepening his meditation practice in between cleaning, reorganizing, and rearranging the thousands of dusty books he had accumulated over the years. We planned to talk weekly.

After Deepak and I hung up, I realized it was still too early to try to reach Maya. My good news would have to wait a few more hours until my sister from another mother was awake. Fortunately, Mom was in the kitchen. I could hear the sounds of food prep and the smell of onions and garlic sautéing, the precursor to her quinoa veggie delight bowl.

"Mom, I've got great news," I said as she stood in front of the stove with her back to me.

No response.

"Mom," I shouted.

She turned while pulling out her earbuds.

"Hey, Honey, dinner's almost ready. How was your day?" she asked without really looking at me.

"My day was amazing. It was perfect. It may be one of the best days of my life. We have to celebrate!" I proclaimed.

Now I had her attention. Tilting her head and her eyes slightly squinting, I could see her brain scrambling to make sense of what I was telling her. Without giving her a chance to speak, I launched into a recap of Jackson's visit, Barry's plea deal, the timing of the hearing, my unfettered joy that I didn't have to testify, and that justice would soon be mine.

Mom's face lit up. She went to the fridge and pulled out a chilled bottle of prosecco. "You're right. This is a reason to celebrate! I'm thrilled this darkness is over. We have to tell Auntie Geeta right away. Oh, it just makes my heart sing when the judicial system works. Why don't you go call her, and I'll finish cooking?"

To properly celebrate, I set two places on the well-worn butcher block island, added a small bunch of mini-sunflowers in a mason jar, lit two candles, and poured the prosecco into crystal flutes. We sat down with steaming bowls in front of us.

Mom placed the blue-checkered cloth napkin in her lap and then raised her glass and said, "Let's toast Agent Jackson for—"

"Mom, stop," I interrupted. "Wait, let me video this, and I can send it to him." I quickly adjusted my phone to selfie mode and framed the two of us, flutes held high. "Okay, go," I instructed.

"Agent Jackson, tonight we are toasting you for a job well done. We are toasting you for being a smart, dedicated catcher of bad guys and for making our world safe again," Mom crowed.

"Yes, ditto to all of that, Jackson. Thank you for being my hero," I said with a wink of my own.

I quickly texted him the video with the line, "Are your ears burning?"

CHAPTER THIRTY-EIGHT

Justice Is Done

"All rise," boomed the bailiff and, with that, the pre-court chatter instantly stopped, creating an almost palpable hush. Auntie Geeta sat to my left, Mom to my right. Both of them grabbed my hands at the same time. Agent Jackson sat behind us.

I realized I had been holding my breath and let out a deep exhale while my eyes scanned the wood-paneled courtroom. I saw Barry in a black suit that seemed to hang lifelessly on his now-even-thinner frame. He was seated next to a man I recognized as a lawyer friend of his, Mel something. I guess Barry had finally come to understand the meaning of the old expression that an attorney who represents himself has a fool for a client. Of course, it was now far too late for him to benefit from that wisdom.

In the next to last row of the gallery, I spotted one of his twin daughters. I was too far away to tell which one. She was seated next to her mother, Barry's first wife.

I was so lost in my thoughts looking around that I missed most of what the judge was saying. Finally, I focused when I heard chairs scraping across the floor and saw Barry and his lawyer stand as the judge spoke.

"Mr. Tavers, have you entered into this plea agreement knowingly and voluntarily?"

"Yes, your honor, I have," Barry said without emotion.

"Mr. Tavers, is there anything you would like to say before I proceed with the sentencing?"

"Yes, your honor, I respectfully ask that I be confined in Southern California so that I can see my family."

"I can make that recommendation, but the final decision is ultimately not up to me," she said dryly.

The judge then spoke about the plea agreement and concluded by saying, "Barry Tavers, I hereby sentence you to ten years in a federal prison, location to be decided by the Federal Bureau of Prisons. I will add that because of your plea agreement, you are waiving all rights to appeal or to collaterally attack your sentence."

With that, she ordered that Barry be taken into custody. He was handcuffed and escorted out the back door by two uniformed officers.

I had fully expected that at this moment, I would feel jubilation, but instead, I felt nauseated. I told Auntie Geeta and Mom I would meet them in the lobby and quickly went to find the closest ladies' room.

Standing in front of the white porcelain sink, I let the cold water run over my wrists while I slowly breathed in and out, willing myself not to vomit.

The nightmare was finally over. Why wasn't I doing backflips? Sure, Barry had stolen from me, lied to me, and used every dirty, underhanded trick in the book to try to get me to take the fall for his crimes. Of course, he deserved to go to prison, but that knowledge didn't make this moment any easier.

I heard the bathroom door open and, in the mirror, I saw Barry's daughter, Lily, walk in. Our eyes met at the same time. She approached me.

"I'm so sorry for what my father did to you, Holly. You never deserved that. He's a monster, more than you'll ever know," she said as she gently placed her hand on my upper arm.

"I came here today to make sure that he really would be put away for his crimes," she admitted as tears slipped out of her eyes. She looked so sad.

I quickly dried my hands and gave her a huge hug. "I'm sorry for you, too. This must be so hard for you," I said. "Where's your sister?"

"Tiffany and I are not speaking. Dad embezzled our entire trust fund and we had to drop out of college. She was always a daddy's girl, craving his attention and approval, and she accepted his crazy lies. When I told her I was finished with him and that I could no longer have him in my life, she tried to get me to believe that the money wasn't embezzled but invested for us offshore and that we'd get it back in a few years," she revealed.

"Plus, Tiffany bought into his story that Grandmother is the real criminal and that he ONLY accepted the plea deal to keep her out of prison in her remaining years. I know he's lying. He's always been a liar. And, I found out that Grandmother knew exactly what was going on and that she was a Nazi sympathizer. It's all too horrible for words. I've moved back in with my mom, and for now, I'm going to community college until I figure things out," she explained, sounding tired and a bit lost. My heart just broke for her. In less than a year's time, she'd lost her father, her grandmother, and her sister. I said a silent prayer that Lily would find a way to leave all this darkness behind her.

I stepped out of the ladies' room to find Jackson, Auntie Geeta, and Mom waiting for me in the ultramodern white and glass lobby.

"Holly, honey, you okay?" Mom asked in her very mom-like way.

I paused for a moment, resisting the urge to say, "I will be." Tuning in to my heart and searching my body for my misery level, I realized I really was okay. More than okay. I felt whole, content, satisfied, and grounded.

"I'm happy this chapter of my life is now over," I said as I playfully bumped into Jackson. "Thanks to this guy, my real-life hero."

Jackson saluted us. "Well, this hero is hungry! Who wants to join me for lunch?"

"You kids go have some fun. We've got to get back to the office," Mom said with a knowing look as she quickly hooked her arm into Auntie Geeta's and walked away.

Jackson took a quick look at his watch. "If we roll now," he said, "I know where we can get some great sushi before the lunch crowd arrives. Are you up for that?"

As if on cue, my stomach growled in response. Jackson burst out laughing. And at once, my neck and face flushed pink.

"Okay, I can take a hint," Agent Jackson chuckled. "Young lady, you are coming with me. Let's go get you something to eat. How about some outdoor terrace dining? Does sushi sound good, or would you prefer an Indian lunch at Bombay Heaven?"

Holy fuck. Jackson wanted to go to lunch. With me. Now. Again. But this time, we were no longer officially on an agent-witness level. I suppressed the urge to do a cartwheel in the lobby of the federal building.

"You had me at Indian lunch," I said with a grin.

It was a little past noon when we walked into the restaurant. I was impressed that the staff all seemed to know him. Evidently, Agent Jackson was a regular here at Bombay Heaven. The lunch buffet offered the usual mix of Tandoori chicken, saag paneer, several curries, rice, raita, naan, and chapati. Tasty and filling but certainly not what grabbed my attention. Way better than the butter chicken was the man who was sitting right across from me: this smart, handsome hottie. It took me a second to realize I had never considered how truly cute Agent Jackson was until this very moment.

Returning to our table with plates piled high, Jackson looked at me with an expression I couldn't quite place. "No more of this 'Agent Jackson' stuff," he said with a smile. "Besides," he added, leaning back in his chair for emphasis, "all my friends call me Spyder."

"All right, so does this mean I get to question you, as well?" I said a bit too flirtatiously. *Whoa. What am I thinking?* I couldn't help myself. Perhaps I was feeling a high that suddenly made me so bold.

"Of course," Jackson said without skipping a beat. "Like all federal agents, I am an open book, totally vulnerable and transparent," he said with no hint of sarcasm. I could feel my stomach do a backflip. I once again stared at his beautiful hands. Resisting the urge to grab them in mine, I practiced the breathing techniques I had learned in India.

"Okay, Spyder." I smiled. "For starters, you can tell me how exactly you wound up with that nickname."

Jackson laughed, obviously caught off guard. Was he blushing? "Well," he began, "for my eighth birthday, my parents threw me a party at a rock climbing gym. At the time, I was sure I was going to grow up to be a professional rock climber."

I smiled, enthralled by how cute little eight-year-old Jackson must have been, and trying hard to suppress thoughts about what our children might look like.

"But being a rock climber wasn't my only dream," he continued, suddenly looking decades younger. "I also wanted to be a superhero. So on the day of the party, I thought, *what could be better than to combine these two aspirations by wearing my favorite Spiderman pajamas?* And that was the birth of my nickname, Spyder."

"Wow," I said, genuinely impressed. "A real-life superhero, complete with an origin story and everything!" Jackson beamed.

I took a sip of tea and tried to refocus.

"I do have another question," I said, with a serious tone.

"Shoot," he said, as though he knew right where I was headed.

"Can you please explain to me how you got Barry to take a plea deal? How did that happen? And what about his mother? Is she going to prison also?"

"Holly, should I officially debrief you?" Jackson asked in his official voice.

"Yes, sir, go right ahead."

"Well, as you know," Jackson began, "the Tavers had insisted all along that they had the provenance papers for each piece of art and had no knowledge that the art was stolen. Before their very public arrest, they actually had the audacity to make a statement to the press stating that they were the victims in this matter and demanded an apology from both the FBI and the U.S. Attorney's office. But the real truth came out during Phyllis Tavers's 'Queen for a Day' interview with AUSA Susan Karson." *Phyllis Tavers also had a Queen for a Day interview with Susan Karson?*

This was news to me.

Jackson took a last bite of Tandoori as the waiter refilled our teas.

"In order for what I'm about to tell you to make sense, I'm going to have to give you a bit of the backstory," he said. "Is that okay with you?"

"Yes, of course," I said eagerly, pushing my empty plate to the side. "When Lassie's home was raided, and he was taken into custody, a thorough search of his home turned up an underground bunker filled with priceless art and an old, well-used, leather-bound ledger with a bounty of details written in simple coded German. Once I obtained a copy of the ledger, I went through Barry's passport and in a matter of minutes was able to determine the dates of every visit he made to Budapest over a five-year period.

"Those dates coincided with the sale of a dozen paintings, the names of which were clearly identifiable in the ledger, and all of which matched up with the art confiscated from the Tavers's estate," Jackson explained. "The only thing the prosecution needed now was undeniable proof that both Barry and his mother knew that the art was stolen."

I nodded, indicating my understanding.

"Marc Russell, Mrs. Tavers's attorney, called AUSA Susan Karson almost daily, trying to get the charges against her dropped. Seizing the opportunity, Karson offered Phyllis a 'Queen for a Day' meeting, and Marc jumped at the chance to see what other new evidence they might have against his client. For his part, Marc was well aware that most of his clients were top-notch liars and he was interested in hearing what Mrs. Tavers would reveal in a no-holds-barred interview where she was sworn to be completely truthful.

"As her defense attorney, keeping Mrs. Tavers out of prison was Marc's only priority and he really didn't care what happened to Barry, whom he suspected had been living high on the gravy train of family money his entire life.

"And so, to get the old lioness to act in her own best interest, he convinced her to agree to the Queen for a Day offer and to not tell Barry anything about it, either before or after."

My eyes widened at the prospect of hearing Phyllis's side of the story. Jackson continued.

"So, on the morning of Phyllis's Queen for a Day interview, she, myself, Marc Russell, and Susan Karson all met in a conference room on the fifth floor of the federal building to hear what Mrs. Tavers had to say about the arts' origins.

"Susan had her laptop hooked up to a projector, and on the giant screen were the handwritten ledger pages detailing the names of the paintings that had been confiscated from Phyllis's home. Next to each one was a dollar amount indicating the sale price for each painting."

"Okay," I said, not really understanding the relevance of that detail.

"You see, per my training, I'd been watching Mrs. Tavers intently as Susan went through each painting and its sale price line by line. As they went through the accounting, I could see the blood practically drain from her face, then rise again, her cheeks flushing with anger.

"And at that moment, I had a strong hunch as to why."

"Yes?" I asked, on the edge of my seat.

"So just as I'm about to ask Mrs. Tavers if the sale prices on the ledger matched her recollection of what she paid Barry for their acquisition, she flies into a rage and screams, 'That fucking no good liar! I paid him twice what he paid for those!'"

Suddenly transported back to the present moment at the Bombay Heaven Café, Jackson and I both looked around a little self-consciously. Thankfully, most of the lunch crowd had already dissipated and the restaurant was nearly empty.

"Unbelievable," I said, even though a part of me wasn't at all surprised. Barry had lied to and stolen from me from the very beginning. What made me think he would spare his mom? Shaking off that distasteful thought, I managed a small smile and urged Jackson to please continue.

"After Mrs. Tavers's outburst, Marc, Susan, and I all looked at each another in silence, realizing that the path to Phyllis's freedom had just been revealed, along with the sure path to Barry's indictment. Then, of course, Marc asked for a moment to consult with his client.

"Marc quietly explained to Phyllis that if she truly wanted to be done with the nightmare of this situation, he could negotiate a plea bargain for her in exchange for her testifying against Barry. Of course, she'd have to forfeit the art, and agree to a probation sentence, probably with an ankle bracelet to keep her homebound for a year or less, but at least she'd avoid prison. And, of course, Phyllis, still seething from her son's betrayal, hissed at Marc to make the deal.

"So Marc turns back to Susan and says, 'If my client can prove that her son always knew the origin of this art, can you grant her full immunity?' Susan thought about this for a minute, then responded, 'First, I'd like to hear the whole story.'"

I listened carefully as Jackson related Phyllis's story.

"It turns out that in 1949, Phyllis traveled to Dusseldorf to visit her cousin Ilona, who was the mistress of an infamous art dealer, Hildebrand Gurlitt—notorious for his role as the head of Hitler's art theft brigade during the war. Even though Gurlitt was guilty of many crimes, he had skated by in a trial by claiming that as 'part Jew' he had been persecuted by the Nazis and was forced to participate.

"During that same trial, he was also able to prove that he had legitimately inherited some of the artworks he possessed. After the war, Gurlitt went on to open art galleries and display over seventy exhibitions of leading modern artists. He would broker the sale of paintings while at the same time dealing privately and purchasing works for his own collection.

"Then, a few years later, Ilona had an illegitimate son with Gurlitt, a cute little boy named . . ."

"Lassie!" I shrieked as previously disconnected bits of information began clicking into place. A grin started to spread across my face.

"You got it!" Jackson said, playfully. "Gurlitt and Ilona are the ones who introduced Mrs. Tavers to the world of fine art and even gave her a small Renoir etching as a gift. This was the start of her love affair with fine art.

"Then, after Mr. Tavers struck it rich as a slumlord, Mrs. Tavers decided to begin collecting art. It had been decades since she had heard from Ilona, so she sent Barry to Budapest to search for her and hopefully gain access to a good deal on some rare art. Barry easily found Lassie, by now a well-known art dealer and collector himself. He explained that his beloved mother had died many years earlier.

Even though Lassie didn't remember ever having met Phyllis, he was familiar with a photograph his mother kept on her vanity table of the two women bookending his birth father, dressed in his Nazi uniform.

"Apparently, Barry was captivated by the photo and brought home a copy of it framed in antique sterling silver as a gift for his mother, along with the first painting for her collection, a rare signed Pissarro that Lassie swore was the deal of a lifetime."

I drifted off for a moment, remembering the official tour Phyllis had given me of the Tavers's home shortly after Barry and I began dating. I couldn't say with any certainty whether they owned a Pissarro, but I knew for sure I'd seen that creepy old photo.

Jackson cocked his head to the side as if to ask where I'd gone. I brought myself back to the present and nodded for him to continue.

"So, at this point in the interview, Susan asks Phyllis if she knew that the paintings were part of the cache stolen from the Jews.

"And after some stalling, Phyllis finally admits that she assumed they were stolen because Ilona had told her all about Hildebrand and what he did for Hitler. With that bit of information, Susan's next task was to find out if Barry also knew, so she asked her point blank, 'Did Barry also know the origin of the artworks?'

"Phyllis again mentioned the photo of herself and Ilona with Hildebrand that Barry so proudly brought back as a gift and confirmed that, yes, Barry knew the origin of the artwork and knew exactly who Hildebrand was to Hitler."

Jackson flashed his wry little smile, and as if reading my mind, he said, "Holly, Marc had taken a picture of that photo with his iPhone days earlier when he met with Phyllis at her home to prep her for the interview."

A little gasp escaped my lips as Jackson said this, and I felt pretty sure I knew where the story was going. "Okay, go on!" I practically begged.

"At that point, Marc pulled out his phone and showed the picture to Susan and me as undisputable evidence that Barry had full knowledge of the art's origins. And Mrs. Tavers confirmed that he had always known." I sat there, speechless, a more complete picture of Barry's evil nature now coming into view. Jackson sat in silence with me, giving me time to process all that he had just said. "Wow. Thank you for explaining all of that," I managed finally, then realized there was still one piece of the puzzle I didn't understand. "What do you think finally convinced Barry to take the plea deal?" I asked.

"Well, Holly, Barry tried every stall tactic in the book to delay the proceedings, but I think he was really counting on having his mother's testimony thrown out. He actually convinced the judge to order a competency hearing, which Phyllis passed with flying colors. Much to Barry's surprise and dismay, Phyllis is still sharp as a tack with an impressive memory. That setback, coupled with the number of federal charges against him which could have resulted in a sentence of more than forty years, finally made him realize that he was going down for this. His best bet was to take the deal."

Jackson paused for a moment, his expression growing brighter. "And, Holly, you'll be happy to know that Susan used that video footage you captured of Barry offering you the hundred grand as the final nail in the coffin, saying that it was further evidence of his attempts at witness tampering," Jackson added, looking satisfied.

"Now, before we leave that corrupt family in our rearview mirror forever, is there anything about what transpired that you didn't understand?" he asked.

"No, sir, I think I got it all. Thanks to you, a very bad, *bad guy* is going to prison for ten years. Did I get that right?"

"Yep, you sure did."

"And I am one hundred percent free and clear from any prosecution or suspicion of illegal activity?"

"Yep, you sure are."

"Then I am all good."

Before I knew it, three hours had flown by. After rehashing the sordid details of Barry's final downfall, we discussed everything from our shared love of watching *Cash Cab* to our favorite Michael Franti tunes to my crazy-busy months in Delhi and the opening of its hottest new restaurant, Moondoggie's.

Jackson listening to me was healing in itself. His questions showed he was genuinely curious about me, and I felt heard in a way that I never had with Barry. I realized that, with Barry, the focus was always on him: his wants, his needs, his plans. It all seemed so exciting at the time that I didn't notice, or didn't want to notice, that it was never about me. I was just a useful pawn in his chess game, distracted by his gifts, traveling, and orchestrated romance, and I had cast him a starring role in my lifelong fairy tale. Ultimately, we had both used each other, and while the cost to me was significant, his would be public disgrace through the media and include ten years' prison time.

I discovered Jackson was amicably divorced with two tween kids, Sam and Zoë, a boy and a girl, and that he co-parented with his ex, who was also an FBI agent. Their marriage had fallen apart when he was assigned to train in Budapest as part of an international art fraud task force. Over the years, he advanced from trainee to instructor, which led to his work chasing Lassie and his sleazy collectors. When Jackson's ex-wife was transferred to San Diego a few years ago, he arranged to be relocated there as well.

It became clear in the restaurant we were sitting at that it was time to go when the only people left besides us were the busboys who were anxious to clear our table for the early evening dinner reservations.

As we reluctantly left the restaurant, my body felt elated, exhausted, exhilarated, and eager to move forward into a new life. I didn't want to salute Jackson this time, so I extended my hand instead, which he warmly embraced with his.

"Do you like the beach?" he asked as he pocketed his phone in his jacket.

I swallowed hard. Was he asking me to walk on the beach like Barry had an eternity ago?

"We live in San Diego. How could I not?" I smiled warmly, hoping I didn't sound too harsh. In truth, I was overcompensating for my heart doing backflips at the thought of seeing Jackson again.

"I'll call you," he said as he escorted me to the parking lot. After he opened the car door for me, I slid behind the wheel, grabbing it with both hands to contain my excitement.

"I'd like that," I replied softly, not knowing where else to look but straight into his gray eyes. His body blocked the sun as I squinted in his direction. Placing his hands in a namaste, he backed away from my car toward his Jeep. *Did he just namaste me?* I wondered as I fired up the ignition. What else do I not know about him? In just a matter of days, I was about to find out.

CHAPTER THIRTY-NINE

A New Rating System

Not even twenty-hour hours after our Indian lunch, Jackson texted me.

"Tomorrow, around 5 P.M., I'm planning to go to Pacific Beach and take a long walk down to the jetty and back. Want to meet me in front of the Plunge?"

Unlike my first walk with Barry, at another beach entirely, this location was a Barry-free zone. He would never hang with the multi-ethnic crowd around Belmont Park. The La Jolla Beach & Tennis Club was more to his liking, and the likelihood of my ever going there again was slim to none.

"Sounds like fun. See you then," I texted back in a flash, then quickly added: "Do you like peanut M&M's?"

It felt like an eternity before he responded. "How did you know?" He included a smiley emoji, which made my heart leap. A certain pleasant dizziness took over my brain. My heart began pounding intensely, like the drum solo from Phil Collins's "In the Air Tonight," as I immediately started trying to figure out what oh-so-casual-yet-cute outfit to wear. Hat or no hat? Certainly, I needed one in the midsummer heat. Not to mention a cool pair of sunglasses. My mouth felt dry, and my mind was spinning with possibility.

By 4 P.M. the next day, I was a nervous wreck as I got ready for my meetup with Jackson. I decided to wear my most comfortable and favorite fuchsia hoodie and black yoga pants. I was hoping the choir in my head would stop torturing me once I got to the beach.

Holly, the last thing you need is another tragic heartbreak, said my wounded inner child.

Maybe the best thing in the world for you is a new romance with a man who has taken an oath to serve and protect, said my optimistic side.

Don't believe every thought you have, said Mom's voice in my head, quoting her beloved Wayne Dyer.

Well, at least you will get in a nice long walk, said my practical Virgo side.

Go have fun and trust the process, said my future self. And there it was!

My newfound confidence propped me up, improving my posture as I stuffed my phone and lipstick into the pocket of my hoodie. I grabbed the jar of M&M's I had recently gotten at Costco and headed out on my newest adventure in my trusty blue Prius.

Traffic was lighter than expected, and I arrived ten minutes early to a near-empty parking lot. With my heart racing and palms sweating, I decided to sit in my car and use the time to do the mindfulness breathing Ritaji had taught me, hoping it would instantly transform me into the essence of cool, calm, and collected.

I rolled down the windows and, following my own directions, I began inhaling through my nose for four seconds, holding for four, exhaling through my mouth for four, dropping my shoulders, sinking into my seat, and keeping my attention on my breath. The plan was to complete ten cycles of breathing. In the middle of the eighth round, I nearly had a heart attack as I heard a rapid tapping on the roof of the car. Leaning in and looking at me with a giant grin was Jackson.

"Fuck! You scared me to death!" I exclaimed without thinking and then instantly blushed at dropping an f-bomb.

"Sorry, but I must say you are fucking adorable," he said with a wink.

My shoulders straightened as he opened the door for me.

"You've got the package, right?" he said with a straight face and a serious tone.

I looked around, pretending to be cautious and nervous.

"Yes, it's all here," I whispered, reaching over to the passenger seat and handing him the big jar of peanut M&M's.

"Thank you. Let's go put this in my car, okay?"

I playfully punched him in the arm and made him promise that he would never sneak up on me again.

"My bad. I shouldn't disrupt a beautiful woman when she is meditating," he said as an apology.

Now I was blushing again. *He is totally flirting with me. OMG.*

"Oh, I don't really meditate. I was doing a mindfulness breathing exercise I learned in India. I suck at meditation. My brain seems to go into high gear, and the chatter is intolerable when I try to meditate," I explained while trying not to appear as unsettled as I felt.

We talked nonstop on our leisurely stroll on the boardwalk. It was fun, effortless, and felt as if we were two people who had known each other forever.

"You know, you have a big advantage over me," I said teasingly.

"Really? Why is that?"

"Well, for starters, you know the intimate details of the worst time in my life, and I only know that you like Indian food and peanut M&M's," I said.

"Holly, you have permission to ask me anything," he said with a sincere smile.

"Okay, so, why did you become an FBI agent?"

He looked out at the ocean and was silent for several seconds as if deciding which version of his story to share with me. An airplane with an advertisement banner sped across the sky. Just when I thought he would never answer my question, he turned to me with a smile.

"I was small for my age as a kid and, in the fifth grade, I was bullied a lot by three punks in my class. It was really awful because I was the smartest kid in the room and they were the dumbest. But, of course, they were bigger and meaner. At the time, I was a big fan of Bruce Lee movies and had fantasies of becoming a ninja." He laughed. "I begged my parents to let me learn karate, but instead, my mother enrolled me in an Aikido dojo, a martial arts gym. She wanted me to have the *skills of a warrior and the heart of a poet*. Aikido is known as the art of *not* fighting."

"Hmm . . . well, how do you defend yourself if you aren't fighting," I asked dubiously.

"Want me to show you?"

I nodded. He placed his hands on my waist and picked me up like I was as light as a feather, and set me over the low containment wall and onto the sand.

He then walked about ten feet away and said, "Okay, Holly, come at me with everything you've got. Like you are going to hit me as hard as you can."

What the heck, I thought. *He wants me to attack him?* At that moment, I thought of a few other physical things I wanted to try out with him. But this?

"Come on," he encouraged. "I promise I won't hurt you. It will be fun."

"Okay, you asked for it," I declared and ran toward him with my right hand in the air, ready to punch him.

The next thing I knew, I was lying in the sand. He had grabbed my arm, spun me around as if we were dancing, and gently laid me on the ground.

"That was Aikido 101," he said with a self-satisfied grin.

"I simply moved you in the direction you were going without causing either of us any pain."

Lying in the cool sand, I became acutely aware of how blue the sky was overhead as I saw Jackson's face peering down at me, his arm outstretched with an offer to pull me up. It was like a freeze-frame moment, my senses firing all at once. I could taste and smell the salty breeze while I heard the squawking of the seagulls flying by and a small inner voice whispering to me. *This is how it happens*, the voice said softly. *Remember this moment*. I squeezed my eyes as tightly as I could. As if the pressure on my eyelids might freeze the memory forever in my brain.

Once I was standing up, we were nose-to-nose for a second. I wanted to kiss him and run away all at the same time. Fortunately, he turned me around and brushed the sand off my back.

"So, learning Aikido gave me what I needed to handle bullies. And it became an important part of my life, teaching me how to be physically, mentally, and spiritually strong," Jackson continued.

"How is this spiritual?"

"My *sensei*, which means 'teacher' in martial arts, taught me to meditate for several purposes. One is to achieve the witness state, which is a state of total freedom, along with the silent state of awareness that underlies all sound, feelings, and thought. The object of another meditation is for letting go, for the elimination of limiting mental and emotional programs. It is the attainment of an unconditional mind and, ultimately, a transcendence of the mind itself, thereby leading to higher states of consciousness such as love and peace," he explained reverently.

"Wow! Deepak and Ritaji would love this explanation of meditation," I said.

"Who are they?"

"Deepak is my friend and sort of guru in Rishikesh. I call him my Love Walla. And Ritaji was my sweet yoga teacher in Delhi," I explained.

"Sounds like you've been in good company. I'd like to know more about them," he said, sounding genuinely curious.

"Okay, but you haven't finished telling me how you came to join the FBI."

After walking and talking for over an hour, we stopped at a rooftop café for fish tacos and wine. We watched a beautiful sunset, and for the first time ever I saw a green flash, which Jackson said was a sign that good things were about to happen.

He told me that his experience of being bullied led him to choose law enforcement as a career and that he loved being able to solve real-life mysteries. To him, it was like fitting puzzle pieces together, which eventually led to putting the bad guys away.

I told him about my love of food and the creativity that cooking allowed. In the end, I revealed to him my plans to care for Dada and Nani through my culinary skills until I figured out what was next for me. It was almost nine o'clock when I got home. Mom was asleep on the couch in front of the TV, so I tiptoed to my room. I felt happy in a way I hadn't felt in forever. Not exactly in a santosha sort of content way, but more like a joyful sukha way. I was both happy and content and grateful to be a complete zero on the misery level. I wondered if it was time to invent a new happiness rating system for myself.

CHAPTER FORTY

Sweet Beginnings

Thus began the slow and sweet beginnings of Jackson and me. Our pattern began by sending very short, friendly texts back and forth every few days, interspersed with FaceTime chats and dates on the weekends when he was in town. While I wanted more, I was trying to pay attention to my inner warnings about not rushing things. Yes, I still wanted the kids and the white picket fence. But now I knew in my heart that whatever life had in store for me, I would be just fine.

On one of our "video dates," he shared with me his collection of Bruce Lee action figures and collectibles, and on another night, we watched *Fist of Fury*, his all-time favorite Bruce Lee film. I gave him a tour of my dollhouse, now living deep in the corner of Mom's garage.

"Where are you?" he asked, twisting his head to one side.

"My mom's super dusty garage," I replied, sneezing three times before stepping over boxes to get to the back shelf where my dollhouse sat. "She asked me to sort through some things to make space. We are going to donate a lot of stuff to the homeless shelter." I had made some progress before Jackson called. Several bags of old towels and sheets filled a corner of the garage.

The white siding of the dollhouse had a gray layer of dust covering its once-bright veneer. It appeared smaller than I remembered it. "I used to play with this thing for hours," I said softly as I wiped the sides off with my hands, careful to run the camera all around it for Jackson to see. "My grandfather made it for me." As I reflected on how much I had learned over the past year and a half, I realized it was time to release my childhood dream of the perfect life once and for all. I lifted the dollhouse from the shelf and placed it next to the bags of clothes. *Perhaps another little girl will find joy in it*, I thought. Turning my attention back to Jackson, I could see him shifting in his chair.

"Where are you, actually?" I asked, trying to figure out why he suddenly seemed to look a bit distorted.

"Now don't go making fun of me, but I am in my BarcaLounger. Her name is Peggy, after my grandmother, and it's the coziest place on Earth," he said as he arranged the phone so that I could take in the full view of his repose. So he had a grandparent who meant a lot to him, too. And I just loved that he named his chair after her.

"You and Peggy look good together," I played along.

"Ah, Grandma Peggy, you would have loved her. She was a true living Buddha. I was her favorite grandchild, and she was convinced that I was, as she always said, 'an evolutionary love being,'" he said with much pride.

"She sounds like an enlightened woman."

"Definitely. She was a nondenominational street minister who believed she was here to give love to everyone she came in contact with and, fortunately, I was the beneficiary of a lot of her love," he said with a sigh.

Of course, he already knew the worst of my baggage, which in many ways made it easier for me to be more vulnerable and revealing. We openly discussed his relationship with his ex-wife and the challenges and rewards of sharing custody of their preteen kids.

"Do you like boats?" Jackson asked me one day over FaceTime. Careful not to offer another snarky response about living in San Diego and the unavoidable interaction with the ocean, I offered him a sweet reply. "I do!" He arranged to meet me at San Diego Bay the next day for a surprise.

San Diego Bay was filled with boats of all shapes and sizes, from a five-masted fully rigged tall ship, to a few naval ships, and several chartered fishing boats. The almost high noon sun was reflecting off the water like sparkling, glistening diamonds and was a match for my quickly brightening mood.

Holding hands, we jumped into a water taxi and headed across the sapphire water of San Diego Bay to Coronado Island. I love surprises, and this was an unexpected delight.

Standing on the bow of the water taxi, the wind was whipping my hair across my face and Jackson's as well. He surprised me when he used his hands to brush my long locks into a makeshift ponytail that he held in his hand.

"We'll both look and feel a lot better for lunch this way," he joked. A few minutes later, we were seated under a massive blue umbrella, where Jackson quickly ordered us a delicious spread of charcuterie, artisan sourdough flatbread roasted with tomatoes and fresh basil, and two baby kale salads dressed with goat cheese and pepitas.

This guy really knows his way around a menu, I thought.

Diving into the feast laid out before us, I shared with Jackson that a few months earlier, I had taken a DNA test to see if I could find my biological dad and my half sisters, which the Nadi readers had told me about.

"My results turned up one woman in Alaska who was a forty-three percent match with me, and after a little social media and google research, I tracked her down, and we got on a call. She was the eldest of three sisters, all a few years older than me. She claimed to have no idea about me and said that her father had died of cancer a few years ago." I paused to take a crunchy bite of flatbread.

"Well, what did you learn about the dad?" Jackson asked with genuine interest.

"Turns out he worked on a fishing boat most of the year. She said her parents had been married for more than forty years, and as far as she knew, they were very happy together. He had even been a rock band manager for several years when she and her sisters were quite young."

"Are you going to meet her?"

"Doesn't look that way. She was pleasant but not really friendly and ultimately wasn't interested in telling her sisters about me or having any further contact," I said.

And then, without meaning to, I began to cry. "Oh, I'm sorry for weeping at this beautiful lunch," I mumbled.

Jackson gently dabbed my tears with his paper napkin.

"It's okay. That must have been such a big disappointment for you. And it's their loss," he commiserated.

"Well, at least now I know. He didn't reject me. He never knew about me, and it makes sense that after all this time, they wouldn't want a total stranger invading their lives. Besides, Alaska was never on my bucket list," I said, trying to convince myself it wasn't that big of a deal.

"From what I can see, the family you have loves you deeply, so while it might seem like having half sisters might have been some kind of a bonus, maybe the Universe has other bonuses in mind for you," he said a bit mysteriously.

And with that, our server, an older, buxom brunette with a big smile and a wide swagger, came at us with a dessert sporting a sparkler.

"Your friend here slipped me a note earlier saying you have a big sweet tooth, so here's the house specialty, our secret recipe, homemade sugar-free, gluten-free churros over vanilla bean ice cream smothered in hot fudge sauce," she crowed, placing the fiery delight in front of me. She then picked my phone up off the table and said, "Let me get a picture of the two of you," and before I could answer, she had quickly snapped a few and walked away as if that was the most normal thing in the world to do.

Jackson handed me a spoon as he picked up his. "Before we dig into this sinful concoction," he said, "I have a very important question to ask you. Okay?"

Not knowing what he was about to say, I nodded yes and whispered, "Okay."

"Holly Grant, the most beautiful and courageous woman I have ever met, would you do me the honor of becoming my official girlfriend?"

I was stunned and, fortunately, I had not yet taken a bite, or I would have had to spit it out all over him. I looked into his eyes to see if there was any hint that I was being punked (or worse), but all I saw was a sincere happy man waiting for an answer.

"Agent Turner, the answer is 'yes'!"

And with that, he leaned over and took a bite of whipped cream and then gave me the sweetest, longest, most delicious kiss I had ever had.

CHAPTER FORTY-ONE

Full Circle

After many long talks and sleepless nights, Jackson finally decided to retire from the FBI and follow his passion and open his own Aikido dojo. His former FBI mentor, Robert Wittman, had made him an irresistible offer to work part-time as a virtual investigator while he ramped up the new business. During his twenty-year tenure with the FBI, Wittman had recovered more than three hundred million dollars' worth of stolen art, which led to the prosecution and conviction of countless criminals from around the world. Jackson was thrilled to associate with him again in his role as investigator.

While searching for a space for the dojo, we found a mixed-use building with a perfect, large ground-floor space, and a beautiful large three-bedroom apartment right above for us to live in. Jackson was a man on fire, excited to be training his young students and embracing his new role as sensei.

During the time Jackson was reinventing his career, I had the same dream for three consecutive nights. I dreamt of a bright pink, orange, and yellow food truck painted with Hindu Gods and Goddesses and floral patterns. It was quite psychedelic in a late sixties Woodstock-era way. I could even see the menu. It consisted mostly of dosas, a cross between a Mexican burrito and a French crepe. They were made of rice and lentil flour, filled with a variety of ingredients, and served with yummy sauces.

Dosas are incredibly delicious and very addictive. One of my favorites was a masala dosa with scrambled eggs, dahl, and highly seasoned Yukon potatoes. In my dreams, the truck always looked the same, but the menu items kept expanding, and I could see long lines of customers.

I decided to turn my dream into reality. After getting all the required regulations and licenses and plunking down the deposit for a brand new, state-of-the-art truck, my dosa food truck business was up and running. And, thanks to the social media prowess of Jackson's daughter Zoë, I had already amassed quite a following, boasting dozens of five-star reviews on Yelp—including one with the headline *"Om Om Good!"* I enjoyed discovering new neighborhoods and meeting families of all nationalities who were loving my dosas. My wild, bright pink, orange, and yellow custom paint job was a magnet for the hungry and the curious. The hardest part wasn't the cooking or the customers; the greatest challenge was learning to drive and park my twenty-foot-long kitchen on wheels.

It was a little before 9 A.M. on a Friday, and I had just settled into one of my favorite shady spots on a hill overlooking the dramatic Sunset Cliffs shoreline, in the hippie town of Ocean Beach. Inhaling the salty sea air as I rolled out my awning, I was filled with gratitude for every single step along my journey that had led to this moment. With the music of one of my favorite artists, Jason Mraz, bumping gently in the background, my usual pre-lunch crowd chores were unfolding in a perfect flow, and I was fully absorbed in the bliss of the present moment.

An unexpected sound broke my trance. Was someone knocking on the window? I opened the front door to find Carly standing there, a sheepish half-smile on her face. My immediate gut reaction surprised me. I wanted to reach out and hug her. It was honestly so good to see her after so long. My mind kicked in a millisecond later. I wondered if she could see the range of emotions playing across my face.

"Um, hi," I said tentatively. "How did you find me?"

"What? Are you kidding? It would be hard not to find you," she said excitedly in that zesty tone I had loved for twenty-something years. "You're blowing up on all of my feeds!" She was beaming love. I couldn't help but smile.

"Have you ever had a dosa?" I asked finally, not knowing what else to say. Food had always been our common ground.

I picked up a large serving tray of freshly made potato masala dosas, soft in the middle and crispy around the edges. As I removed the foil from the pan, the scent of Indian spices warmed the air. Placing two on a plate alongside a trio of mango, coriander, and chili chutneys, I motioned for her to sit on one of two chairs I had placed outside.

Carly reached for the plate. "Promise you're not going to poison me?" she said, only half-jokingly.

I felt my heart melt.

Seated side by side on the bluff, I watched Carly drench a dosa in the mango and chili chutneys before taking a big bite. "Oh my God," she said, still chewing. "Holly, this is incredible!"

I thought about the evolution of my cooking skills since I had last seen her and about the radical change in the trajectory of my life.

There was something very full circle about the moment. Me sitting here with my childhood best friend, now about to begin a whole new chapter in my adult life.

"Carly," I began, turning my chair toward her. "I need you to know that even though everything that happened between us broke my heart, it also saved me from a lifetime of even greater heartbreak."

Carly broke down crying, but I continued.

"I owe you a lot, actually, because you helped to expose Barry for who and what he really is. Thanks to everything that happened, my old life was turned completely upside down. Thanks to you, I spent months in India, learning not only a new way of cooking but a whole new way of looking at life. Thanks to you, I dodged a bullet and in the process met the true love of my life."

"Oh, Holly . . . I'm so sorry for everything," Carly sobbed, tears streaming down her face. "I was stupid and jealous, and I've prayed that someday you would forgive me."

"Yes, yes, of course. I forgive you," I reassured her. "I know better than anyone how seductive that motherfucker can be. Neither of us ever stood a chance against his narcissistic ways."

And then, suddenly, I felt like a two-ton lead jacket had dropped from my shoulders, and all I could feel was love and compassion for my old friend.

Would we ever be close again? Only time would tell, but at that moment, all I wished for her was a happy life with someone who would love her the way Jackson loved me.

CHAPTER FORTY-TWO

Happy at Last

Breaking with tradition never felt so good. Jackson and I were snuggled up under the white, fluffy comforter in our cozy hotel room across the street from our wedding site. The warmth of his body and his gentle breathing filled me with a sense of joy, as if I was wrapped in a cocoon of love and safety. I smiled as I tried to give this feeling a name. Yes . . . it was sukha and, yes, it was santosha. I was happy and joyful, totally content, and it was also something more . . . a sense of destiny, a feeling of "meant-to-be-ness."

With the bright morning light seeping in through the bamboo blinds and the gentle sound of emerald green and turquoise waves lapping the shore, I felt the certainty of this magical day. Whoever said the bride and groom should be apart the night before the wedding was completely lacking in romance and imagination.

We had splurged on a suite with a large wooden deck and a totally unnecessary fireplace. The furniture was beachy kitsch, but we didn't care. This was our little slice of heaven on earth for a couple of nights. Besides, we had already been living together for a few months.

Just before 7 A.M., Jackson woke up smiling and cheerful when he announced, "Did you know, my soon-to-be Mrs. Turner, that according to ancient mythology, a wedding day that begins with lovemaking is destined to bless the bride and groom with happiness for eternity?"

"Yes, of course, my soon-to-be husband, everyone knows that," I teased as I rolled over on top of him. "And did you know that it's a good omen to make the bride as happy as you would like to be?"

"I plan to devote the rest of my life to making you the happiest woman alive," he said and proceeded to do exactly that.

Our wedding was scheduled to begin at 11 A.M. in a postage-stamp-sized park affectionately known as the Wedding Bowl. Tucked several feet behind the street that ran along the La Jolla shoreline, it was a circular patch of grass surrounded by an array of palm trees and pretty succulents. These provided a sense of intimacy and privacy. The theme of our wedding was "Super Casual, Love, and Happiness," meaning no dress code for our small group of thirty-three friends and family.

I found a pretty ankle-length white satin slip dress. And Maya, whom I had naturally asked to be my maid of honor, bought me a stunning 22-karat gold and pearl choker. Jackson decided to wear a white linen suit with his favorite baby-blue knit T-shirt underneath. We both wanted to wear our most comfy flip-flops.

When I had told Deepak about the upcoming wedding, he uncharacteristically invited himself. "I need to book a visit to Michigan to see my kids," he said cheerily, "and I've always wanted to see San Diego. Do you have room for one more guest?"

My heart just about exploded with joy when I realized I had been harboring a fantasy. "Okay, Deepak, I'll make you a deal: you can attend my wedding, but only if you will walk me down the aisle."

"Oh, Holly, I would be so deeply honored," and I swear I heard him sniffle as I began balling my eyes out. I may have grown up without a dad and had my heart shattered by a love thief, but now I had my own personal Love Walla, someone who had shown and taught me what real love is.

With Deepak, I found what it was like to have a real, mature man love, care for, and nurture me. Yes, he was a father figure, and even better, he was my friend. I marveled about how fortunate I was to have manifested two incredibly loving, trustable men like Deepak and Jackson. In a strange way, I came to realize that without having suffered through Barry's betrayal, I would have never ended up here, on my wedding day, happier than I ever thought possible.

Deepak and I stood arm-in-arm at the top of the entrance to the Wedding Bowl. Jackson was standing beneath our gorgeous floral wedding arch, big turquoise waves cresting just behind him. His two kids, Sam and Zoë, were positioned one on each side of their dad, holding his hands. And our guests were now standing on both sides of a sloping pathway strewn with rose petals, waiting for the processional music to begin.

Taking in the small gathering of smiling faces below, my eyes landed on Mom. She looked happier than I'd seen her in a very long time and somehow younger and more beautiful, too. I looked back at Deepak and realized that the two of them were locked in a gaze, probably in their shared love for me, but maybe it was something more?

I drew in a deep breath as if trying to physically make space inside me to contain the big emotions of this moment.

I was beginning to feel as if I had entered an otherworldly state. Part of me was floating above it all, looking down and noticing the sea breeze moving through. I was intensely aware of the sounds of the ocean mixed with the music of the harpist, who was gently plucking the strings and playing a heavenly angelic tune. My heart felt like it was beating in a rhythm of a conga drum. Deepak whispered in my ear. "It's time."

This wise, compassionate man had become the father figure I'd always dreamed of. This moment felt so right, so perfect.

Then, we were suddenly walking down the aisle as if in slow motion. The smile on my face was so big it nearly hurt. I could see all of those beautiful eyes of my most precious friends and family staring at me, lavishing me with their affection, and I was experiencing a tsunami of love. And then I found myself standing next to Jackson, my soon-to-be husband, who whispered to me sweetly, "Holly, you have never looked more beautiful."

At that moment, Mikey took over his role of official wedding emcee. "Welcome, everyone," Mikey began with his signature radiant smile. "I'm Michael Watt, better known to most of you as Mikey, one of Holly's oldest friends and certainly her biggest fan. We are all blessed to be here today in the presence of love, the love of Jackson and Holly, and our love for them. We are thrilled to stand as witnesses to the vows they will soon make to each other.

"Before we officially begin, I'd like to invite Jackson's son and daughter, Sam and Zoë, to recite a Dr. Seuss–inspired tribute to our bride and groom."

Jackson's two children looked both a little nervous and a little giddy as they stood in front of the wedding guests. Then Jackson's son, Sam, holding a piece of paper, looked up at us and said, "Dad, Holly, we love you so much, and we want to say . . .

Dad and Holly, congratulations on this most special day, as you stand before us committing to love each other all the way. And Holly, we must say, we are super thrilled to have you as our amazing bonus Mom.

Today is the day when you share these sacred vows: You will choose to love each other rich,

You will love each other poor,

You'll even love each other when someone starts to snore!

You will love each other on good days and bad

'Cause you are now soulmates and the best friends you've ever had. You love each other with all your heart.

You'll love each other till death do you part.

And you will even choose to love each other when someone farts.

We wish you a life full of wedded bliss, filled with love, laughter, and happiness, sealed with a tender kiss.

May your love be like a fire, burning bright and strong and may it light up your lives for an eternity long.

Mikey gave both kids a hug and again addressed the wedding guests. "I will now turn the ceremony over to our very special guest and officiant, a holy woman from Rishikesh, India, Sadhvi Bhagawati Saraswati," Mikey said, bowing in a namaste to Sadhviji.

Sadhviji, looking radiant in her orange holy woman robes, began by asking us to turn and face each other and to hold hands. I handed my bouquet to Maya and clasped the hands of my amazing hero: the man who had proven to me that real love is possible.

"You stand together, here today, at the beautiful intersection of the ocean and the sky and the earth and heaven and that which is beneath us, supporting us, holding us, nurturing us and that which provides us, enlivens us, and surrounds us. As you stand here, you come together not just as two individual souls but as two expressions of one soul, as two reflections and the manifestation of love, itself.

"You are two wholes, recognizing in each other, Oneness. In marriage, as in life, there are challenges, and there are opportunities. It's up to us how we want to face and embody these. There will be issues of egos and the opportunity to overcome them, remembering in every moment, regardless of the challenge, you always have the choice to pick love.

"You always have the power to choose peace. You have free will, and it's up to you. You can choose to be right according to your particular ego drama, or you can choose love. In the Indian Hindu tradition, the householder life, the time of being married, having children, having a career, is the time in which we see God and get closer to God through marriage.

"I know that both of you have come to this day on your separate spiritual paths and practices. Now it's time to recognize and know your marriage is a single vessel, beginning on a lifetime voyage.

"Your spiritual practice and your marriage are not separate; your marriage is the path through which you will expand and blossom and grow spiritually. Can you see the divine in each other? Right now, look into each other's eyes, and instead of just seeing Holly and Jackson, keep looking. What else can you see?" She paused for a moment.

"What you see is the depths of each other. The joy, the sadness, the fear, and the beauty . . . keep looking until you see yourself in each other's eyes. Look until the spirit of you sees itself in each other.

"Keep looking. When you recognize yourself in each other, keep looking and allow in that recognition the individual looker, the individual watcher, and the one that is being watched, allow those distinctions to disappear, to melt away. Until there is no Holly. There is no Jackson. There is just the soul. Just divinity. Just God. There is just Love.

"Allow your union to be your vessel, to be your path to realize that your marriage is a way to experience God in your own self through another being. And together you are being, melting, emerging, and expanding into Love.

"Every day when you wake up, choose love, choose your marriage, choose each other and choose to walk toward God through and with each other."

With Sadhviji's guidance, Jackson and I exchanged vows and rings, and then she proclaimed us husband and wife. She turned to Jackson.

"You may now kiss your bride."

Jackson took my face in his hands and kissed me gently but deeply as I wrapped my arms around his waist. I was lost in the blissful moment until suddenly I became aware of everyone yelling "Look! Look! Look up!"

Jackson began laughing as he turned me toward the ocean and tilted my head up, and said, "One last surprise for our special day, my darling Holly. I will love you until the end of time."

Flying overhead was a bright yellow, single-engine biplane towing a banner that read, "Holly and Jackson Forever."

I marveled at the journey I had taken to be standing here in the arms of this loving man. In spite of (or maybe because of) having my heart broken and my dreams crushed, through the healing power of love, and the wisdom of loving guides, I stood before the altar and on the precipice of a new life with an overwhelming sense of peace. My forever had finally begun.

Acknowledgments

In the fall of 2018, this story began to unfold in my head like a movie, a movie that takes place in Rishikesh, India.

The first sentence, "My mother was right," began to flash inside my mind, over and over and over again. Ugh. How can I make this go away?

Soon after, I received an email from www.masterclass.com offering a video course from Dan Brown on how to *Write a Thriller.*

I signed up. I worship Dan Brown. And I knew that watching this would be just for fun. Writing a thriller was not something I aspired to do.

I loved seeing Dan sit in his living room seemingly speaking directly to me.

Video #3 was about location as a character in the book (ala Florence in *The Da Vinci Code*). I began fantasizing about going back to Rishikesh to absorb the colors, sounds, and vibe of that holy city on the banks of the Ganga.

Stop it, I told myself.

This is stupid.

You don't need to torture yourself and write another book, especially fiction!

Still, haunted by the ongoing movie in my head, I spoke to God and told him/her that if I was meant to go to Rishikesh I would manifest a roundtrip business class ticket.

Forty-eight hours later, that happened! (Blessings and thanks to my dear friends Mike Koenig and Vivian Glyck.)

A month later, I was in India where miracle after miracle occurred. The places and events I had seen in my head I was now experiencing, finding, tripping over.

On an earlier visit to India, with my friend Deepak Chopra in 2003, we were at Ramana Maharishi's ashram in Tiruvannamalai, preparing to circumambulate Mount Arunachala with a half million pilgrims to celebrate the Full Moon of Pongal.

As we began walking, Deepak spontaneously said to me: "In India, Spirit is not difficult to find . . . it's impossible to avoid."

I never forgot that. Now I know why.

My first morning in Rishikesh I realized Deepak was right. I heard music, gongs, and chanting outside my hotel room. I ran to the balcony and beneath me were a dozen men in orange and white robes carrying a deceased guru on a white stretcher on their way for a cremation. Spirit was indeed everywhere.

I heard the road traffic, the *beep-beeps* of the autorickshaws and motor bikes. I also heard my dear departed friend, Nancy De Herrara, whisper in my ear from the other side, "go visit my ashram." So I did.

Nancy met Maharishi Mahesh Yogi in the early 1960s and she became his right-hand person for many years; she was responsible for overseeing the Beatles' visit to the ashram. My dear friend and holy woman Sadhviji (yes, she is real) and I took the fifteen-minute walk from her ashram to Maharishi's, now often referred to as the Beatles' ashram. The beautiful, lush grounds are filled with all kinds of trees and winding pathways and unusual stone teepee-like meditation huts. However, all of the other buildings are in disarray, no doors or windows . . . deserted for decades now.

In the main hall were several brilliantly painted murals of Maharishi and the Beatles. Having read Nancy's memoir, *All You Need Is Love*, many times, it was so much fun to actually see it all for myself. It would have been even better if Nancy were there with us, regaling us with her wild and crazy true stories about John Lennon, Donovan, Mike Love, and the gang. Hard to believe that all happened more than fifty years earlier and was the inspiration for the Beatles'

White Album. The song "The Continuing Story of Bungalow Bill" was written about Nancy and her eldest son, Rik Cooke. If she were still alive today, she would be past one hundred.

One of the amazing things that began to happen in Rishikesh is that when I desired something it manifested before I even realized the desire was there. One afternoon I was very hungry, craving rice and mildly cooked veggies. Within an hour, Sadhviji sent a messenger with the most delicious meal in a traditional tiffin package. While walking through the main area of Rishikesh, Tapovan, I was wishing for a red string blessing from a Sadhu and, voila, a man dressed as Hanuman appeared before me and did just that.

Nearly every day I experienced unexpected magic and guidance. The magic continued when I arrived home and began writing. Having written eleven nonfiction books, I had no idea how different writing a novel would be. I always considered myself a strong writer, but this, well, this was something else and I am glad I had no idea just how hard it would be or I wouldn't have attempted it. Writing a novel was never, ever, on my to-do list.

In the creation of this book, I have been beyond blessed to have three talented and amazing "Book Godmothers" who helped birth and push this book out of me. Much love, gratitude, and appreciation to my agent, Margret McBride, and freelance editors Danielle Dorman and Christine Hohlbaum. Their enthusiasm, creativity, and ability to nudge me without pissing me off have been great blessings.

Special thanks to my dear friend Neale Donald Walsch for so graciously allowing me to interview him and incorporate his wisdom as part of this book. Thanks also for the expert advice from Vedic palm reader Steven Highburger; to Nadi reader provider Dr. Q (yes, he's also real); to betrayal therapist Debi Silber; to Nimisha Amin for superb Indian cooking classes; and to Ashley Ford-Wells, thank you, for inventing the signature cocktails for Moondoggie's.

I am indebted to Holy woman and soul sister Sadhvi Bhagawati Saraswati for her generous sharing of her healing and powerful words; to psychologist Dr. Ken Druck for allowing me to incorporate some of his creative healing processes; and to my beautiful friend and go-to fashion expert Liana Chaouli who envisioned Holly's Budapest wardrobe.

Peter Guzzardi, this book got done because, as the first one to read the earliest pages, you believed in me and encouraged me to keep going. Thank you.

Suzanne Todd, I am forever grateful for your support and vision to turn this into a streaming series. Your passion and talent is the reason why your movies earn billions and delight audiences around the globe.

The only thing harder than writing a book is marketing it. I am fortunate to have three dear friends who not only love me but just happen to be marketing geniuses. Thank you, Claire Zammit, Marci Shimoff, and Christine Kriner.

I am blessed to have many gracious friends who offered advice, deeply personal stories, input, encouragement, connections to experts, feedback, and so much more along the way.

Mille grazie to my brilliant legal and FBI experts Terri Hilliard, Mark Eiglarsh, Mark Stern, Benjamin Jolley, Robert Whitman, and Tom Mueller (and thank you Krista Linza for connecting me to Tom).

The early readers and supporters of this book were more meaningful to me than they will ever know. Beyond taking the time to read, they offered little gems of inspiration and useful details and kept me going when I often was besieged by thoughts that I was in crazy land attempting to write fiction. In no particular order, my blessings and thanks to my dear friends: Heide Banks, Nancy Deville, Laurie Sue Brockway, Divina Infusino, Becky Robbins, Marianne Williamson, Natalie Ledwell, Lynne McTaggart, Debra Poneman, Sheri Salata, Iyanla Vanzant, Mary Morrissey, Laura Berman, Ken Page, Damona Hoffman, Linda Sivertsen, Carol Allen, Nancy Levin, Marni Batista, Dr. Diana Kirschner, Colette Baron-Reid, Peggy McColl, Liz Dawn, Jonathon Aslay, Cynthia James, Barbara Biziou, Christy Whitman, Puja Shah, Susie Collins, Helen Powers, Amorah Kelly, Lisette Omoss, Barnet Bain, Heidi Metcalfe, Minda Burr, Joan Borysenko, Kelly Sullivan Walden, Cheryl Richardson, Donald Altman, Terri Britt, Jennifer Joy Jimenez, Charlie Wagner, Kailen Rosenberg, Bela Gandhi, Heidi Krupp, Erin Saxton, Patty Aubery, Allison Maslan, Sarah Ford

Brammer, Eve Ford Davenport, Leslie Powell, Carla Picardi, Jessica Baum, Gay Hendricks, Janet Mills, Susan Pohlman, Betsy Chasse, Leize and David Perlmutter, Lissa Rankin, Annie Kagan, Fauzia Burke, Debra Evans, Cathy Carpizo, Laurie Larson, Tina Cameron, Kurt Koontz, Julie Ferman, Barbara Beltaire, Candice Chen, Shelley DeAngelis, Veena Sidhu, Gareth Esersky, Shabnam Miglani, Jean Courtney, Kait Hilliard, and Kailen Rosenberg.

Sincere thanks and appreciation to the behind-the-scenes support of Kevin Anderson & Associates, Jericho Writers, cover designer Laura Duffy, webmaster (and more) Andy Huguenard, copyeditor Nina Shoroplova, and the dynamo team at Hasmark Publishing.

Finally, and most importantly, I am grateful to my beloved husband/soulmate/life partner of twenty-five years, Brian Hilliard. His endless deep love and unlimited support fill my heart and blow my mind. Bri, you truly are my personal Love Walla!

About the Author

Arielle Ford is a leading personality in the personal growth and contemporary spirituality movement. For the past thirty years, she has been living, teaching, and promoting consciousness through all forms of media. She is a celebrated love and relationship expert, author, and speaker. Her mission is to help people Find Love, Keep Love, and Be Love.

Arielle is a gifted writer and the award-winning author of eleven nonfiction books, including the international bestseller *The Soulmate Secret: Manifest the Love of Your Life with the Law of Attraction*, which was published in twenty-one languages and forty countries.

She has also written many groundbreaking books, including *Turn Your Mate into Your Soulmate: A Practical Guide to Happily Ever After* and *Wabi Sabi Love: The Ancient Art of Finding Perfect Love in Imperfect Relationships*.

Arielle has been called "The Cupid of Consciousness" and "The Fairy Godmother of Love." She lives in La Jolla, CA, with her husband and soulmate, Brian Hilliard, and their feline friends.

The Love Thief is her debut novel.

Find her at **arielleford.com**.

Reading Group Guide

While in India, Holly encounters many people who point her in the direction of self-discovery and healing. Do you see these as coincidence or as universal guidance? What one person or experience significantly altered the direction of your life?

Early in the book, Holly entertains visions of revenge upon Barry (and with Mikey's help, vicariously acts one of them out). In the end, she forgives Carly, and herself. Share a story of a time when you forgave yourself for something.

What are some red flags about Barry that Holly ignored early on in their courtship? In your own life, how have you learned to recognize and honor your intuition?

In one of their first conversations, Deepak tells Holly that from a divine perspective, there are no mistakes. What experiences have you had that seemed like mistakes at first, but turned out to be blessings in disguise? Was there a time in your life when something devastating turned into the best thing that ever happened to you?

If you could have shared words of wisdom with Holly in her hardest moments, what would you have said?

In what significant ways has Holly changed by the time she begins a relationship with Jackson? How have her life experiences prepared her to co-create a life with her soulmate?

What qualities or characteristics did Holly embrace on her journey that you would like to tap into and express in your own life?

What was your reaction to Holly's blunt expression of rage? What role did embracing her anger play in her ultimate healing?

It's left undecided at the end of the book what becomes of the relationship between Holly and Carly. If you were Holly, would you invite Carly back into your life? Why or why not?

What new possibility opened up for you in your own life after reading *The Love Thief*?

What is your own vision for BIG love in your life?

Nadi Readings

More than twenty years ago, Brian and I traveled through South India with Deepak Chopra. One of the highlights of our journey was to experience a "palm leaf reading," also known as a Nadi reading, where a priest and an interpreter found our life history written in old Tamil, on a palm leaf.

Nadi forecasts were created thousands of years ago by enlightened sages and include everything from your name, your life history with extraordinary details, and your past life information that impacts your karma in this life (for instance, I was told I wouldn't have kids in this life because in my last life I performed illegal abortions!). You also discover what is predicted for all the years you have left on the earth.

These readings contain information that cannot be found on the internet and the priests who do the readings don't read or write English. We were in a forest, six hours from the next city, in a concrete block room with a single light bulb overhead and no other electronics—and only an outhouse!

It all begins by providing your thumbprint. With that thumbprint (they do not know your name or date of birth, just whether you are male or female), a search begins for the bundle of palm leaves that may contain your leaf.

At my reading in the forest, my priest was named Ravi and my translator was Babu. It took about forty-five minutes before Ravi finally had the right leaf for me. We knew he had the right leaf because it contained the names of my parents and husband (all badly mispronounced—imagine hearing *Sheila* and *Harvey* in Hinglish). They told me my name was Arielle and that I was born early on a Monday morning (which even I didn't know til I got home and looked it up), that I have a younger brother and sister, and that my father had two wives (all of which is true). Ravi then proceeded to give me precise details about the remainder of my life, including the kind of work I do, business things to beware of, dates for auspicious things to do, upcoming physical ailments, and so much more.

Until recently, having a Nadi reading was impossible unless you went to India and had the right connections.

A few years ago, I met an amazing man, Dr. Q, who has created an organization to provide Nadi readings from South India via Zoom. My reading with his group was as real, authentic, and mind-blowing as my in-person reading.

Learn more about it at *www.mynadireading.com* and then decide if it's right for you.

Please note: There are many fraudulent practitioners of Nadi readings in India and online. Dr. Q's organization is the only one I can vouch for.

About Sadhvi Bhagawati Saraswati

Meet my dear friend and soul sister, Sadhviji.

In the fall of 2010, Brian and I took a group of friends to some of our favorite places in India, including a Ganga aarti ceremony at Parmarth Niketan ashram in Rishikesh. On that auspicious evening, we met the holy woman Sadhvi Bhagawati Saraswati, Ph.D., who welcomed us "home" and immediately took us to sit with her guru, Pujya Swamiji. It was love at first sight.

I'm delighted that you have now experienced her wisdom and divinity through the pages of this book.

Sadhviji is a spiritual leader, motivational speaker, author, and social activist, based at Parmarth Niketan, the largest ashram in Rishikesh. She is also president of Divine Shakti Foundation, bringing education and empowerment to women and children. And she is secretary-general of Global Interfaith WASH Alliance, the first alliance of religious leaders for Water, Sanitation and Hygiene, as well as director of the world-famous International Yoga Festival. She has received numerous awards for her humanitarian work, including the Lifetime Achievement Award by U.S. President Joe Biden. She is also the author of the #1 best-selling memoir *Hollywood to the Himalayas: A Journey of Healing and Transformation.* Originally from Los Angeles, and a graduate of Stanford University, Sadhviji has lived at Parmarth

Niketan for more than twenty-six years, where she gives spiritual discourses, satsang and meditation, leads myriad humanitarian programs, and serves as a unique female voice of spiritual leadership throughout India and the world.

Going to India? Visit Sadhviji. Learn more at: **https://sadhviji.org**

Parmarth Niketan is nothing less than a spiritual haven that is attended annually by tens of thousands who seek rejuvenation. Pujya Swami Chidanand Saraswatiji Maharaj is the president and spiritual head of Parmarth Niketan, which is situated along the banks of the Ganga and has 1,000 comfortable rooms, complete with delicious vegetarian food, daily yoga, healing courses, meditation, and Western toilets!

Visit: **www.parmarth.org** or email **reservations@parmarth.com**

Hay House Titles of Related Interest

YOU CAN HEAL YOUR LIFE, the movie,
starring Louise Hay & Friends
(available as an online streaming video)
www.hayhouse.co.uk/louise-movie

THE SHIFT, the movie,
starring Dr Wayne W. Dyer
(available as an online streaming video)
www.hayhouse.co.uk/the-shift-movie

THE PROPHETESS: The Return of The Prophet from The Voice of The Divine Feminine, by Chelan Harkin

THE DALAI LAMA'S CAT AND THE ART OF PURRING: A Novel, by David Michie

A TIME FOR GRACE: Sacred Guidance for Everyday Life, by Caroline Myss

ASK YOUR GUIDES: Calling in Your Divine Support System for Help with Everything in Life, by Sonia Choquette

All of the above are available at your local bookstore, or may be ordered by contacting Hay House (see next page).